299 Days VIII: The War

by

Glen Tate

Book Eight in the ten book 299 Days series.

Your Survival Library

www.PrepperPress.com

299 Days VIII: The War

ISBN 978-0615994451

Printed in the United States of America.

Prepper Press Trade Paperback Edition: March 2014

Prepper Press is a division of Kennebec Publishing, LLC

- To the real Team. Few men, especially civilians, ever get to know what it is like to be in a band of brothers. Very few ever get to experience knowing that you will die for a brother and that he will die for you. I have been given this extremely rare honor and will treasure it my entire life. I thank God for putting these men in my life.

This ten-book series follows Grant Matson and others as they navigate through a partial collapse of society. Set in Washington State, this series depicts the conflicting worlds of preppers, those who don't understand them, and those who fear and resent them.

The War is the eighth book in the *299 Days* series

For many people at Pierce Point and the rest of Washington State, the upcoming New Year is a time for hope, and belief that life is going to improve and the Collapse will end. For Grant Matson and the 17th Irregulars, the New Year means only one thing – war. The time has come, and they have received their orders from HQ. Grant must come clean with Lisa and tell her the truth about his work as he plans to abandon his family once again.

While the Loyalists drunkenly and selfishly celebrate New Year's Eve, the Patriots mount a surprise attack on Frederickson, making way for the 17th Irregulars to move toward Olympia. As the battle moves on, the men quickly realize the importance of everything they have been training for when they find themselves ambushed. Doing everything he can to suppress his own fear and lead the 17th Irregulars, Grant motivates them to persevere as they fight for liberty and restoring the country to the greatness it once was.

Books from the 299 Days series published to date:

Book One – *299 Days: The Preparation*

Book Two – *299 Days: The Collapse*

Book Three – *299 Days: The Community*

Book Four – *299 Days: The Stronghold*

Book Five – *299 Days: The Visitors*

Book Six – *299 Days: The 17th Irregulars*

Book Seven – *299 Days: The Change of Seasons*

Book Eight – *299 Days: The War*

For more about this series, free bonus chapters, and to be notified about future releases, please visit **www.299days.com**.

About the Author:

Glen Tate has a front row seat to the corruption in government and writes the *299 Days* series from his first-hand observations of why a collapse is coming and predictions on how it will unfold. Much like the main character in the series, Grant Matson, the author grew up in a rural and remote part of Washington State. He is now a forty-something resident of Olympia, Washington, and is a very active prepper. "Glen" keeps his real identity a secret so he won't lose his job because, in his line of work, being a prepper and questioning the motives of the government is not appreciated.

Chapter 251

HVT

(December 17)

"We're hit!" screamed helicopter co-pilot, Lt. Francisco "Paco" Mendez, into the radio. "AC shot!" he said, referring to the aircraft commander, Nedderman, who was slumped over in the pilot's seat to the right of Mendez.

"Small arms fire!" Mendez screamed some more. By now, eight military, contractor-looking soldiers had swarmed the helicopter. Mendez looked at one of them through the helicopter's windshield and gripped his pistol. He was terrified.

The soldier came up to the windshield and flashed Mendez seven fingers, followed by a fist, and then two fingers. This was the code they used to identify themselves as friendlies and proceed with the mission as planned. Mendez sighed in relief. He was 99% sure he knew who these soldiers were, and that shooting Nedderman had been necessary, but he was glad to know for certain.

Mendez motioned for the soldiers, or contractors, or whoever they were, to get into the helicopter. As they poured into the helicopter, Mendez got back on the radio. He called in his location, standard operating procedure for when an aircraft was hit.

"I'm getting the hell out of here," he screamed into the radio.

"Go! Go! Go!" someone screamed on the radio in a panic.

The apparent team leader, who was the first in the helicopter, got on the helicopter's intercom and said, "You're going to St. Pete's Hospital."

"Really?" asked Mendez. He wondered if this was to get Nedderman medical care, although Nedderman was supposed to be shot in this mission.

"Yes. Trust me," the team leader said. "Seven, zero, two, bro, 7-0-2." That meant that this was the ultimate destination for the pick-up, as called for by mission number 702. Mendez had been told that the pick-up location would not be disclosed until they were in-flight.

Mendez wondered why they would steal a Blackhawk helicopter and shoot the lead pilot, just to go to a hospital. He wondered what he'd gotten himself into.

"Bearing is 230," the team leader said into the intercom, telling Mendez which direction to go to get to the hospital.

"They have a helo pad?" Mendez asked, suspecting that the hospital probably did.

"Affirmative," the team leader said. They flew in silence for about thirty seconds.

"Tell the TOC," the team leader said, referring the Tactical Operations Center back at Camp Murray, "that you're getting the pilot to the hospital. Leave it vague."

Mendez got on the radio to the TOC and said, "I'm taking Kevin to the hospital," he said, using Nedderman's first name to make it seem like they were close friends and on the same side.

"Do it," the scared voice from the TOC said.

"Tell them it's St. Pete's and that you'll land on the roof," the team leader said into the intercom. Mendez followed orders.

"What's going to happen at the hospital?" Mendez asked into the intercom, double checking that he was talking on the intercom and not the open channels that could be heard by the TOC.

"We're going to drop off your pilot," the team leader said, "And pick someone up."

"Why?" Mendez asked, realizing he didn't need to know that now.

"HVT," the soldier said, meaning a "high-value target."

"Just our luck," he continued, "an HVT is at the hospital and we have a great reason to land a helicopter on the roof. Pretty cool, huh?"

Then Mendez remembered what the team leader said when he first got into the helicopter: they were going to "see the Attorney General." That must be the HVT.

"Okay," replied the team leader as they approached the hospital's roof and prepared to land. "Don't leave without ten guys: the eight of us, the HVT, and another guy."

"Copy," Mendez said.

"We'll take the pilot out and into the hospital, and then, once we're in there, we'll go get the HVT," the team leader said. "If anyone asks why you have eight guys on board that you didn't report, tell them that you were freaked out by the pilot getting shot."

"Roger that," Mendez said.

"TOC," Mendez said into the open channels, "ETA to hospital is one minute. Tell them we're coming."

"Copy," said the TOC radio operator, who then realized

Mendez had said "we" were coming. "How many you got on board?" she asked.

"Kevin and some operators who were at the landing site and taking fire," Mendez answered.

"Proceed," she said.

"Now the hospital won't be surprised to see us," the team leader said on the intercom. "Nice." That would mean a lower chance of having to shoot innocent hospital staff when they were in there.

Mendez had never landed on this particular helo pad. He was a good pilot, but every landing on an unfamiliar surface required total concentration.

As soon as they touched down, the soldiers got out and were met by hospital medics with a gurney. The soldiers removed Nedderman out of the pilot's chair and made it look like they were rendering first aid.

The hospital staff did not have any security. Why would they need it? This was a Loyalist helicopter making an emergency landing at a Loyalist hospital. Camp Murray had radioed in and told the hospital to expect several soldiers in the helicopter, so no one was alarmed that eight extremely well-armed operators were now entering the hospital.

As soon as the operators were inside, the team leader found the stairs and went down to the sixth floor, with his seven teammates right behind him. They quickly found Room 612.

They walked down the hall and past the nurse's station. No one even looked up. The operators looked right at home there. St. Pete's often had soldiers and contractors milling around.

The team leader knocked on the door to Room 612 and said, "Trigger?"

"Seven, zero, two," a male voice said from behind the door.

The team leader pointed to two operators and motioned that they stand guard at the door. Another two took up a nonchalant position facing the elevator. The four remaining operators went into the room.

When they walked in, they found Roy "Trigger" Chopping holding a pistol on a small, well-dressed man with duct tape over his mouth.

"Mr. Attorney General," Roy said to the well-dressed man, "your ride is here."

The team leader motioned for the medic on his team to approach the Washington State Attorney General. The little man in the suit was terrified, but couldn't scream because of the duct tape.

3

"Sir," the team leader said to the Attorney. "Don't make me do this," as he made a fist. The Attorney General tried to run away. The team leader grabbed him and punched him in the face. The Attorney General dropped to the ground.

One of the operators took a big, body-length bag out of his backpack and another operator helped him unfurl it. They gently put the Attorney General inside and hoisted him up on their shoulders.

"Let's boogie," the team leader said and motioned for Roy to join them, which he did and then they all left the room.

Before they left, an operator in the room knocked three times on the door to let the two standing guard outside know that they were coming out.

The operators walked calmly out of the room with a heavy bag on the shoulders of two of them. It didn't look out of the ordinary. Soldiers carried heavy things all the time, especially during wartime and in the state capitol hospital that catered to the VIPs in state government.

Roy, a former NYPD detective who moved to Washington State for a job in the Attorney General's office as an investigator, felt a surprising calm wash over him. Not only was he calm – he had done years of undercover work and been in some extremely dangerous situations – but he was actually enjoying himself. He was so at ease that he even winked at the pretty nurse at the nurse station as he walked by. Roy's sense of calm was contagious; the team leader started whistling a song like he didn't have a care in the world.

They took the stairs up to the roof, which was locked. That was the one thing they hadn't planned for. Someone should have noticed that when they came down the stairs from the helo pad, but that detail had been missed.

"Shit," the team leader said.

"I got it," Roy said as he went back down the stairs and to the nurse's station.

"Hey, beautiful," he said in a New York accent, "My security detail needs to get back in a helicopter that's on the roof, burning a gallon of very expensive fuel every few seconds it's sitting there. The roof door is locked. Could you call someone? Quickly?"

The nurse, who got hit on all day long, but was charmed by this New Yorker with silver hair, said halfway flirtatiously, "It depends. Who are you?"

Roy got out his Attorney General's investigator badge and flashed it. The nurse smiled and picked up the phone and gave him the thumbs up after thirty seconds.

"Thanks, beautiful," he said as he ran toward the stairwell. He caught up with the operators and they got into the helicopter. No one tried to stop them.

As they lifted off and got out of small-arms range from the hospital, the team leader started to relax slightly. He handed Roy a headset and said on the intercom, "How the hell did you do that?"

"The door?" Roy asked. "Cute nurse."

"No," the team leader said, "Get the Attorney General into a hospital room so we could get him."

Roy smiled and said, "Ah, well, that's a story I can tell you over a beer sometime."

Chapter 252

Tet

(December 21)

It was late afternoon and Jim Q. was getting hungry. He was thinking about what was for dinner that night when his radio crackled. "My shoe is green," he heard his cousin say in their language. It sounded so sweet to hear his language from a familiar voice.

Jim Q. had been instructed to test messages from HQ to ensure they were valid, even though they were in a language only about three dozen people in the state understood. He opened his code book and looked at the letters written in his native language, which was in an obscure alphabet only those three dozen people in the state, and maybe a Near Eastern linguist professor, would even recognize.

Jim Q. found the appropriate test phrase for an instruction coming from HQ "When do the birds fly south?" he asked in his language, one he only spoke on this radio.

"My birthday is fourteen days after the Festival of the Harvest," his cousin answered. This was the proper response, meaning the person on the other end had the same code book. Of course he did: no one else spoke this language and Jim Q. recognized his cousin's voice. But it was easy to take the extra precaution of code phrases. The 104 soldiers in the 17th Irregulars counted on secure communications.

"Go ahead," Jim Q. said, meaning it was safe to start the message, now that the sender had been authenticated.

"The ocean is purple," his cousin said.

Jim Q. looked at his code book again. This meant "an all unit-commander meeting tonight at midnight at Boston Harbor."

"My kitten is green," Jim Q. said, which meant, "Message received: there will be an all unit-commander meeting tonight at Boston Harbor."

Jim Q. wrote down the message about the meeting at midnight just to make sure he got it right. Naturally, he wrote it in his language. Even if that message, the code book, or the radio transmissions were intercepted, no one would have any idea what language was involved, let alone what was being said.

Jim Q. and his fellow code talkers were essential. The Limas were monitoring the radio frequencies and would love to know that all the Patriot guerilla commanders would be in the same place at the same time.

"Horse seven out," his cousin said, which was his call sign. They used English for "out" because there wasn't a word in their language for "end of radio transmission." Besides, let the Limas know that the speakers of this strange language used one English word. It would just confuse them more.

"Bear two out," Jim Q. said in their language, before going to find Ted.

When he caught up with him, he mentioned the meeting that night. Ted nodded slowly. It must be the meeting about the offensive. Finally. Ted had been waiting for weeks for the green light.

"My guys are ready," Ted said out loud to himself. They were. Not ultra-ready, but as ready as they could be. They were ready enough for the mission best suited for the 17th Irregulars that he and Lt. Col. Hammond sketched out from the beginning: rear-echelon occupiers of Olympia with a strong civil affairs emphasis. Ted just hoped that this was the same mission they would receive. He was hoping his semi-rag tag unit wouldn't be tasked with taking a fortified Lima facility.

Ted got on the radio and called Grant. "Giraffe 7, Giraffe 7, Green 1."

After a few seconds, Grant answered, "Green 1, Giraffe 7."

"Supper at the ranch," Ted said. He added, "Bring a toothbrush," which essentially meant that he'd better plan to spend the night.

"Roger that," Grant said. Another evening and night away from the family, he thought. Oh well. That was becoming more and more common for him. For the most part, his family was understanding. He had to get the "rental team" up to speed to get some food and gas coming to Pierce Point. It was a worthy cause, even if it was a lie. The actual cause was even more worthy, but his family wouldn't understand.

"Should I bring my cousins?" Grant asked. This was code for the Team.

"Negative," Ted answered.

"Copy," Grant said. "Giraffe 7 out."

"Green 1 out," Ted said.

It was about 4:30 p.m. Dinner was always at 5:30 p.m. It was earlier than most civilians were used to, but the unit got up at 5:00 a.m.

Grant arrived at Marion Farm about a half hour later. He flashed the guards the unit's "1-7" sign and they let him in. The sign was just for fun. The guards recognized Grant.

Grant checked his watch. It was a little after five. That gave him some time to talk to Ted and see what was going on. Grant could sense that something big was up. He, too, had been waiting for the green light from HQ This must be it, Grant thought.

"Hey, what's up?" Grant asked when he saw Ted.

"All unit-commander meeting tonight at HQ," Ted said. "You know what that means."

"Yep," Grant said. His marriage was about to finally end, he thought. That's what's up. Oh, and he might be killed. There was that, too.

Grant had dinner and talked to the troops all night. Around10:00 p.m., he took a caffeine pill, anticipating a long night. A little while later, he and Ted got their kit and rifles and headed out to the beach landing. There was the Chief ready to take them to Boston Harbor.

They still hadn't found Paul's body and Mark was still insane. Every time Grant got out on the water, he thought about Paul and how dangerous it was just to move around now. Grant would inquire with HQ tonight about a Purple Heart for Paul. He died during operations. No one was shooting at him, but he was out on the water doing something dangerous for the unit. Grant would also inquire if there was some commendation for a training injury for Tony Atkins, who was still recovering. A commanding officer had the duty and responsibility to get his men recognized by higher ups when they deserved it. Tony and Paul surely did.

The boat ride to Boston Harbor was uneventful. Grant remembered the last one back in the summer, which had been his first trip to Boston Harbor. Everything seemed magic on that trip. It was a brand new adventure, going to meet with a Special Forces commander and finding out you are commanding a guerilla unit. That had been an amazing trip.

This trip was not like that. This was all business. Comparing the first trip to the second, Grant realized how much he had changed in the past few months. He had gone from thinking it was amazing that he was part of this guerilla adventure to thinking he was going to see his boss and get a big work assignment.

Grant had become a soldier in the past few months, a professional soldier. Not in the sense that he was particularly good at it, but that it was his job to be a soldier. Now he thought of soldiering as his job rather than an adventure.

Security was particularly tight that night. The Chief had to make several radio checks at various points with code phrases. The picket boats were farther out and more numerous than the first time. There were soldiers on the bank along the entrance to the marina. And the marina itself was bristling with soldiers, very well-armed soldiers. They had medium, and even heavy machine guns and grenade launchers. Grant hadn't seen that the first time he was out at Boston Harbor. The Patriot forces were getting much better armed as they captured Lima weapons.

When they pulled into the their slip at the marina, a sergeant—in an actual uniform consisting of FUSA Army fatigues, but with a "Wash. State Guard" name tape—came up to them and said, "Unit, please?"

"17th Irregulars," Grant said.

The sergeant looked at his clipboard.

"And you are?" he asked.

"Lt. Matson and Sgt. Malloy," Grant said as he realized that he was in civilian clothes and had no insignia, except for his small homemade 17th Irregular unit patch, which would be next to impossible to see in the dark with the poor lighting of the marina.

"Call signs, please," the sergeant said.

"Giraffe 7 and Green 1," Grant said. He was glad that they had so many security checks. It took two seconds to give a call sign, but it was an easy way to uncover a Lima spy who could get all of them killed. It was an excellent use of two seconds of time.

The sergeant checked his clipboard. "Yes, sir," he said, saluting Grant. Grant wasn't used to saluting since they were under battlefield rules out at Marion Farm even though no one was actively shooting at them. But it must be okay to salute here at HQ since the sergeant saluted first. Grant returned the salute.

The sergeant told them to go to the building where they met the first time he was out there. The Chief took off from the slip to make room for the next boatload of meeting attendees. Grant and Ted started walking toward the meeting building. Grant was amazed at how … "military" the place was. Everyone had uniforms – actual uniforms. Grant felt a little out of place in civilian clothes, albeit contractor clothes, and his tactical vest. Ted was a little more in place with his Army fatigues, but also with a tactical vest and a baseball cap. Grant and Ted had their rifles, which made them stand out. Except for the guards, most of the uniformed troops at Boston Harbor did not have rifles.

There were several other contractor-looking guys among the much larger number of men and women in actual uniforms. Grant assumed that the contractor-looking guys, who all had beards, must be from guerilla units, like Grant and Ted.

The closer Grant and Ted got to the well-lit meeting building, the more they could see people's faces. There was a seriousness on most faces, not worry or stress. People had their game faces on. It was go time. They were serious people about to perform serious business. There was a slight air of nervousness. It wasn't a lack of confidence, rather an air of "this is really going to happen – and soon."

At the door to the building, a soldier was checking rifles to make sure the safeties were on, which Grant thought was odd. Of course Grant's and Ted's safeties were on, but maybe there were some guerillas attending who had only recently learned how to handle guns.

A second soldier, actually, an airman in Air Force fatigues with the State Guard name tape, was at a card table at the entrance asking for each person's unit and once again verifying call signs.

"Take a seat wherever you'd like, Lieutenant and Sergeant," the airman said.

Ted's eyes lit up and he ran over to some guys and gave them a "bro hug," the kind of mild hug and pat on the back guys do. Ted introduced them to Grant. They were former colleagues of Ted's from his Ft. Lewis Special Forces unit.

They chatted for a while. Ted's colleagues were doing the same as Ted, leading and training guerilla units nearby. Some units were out in the rural areas even farther away from Olympia and the Seattle metro area than Pierce Point. Quite a few were located on or near the water, like Pierce Point. Some units were surprisingly close to the Seattle metro area. One of Ted's colleagues, unarmed in jeans and looking like a non-descript civilian, just said, "I'm with some guys behind the JBLM line," referring to the ring of fortifications surrounding Joint Base Lewis McChord. "That's about all I'll say." Fair enough.

Ted's colleagues talked about how they got from their areas to Boston Harbor. For many, it was quite a journey. For the ones from rural areas, they had to take back roads because I-5 was sealed off. Some had to walk from a drop-off point to a beach where they were picked up by a boat from Boston Harbor. For the guy in jeans who was operating from behind the JBLM line, it took two days and two fake

IDs to get there. Grant and Ted realized how easy they had it, just taking a short boat trip there.

Grant was reminded how strategically located Pierce Point was, especially with its proximity to Olympia. No wonder Lt. Col. Hammond had been so excited to have a unit out there, especially one built around personal friends of Ted's. And one that was running its local community so well.

The meeting started right at midnight. These military personnel were very precise about time. No one strolled in late. "Early is on time and on time is late," was their saying.

The captain from the first meeting took the podium. Grant recalled that his name was Morris.

"I need each irregular unit to count off," Morris said.

The highest ranking person from each unit stood up and gave their unit's number. There were two units missing, the Fourth and Fifteenth. Quite a few of the commanders were women, more than had been assigned as commanders at the first meeting. Grant wondered why.

After the Sixteenth, Grant stood up and said with a strong and confident voice, "Seventeenth." They went to the Twenty Fourth and that was it.

Some in the audience, like Ted's friend in jeans, didn't count off. They must not be in irregular units. They were probably "special specials" as Ted called them, meaning "special special operations."

"Thank you," Captain Morris said. "We have representatives of all but two of our irregular units. I would like to thank the women who are here in particular. Some of the units could not get their commanders out here given the travel conditions so they sent women who would look less suspicious to the Limas and could get through the checkpoints. These 'nice ladies' wouldn't hurt a fly, right?" People laughed.

"Now I give you our commander, Lt. Col. Hammond," Capt. Morris said.

Ted and the other Special Forces guys clapped. They loved Hammond. Everyone else joined the applause. That was not military custom, to applaud a speaker about to give a briefing, but Hammond deserved it.

"Thank you, ladies and gentlemen," Hammond said. "You know how a speaker will often thank people for coming. Usually that's just polite talk. Not tonight. Thank you. Each of you. You risked your lives to be here. I'll try to make it worth your while. We have some important business to discuss."

Hammond went from the podium to a large map of Western Washington, holding a pointer, which was all he needed. A microphone was unnecessary with his deep, booming voice.

"We are here," Hammond said, pointing a few miles from Olympia on the map. "You are from all over here," he said pointing to various points in western Washington.

"We're going to take Olympia," Hammond said, in a flat, matter-of-fact tone. The crowd digested that for a moment and then some started to clap and cheer. Pretty soon, the crowd was whooping and hollering.

"God damned right," Hammond yelled in response to the cheering. "We're going to take the capitol and drive those bastards out." This was followed by more cheering.

"This is our state and that's our capitol!" Hammond yelled, accompanied by even more cheering. This was no typical military briefing which would not include cheering. But this wasn't a war in some far off country, either. This was America. This was a war for *their* country. They had been treated like shit by those bastards in Olympia. The government and gangs had been taking whatever they wanted. More than one solider in that room had a wife or daughter taken by the gangs. Nothing made a man fight harder than that. Most people in the audience had friends or loved ones thrown in jail by the Limas. Several had their spouses or children killed. Every single person in that room was there to end it. They had been preparing for a long time to stop it. The hatred and revenge had been boiling over and over. They had nightmares. They cried uncontrollably at the kitchen table when they saw the empty seat formerly occupied by their dead or missing family member. They could not sleep trying to keep out the thoughts about what the gangs were doing to a wife or daughter. It was time to finally fix the mess that had been made. It had to end.

Hammond let the cheers die down until it was silent. "Here's how we're going to do it," he said, with obvious pride. He had been working on this for months. "You're all a part of it," Hammond said. "A big part." Grant swelled with pride. He felt important, not in an egotistical way, but in a small part-of-something-big way.

"But before I describe how we'll do it," Hammond said, "I will first tell you why we're doing it." It was important for the unit commanders to know why they were doing this, not just how.

Hammond shrugged and said, "Simple. You already figured it out: Olympia is the state capitol. It's symbolic, the seat of state government. I don't mean symbolic as in 'just a meaningless symbol.' It's hugely important to have the capitol. We will implement an interim state government—we have one in place already and they're ready to start governing—and then we'll rightly claim to be the 'legitimate authorities' in the state. We'll have pictures of the new management of the state sitting in the Legislature and we'll get it out to the rest of population who are trapped in Seattle and the suburbs. Us sitting in the House and Senate chambers. That's a very powerful message." Grant pictured that in his mind. It was exhilarating. It was why they were doing all of this.

"That photo of Patriots sitting in the Legislature's seats," Hammond said, "will prove to the remaining Limas that we're winning. It will make it even more obvious to everyone that Seattle is their only stronghold. More and more of them will go to Seattle, which is fine with us. We'll be herding those bastards to a big pen. We can either go take Seattle when the conditions are right or just leave them in their pen, where they can't hurt us and screw things up like they did last time." More applause exploded from the room.

"Olympia as an objective makes sense on two more levels," Hammond said. "First, as I'll describe more, Olympia is weakly defended. Most of their beef is up in Seattle. Second, we have lots of assets south of Seattle, near Olympia. That's the beauty of JBLM being nearby. We have lots of Patriot FUSA troops here in the neighborhood." He smiled and pointed at members of the audience in military uniforms.

"Here's the plan in a nutshell," Hammond said, "We start off with irregular units north of Seattle, in Seattle itself, and over here in the eastern Washington farms. These units start diversionary guerilla attacks. We give the Limas a day or two to move their forces there. Then we have regular units come from here," he pointed to several areas on the map, demonstrating that the regular units would be coming from all over the area. It looked like they were pretty widely disbursed.

Hammond smiled and said, "And here." He pointed to JBLM. There are Patriot regular units at Ft. Lewis? What the hell?

"That's right," Hammond said pointing again at JBLM, "we have regular units right under the Limas' noses." He let that sink in with the audience.

"I won't give details," Hammond said, "but there are bunch of sit-out units." He was referring to the term for units sitting out the war. Usually for a price. But apparently, the Limas couldn't buy ultimate

13

loyalty from these units. Or the sit-out units were figuring out that the Limas were losing and the sit-outs wanted to be on the winning side. Either way, some of the sit-outs would be joining the Patriots, so who cared what their motivations were. News that some sit-out units would be joining the Patriots drew some more whooping and hollering.

"The regular units will spearhead the drive to Olympia, but," Hammond paused, "their main job will be to fight the Lima regular units rushing down from JBLM to reinforce Olympia. We want our regular forces facing their regular forces, but that leaves lots of the street-to-street fighting inside Olympia up to the irregular units. That's why you're here tonight."

Hammond paused again. He was about to launch into the main message, so he gathered his thoughts.

"I want to start," Hammond said, "with a philosophical overview that will explain the operational details of why we're going to attack the capitol."

He put his finger up for emphasis and said, "The philosophical overview is the difference between chaos and order." That got some people curious.

"When you're in control," Hammond continued, "minimize chaos. When you're trying to take control, maximize chaos." He let that sink in.

"At the beginning of any insurgency," Hammond said, "the insurgents — by definition — are not in control of the government. They are the underdogs. The rebels. They need to maximize chaos. That's what we do. Maximize chaos. Hit soft targets at first. Make them divert troops from other battles to protect their soft targets. We also steal all the shit we can haul away. Blow up fuel supplies. Disrupt communications. Get their uniforms and, wearing Lima uniforms, go shoot them up close so they never trust their fellow soldiers in uniform. That's some powerful chaos. They have to devote guards to protect themselves from people in their own uniforms. Chaos. Maximize it."

Hammond paused and continued, "Then, after we've dished out all that chaos, we'll be winning. We'll start to be in control. That's when we'll switch roles with the Limas. They'll be the insurgents and we'll be the government."

Hammond put his finger up again and said, "That's when we switch to minimizing chaos. When we've taken Olympia and occupy it, then we're about order and stamping out chaos. That's when we set up law and order and feed hungry people and get them medical care. We establish order and then we go after any remnants of Limas who, now that they are the insurgents for a change, are trying to create chaos for us."

"So our mission," Hammond said, "has two halves: chaos first and order second." He gave his audience a few seconds to take that in.

Hammond put up his hand with three fingers out and said, "There are three fundamental points about this operation that you need to know." Anyone could have heard a pin drop in the room.

"First," Hammond said, "our enemy is extremely weak. We still need to respect the enemy. They will cause us some casualties. You can count on that, ladies and gentlemen. Count on that," he said a second time to emphasize the point. He paused.

"But," he said dramatically, "Our enemy is crumbling. They are running out of supplies. I'll touch on their lack of military supplies in a moment. But they're running out of every kind of supplies, like food. It appears that their stupid-ass socialist system is not producing any food. Huh? Who saw that coming?" This was about as political as Hammond ever got. He was a soldier, not a politician. But politics affected the military situation by having a system that caused the Limas' food supplies to run low.

"So what are they doing?" Hammond asked the audience. "They're doing what dictators always do, limiting food to the civilians and taking it for themselves. That's the whole FCard 'clearance' system. It is a hierarchy of who gets how much food. Well, guess what? The civilians in the Lima areas like Olympia don't appreciate this. They see it all day long. The regular people see connected people having plenty while their kids go hungry. I don't want to exaggerate, there isn't massive starvation in Olympia, but there is hunger. And it's winter. Early winter. The civilian population, even those who were big time Loyalists a few months ago or even a few weeks ago, are realizing that they're getting screwed. This is a big part of our strategy, as I'll discuss in a moment."

"The resentment by the civilians and the lack of supplies overall," Hammond said, "means that the population will either be receptive to us or neutral. I'm not expecting a ticker tape parade when we go in, but I bet many civilians will just hide in their houses and come out only to get food. That's been our experience in the other countries where some of us in this room have fought." A few of the Special Forces guys were nodding.

"Humans are humans anywhere on the planet," Hammond said. "Civilians in Olympia won't fight to the death over ... what? Devotion to a political party? Some belief in a Keynesian economic model?" Hammond was very well-read.

"Now, this won't be a cakewalk with the civilians," Hammond cautioned. "There will be some who are hardcore Limas. They really believe the Patriots are Klansmen out to get them." Hammond paused and swung around to a member of the audience.

"Thompson," Hammond said with a smile to a black soldier, "You a Klansman?"

"Hell no, sir," the solider said. That got a laugh.

Hammond wanted to get back to serious business. "Okay," he said, "Here's what we know about their weaknesses. They have a huge AWOL problem. With Christmas coming, they're melting away to be with their families and get the hell out of outlying areas, like Olympia. They're going to Seattle by the busload. Most of the FCorps and National Guard are either gone or are combat ineffective like when they sell their weapons for a carton of cigarettes." Hammond winked and said, "Based on a true story, ladies and gentlemen. Several of them, actually."

Hammond pointed outside. "This illustrates my point exactly. We're in Boston Harbor, about six miles from the Olympia city limits. Do you see any Limas around here? They probably know we're here, but are too weak to do anything about it." What Hammond didn't say to the crowd was that the Patriots had people in the Lima organizations and would instantly know about a pending attack. On the other hand, and something else Hammond didn't say, was that one well-coordinated Lima helicopter attack would level Boston Harbor in about fifteen seconds. There was no need to alarm people.

"But this is the capitol," Hammond said, still pointing toward Olympia, "Where lots of Lima forces are concentrated. The state police are still a pretty cohesive unit. There are a surprisingly high number of National Guard troops in Olympia — more than I would have stationed there, but we have to play the hand we've been dealt. They are pretty crappy troops in general, the ones who are left in the National Guard. Lots of young kids just doing this for that big college money they still think they'll get, even though all the colleges are closed. These police and National Guard units have nothing to lose now. They've picked sides. They know what will happen to them when we win. So they'll fight pretty hard. Not necessarily well, but hard. But they're not up to our standards."

"There is one formidable foe in Olympia," Hammond said. Everyone was paying attention. "The gangs. They are pretty much running the place. They are well-armed, as well-armed as we are in many cases, but they're not trained. Well, mostly not trained. The ethnic gangs aren't trained, they're street criminals with AKs and some ARs. Lots of them are on drugs or have venereal diseases. They are not exactly combat effective. They're just thugs who we can take out relatively easily."

"But this isn't a cakewalk," Hammond said again. "Some of the gangs are comprised entirely of former law enforcement and even military. They will be a big problem for us. And some of the ethnic gangs have former LEO and military 'security contractors' working for them." What Hammond didn't say, because he didn't want his troops to be overconfident, was that the gangs' "security contractors" would probably cut and run at the first sign of Patriot regular units or even irregulars. The gangs' "security contractors" were just mercenaries who wouldn't die for the gangs. Hammond wanted his audience to take the gangs seriously.

"But," Hammond cautioned, "Going back to the untrained gangs, what they lack in training, they make up for in viciousness. This is a huge equalizer. You don't have to be well trained to kill our guys if you spray fire into a crowd of civilians and happen to hit our soldiers. Or if you torture people so they don't talk to us when we come in. So don't think of the gangs like traditional enemy soldiers. This leads to my second point." He put up his hand with two fingers up.

"The second difference between this operation and what you might have trained for in a regular unit," Hammond said, "is that this is not a traditional military operation. Okay? Everyone hear that. There's no air support, no artillery, no armor, nuthin'."

Hammond continued, "Yes, they have a few helicopters and some arty," which was short for artillery, "but very little of it. Most of the Lima units that maintain aviation assets or move around artillery pieces have gone AWOL, are sit-outs, or are concentrated in Seattle, so they can't really use these technological marvels on us in Olympia. Same with armor. Maybe they have some armor around, but they don't have the fuel or spare parts for them to be mobile. Our observers on the ground tell us that the Limas have some armor guarding their major facilities, but they don't have any running around intercepting our infantry, which is damned good news." That got a few claps. There was nothing more terrifying to ground troops than enemy tanks.

"If we were going to take Baghdad or Kabul or whatever," Hammond continued, "we wouldn't try it with as small a force as we have. Let's be honest about that. We have a pretty lean force. But this isn't Baghdad or Kabul. This is Olympia, Washington. This leads to the third fundamental point: civilians."

"The civilians in Olympia are Americans," Hammond said. "Our people. Our neighbors—hell, our families—in some cases. They are our fellow citizens in all cases, which means a couple of things."

"First of all," Hammond said, "we always try hard not to hurt civilians, even in foreign countries, but the stakes are higher here because these civilians are Americans. This means we have to have rules of engagement, as much as I hate those things. Basic stuff, though, not lawyer shit. You know, don't shoot unless you can reasonably identify your target. We won't go overboard on ROEs." Hammond, and most of the regular military in the room, had been hobbled in foreign deployments by ridiculous ROEs, as they called Rules of Engagement. Ridiculous ROEs created by liberal politicians let enemy fighters get away with murder. Literally.

"A second thing about our objective being full of American civilians," Hammond said, "is that we will have a strong emphasis on civil affairs." Hammond looked at Grant.

When Hammond said "civil affairs," he put up his hand as if to say "don't start whining." He continued, "Not the 'civil affairs' stuff where we give money to corrupt contractors to build schools in foreign countries that the insurgents use to fire mortars at us." He shook his head. "No, we'll get the government services up and running, especially food, so our own people, Americans, can make it through this. I guess what I'm saying is that we always care about the civilian population, but we care more in this operation because they're our own people."

"Any questions so far?" Hammond asked. There were none.

"Okay, here's the basic overview of the plan," Hammond said. "I should note that you are getting a basic overview. This isn't like the traditional military operations we do where we spend days planning how to coordinate armor, air, artillery, medevac, logistics, and all that. We're going to freestyle this a bit."

Freestyle? That got some concerned looks from the regular military people. That was the opposite of precise military planning. Hammond had anticipated this.

"Here's the deal," Hammond said almost defensively. "We don't have any armor or air to coordinate. We don't have a traditional enemy. They don't really have any command and control that we need to smash. Plus, we have lots of civilians to protect and get back on their feet. This is why I said this isn't a traditional operation at all."

What Hammond didn't say was that Patriot command at the

national level had decided that the time to strike was now. The sit-out units were getting restless. It was now or never for the Patriots. The timing wasn't perfect because the Patriots didn't know if they had superior forces and supply, but it was a "use it or lose it" situation with the sit-outs.

"Regular units will start to move in toward Olympia from all directions," Hammond said and used his pointer on the map to illustrate. "They will lead the assault." Hammond realized he was repeating this part, but wanted the audience to hear it a second time.

"But you folks are here tonight," Hammond said, "because you're the irregulars. Here's your role: come in behind the regular units and occupy the objective. Mop up. Get government services up and running. Let the regular units go after the entrenched facilities and deal with the high-tech Lima threats, like aviation, artillery, and armor, if there are any."

The Special Forces soldier in Hammond took delight in the next point. "Some of the irregular units will be doing traditional guerilla work: sabotage supplies and diversions." Grant knew that the 17th wouldn't be doing these things. He knew what role his unit would have. It was pretty obvious.

Hammond pointed to Captain Morris, who started to gather up packets of documents, each one in a large mailing envelope. "Each unit will have a plan, of course," he said as Morris handed them out.

"There are two kinds of documents in your packet," Hammond said. "One in English and one in your Quadra's language. The one in English has simple things, like radio frequencies and some basic info. The very detailed plan is written in Quadra. This is the sensitive stuff that we really don't want the Limas to get. Your Quadra back at your unit will be able to tell you what's in the detailed plan." Hammond didn't mention that the plans in English were to allow a unit commander to know if a Quadra was a spy and lying about the detailed plan. Hammond wasn't concerned about this, but they had a plan for everything.

Hammond continued, "In this non-traditional operation, we will use radio communications, via the Quadras, to provide a lot of the instructions to you. So you'll have a basic plan, some way-point objectives along the way, and you'll get last minute and detailed instruction from HQ via the Quadras."

"Any questions so far?" Hammond asked. Grant was handed his packet. He looked it over. The Quadra language was in some weird alphabet Grant had never seen. The letters looked like a cross between the Arabic, English, and Russian alphabets.

"We have someone here tonight for each of the units who will verbally give you your specific plan," Hammond said. "Nothing complicated, but we don't have to be complicated. This is more like fighting about a hundred fifty years ago, during the Civil War, than anything you've seen since then. I can't stress this enough: do not view this as a traditional military operation. It's more like a giant law enforcement operation, kicking out some gangs from a city. Because that's basically what it is."

"Any questions?" Hammond asked again.

"Will this be coordinated with attacks in other states?" a contractor-looking guy asked.

"Negative, Brainard," Hammond said. "Each state is pretty much on its own. The Free States," which meant the South and mountain West, "are in the best shape, of course. But even they have their hands full keeping the Limas under control. There are Lima terrorists and even Lima guerilla bands in the Free States. Plus, the Free States are spending all their resources getting food to their people. They are offering political support by recognizing our new state governments, but for now, that's all they can do." What Hammond didn't say was that the logistics of moving Free State forces hundreds of miles to a neighboring state was just too hard with fuel being so scarce.

There was another reason why the national Patriot plan was for each state to kick out the Limas on their own. The basic idea was that if a state had enough political support for the Patriots to mount up an operation, then it could muster up the strength to take back its own state. If the Patriots didn't have the political strength, then that state was a second priority for the Patriots. The Patriots only wanted to try to take areas where they had the support of the population. They weren't interested in taking an area just to say they won it, and then having to fight the population for years. Why bother?

There would be states like California that were too far gone and would never have enough popular support to allow the Patriots to take over. The Patriots would write those states off. There had been a debate in the national Patriot command whether to eventually liberate the "hopeless states" as they had become known. The consensus was to not even try. Most of the Patriots had gotten out of the hopeless states already. Regardless, the Patriots didn't have the strength, or the fuel, to go hundreds of miles and try to take, and then occupy, a place as large as California. The Limas could have it. Let them have their socialist paradises in California, the Northeast, and strongholds like Seattle, Denver, Phoenix, Houston, and Chicago. Enjoy your paradise and stay the hell away from the rest of us.

The Patriots wouldn't try to unify the whole country. The United States was too long. That was one of the biggest reasons the states broke away. It took a bloated and oppressive federal government to make sure the same things that made sense to politicians and bureaucrats in Washington, D.C. were forcibly imposed on a small Alabama town and Los Angeles at the same time. The Patriots had no desire to duplicate this mistake by trying to reunite a country that was too big and diverse to start with. The "United States" was just a bunch of lines on a map, lines that were too big. Americans had common cultural ties, but they were not beholden to lines on a map.

A soldier raised her hand.

"Yes?" Hammond said.

"When will this happen?" she asked. It was an obvious question no one had yet asked.

"Soon," Hammond responded. "Exact date is still being worked out. Be ready to go on a moment's notice. Soon. Very soon." Hammond knew the exact date—New Year's Day—and it had been decided long ago. But he didn't want to say it out loud in case there was a spy there. Each unit would be told the date in a secure Quadra radio message. Besides, things might change at the last minute and the date might need to be adjusted.

A second soldier raised his hand. "What's the name of this operation, sir?"

"Tet."

Chapter 253

A Predictable Mission

(December 21)

Tet. Grant thought about that.

Tet was the surprise offensive by the Viet Cong guerillas during the Vietnam War. The guerillas had an elaborate system of underground tunnels and the government they were fighting was corrupt and unpopular. On the Vietnamese New Year holiday called Tet, guerillas throughout South Vietnam simultaneously attacked. Since it was a holiday, most of the government forces weren't at their jobs. The guerillas primarily destroyed soft targets, like police stations and government buildings, and economic targets. They focused on political targets by assassinating enemy officials and taking symbolic facilities, like government buildings. They even attacked the U.S. embassy and blew a hole in the outer wall of it, which was an unheard of feat for supposedly harmless little guerillas.

Tet was a gigantic shock to the government and the population. The "ragtag" guerillas weren't supposed to be able to do things like that. The population looked at the guerillas in an entirely different light after that. They looked at them as potential victors. People on the fence started to take the guerillas seriously. They started to cooperate with the guerillas, not because they believed in the guerillas' cause, but because they feared the guerillas might win because the Tet offensive proved they could pull of major attacks.

Tet wasn't perfect for the guerillas. The Viet Cong tried to use the guerillas in Tet against hard targets like regular military units, and got cut to pieces. Hammond and others studying Tet had learned that the soft-target part of Tet worked spectacularly well, but the hard-target part failed. Lesson learned.

But the Vietnamese guerillas ultimately won. Many credited their victory in Vietnam to the bold guerilla attacks during the Tet Offensive.

Grant assumed that was what Hammond was going to do, attack soft targets and get the population behind the Patriots. Olympia must be a "soft target." That made far more sense that some stupid attack on the Limas' fortified regular forces. The strategy behind Tet in

22

Vietnam was all about politics, not traditional military victory. Grant was glad Hammond was thinking that way.

Grant could tell that Hammond was a non-traditional warfare guy, not some tank commander who thought that winning was waiting until you had more tanks than your enemy and then having a big battle. Hammond's non-traditional warfare approach made sense: he was a Special Forces guy. They went out, lightly armed, into the boonies in some far off country and got the population to rally behind their side. They used military force as a way to beat the other side's forces, but their ultimate goal was for the natives in their area to want to kick out the opposing side. Hammond was applying this philosophy to someplace he never thought he'd be fighting: Olympia, Washington.

"A final thought," Hammond said. "I know about every single one of you and your units." Grant knew this was true. In his first trip to Boston Harbor, Grant was stunned at how much Hammond already knew about him and Pierce Point. Hammond put his pointer down and folded his hands. It was like he was about to pay respect to someone.

Hammond nodded to the audience and said slowly, "I am extremely confident that each and every one of you will do a magnificent job during Tet. I wouldn't send you out if I didn't know you'll do great and that we'll win." He looked up and then said, "Each of you is supposed to be here and supposed to do what you're about to do. Go do it. And let's take Olympia back!"

A cheer went up. It was the kind of cheer that comes from pent-up, raw emotion, a cheer from men and women who had been working hard for months and hadn't had a room full of like-minded people to cheer with until now.

"Captain Morris will now assign a briefer to each of you," Hammond said. "Thank you. Every single one of you."

The audience applauded, with someone yelling to Hammond, "No. Thank YOU!"

After the cheering died down, Captain Morris came to the front of the room and said, "Each unit line up in number order along the wall starting over here," he said, pointing. The units started to get up and find their places.

After a few minutes, a sergeant came up to Grant and Ted.

"The 17th?" the sergeant asked.

"Yes," Grant said.

The sergeant opened up a sealed envelope that had "17th" written on it and took a look at the map that was on the inside.

"You guys," the sergeant said, "Are going through

Frederickson first and then down Highway 101 straight into Olympia. Pretty simple. You'll also be defending 101 against any Limas coming down south from Bremerton trying to reinforce Olympia." Bremerton was about thirty miles north of Pierce Point. There was a giant Navy base there. The Limas would have forces there guarding the ships and subs. It seemed like a long haul for Limas to come down from Bremerton all the way through ambush country just to reinforce a secondary city like Olympia, but the Limas just might try it.

Grant and Ted nodded. They figured this would be their mission. There was nothing complicated about it, except maybe getting through Frederickson, although Rich had filled him in on Bennington's offer.

"Your Quadra," the sergeant said, "will get you more detailed instructions and be able to relay your specific questions to us."

The sergeant handed Grant the map and then got out his clipboard. "Do you have any specific plans on how to get through your first objective, Frederickson?"

"Yes," Grant said. "We promised him secrecy, but we have a very highly placed source there that is waiting to be activated and will take out the county government's leadership." Ted nodded as if to say, "Seriously."

The sergeant's eyes lit up. "That's awesome, sir." He made a note on his clipboard. Grant and Ted had previously radioed this in to HQ via Jim Q., but that had only been a couple of days ago; maybe this news hadn't gotten to the planners charting out the 17th's mission. As squared away as HQ was, no organization this big, and operating in such semi-primitive conditions, could be perfect.

Then the sergeant looked concerned. "Does this source know about the 17th?" he asked.

"Nope," Grant said. "The source doesn't know a thing. Our contact with the source is via someone in our community who, in turn, is working with us."

The sergeant smiled. "Nice," he said.

Ted said, "We plan on activating the source a few hours before we head out. That'll be okay, right? I mean, we don't want to let people outside of our unit know that an offensive is coming unless we have to. But, in order to take out the county's command and control, I think it's worth the risk."

"A few hours is fine," the sergeant said. "The Limas will be hit with diversions elsewhere a few hours in advance, so it's okay that they know the whole state is erupting on them. Just fine."

24

That was it for their briefing. Grant and Ted left together and then Grant walked off to learn how to get Paul and Tony a medal. Ted was very glad to see this civilian lawyer lieutenant had the instinct to look after his men in such a way. You can't teach that, Ted thought. This was all coming together.

Chapter 254

Collapse Christmas at Camp Murray

(December 24)

For the obvious reasons, the "Collapse Christmas" was different than any other Christmas. Very different. Unforgettable.

Christmas is full of traditions: opening presents, Christmas dinner, wearing a Santa hat, and going to a Christmas Eve church service. There were countless individual Christmas traditions.

Those traditions clashed with the reality of the Collapse. Many traditions could not go on. There were far fewer presents. For some, the cherished Christmas dinner was going to be oatmeal. Some Christmas Eve church services were cancelled because those churches were refusing to play ball with the government and it was too dangerous to leave the house anyway. The football games had been cancelled all season. The government desperately wanted the teams to play to project a sense of normalcy, but most of the players, like the AWOL soldiers, had just gone home to be with their families instead of reporting for work.

Then again, Grant noticed some traditions carried on. Little things seemed to mean more during the Collapse Christmas. Presents were things like batteries, a deck of playing cards, and a can of soup. Some weren't wrapped, and some were wrapped in black and white newspaper, rather than colorful wrapping paper. Everyone did their best to keep their chins up and hope that the next Christmas would be better.

With that hope, however, many wondered whether the Collapse would still be going on next Christmas. They didn't like the idea that it would, or that every Christmas might be as bad.

Christmas made people think about kids—whether it was their kids or remembering what Christmas was like when they were kids themselves. Would kids have more crappy Christmases in their future? Forever? Was traditional America, and wonderful Christmases, over forever?

People who had never thought about the "temporary Crisis" really being a war started to think about it for the first time. Many had been going with the flow up until the holiday. While they thought the government was inept, what was the alternative? The government they had was ... well, the government. There could only be one government at a time. It wasn't like there could be a competing one. Could there?

The thought of competing governments started to make more sense when people heard about the Southern and mountain West states essentially striking out on their own. There was no giant civil war with two huge armies, one in blue and one in gray; nothing like that, but it was pretty clear that there were two competing governments. One seemed to be working well and the other didn't.

Jeanie Thompson had come to this conclusion long ago. She got to see how awful the Loyalist government was. She was in the building where most of the decisions were being made. She saw everything. They weren't even trying to hide things from her any more.

Jeanie was still doing the menial job of giving tours to NSVIPs — Not So Very Important Persons, as she called them. Not even the mayors and mid-level government officials who came to Camp Murray to get a "briefing" on how great things were going were upbeat anymore. What a joke. By now, everyone she was giving the spiel to knew everything was a lie and she knew that they knew. She kept doing the tours anyway. It was her job. If she lost her job, she would have to leave Camp Murray. And if that happened, she'd be dead in ten seconds "outside the wire."

Jeanie's boss, Rick Menlow, had finally realized his dream. He became the Governor. The former Governor resigned for health reasons. She was a wreck and had several nervous breakdowns. At least, that's what everyone said. But, maybe she was shoved aside for political reasons. Who knew? Who cared?

Jeanie shrugged when she heard the news. Her whole career had been built around the dream of her boss being the Governor and she being the press secretary for him. That was ... months ago? Was that all? It seemed like a lifetime ago.

Now Jeanine didn't care. Her boss was a tool. He would just do whatever D.C. told him. He had gone from the fresh reformer conservative who miraculously got elected as the State Auditor to what he was now – a tool.

Jeanie reflected on her enthusiasm when she and her boss bugged out of Olympia and first came to Camp Murray. Back then, she felt like she was going to help the state in a time of need. She was going to do all these wonderful things to help people.

Now, Jeanie was a prisoner. Everyone in that building was a prisoner, even the people running the state. They couldn't leave the protections of their government facilities. They had plenty to eat in those facilities, but they couldn't leave.

Something had to change. People couldn't live that way much longer.

Jeanie, who was out of the official loop because she had ties to some POIs, still overheard conversations about a war. A "war"? Not the little terrorism stuff or the police rounding up teabaggers. This was an actual war. They were calling it a civil war. That term sounded so outlandish. A "civil war"? C'mon. In America? That was crazy!

There was constant talk around Camp Murray about which military units were still "sit outs" and which ones were going over to the teabaggers. Loyal units were highly sought after. They could have anything they wanted for their services. There were some stories of very nasty behavior by the loyal units.

The rumors Jeanie overheard seemed to be that the teabaggers were about to launch something in Washington State. There were conflicting reports of what it would be. The legitimate authorities had spies in the teabagger army, but they were getting conflicting reports. Jeanie wondered if some of the spies were double agents sending out intentionally conflicting reports. Some said there would be a New Year's Day limited attack that would bypass Seattle entirely. Others said it would be a full-on attack in February. Others said it would come in the spring and would be from units currently sitting out that would go over to the teabaggers. No one knew for sure.

There was also continuous talk at Camp Murray about how the farms were not producing enough food to feed people. Jeanie learned that, before the Crisis, America had imported over half of its food. Over half! Most people couldn't believe it. Those supplies were now cut off. The dollar was worthless and there wasn't enough fuel to ship food. America had the most farmland in the world, right? Well, yes and no. America had the most land capable of farming, but for years, farmers had been living on government subsidies instead of actually growing any significant quantities of food. Before the Crisis, the government actually paid farmers not to farm. That amazed Jeanie.

Even the farmers who still farmed didn't help the situation much. Before the Crisis, Jeanie learned, the government paid them to grow crops, such as corn, to be used for ethanol. The fields to grow corn were still available — but many of the processing plants to turn the corn into food were not. They had been retooled to make ethanol. The processing plants to make cornbread and other things were shut down. Try as they might, the government couldn't get enough of them back up and running to make cornbread.

Jeanie also found out how devastating America's pre-Crisis dependence on foreign goods had been. It wasn't just that over half of the nation's food came from overseas. It was that a bunch of the domestic food production capabilities had been shut down, much like the corn processing plants. For example, when it was cheaper to grow peaches in China and send them on a ship to Atlanta, all the Georgia peach orchards a few miles outside of Atlanta were plowed under. It takes years to grow a mature peach tree that will produce peaches, so it would take years to bring America's food production capacity back. If it ever came back.

But the government urgently needed food. The political and military people at Camp Murray constantly talked about food riots. They were all trying to calculate the point at which FCard food would reach such a low level that people would have nothing left to lose and would start rioting. Would the Legitimate troops—they preferred the term "Legitimate" to "Loyalist"—shoot fellow Americans? That was a constant topic of discussion.

It was Christmas Eve. Jeanie sat in her tight barracks room with a little stocking that all the staff got. It looked so pathetic, so small, and so fake. It was nothing like her real stocking at her parent's house. She wondered if they were okay. Probably. Hopefully. She missed going home each Christmas and going to the Christmas Eve service at her parents' church. She had so many memories of that, like when they turned off the lights, everyone lit a candle, and they sang *Silent Night*. She could hear that in her head. It was sweet and warm, wonderful.

But there was no Christmas Eve service at Camp Murray. That would be too divisive. They couldn't even say the "C" word (Christmas) there. Instead, they had a "winter solstice" event. That wouldn't offend anyone … except the 99% of people at Camp Murray who weren't Wiccan.

Jason felt like he was in prison, too. He had gone from being the ultra-cool and confident briefer to be being a terrified liaison with the federal government. He had special communications equipment that let him talk with the intelligence community in D.C. He received their dispatches and told them what was going on in Washington State. He knew just about everything that was happening, which was why he was terrified. The federal government had essentially ceased to operate. Almost all federal resources were devoted to the military, FEMA, and federal law enforcement agencies. No one really knew what the "military" was anymore. There were military units on paper, but most had simply vanished or were sit-outs. Some units were run by seemingly loyal officers but, on occasion, a seemingly loyal unit would just disappear or announce it was sitting out. Some went over to the Patriots. Command and control? The federal government had neither.

Jason didn't know who he could trust. Was this Washington National Guard unit guarding them secretly a Patriot unit? How could he tell? Were the federal agents who were guarding him secretly paras? Or taking bribes to kill him? He couldn't sleep at night. He cat napped all day long. And each day was so long. He was up most of the time. He lost track of time. It was like one long blur. He had aged ten years in ten months and lost so much weight that his tailored suits no longer fit.

Jason knew it was over. Whether the Patriots won or not, it was over. There was no way the Legitimates could continue. Food would get dangerously low over the winter. Rioting would ensue and most military and police units would not fire on the crowds. Some, like the mercenaries and psychos who enjoyed it, would, but most would not.

Despite all of this, there was a strange sense of hope. Seattle was a stronghold, one of the strongest in the country. Things were relatively calm there. The population seemed to actually like the government. Most of the individualists had left, and Loyalists poured in from other parts of the state, even from other states. There were genuine rallies in support of the government there.

Jason had reported this to his superiors in D.C. They came back with a plan: move the Governor and senior staff to Seattle. They would use the ultra-secure federal courthouse in Seattle as a headquarters. This was the first good news Jason had heard in months.

They would move out—secretly, of course—in the middle of the night on Christmas Eve. No one would be paying attention at that time and, according to D.C, something might be happening on New Year's Day in Washington State. No one could know that the Governor was abandoning Camp Murray, which was supposedly safe behind the super- fortified JBLM ring. If Camp Murray wasn't safe enough for the Governor…

Jason was one of about ten people who knew the plan. They would go in one of the commercial buses taking people into Seattle. There was no need to have a big motorcade that was a big fat target.

Jason didn't trust even the FBI or state police EPU unit guarding the Governor, so he arranged for a diversion motorcade to go out first. He let it slip that the Governor was going in a motorcade from Camp Murray to the airfield at McChord Air Base to take a flight to

D.C. to meet with the President. If there was a leak, that diversionary motorcade would get hit. Too bad for the guys in that motorcade. Oh well. This was tough business.

Jason was packing up his things for the bus ride to Seattle that night. He realized he didn't have a single personal item from his months at Camp Murray. Then he saw it. His stocking. His cheesy little stocking. He took it and put it in the inside pocket of his tailored suit jacket. At least he had one souvenir from his time in that God-awful place.

Chapter 255

Todd & Chloe Part II

(December 24)

"So, how much are we talking?" Todd asked the former police officers who were being paid to guard his posh Bellevue neighborhood.

"Depends," one of the former officers said. "Where, exactly, do you want to go?"

"Wenatchee," he said.

"Let's come up with a plan first and then we can answer the 'how much' question," said another of the former officers. They looked around their makeshift guard shack for a few seconds and then asked Todd, "You got a map?"

"Yep," Todd said, swelling with pride. For once, he was the one who was prepared. He went back to the Range Rover and knocked on Chloe's passenger-side window.

"What is it?" she asked with concern.

"I need the map in the glove box," he said. "They're going to help us get out of here." She smiled, glowing with joy. This was going to work, she thought. They were finally going to get out of this terrible place and to a safe cabin in the woods with their former neighbors, Ken and Kim. She opened the glove box and found the old highway map and handed it to her husband, who was finally being a man, six months into this nightmare. Better late than never, she thought. She leaned back in the plush leather seat of the Range Rover and felt like she could finally relax. They were getting to safety. She smiled for the first time in a long time.

Todd took the map over to the guard station. The three officers unfolded it and started talking among themselves.

"Once you get a mile from here, it's bad," one of them said. "Going through Bellevue proper is extremely dangerous," another said, "and the highway from there out to I-90 is spotty."

"Robberies?" Todd asked, hoping that was the only problem, but knowing that rape and kidnapping were also common.

"And worse," an officer said. "But your main problem, and the main thing we can help with, are the roadblocks."

"Roadblocks?" Todd asked. "Who's blocking the roads?"

"FCorps," another officer said. "They want to keep people in the cities where the government services are." What he didn't say was that they were stealing people blind and, on occasion, grabbing women and children for the gangs.

"Gee," Todd said. "How do I get through the roadblocks?"

One of the officers reached under his jacket and pulled out his badge that was hanging from the chain around his neck.

"This is how," he said with a smile. "One of us will come with you."

Great! Todd thought. Not only will they have the badge to get through the roadblocks, they'll have a well-trained and armed police officer. Chloe will be so happy.

"Will you have a gun with you?" Todd asked, instantly realizing what a stupid question that was. Chloe wouldn't want a gun around the girls. A gun could go off and hurt them.

The officers tried not to roll their eyes. "Yes, sir," one of them replied. "A couple of them."

"And you'll have one, too," the third one said. "It's a package deal: one of us goes with you and gets you through the roadblocks, and we get you a gun you can have for use at your ultimate destination." He paused. "It's a package deal, sir. You *need* a gun."

Todd thought about what these men were saying. He realized his family could get to Ken and Kim's cabin with these escorts who were former police. And he really needed a gun; even Chloe agreed to that now. The savvy businessman in Todd kicked into gear.

"How much?" he asked. He expected it was going to cost him several thousand dollars.

"Your house and everything in it," one of the officers said.

Todd felt he'd been punched in the stomach. He could barely speak. Finally, he managed to blurt out, "Everything? Seriously?"

"Seriously, sir," one of the officers replied. The other two nodded.

"If this is some kind of joke, I'm really not in a great mood for that now," Todd said, attempting to gain control of the situation.

"You and your family are dead," one of the officers stated, without emotion. So much for taking control of the situation, Todd thought.

They had him. His mind raced to figure out how he would make this work without giving away all of his worldly possessions.

"Surely, you guys are open to negotiation," Todd said, after he realized he had zero bargaining position.

"No, sir, we're not," the first officer said. "We would be risking our lives and using an extremely valuable asset only we have: our badges."

"Take it or leave it," the normally quiet officer said as he walked away. The other two started following him.

"Wait!" Todd yelled out. He instantly realized he was desperate, which was a bad negotiating strategy. He said more calmly, "Surely we can work something out." The officers kept walking.

"Okay!" Todd yelled. "You can have everything, but I want some guarantees." The officers stopped and slowly turned to face Todd.

"Like what?" one of them asked.

Todd had no idea what "guarantees" he could obtain. He said it without thinking.

"You'll see when we get back to my house," he said, trying to buy some time. He added, "Oh, and I need to ask my wife if this is okay."

The normally quiet officer started laughing. "Why?" he asked.

"Community property," Todd said. "She owns half the house."

The first officer intervened to make sure the quiet one wasn't scaring off a very good-paying client.

"We understand," the first officer said. "Makes sense."

Todd nodded and pointed at the Range Rover and said, "Be right back."

Then it hit him. He actually had to go ask Chloe for permission to give away all of their things – the house, the BMW, the art, the boat, everything – in order to do something that he could have done for almost free six months ago. That house was everything to her. In that moment, he was more afraid of her than of the carjackers a mile way.

"Is everything okay?" She asked him as he walked up to the passenger side of the Range Rover.

"Oh, yes," he said with fake enthusiasm. "They will give us an escort to the cabin."

"Oh, thank God!" she shrieked. "I'm so glad they're doing that for us."

"Well why don't you step out here for a moment," he said, not wanting this argument to be seen by his little girls.

"Be back in a minute, girls," Chloe said cheerily, although it was apparent she was concerned something was very wrong.

When they were far enough away from the Range Rover, Todd said, "The cops aren't doing this for free."

Chloe looked at him with amazement. Of course they would do this for free, she thought, they were public servants. Or former ones, or whatever, but it was their job to take care of people like her.

"How much?" she asked. "I hope it's not more than a few hundred dollars because that's all the cash we have since the bank closed."

"It's a lot more," Todd said, hoping to break the news to her gently. "Like, way more." He was trying to lower her expectations.

"But we don't have any more cash," Chloe said, perplexed at how they could pay more than a few hundred dollars, and still wondering why public servants would want cash in the first place.

"It's not cash," Todd said, "That's the good news."

"What's the bad news?" Chloe asked.

"They want the house and everything in it."

Chloe nearly fell over. She grabbed onto Todd's arm and softly whispered, "What?"

Todd nodded.

"Sure," Chloe said, without blinking an eye. "Let's do it."

Now it was Todd's turn to nearly fall over.

"Yes," Chloe said, "We have no choice. Let's do it."

"What?" Todd stammered.

"Don't you agree?" Chloe asked.

"Well, yes," Todd said, still in shock. "But I didn't think you would."

Chloe hugged Todd and whispered to him, "A lot has changed since yesterday. You're being a man and taking care of us. I need to do whatever I can to support you."

Now Todd was in even more shock. What explained her sudden change of heart? "Huh?" is all he could say.

"We'll talk about it at the cabin," Chloe said and hugged him tighter. "I'm thankful that you're handling this. Let's do it and get going."

Todd felt like he was floating on air. He was elated. This was going to work out. They would make it.

After a few seconds of hugging, Todd realized the officers were waiting for him. "I have a deal to close," he said to Chloe, who hugged him tighter.

"That's my man."

Todd still felt like he was walking on air as he walked over to the officers. He couldn't contain his happiness, despite trying to mask it for negotiating purposes.

"Follow me to the house and I'll get you all the keys you need," he said.

The officers nodded. The first one said, "I'll come so these two can stay as guards."

"You need to get a ride?" Todd asked the officer.

"Nope," he said, "I'll ride on the rear bumper of the Rover. I can hold onto the roof rack."

"Okay," Todd said. When he came up to the Range Rover, he motioned for Chloe to lower her window. "He'll ride on the rear bumper."

"Okay," she said, to Todd's surprise. He expected her to question if that was safe. She had completely changed since yesterday. Todd knew from years of marriage that she had a personality that allowed her to change her mind on a dime. When she realized she had been wrong, she could just switch gears and go on with life. Todd was enormously relieved that she was fine with the AK-47.

"Girls, a nice police officer will be riding on the back of the Rover with us to our house," she said to the girls in the rear seat. "Don't worry. It's safe."

Todd got into the Range Rover and felt a weight on the rear of the vehicle and then two light taps on the roof, which he assumed signified that the officer was ready to ride. Todd slowly drove off, back toward their beautiful home.

"Hey, girls," Chloe said as they pulled into their long, beautiful driveway, "We'll stay in here while Daddy and the police officer talk about how they'll get us to the cabin!" She wasn't prepared to tell them that their house, and everything in it, would no longer belong to them.

"Yeah!" the girls cheered.

Todd stopped the Range Rover and got out silently. He still couldn't believe he was going to do what he was about to do. He felt a weight released from the rear of the Range Rover as the police officer got off the bumper. "A weight off our shoulders," he said to Chloe, who smiled and nodded.

Todd wanted to make this quick. "I'll get you all the keys," he said. The officer nodded.

Todd went through the garage and saw his prized possession, his boat. It was a twenty-five foot 2005 Pursuit with twin Yamaha four-stroke engines, to be exact. It was beautiful. That boat was Todd's escape from all the pressures of being a corporate executive. It was luxurious and comfortable.

To Todd's horror, the officer let out a whistle and said, "That's nice. Very nice."

"It's not part of the deal," Todd impulsively replied, surprised by what came out of his mouth

"You're right," the officer said with a slight smirk. "It's not part of the deal for getting you guys past the roadblocks," he said. Todd was so relieved he was short of breath.

"Nope, the boat is what the AK will cost you," the officer said.

"The what?" Todd asked.

The officer pulled a frightening-looking rifle out of his long backpack. "It's an AK-47. You'll need it. Very rugged. Perfect for what you'll need at the cabin."

"A $150,000 boat for an AK-47?" Todd asked. He knew the answer, but asked the question anyway.

"Yes, sir," the officer said. "This boat won't do you any good here, anyway."

Todd realized that the officer had a point, a really good one.

"Don't let my wife see that," Todd said and, almost on queue for bad luck, Chloe walked into the garage.

"Oh, cool," she said, pointing to the AK-47. "That's just what we need, an Army gun." She was serious.

Todd still could not believe what he was hearing and seeing, but he was glad everything was working out.

"I just needed to use my bathroom one more time," Chloe said. She walked into the house.

"Let's label all the keys," the officer said. Todd found some painters tape and a Sharpie marker and started labeling the keys, remote entry devices, and garage door openers. It took almost a half hour. Todd and Chloe had a lot of stuff. At least, they used to, Todd thought.

The officer's radio crackled, "What's your ETA back to the shack?" one of the officers asked.

"Just wrapping up," the first officer responded into the speaker mic clipped to his jacket. The officer looked at Todd and asked, "You got a piece of paper we can write on?"

"Sure," Todd said, heading to the office supplies in the study. "Why?" he asked as he was walking.

"You're going to write up a deed," the officer said. "Your wife will need to sign it because she owns half of this."

"A deed?" Todd asked. "Are those even necessary anymore?"

"Not now," the officer said, "but normal life might return and we need a deed, even a handwritten one, to prove you gave this to me."

"Seriously?" Todd asked.

"Seriously," the officer said. "Probably will never need it, but it's nice for me to have."

For some reason, Todd found that writing out a deed seemed to be the most surprising thing of all that morning, despite all the craziness that had already ensued.

Todd knew that a handwritten deed didn't even come close to complying with the law for a deed, but he wanted to do it so that he and Chloe would, symbolically at least, make it official that they had given the house away. Todd and the officer quickly scribbled a two-sentence deed and Todd took it to Chloe in the Range Rover to sign. She was surprised, too, but signed it anyway. The house was no longer hers in her mind.

Todd read the deed to see the officer's name hand printed above the signature. "Christopher Willden" it said.

"Christopher or Chris?" Todd asked him. "I might as well know the name of the guy who's getting everything I own."

"Chris," Willden said. He felt bad that he was stripping this guy of everything that he owned, but he had to take care of his family and his fellow officers guarding the subdivision. It was just business, he thought.

"Heading back," Willden said into his radio, and then said to Todd, "Let's start getting you guys where you need to go." Those words sounded so sweet to Todd's ears that he almost began to cry.

Willden got back on the Range Rover's rear bumper and they drove back to the guard station.

"How many of you guys are coming with us?" Todd asked two of the other officers. They pointed to Willden who pointed at himself and said, "Just me."

"Oh," Todd said disappointedly. Then he realized that the other two needed to stay at the subdivision to guard it.

"What car are you going to take?" he asked Willden.

"I'm not," Willden said. "Waste of gas."

"So how are you getting back here?" Todd asked.

Willden pulled out his badge and said, "I can get rides pretty easily."

They discussed the logistics. Willden would drive the Range Rover and Todd would be in the front seat. Chloe would sit in the back with the girls; she was very slender so she could fit back there much better than Todd, who was fit, but an average sized man. Willden sitting in the driver's seat would allow him to flash his badge at the roadblocks.

Todd was still nervous about the AK-47 being in the Range Rover. He asked Willden, "How do I handle the gun you got me?"

"I'll show you how to shoot it," Willden said.

"No," Todd said, "I mean how do we announce to Chloe and the girls that it's in the car?"

Willden was puzzled. He felt sorry for Todd for being such a wuss.

"I dunno," Willden said, trying to stay polite. "You have it in the passenger seat so you can use it for threats on that side of the vehicle."

"What?" Todd said, "Me? Shoot a gun?"

"Yes," Willden said, this time unable to hide his displeasure for Todd. "That's what you do when people are shooting at you. You shoot back."

"I don't think I should be doing that," Todd said. "It seems dangerous."

Willden called over for Chloe who got out of the Range Rover and came over.

"You okay with riding in the front and shooting that thing?" he asked, pointing toward the AK-47.

"Sure," she said. "Why isn't Todd doing it?"

"I will do it," Todd said, horrified that his wife was being more of a man than he was. "I'll ride shotgun, or 'AK' if that's what you call these things."

"Problem solved," Willden said, somewhat sarcastically. Rich people are so high maintenance, he thought.

They went over the plan one more time, but they had it down by now.

"We'll go at sunrise," Willden said. "That'll be in an hour or so. You didn't want to be out in this stuff in the dark," he said, wondering why these nice, but naïve rich people had been planning to leave before light.

"Stretch your legs while you can," Willden said. The girls were getting restless being in the Range Rover for so long, thinking they were going on a big trip to a cabin, and then not going.

"Hey, girls," one of the other officers said, "you want to see all about being a real police officer?" The girls ran over to the guard shack and the officers began to entertain them.

"What is Santa getting you guys?" one of the officers asked

them. It was Christmas Eve, after all. The girls began talking a mile a minute about all the toys they wanted.

"I bet Santa brought all those things to the cabin," the other officer finally said when the girls stopped talking. "He knows where you'll be tonight." He realized what he just said and suddenly got very quiet. Todd couldn't understand why the officer was so disturbed about where the girls would be tonight.

"Time to go," Willden said as it was getting light at about 8:10 a.m. Before getting into the Range Rover, Chloe announced to the girls, "Daddy has a pretend gun to scare any bears away."

"But don't worry," Todd said. "There won't be any bears. Know why?"

"Because they're scared of Daddy's pretend gun!" his youngest said.

"Let's hope so," Willden muttered under his breath.

Everyone was anxious to get the dangerous journey started; they had been waiting all morning to get on their way. When it was finally time to go, time to leave everything they ever owned, Todd and Chloe were ready.

"One last thing," Willden said before he and Todd got into the Range Rover. He handed Todd the AK-47. At first Todd didn't want to touch it, but then he saw Chloe was watching. He couldn't wuss out in front of her, so he took the AK, but touched it softly so it couldn't go off by accident.

Willden saw Todd was afraid of the AK. "They don't go off by themselves," he said.

"Does this have a safety?" Todd asked.

"Yes," Willden replied. "It's that lever there," he said pointing to the right side of the rifle. "When it's up, like it is now, it's on safe. So push that lever down when you want to fire."

"Okay," Todd said, knowing that he never wanted to fire it.

Once they were ready to go, they slowly left the safety of the subdivision. The other officers waved goodbye to them. Willden seemed very serious about the journey ahead. He didn't talk at all.

Todd and Chloe hadn't been out of the subdivision in weeks. The subdivision next to theirs was also nice. They drove to a gate that was manned by private security contractors and Willden flashed his badge. They rolled right through.

Todd had to break the silence. "That thing works pretty well," he said, pointing toward the badge.

"Yep," Willden said. "That's what you're buying."

They went through another few subdivisions, with Willden flashing his badge each time. The neighborhoods were becoming less and less expensive as they headed to the streets that fed into the highway. Each neighborhood seemed more and more crime-ridden. There were a few burned out cars and garbage was strewn everywhere. One subdivision had a huge pack of wild dogs running around on the hunt. Todd was glad they were in a vehicle and not out in the open.

They came to what looked like an official police roadblock. Willden flashed his badge and they breezed through. No other vehicles were allowed through it. Todd was thrilled that he was renting that badge, even if it did cost him everything he'd ever owned. Unfortunately, it appeared to be the best deal he'd ever made.

The streets were deserted except for a few small packs of dogs. Many stores were burned out and had been looted.

"Did someone break that window, Mom?" one of the girls asked.

"No, silly," Chloe said, "It broke when something fell on it."

"Did that building get burned?" the other girl asked.

"No," Chloe said. "They just painted it to look that way. Kinda silly, huh?"

The girls nodded, and then Chloe changed the subject and got them talking about the Christmas presents Santa was bringing to them at the cabin, which occupied them for long enough.

When they came up to I-405, there was a huge roadblock with military vehicles that looked like tanks and had machine guns on them.

"Why are the Army men here?" one of the girls asked.

"To help us," Chloe said, and then she changed the subject back to what Santa was bringing.

"You might want to put something over the AK," Willden said to Todd. "These are National Guardsmen. They are under orders to seize assault rifles. Remember that you're working with me on an official law enforcement assignment. Got it?"

"You're going to lie, Daddy?" one of the girls asked.

"Of course not," Todd said as Chloe handed him a jacket to put over the AK. "I'm helping the police by scaring away bears."

The girls cheered.

A soldier came up to them. Willden had his badge out the window. The soldier carefully scrutinized it to make sure it was a legitimate badge.

"What brings you out here, officer?" the soldier asked.

"We're transporting the family of my chief," Willden said, very convincingly. "Paras are..." he paused and pointed at the girls and implied that he didn't want to say everything in front of the girls. "The paras are, you know, making trouble."

"Who is your chief?" the soldier asked.

"Nick Moyes," Willden answered. "Want to confirm all this?" Todd froze.

The soldier kept looking at Willden and Todd, and then Chloe and the girls. He didn't want to waste his time talking to some police chief.

"Aren't they a little young to be the family of a police chief?" the solider asked. Todd felt his stomach knot up.

"Second marriage," Willden said. "And he's pretty young. You know, with all the para activity, there have been a lot of replacement chiefs lately." He put his finger up to his lip to signal to the soldier that he didn't want to say anything that would disturb Chloe or the girls.

"Oh, right," the soldier said. His shift was over in ten minutes and he didn't want the hassle of confirming all this. Besides, the second marriage thing kind of made sense. Everything Willden said to him appeared to make enough sense for him to let these people through.

"You know we cannot guarantee anyone's safety," the soldier said like a robot. He used this phrase a hundred times a day.

"Understood," Willden said. "Is there anything I should know about down the road?"

The soldier didn't have the time or patience to tell this cop about all the threats out there. Besides, he didn't want to scare the girls.

"Just the usual," he said. Willden nodded.

"Good luck, officer," the soldier said as he waved them through.

As they went through the roadblock, soldiers on top of the tanks – or MRAPs, as Willden corrected Todd – were pointing machine guns at the Range Rover the whole time.

Interstate 405 was empty, which Todd had never seen. "We'll take I-90 east to Wenatchee," Willden said. "We have enough gas if we don't get delayed."

Everyone was silent, except the girls and Chloe, who were talking about Santa. Willden and Todd were tuning it out.

They went through another military roadblock similar to the one on I-405. Willden used the same story about evacuating his chief's family.

Interstate 90 was empty, too, except for occasional police cars and military vehicles. There was one long convoy of semi-trucks with

42

military escorts. "Food and fuel," Willden said.

They drove about twenty miles. As they went under an overpass, several vehicles zoomed down the on ramp and started to chase them.

"Hold on!" Willden yelled and he punched the gas pedal. The Range Rover sped up, but it was no race car. As the vehicles came up behind them, Willden slammed on the brakes and the chasing vehicles sped on by. Their brake lights quickly came on. Todd was terrified.

"Get out and point that AK at them!" Willden yelled. The girls were crying and Chloe was screaming.

Todd did as he was told. "Use the Rover for cover!" Willden yelled. He had his AR pointed at the brake lights, which stayed on for a minute or so. It was the longest minute of Todd's life. Finally, they went off and the vehicles drove off.

"Whew!" Todd said.

"Except that they're up there and we'll probably meet up with them again," Willden said. He was starting to regret taking on this job, despite how profitable it was.

"We'll have to go slower now," Willden said. They crept along at 35 miles per hour for a few miles. They saw the pack of vehicles speeding back the other way.

"Are they coming back for us?" Todd asked.

"Nope," Willden said. "If they wanted us, they would do a roadblock up ahead." They kept driving and didn't see the vehicles again.

After about an hour, Willden looked at the gas gauge. He had just over half a tank. "Let's get out and stretch our legs," he said. That sounded good to Todd. The family got out and walked around for a bit.

Willden seemed nervous. "Stay here," he said, as he got into the Rover. He started it up and drove up to the family.

"Hey, this isn't working out," he said, as he rolled down his window. "I'm heading back."

Todd laughed. Willden didn't.

"We're not at Wenatchee yet," Todd finally said.

"That's your problem," Willden said. "I gotta get back before dark. See you guys."

This isn't funny anymore, Todd thought. Before he knew it, he had lifted the AK to his shoulder, pointed it at Willden, and yelled "Stop!" The girls started screaming.

Willden laughed. Finally, he said, "Go ahead and shoot, Todd."

Todd pulled the trigger, but the gun didn't go off. Then he remembered that the safety was on. He pushed the lever down so it would fire, re-shouldered the AK and pulled the trigger again.

Click.

Willden started laughing. "It's not loaded, dumbass."

Todd tried pulling the trigger again, but the gun did nothing.

"The magazine has been empty the whole time," Willden said.

"Take care," he said as he drove off.

Chloe was screaming and the girls were crying.

After an hour of arguing and trying to figure out what to do, Todd and Chloe finally sat down on the shoulder of the highway. Not a single vehicle had gone by the whole time.

After a long while of sitting there silently, Todd and Chloe heard the sound of approaching cars. They felt a sense of relief.

Until they saw that it was the same pack of vehicles that chased them. Todd shouldered his AK again and felt a hot punch in his chest and then heard a loud noise. He saw blood everywhere and it felt like someone spilled hot soup on his chest. Then he realized he'd been shot. The last thing he saw before he was swallowed by darkness was a group of men grabbing Chloe and the girls.

Chapter 256

Winter Solstice in Seattle

(December 24)

Professor Carol Matson was having a delicious cup of hot cocoa and listening to winter solstice music on NPR. She loved NPR. It was so soothing and civilized.

Carol was in a great mood. Winter solstice was a marvelous time. It was a time to reflect on the year. There had sure been some scares this year. The initial shock of the empty store shelves and all the teabagger violence. All the people recently coming to Seattle to escape the right-wing terrorism. She had heard that the so-called Patriots were rounding up minorities and killing them. But that wasn't happening in Seattle. People were treated right in Seattle. People were taken care of. They had equality there: free health care, free food, free everything. Well, when those things were available, which meant when the terrorists hadn't interfered with the supplies. The government was doing its very best to provide for everyone, but the terrorist teabaggers were sabotaging that, which was why there were supply problems.

Carol loved diversity; people of all races who, thankfully, all seemed to agree on things. In Seattle, everyone agreed that the government was doing the right thing. Instead of her being a "liberal" in redneck country, now everyone in Seattle seemed to think like her. Progressive. Smart. Open-minded. Caring. She felt like the decent people were finally in charge. People like her.

Carol looked forward to a great new year. Things were on the right track. There was way too much suffering out there, but people could still make it into Seattle. They would be safe there. They could have their own little country there. There would be no more rednecks telling them what to do.

The news—NPR was the only station left—was positive. There were small groups of terrorists in the South and mountain West, the "Confederates" as the news called them, who were still performing their killings. New Congresspersons and Senators had been appointed for those states and Congress was meeting again. Somewhere.

But, order had been re-established. The federal government

was functioning just fine. There were lots of news stories about national parks being open and full of visitors. Well, a few visitors on camera. The postal service was working. There were long delays because of the restrictions on using the freeways and the gas rationing. Carol hadn't actually gotten any mail, but she'd heard on the news that the postal service was working. There was no more junk mail; one good thing to come from the Crisis. There were lots of stories on the news about celebrities and how things were just like the old days for them. Shopping, having parties. Just like normal.

Seattle was certainly doing fine. While food was in short supply, Carol, as an FCorps employee, had plenty of credits on her FCard. And the utilities were on. Not bad.

But all the good things in Seattle came at a price. Carol wondered how her brother was doing. She hoped he had just grown out of his rebellious "Patriot" nonsense. He was always a practical guy—a survivor. She and he had survived their terrible childhood, so he would probably be fine. Besides, he was smart. He probably realized the right-wing stuff was a lie. He had probably renounced it and was pitching in for the Recovery there in Olympia. He would be fine. And so would his great kids. She missed them, too.

Carol started thinking of little stocking stuffer gifts for her FCorps students. While they didn't have anymore "Christmas" traditions in Seattle—that was so divisive—they could still do stocking stuffers. She had heard stockings were a Scandinavian pagan tradition for winter solstice, so it was okay.

Carol got her coat on and went out for a walk. She was getting a latte at the university bookstore. As long as there were lattes, everything was fine.

Chapter 257

Christmas Moonshine in Forks

(December 24)

The "Collapse Christmas" in Forks was truly memorable. Steve Briggs knew people would talk about it for generations thereafter. It was an amazing mix of being incredibly different than other Christmases while, at the same time, being very similar.

Christmases in the few years leading up to the Collapse had been slowly changing in Forks. With D2, the Second Great Depression, going on before the Collapse, Christmases became poorer and poorer. So a sparse Christmas, when it came to presents, not traditions, was not new in rural Forks.

This was true in Steve's family. A big part of his pay as the manager of the local parts store was his performance bonus that was given out on the first of December. Steve would wait all year for it and planned his household's major purchases around it. He tried to split the bonus between necessities — new tires for his wife's car and a new water heater — and nice things. The year before the Collapse, he managed to get his wife the really fancy food processor she wanted. He got himself a gun safe, which turned out to be a very valuable thing to have.

Needless to say, there was no "performance" bonus this year from the auto parts store. Hell, there was no job at the auto parts store after the Collapse in May. So there would be no food processors or gun safes. Of course, there were no trucks making deliveries to Forks, so there weren't any gifts coming in even if people had money.

The total absence of big gifts this year was really different. Steve, who prided himself on self-reliance and not needing "stuff," was surprised by how ingrained the "stuff" part of Christmas had become for him. He even looked at the calendar to make sure it was really December 25 because he couldn't believe it was actually Christmas without all the usual holiday shopping.

That being said, the gifts were better this year because they actually meant something for a change. He went to one of the many "garage sales" in Forks, where people bartered their things to each other, and got a nice rolling pin for his wife. It cost him 10 rounds of

.22. She had mentioned that she needed one to make pies.

His wife made him a gift, a comforter cover sewn out of pieces of their old clothes. A scrap of shirt here, a scrap of a pair of shorts there. Each scrap had a memory to it. He remembered wearing a shirt or her wearing a dress that was now part of the comforter. Best of all, his wife told him that they could snuggle under the new comforter cover anytime the kids were asleep and, as she put it, "you might get lucky."

That was one thing that was way better for Steve these days – sex. Lots and lots of really great sex with his lovely wife. They had way more time now that they weren't rushing around all the time. They spent most of the day together and that turned both of them on. On top of that, they both really needed each other now, and they appreciated each other. Not to mention that it was cold, and they needed to make the best out of some bad circumstances. Steve would take the comforter — and all that getting lucky — over a gun safe any day.

The traditions of Christmas were back in the Briggs' home and Forks, in general. One was the Briggs' tradition of the kids opening a little present on Christmas Eve and putting milk and cookies out for Santa. There were only a few dairy cows in town. The owner made sure all the kids in town had a little bit of milk for Santa that year. Steve almost cried when he saw the kids putting the milk and cookies out. Some things were the same, even with all that was going on around them.

Steve had hope for the future. Despite the Collapse, his kids could put out milk and cookies for Santa. And their kids would also be able to years later. There was continuity between the generations, even with all the massive changes and misery.

The community made a big deal out of Christmas this year. It was a time for them to pull together. They'd been doing that all year long, but instead of pulling together to shoot some looters, now they got to pull together for something positive.

The local churches started caroling. They'd never done that before, and it really was quite magical. When they came by the Briggs' house, the whole family stopped doing what they were doing and just listened. They listened to the words of the carols and thought about their meaning. No one in the family said a word for half an hour after the carolers were gone.

Christmas Eve services at the Forks churches were packed. Lots of people who hadn't been to church in decades were back in the pews during the Collapse. In fact, most of the town was attending church, including the Briggs family.

Steve had never felt closer to his family and his community than he did that first Collapse Christmas. Things seemed so much more real and were boiled down to what mattered, which wasn't food processors.

The gentlemen of Forks decided to start a new Christmas tradition. Steve and his friends snuck out of their houses after Christmas dinner and went to city hall, which had become the guard headquarters. They cracked open some moonshine. With all those hillbillies living in Forks, there were plenty of people who remembered grandpa's 'shine recipe. Some guys had been making 'shine all summer and fall. It was a good business to be in. People needed it, especially now.

They sipped moonshine that night and talked about the past year and the coming year. Through Don Watson, the local ham radio operator, they got dispatches from the rest of the world. Landline phones usually still worked, but cell service and long-distance texting. The internet didn't work because the only service provider out there went out of business. One person in town had some spotty satellite internet service, but it was nothing to count on. Ham radio was the main link.

Don, sipping some 'shine with one hand and holding his handheld radio in the other, got real serious at one point.

"You know, guys," Don said, "there are tons of rumors out there that there's going to be something big in a few days."

"Will they try to cut off the utilities again?" someone asked.

"No one is saying for sure what's coming," Don said, "but if I had to guess, I'd say it's a Patriot military move of some kind."

The room fell silent. Everyone thought about what that meant for them in little, and totally isolated, Forks.

Not much, Steve thought. This would have very little effect on them.

"No government here in Forks to overthrow," Steve said as he raised his cup of moonshine.

"Cheers!" everyone said. They'd drink to that.

Chapter 258

Christmas at Prosser Farm

(December 24)

The EPU team and Carly seamlessly fit into the WAB families out at the Prosser Farm. Everyone there was doing all they could to give the kids as normal a Christmas as possible. Everyone spent time figuring out little gifts to give each other. There was no access to stores, so they were on their own.

There was one exception. Dennis, on one of his runs into Olympia to secretly distribute the Rebel Radio CDs, got some candy canes. They were left over from a prior year and some street vendor was selling them. They cost Dennis a fortune (a box of 12-guage shells), but it would be worth it to see the look on the kids' face, when they had a real candy cane. That would make Christmas "normal." Sorta.

Things settled into a day-to-day routine after the EPU agents arrived. There were still a bunch of chores to do every day on the farm, so that kept everyone busy. The agents pitched in, of course.

When they arrived, the agents started setting up communications and a very sophisticated guard system. They still used the Prosser neighbors for guards, but as a first ring of defense. The agents were the second ring. They came up with detailed escape plans and trained everyone on how to start running down the escape paths on a moment's notice. They had supplies and weapons pre-positioned in two sets of vehicles. If they had to evacuate people, they would essentially drive out the back pasture into the forest and take a logging road to the power lines, which were cleared of brush. From there, the Delphi guards would pick them up after being alerted. The Delphi guards didn't know who the families were. They just knew that if Jeff Prosser said they needed to be at the power lines and used a certain code phrase, a select team of guards needed to be there. And they needed to be ready to fight their way back to a safe house, which was the home of Ned, the guard commander.

All that Ned knew was that Jeff was a Patriot, he had guests from Olympia, and some Secret Service-type people were out there with them. Ned was starting to think some Patriot big shot was hiding out there … until Ned found out about Tom's rich father.

The Prosser Farm neighbors and the leadership of the Delphi guards were told that Tom Foster had a rich father who had hired these people to protect Tom. That story, which would have been absurd before the Collapse, explained everything to Ned.

Now, when anyone with a gun, and especially a badge, could be rented — this story made perfect sense. What would have seemed outlandish was that the Patriot's future governor was living right under everyone's noses and a bodyguard team of defecting state police had been sent to protect the new governor. That would have been crazy.

The EPU agents had amazing radios and even private email devices that didn't use the internet and were totally secure. They could email with the Think Farm and other Patriot headquarters. It was some data packet ham radio thing; pretty clever.

"We need to talk in private," Brad Finehoff, the leader of the EPU team, said to Ben. Brad seemed very serious. The families had just celebrated Christmas Eve. The kids put out milk and cookies for Santa. They had fancy desserts made from the meager sugar reserves they had out there. It was an amazing time. The kids really enjoyed having a "normal" Christmas; it was much needed. So did the adults. Ben could tell that Brad had waited until the festivities were over before giving him something to worry about.

Ben and Brad went out to the shed closest to the house. "What's up?" Ben asked.

"We'll be moving out in a few days, probably the day after New Year's," Brad said. He seemed a little nervous.

"Where to?" Ben asked.

"Olympia," Brad said and then smiled, "Your new office in the capitol, Governor."

Hearing "Governor" still stunned Ben. It took him a while to get his senses back.

"Let me guess," Ben said, "We're not just strolling down the road to Olympia. We're waiting for some people to go ahead of us and clear things out."

Brad nodded.

Ben was silent for a while as he was trying to comprehend what they were talking about. The Patriots would fight over Olympia. If they won — and that was a big "if" to Ben — then he would be the new governor. At least, he would be in the interim, until there were elections that he would probably win.

It was hard to comprehend, even though Ben had known for a

few weeks that he was the Patriot's designated interim governor. But this—actual plans to move into Olympia—seemed so much more real than the talk about Ben being the governor "someday."

Ben was no military guy, but he was curious. "How's this going to work?" he asked Brad.

"Patriot units from the areas all around Olympia will move in on New Year's Day," Brad said. "While the Limas and gang bangers are hung over," he added with a smile.

"And there's political significance," Ben said, "to a new year. A new year and a new set of leaders. New, new, new. People want something new. Last year sucked; this year, with new leaders, things will be better." Whoever thought of a New Year's Day attack understood politics, Ben thought.

"Patriot regular units will concentrate on the north, to prevent Lima regulars at JBLM from coming down I-5," Brad explained. "Patriot irregular units …"

"What's an 'irregular' unit?" Ben asked and Brad explained the term.

"Irregular units will be coming from all around here," Brad said pointing around the farm. "Some will be coming very close to here, right down Highway 101."

"Will they come here?" Ben asked.

"Nope," Brad said. "Not unless we need them to." Brad hadn't talked to HQ about having an irregular unit come to the Prosser Farm, but he knew he could call in to HQ and have them divert one, if absolutely necessary.

Brad continued, "The most dangerous time for us is when the irregular units are nearby. The Patriot forces near us will make a big fat target for the Limas, who supposedly don't have much in the way of helicopters or aircraft, and their artillery can't reach here. But still, the Patriot units will be a target. There could also be some confusion. You know, the 'fog of war.'" Brad had been a paratrooper in Desert Storm and had seen the "fog of war" up close. It was deadly: sleep deprivation, adrenaline, and an overload of information. Bad things happened.

"What do we do when all this starts?" Ben asked.

"When the Patriot forces," Brad said—he almost slipped and added "or God forbid, the Lima forces" but he didn't—"when the good guys get near us, we'll activate the evacuation plan. We'll take you, Tom, Brian, and Carly and get into one of the vehicles and take the route. The second vehicle and half of my team will stay here to get the families out, if that's necessary. I doubt it will be necessary, they'll probably stay here until it's safe for families to go into Olympia and join you."

Ben nodded. This was like part of some movie, but it was happening for real.

"We'll take you slowly and safely," Brad said, "instead of the mad dash we've rehearsed. We'll wait near the Delphi guard station until we have confirmation it's okay to go there. When the coast is clear, it'll be okay to go down 101 to Olympia. Then we cruise there in your first motorcade, Governor."

Ben, once again, was trying to take all this in.

"What do I need to do to help?" Ben asked.

"Get your family mentally prepared," Brad answered. "Make sure their head is in the game, and that they're not afraid and they trust us to get them through it safely."

Brad put his finger up in the air like he had forgotten something. "Actually," he said, "don't tell them what's going on by yourself. We'll have a big meeting with my whole team and we'll use maps to show them what's happening and let them know about all our communications and other capabilities. When they're done listening, they'll understand that we're pros at this." Brad smiled. He was very proud of this plan and his team's abilities. They were good, and they were doing something incredibly important for the cause. Brad couldn't wait to get started. He knew it would work. He just knew it.

"So I just show up and take a ride with you guys?" Ben asked. There had to be more to it than that.

"Well, you need to pack some suits. Do you have any?" Brad asked.

"Nope," Ben answered, and Brad took a note. He'd make sure the Think Farm had some suits for Ben when he got to the capitol. The new governor had to dress well.

"There's one more thing you need to do," Brad said.

"Sure," Ben said, "name it."

"Study those binders we brought out," Brad said. Those were the briefing binders the Think Farm had prepared. They detailed what the Patriot's plan was for governing. How the new, interim government would be formed, who the interim legislators would be, and the political messages the new governor would be giving. And, most importantly, the Patriot plan for a new state constitution and elections.

"Homework?" Ben asked with a smile. "I have frickin'

homework?"

"Yes, Governor," Brad said. "The content of those binders is why we're going to all this trouble."

And by "trouble," Brad meant all the lives that would be lost.

Chapter 259

Collapse Christmas in Olympia

(December 24)

Ron Spencer wasn't even thinking about Christmas this year. He was completely preoccupied and busy preparing for a mission.

Leading up to Christmas, Ron had noticed some big changes in the government-employee enclave of Olympia. Regular people, like him, had been civil to the Loyalists for months, but that was starting to change. Regular people were not taking it anymore. They were no longer accepting that some people got more FCard credits than them. They could sense that the Loyalists wouldn't be running things much longer and they weren't afraid of the Loyalists as much as they used to be. They had seen that the FCorps were a joke.

Ron could tell that the Loyalists were stunned the "temporary Crisis" was still going on. With the whole government focused entirely on the recovery, why was it taking so long? It was almost like government couldn't solve a problem, which was impossible in their minds. The Loyalists were dismayed at the news of states and parts of states joining the Patriots. They were amazed when blacks and Latinos joined, too. How could minorities possibly be part of the racist teabagger movement? And how could stupid hillbillies be winning?

The most tangible evidence of Loyalists losing faith in their side was all the families in Olympia who were abandoning their houses there and getting on buses to go up to Seattle, where they felt more safe. The Loyalists had tight control of things up there.

But not in Olympia. People could tell — and were betting their own lives and their families' lives — that Olympia was about to be in Patriot hands.

A few days before Christmas, Ron received word that he and his fellow "gray men" had a mission. Finally! A mission. Ron was so excited he couldn't sleep.

Their weapons? Cans of spray paint. But not for the graffiti Ron had been doing.

Matt Collins, Ron's friend who was the gray man organizer in the area and got spray paint to Ron, told him before he got arrested that something big was coming up in a while. They were tasked with some "preparations" for the big event.

Matt explained a few weeks before that each gray man would go into his or her neighborhood and spray paint a huge "L" on the houses of people they knew were Loyalists. To get an "L" spray painted on their house, a person had to be more than just a person who went through the motions of supporting the government. A person had to be a hardcore Loyalist to get an "L." This had several purposes.

First, it would inform the Loyalists that the Patriots knew who they were and could strike anytime. This time it would be some spray paint. Next time, it might be a shotgun or a Molotov cocktail. Ron remembered how terrifying it was when Nancy Ringman spray-painted "POI" on the Matson house. Well, it was time for the Loyalists to be terrified. Every day, when Ron walked by the Matson house, he saw that "POI" and was afraid for them. He wondered what happened to them. He figured there was a good chance Grant was dead by now. He hoped Grant's family was still okay.

The second purpose of painting an "L" on Loyalist houses was to allow Patriot forces, who were rumored to be coming into Olympia, to know which houses were safe and which could be trouble.

The third purpose was to let all the people who just pretended to be Loyalists know that they were okay and that Patriots would not harm them. The masses—the "Undecideds"—living in government-controlled areas, like Olympia, were superficially supporting the government. Many Undecideds had "We support the Recovery!" signs in their yards, for example. But they really didn't care about the government—they just wanted their FCards to stay full of credits.

The Patriots would need the support of the Undecideds. They were, after all, the majority of the population. But the Undecideds were scared of the Patriots. They had been told all kinds of wild tales about how the teabaggers were racist, right-wing whackos. The Patriots needed to demonstrate to the Undecideds that they would not harm them, just the Loyalists. When the Undecideds woke up and found their door wasn't tagged but the hardcore Loyalists' were, they would know they were being spared.

A final, and grisly, purpose was to let the population know which houses to loot and whom to drag out of their houses and … Ron tried not to think about that. Reprisals were part of every collapse and war everywhere in the world throughout history; modern-day America was no exception. It was human nature to hurt those who brutalized a person and their loved ones. It was human DNA.

However, Ron fervently hoped the reprisals would be as

limited as possible. He didn't want to be part of revenge killings, but he couldn't deny that the Loyalist bastards—who had taken everything from people—deserved to at least have people know who they were. The decent people who had everything stolen from them and had been put down for so long would have to make up their own minds about whether they'd go over to their neighbor's house, now painted with a big "L," and settle the score. It was up to them; Ron couldn't control that.

He wondered if the Patriots would be coming tomorrow. He knew it would be soon. They wouldn't show their hand by tagging the houses and then waiting too long to follow through on the tagging. So the liberation of Olympia would be coming soon … very soon.

Ron started to think about people in his neighborhood, former friends in some cases, whom he wanted to kill. He thought about how he would do it, in great detail. Then he'd catch himself. He was supposed to be better than that. They were the bad guys; he couldn't stoop to their level, but he couldn't deny that he wanted revenge. He prayed for forgiveness, for the sin of thinking about what he'd do to them if he couldn't control himself – and for forgiveness if he carried out what he was thinking about doing to them.

A few days before Christmas, an envelope appeared on Ron's front porch. It contained the code phrase, "The chair is against the wall," which was a line from the movie *Red Dawn*. It meant that it was time to tag houses that night. There was a handwritten note on it, "This is for Matt Collins, RIP. Clover Park massacre." Ron closed his eyes and prayed that this was a mistake, but he knew in his heart that Matt was now gone.

After pacing around the house all night, it was finally "go" time. Ron snuck out of the house at 2:00 a.m. He had to have personal knowledge that each house he tagged was definitely a Loyalist. The Patriots wouldn't leave this up to making a map and having someone else do it, which could lead to mistaken taggings. That would show that the Patriots had faulty intelligence or faulty execution, and could get innocent people killed. Therefore, a tagger had to know, firsthand, that the occupant was a Loyalist who had committed crimes against the population.

Ron selected three houses in his neighborhood to tag. The first was Carlos Cuevas, a former state Department of Labor official. He had taken over as the FCorps organizer for the Cedars and was a real prick. He went around to people's houses having "impromptu" conversations about politics and taking notes. He wasn't even subtle about it. Carlos thought all Patriots were bigots out to get him. He and his family had an FCard chock full of credits.

Carlos had arranged for some FCorps goons to "visit" Len Isaacson, one of Ron's good neighbors, after Len gave Carlos some "wrong" answers in a political conversation. Len didn't get sent away to prison, but he might have. Len's FCard suddenly had zero credits on it. People in the neighborhood, like Ron, gave scarce food to Len's family. Carlos mocked Len by saying there must be a "glitch" with Len's FCard and he "would get right on that." That was such classic, passive-aggressive behavior of a weak bully who temporarily had power. Carlos loved the power. He was about to find out the other side of that coin.

The second house was Rex Maldonado's. He was a former hippie who became Assistant Director of the State Unemployment Agency. He was Carlos's right hand man. Rex wore Che Guevara t-shirts and, with his gray pony tail, lectured everyone about "social justice." He was all about "peace and freedom," but would send the FCorps to your house if you disagreed with his version of "peace and freedom."

The third house was Scott Baker. He was not a government employee. He worked for some insurance company before the Collapse. Scott was taking maximum advantage of the situation for his personal gain. He volunteered with the FCorps to spy on his neighbors. At first, no one knew he was doing it. People would talk freely to him about politics and how awful things were. Scott would nod and sympathize. Those who talked to him started to get visits from Carlos and Rex. It took a while for them to figure out it was Scott who ratted them out. A few weeks before Christmas Eve, with his cover blown, Scott quit trying to pretend he wasn't a spy. He started going around with Carlos and Rex to talk to people. Scott was handsomely rewarded for his work. He had plenty of FCard credits. He got government gas, which he sold to people in the neighborhood.

There were more people in the neighborhood who Ron suspected of being Loyalists working with the "Carlos cabal" as they called them. But Ron didn't have proof. His instructions from Matt Collins were very clear: only clearly established Loyalists got tagged. Carlos, Rex, and Scott certainly qualified.

The actual tagging of the houses was anti-climactic. Ron left the house with his can of black spray paint. He was careful to take the route as far from the street lights as possible to stay out of the light. Ron was getting good at this. He went out a few times a month and painted Patriot graffiti messages in his area with yellow spray paint.

There were no guards to worry about anymore. After the looters were shot and Grant left the neighborhood, the FCorps took over guard duties. They were pathetic. Soon, they no longer were guarding and—to everyone's surprise—there were no break-ins. How could the FCorps pull that off? Was this a government success?

Nope. It turns out that the FCorps in Ron's neighborhood, and surrounding ones, made a deal with the gangs. Under the direction of the police, the gangs divided Olympia into sections, one gang running each area. The FCorps would pay the gangs to make sure the neighborhoods of government officials, like the Cedars where Ron lived, were left alone. The gangs were given free rein to kill all amateur competitors in their sector, and they did. Ruthlessly.

The FCorps paid the gangs by allowing them to sell "gang gas," guns, and anything thing else they wanted. So the apparent government "success" of some safe neighborhoods was achieved by the government simply buying off some very bad people.

Ron went to the farthest house first and then worked his way back toward his house. The first house was Scott Baker's. Second was Carlos's, then Rex's. There. That was it. Now he waited for the Patriots to come in to liberate his neighborhood.

It wouldn't be long.

Chapter 260

Be Careful What You Wish For

(December 24 - 25)

Jim Q. couldn't believe what he was hearing. It was his cousin saying, "The cow has two heads," in their language, which was code for the big operation starting on New Year's Day. The time had come after months of planning. It was really going to happen. Jim Q. was simultaneously excited and scared.

"My uncle has a brown mustache," Jim Q. replied to his cousin through the radio. This meant that the 17th had confirmed that it would be moving out at midnight on New Year's Day.

Jim Q. hoped he'd see his cousin at their people's New Year celebration of Kha b-Nisan, which was on April 1st. He hoped that the ordeal would all be over by then and they could have their usual family feast. Hopefully.

Jim Q. went and told Ted and Sap who both figured it would be New Year's Day when Lt. Col. Hammond had said the name of the operation was "Tet," which was the Vietnamese New Year's Day.

Grant wasn't at the Marion Farm because it was Christmas Eve and the plan was for him to spend Christmas Eve with his family and come out to Marion Farm on Christmas Day for dinner. Grant wanted to spend more time with the unit, but he had an obligation to his family. Ted understood and wished he could be with his kids and grandkids on Christmas. Not this year. Maybe next year.

Thinking of how Grant should spend quality time with his family led Ted to make a decision. Against all military protocol, he decided not to tell him about New Year's Day until after Grant got a stress-free Christmas Eve with his family. Grant could start worrying about the mission on Christmas Day, when he came out to Marion Farm. Ted smiled. At least one family would have a good Christmas Eve this year.

Indeed, Grant's Christmas Eve was fantastic. He had become really good at "compartmentalizing" information. He could put an imaginary box around bad news or worry in his brain and forget about it for a while to have a good time. Then, when the good times were over, he could unpack the bad news and address it. He could turn the worry switch on and off.

Grant had to do that a lot during the Collapse. He had to pretend, for example, not to know that he would be leaving his family soon while he played with his kids and spent time with his wife. He was lying to them the whole time, but, somewhat sadly, he could compartmentalize it. It was a survival skill.

One thing Grant had to compartmentalize was how hard of a time Manda was having after shooting Randy Greene. She was still having nightmares. She would get depressed for a day or two. Sometimes she wouldn't talk to anyone and then she'd be okay. She wasn't the same spunky girl who had come to the cabin that spring. Grant felt like he'd lost a part of his daughter.

Manda was in a great mood on Christmas Eve, though. She had been looking forward to Christmas for so long. She really wanted the "normal" feelings of Christmas. She was fine with some differences this year, like having Christmas at the cabin instead of their home in Olympia, but she wanted to feel like things weren't entirely different now. She could handle mostly different, but not entirely.

The Matsons had a big Christmas Eve dinner, which was a new tradition. They'd have a big Christmas family dinner, too, but the Christmas Eve dinner was for friends to come over and visit. Everyone brought food.

The Morrells were the first to arrive. Mary Anne brought a boom box, several CDs of Christmas music, and some cookies. They played Christmas music for hours. It was magical listening to songs they all remembered. Grant had the wood stove going and it put out a tremendous amount of heat. It was warm, bright, and joyous in the Matson cabin.

Jordan arrived next with his parents who came for a short while before leaving. It had the feel of the first of many Matson Christmas gatherings with the Sparks' family.

Next to come over was the Team and the Team Chicks, Gideon, and Chip and his new girlfriend, Liz. She was very nice, and cute as a button. She was a gregarious brunette divorcee with three teenage sons. Chip saw her at the Grange and was too shy to strike up a conversation, which was strange given that he could talk to anyone, but he knew he really wanted to be with her and that scared him. Life was hard enough during the Collapse; Chip didn't want a broken heart on top of everything. However, he underestimated what a catch he was. Liz was attracted to him and realized her boys needed a good man like him as a role model. She asked him out at the Thanksgiving dinner and they'd been together ever since. At the Christmas Eve dinner, he was acting like a puppy dog in love.

Grant realized that the Team, Gideon, Chip, and Liz had one thing in common: they didn't have a family out there, but now they did.

The last guests to arrive were Tammy and Missy. It was one of the only times Tammy had been out of the house, except to visit Mark in the mental ward and go to work. She really needed to see some smiles. She needed to know that life was going on as normal somewhere. Maybe there wasn't any joy in her dark, dreary, and nearly empty house, but there was somewhere else. Tammy needed to see that, while her son was missing and her husband and daughter were mentally gone, she still had a family, her Pierce Point family. She forgot about a lot of the negativity in her life for those few hours at the Matson Christmas cabin.

The stockings were up. They were the ones they made for this year, not their normal ones, because their normal ones were back at their abandoned house in Olympia. But, even though they were different than the usual ones, just hanging them made it a "real" Christmas. Christmas would continue; no Collapse could stop it.

Best of all, they had a Christmas tree. There were plenty of small evergreens growing all around Pierce Point. In fact, one of the houses in Pierce Point was actually a small Christmas tree farm and they decided to give away free Christmas trees, mainly because no one had any money to buy them.

Grant didn't get a tree from the tree farmer. Instead, he, Manda, and Cole went out a week earlier and cut their own tree on a nearby vacant lot. They hauled it home, which was a lot of work without a truck. Grant remembered past Christmases when they'd strap the tree to the roof of his Acura. It looked so pathetically suburban, a tree on top of an Acura.

Cutting their own tree this year was glorious, it was a memory that would last forever. They even had hot cider when they got back. Cole couldn't stop talking about it, which was the best part of the experience for Grant.

Everyone ate and ate at the Christmas Eve party. They hadn't been full in … well, since Thanksgiving. Before Thanksgiving, they'd gone all summer and fall without ever being full, which made feeling full a very big deal.

They tasted foods they had forgotten existed, like sweet pickles. Mary Anne brought some over that she'd canned. Who would get excited about sweet pickles? Anyone who hadn't had sugar in a month. They saved the pickle juice to make tuna sandwiches. They had plenty of canned tuna. They lacked mayonnaise, but tuna and sweet pickle juice had become a delicacy. Even for people like Lisa who hadn't liked tuna before. Now—after cornbread, beans, and rice every day—it tasted like the Mahi-Mahi she had at a fancy restaurant in Maui when the family went on vacation.

Chip and Liz capped off the day with some homemade wine. Liz had made it out of wild strawberries and huckleberries. It was amazing, so sweet and flavorful. Grant had never tasted fruit so flavorful. The adults quickly became tipsy as they made their way through several gallons.

It was dark—the sun started setting at 4:30 p.m. in late December this far north—and people were heading home. Grant was exhausted, full and half drunk. He fell asleep on the couch a little after 7:00 p.m. The kids went to bed a little while later. Then Lisa, who was drunk on wine, dragged Grant into bed. He wasn't too tired for what came next.

Lisa got up in the middle of the night and put the presents out. She always did that; Grant slept too soundly, so she had always done it. This year was no exception. On Christmas morning, the kids got up early, as usual. They came down to find their presents by the woodstove. Grant was wearing one of his "World's Best Dad" t-shirts that the kids had given him for a Father's Day gift when they were little. For a split second, he thought about what a lie that shirt was. He was leaving for war very soon and had been lying to them. He didn't deserve to wear that shirt. Then, just as quickly, the bad thoughts vanished and the compartmentalization kicked in. He was Grant, the good father, again.

Manda exploded with joy when she opened her present, a new dress. Eileen and Mary Anne had been secretly making it for her. She loved it. It wasn't the flashy kind of prom dress she had always dreamed about it, but it was great, and nicely made. Nothing was ever fancy out there at Pierce Point, just practical. It was nice to have something fancy for a change.

Cole went crazy with joy, too. He got two new games for his handheld game player. Grant got them by sending some .22 ammo with Rich on one of his grocery runs into town. Rich got the games from a guy selling them at one of the garage sales in town. They weren't at people's houses like in the past, but in the parking lot of the grocery store where the Blue Ribbon Boys maintained order. That was the only safe place where sellers knew they wouldn't be robbed. Commissioner Winters got a cut of all the sales in the crime-free parking lot.

On that same run into town, Rich got Grant some soap and perfume, which cost a half a brick of .22. Grant thought he got ripped off, but he wanted Lisa to have a great Christmas. He wanted her to have "normal," chick things. He wanted to make her feel beautiful and pampered. It was so important to Grant that he didn't mind getting ripped off. Besides, he had plenty of .22 ammo.

Lisa got Grant a wonderful gift: a nice Swiss Army knife. It was beautiful, new in the box. Lisa had no idea how much it was worth. Neither did the patient she treated who gave her the knife as payment. Grant was thrilled. It felt so amazing to have something new in his hand, something fancier than it had to be. He knew he would have that knife with him at all times in the coming days, perhaps, the rest of his life. It was a real keepsake.

Manda and Cole made Grant a heart-shaped clump of glued clam shells. Grant almost cried. It was genuine and meaningful. Grant would treasure that for the rest of his life.

Drew and Eileen got the kids a bracelet for Manda and a nice pocket knife for Cole. Drew was using that stash of pre-Collapse cash and having people go into town to get things. By now, the cash was almost worthless, but it still bought trinkets.

After they opened gifts, they had their traditional Christmas morning breakfast—kind of. In previous years, Grant would go out on Christmas Eve and get donuts and they'd have them for breakfast on Christmas morning. It was the only morning in the year they'd have donuts for breakfast.

There were no donuts this year, so Grant got some of the MRE desserts he saved from the meals he ate out in the field. He stashed them away all year long for just an occasion like this. So, in lieu of donuts, Grant handed out MRE desserts, a fudge brownie, cinnamon scone, chocolate banana muffin top, vanilla pound cake (Grant's favorite), shortbread (his second favorite), cherry blueberry cobbler, raisin nut mix with chocolate candies, and Chips Ahoy-like cookies.

The Matson family loved the unorthodox Christmas morning "donuts." It seemed fitting for this Collapse Christmas.

Grant knew that next Christmas he would either be eating real donuts, prison food, or be dead. He just hoped that if he were eating donuts, it would be with his family, though he suspected it wouldn't be.

The family Christmas dinner was largely a continuation of the Christmas Eve dinner. They had the same great food. They talked about the past year and all they'd accomplished. It was a marvelous, marvelous dinner. Grant had never felt as close to his family as he did right then.

Before he knew it, it was getting dark and time for Grant to go. After dinner, Grant excused himself and got his kit, AR, and his new Swiss Army knife.

"Gotta run out and do some morale stuff with the rental team," Grant said to Lisa. "I'll be back in the morning, or thereabouts."

Lisa nodded. She understood, but only because she didn't know where he was really going.

Grant went over to the yellow cabin where the Team, Team Chicks, Gideon, and Chip and Liz were finishing up their Christmas dinner. It was getting dark.

The Team kissed their women goodbye, because they'd be staying the night "out in the field," as they called it. They told their girlfriends that, in the next few days, they would be going away for a while. The goodbye kisses were long and difficult. Some of the girls were crying.

Grant could feel a definite change. Things had been so magical for the past day or two with all the Christmas celebrations. Now things were going to get grim. It was like a Monday morning after a great weekend.

This was the first time Grant wasn't thrilled to go to Marion Farm. He could sense that all the camaraderie and adventure of the 17th Irregulars was about to turn into some very nasty business. He was glad they had the good times of Christmas, but he knew that bad times were ahead.

The Team got into Mark's truck. Bobby was driving it while Mark was … gone. Seeing Mark's truck without Mark in it reminded everyone about the tragedy of Mark and Paul. And Missy. And Tammy.

The rest of the Team was feeling like Grant, like they were heading into a very serious time in their lives, a time to do what they had been training to do for months, to do what they needed to do. They were doing a job very few were capable of doing, a job that desperately needed to be done. They were glad that they got to do it, but they were anxious about the bad things they knew lay ahead. Each of them had been thinking a lot lately about dying and how to deal with their friends dying.

As they piled in the back of Mark's truck, it was one of the only times Grant didn't say, "This never gets old." And Pow didn't say, "Beats the shit out of selling insurance." They were silent on the way to Marion Farm. Not depressed, just thoughtful. It reminded Grant of scenes in WWII movies where troops were heading out on landing craft to D Day.

It was cold and pouring rain. It was an unpleasant ride, but the Team didn't notice that. They were thinking about what lay ahead in the next few days.

They pulled into Marion Farm and headed to the equipment shed for yet another Christmas dinner followed by one of Pastor Pete's services. They had planned the unit dinner and service for the evening on Christmas Day because Pastor Pete was giving the Christmas Eve and Christmas morning services in Pierce Point. The evening of Christmas day was the only time he had to come out to Marion Farm.

The equipment shed was a happy place. It was decorated, brightly lit, and warm. Everything was genuine there. The decorations were homemade: tin foil stars, strings of popcorn, and a deer archery target with a red nose and a Rudolph sign. There were a few Christmas lights that someone had found in the attic of the farmhouse. They had a Christmas tree that was sparsely, but very tastefully, decorated.

The troops were energized. They had been taking it easy on Christmas Eve and Christmas day. They were relaxed and had been exchanging gifts and hanging out with their new family. The joyous atmosphere of Christmas dinner perked up the Team. They realized how lucky they were to have a second Christmas out there with their comrades.

Pastor Pete arrived and started the service. Nearly everyone attended. Only about a quarter of the troops attended his first service a few months ago.

Everyone could sense that something serious would be happening in the next few days. Many people who weren't religious were thinking that it couldn't hurt to try it out. Just in case.

Pastor Pete, as usual, kept the theology generic. He had Evangelicals, mainstream Protestants, Catholics, Mormons, and a bunch of Agnostics. And he had lots of "sprinklers," which was his term for people who rarely attended church. Their only time in church was when they got water sprinkled on them when they were born, rice sprinkled on them when they got married, and dirt sprinkled on them when they died. "Sprinklers" were warmly welcomed at this service, the last one for some of them.

Pastor Pete tried to make each person feel welcome. He even arranged with Rich on one of Rich's runs into town to get some of the candles with the Virgin Mary for the Hispanic Catholics in the unit, which was a huge spiritual boost for them. They felt like folks were trying to help them have their own "normal" Christmas Mass with that special effort. Pastor Pete even learned a few lines of Spanish and read a small portion of the Christmas Mass prayers in Spanish. While it wasn't the same, they appreciated the effort.

Soldiers took turns reading the familiar Christmas story from the Bible. It was amazing to see a soldier who normally carried a rifle now unarmed and reading from the Bible. It showed two sides of human beings.

It was Pastor Pete's turn to deliver a message. He needed to boil the Christmas message down to its most common denominator and he did. He made the point that the Savior came here for each of them and that it wasn't too late to accept Him. After the service, a dozen or so soldiers were huddled around him, which was extremely gratifying to Grant.

And me. The outside thought seemed to be smiling. It was more of a warmth than a smiling. It was satisfaction and joy for people who had found their way home.

Now it was dinner time. The Team was already stuffed from eating the past two days. They volunteered to serve dinner so everyone, including the KP detail, could all eat at once together. Grant thought that it was particularly important that he, the commanding officer, show his appreciation for his troops by serving them dinner.

Grant was walking over to start serving when Ted came up to him. Ted motioned for Grant to come over and talk out of earshot of everyone else. Grant knew what this was all about.

"Hey, we're moving out at midnight on New Year's Eve. That is, the first minutes of New Year's Day," Ted said.

Grant just nodded. He'd been expecting this. "Figured it would be around New Year's if it was named 'Tet,'" Grant said. Ted was impressed that a civilian knew that Tet happened on the Vietnamese New Year.

It was anti-climactic. Grant had been worrying for weeks about the day he'd have to tell his wife about all the lying and that he was leaving. That day would be very soon.

"I wanted to give you Christmas with your family without knowing this," Ted said. "We got word from HQ two days ago."

"Thanks, man," Grant said. "I needed those two days."

Grant and Ted immediately started thinking about all the planning they'd need to do in the next few days.

"Let's have a nice Christmas dinner with the unit and then we'll deal with this," Ted said.

Grant nodded. There was nothing else to say so he just went back to serving dinner. It cheered him up to see each of the soldiers, knowing they were all risking their lives to make things right again. They all were sacrificing as much as he was and they were in this together. Grant wished each of them a Merry Christmas as he served them mashed potatoes. Someone gave Grant a Santa hat that he wore as he plopped mashed potatoes on everyone's plates. He felt at home with these men and women.

Well, this is my new home, Grant thought to himself. He'd tell Lisa in a day or two and he'd be thrown out of his cabin. He'd come here, to his extended family. Oh well. At least he had a place to go, and a really good reason to be kicked out of his family. Fighting to restore a decent life for his family and people in his state was better than the usual reasons for getting kicked out of your house, like booze or cheating.

"Lives, fortunes, and sacred honor," Grant thought to himself once again as he was serving up mashed potatoes. He frequently came back to this phrase. Grant had always revered the Founding Fathers for the sacrifices they had made. And Grant had always said — words he now regretted — that he wished he could make a similar sacrifice.

Be careful what you wish for.

Chapter 261

Christmas Dinner at Marion Farm

(December 25)

The 17th Irregulars had a magnificent Christmas dinner. Morale had never been so high. They were one cohesive group of 104 people, and together, they sang Christmas carols. Someone handed out candles and they turned off the lights. They sang by candlelight. It was amazing. Grant had goose bumps, actual goose bumps. Everyone knew they were about to do something very, very big. This would be the most important thing they would do in their lives. They would do it together, and would do it well. They would never be closer to a group of people than they were to each other right then.

"Aren't you guys heading back?" a soldier asked Grant and Bobby. The soldier knew that Grant tried to stay at his cabin as much as possible, even though driving him there and back was a big use of precious gas.

"Nah, I'm staying here tonight," Grant said. He wasn't being a devoted commanding officer;, he was scared to go home. He didn't want to be anywhere near Lisa. He was afraid he would blurt out the New Year's Day plan and blow operational security. He wanted to put off his announcement of leaving for as long as possible.

As the Team was cleaning up the dishes, Ted came over to Grant.

"We need to go over all the planning that we need to do," he said.

Grant nodded. It was 11:00 p.m. and he was tired. He was hoarse from talking to so many people. "Tomorrow morning, okay?" he asked.

Ted would have preferred to talk at that moment with all of the operational details that were racing through his mind. He could tell Grant was worthless right then, so he didn't push it.

"0500," Ted said, meaning 5:00 a.m. "The den." That was the little office in the farmhouse they used when they had to close the door.

"Roger that," Grant said as he finished scrubbing a pot. He showed it to Franny, who looked at it carefully and gave the thumbs up for a sufficiently clean pot. Grant's hands were red from being in hot water all night. KP duty was hard, hard work.

The Team was dragging, too. They finished at half speed and headed to their cots in the barn. Grant, as CO, had a few special privileges. One was that he got to sleep on a couch in the farmhouse instead of the noisy barn. The reason was that the CO needed to be as rested as possible. The others who got to sleep in the farmhouse were Ted and Sap and the females, who were in the two bedrooms. Grant fell asleep in thirty seconds on his "home away from home" couch.

Grant was on patrol outside Marion Farm. It was perfectly silent, except for some faint, but terrifying, rustling in the bushes. He sensed there were several Limas nearby. Suddenly, a Lima with a snarling and demonic face jumped out of the bushes and lunged at him with a bright, almost glowing knife. Grant drew his pistol but the demon Lima was blocking his arm. Grant fought him but the Lima was strong.

"Wake up!" Ted was yelling. "It's me, Ted!"

Grant realized he was fighting Ted in his sleep. He was a little embarrassed.

"Did I draw on you?" Grant asked.

"Almost!" Ted said. "This job is dangerous enough without getting shot by my CO. Shot by a lawyer. I'd be laughed at forever."

"Sorry, man," Grant said. He realized others might be around hearing him so he shouldn't call Ted "man." He was a CO, not a drinking buddy.

"0510," Ted said. "Time to get to work."

"Okay," Grant said. He looked for his boots, which were already on his feet. He had fallen asleep with his boots on. He found his kit and AR on the rack where the Team stowed their gear the night before. He always had to know where his kit and AR were. It was crucial to be ready to run out of the house with them at a moment's notice.

Grant wiped the sleep from his eyes and headed to the kitchen. He wanted a cup of coffee, but they only got coffee on Sunday mornings. A cup of water would do. He had a caffeine pill on him, and he knew he'd need it. He needed to be fully alert at this meeting. He took the pill and headed to the den where he found Ted and Sap with a highway map on the desk. In the movies, military personnel planning a mission always had a detailed topographical map or a huge computer screen. Not this time. All that the rag-tag 17th Irregulars had was a standard highway map, the kind most people have in their car. That would have to do.

Ted was telling Sap about Grant fighting him in his dream

when Grant walked in. "Glad no one got shot this morning," Sap said. "We need every man for what's ahead."

Ted and Sap went over the plan with Grant, and it was obvious that they knew what they were doing. Over the next few days, they would make sure every single person in the unit was ready to go. This meant, ready physically, mentally, and emotionally.

They discussed the vehicles they'd need, what to pack in them, and how they'd carry fuel. They went over comms for each squad. They didn't have enough radios for each squad, so they'd double up.

"Not ideal, but …" Ted and Sap kept saying. Grant was getting a little concerned about how many times they said that.

They went over organizational structure. Who each squad leader was, which they all knew by now. Who the medic was for each squad; not a fully trained medic, of course, but the best trained and equipped one for that squad. They went over the three specialty squads.

The first specialty squad was the 11B squad of infantrymen. In addition to the full squad of ten 11Bs, there were six others with infantry experience. They went to the other squads to beef them up. Most of the six were squad leaders of the regular squads.

The second specialty squad was called the HQ/Team. They were the HQ people: Grant, Ted, Sap, and Jim Q., and then the Team, and Nick, the medic. Nick roamed around among all squads, but was technically assigned to the HQ/Team squad. If this were a real unit, the commanding officer and the NCOs would not technically be in a squad, but this was an irregular unit, so they broke many standards.

Just as Ted and Lt. Col. Hammond had originally thought, the Team would serve as an MP SWAT team and help with the civil affair things Grant would be doing. The Team would also serve as the PSD(Personal Security Detail) for the unit's leadership. If things were calmed down enough in Olympia, the Team could be loaned out to be the PSD for other vital personnel.

The third specialty squad was the "chairborne" squad, a play on the term "airborne," which referred to paratroopers. The chairborne squad were the administrative soldiers who sat in chairs (not really, but that's where the joke came from). They performed supply and food service tasks. They were the least combat capable. This didn't mean that they were combat incapable; they could still kick ass on the average gang banger, but compared to the other squads in the 17th, the chairborne unit was less capable.

This did not mean the chairborne squad was not valuable. An

army travels on its stomach, as Napoleon once said. The 11B squad, or the Team, could not perform well things when they hadn't eaten for two days. Similarly, they could not accomplish their mission when there was plenty of food but no one to get it out to the hungry troops, or when they need ammo but no one knows where it is and how to get it to them.

"The night of New Year's Eve," Ted said, "We'll be ready to move out. We'll need Rich to activate Bennington and have Bennington take down the Frederickson Limas."

"I'll tell him," Grant said.

"I'd rather have Rich come out here and get the whole plan," Ted said. "I also want him to see all of us so we can impress upon him that activating Bennington is more than just an errand. It's a vital part of this mission, and all these guys," Ted said pointing toward the troops, "are dead if Bennington doesn't do his job."

"If Frederickson isn't cleared out," Sap said, "we're done for. We won't get past Frederickson," he said pointing to the map, "which means we won't get to Olympia to help, or we'll get there too late or too shot up to be any good."

"We didn't train this hard and suck up this many vital supplies," Ted said, "just to liberate some little hick town from a corrupt political boss. Nope, the Frederickson part of this is too important to be handled by just telling Rich to talk to Bennington."

They had a point, Grant thought.

"I'll get Rich out here whenever you need him," Grant said.

"We'll let you know when we need to talk to him," Sap said.

Next, they went over, in great detail, the path they would take to Olympia. It was pretty much straight down Highway 101.

The plan, which they had come up with weeks ago, was to take a semi-truck full of soldiers and a few pickup trucks.

The idea to use semis came from one of the guys in Ted and Sap's former Special Forces unit at Ft. Lewis. Semis blend in and hold an enormous amount of cargo, almost 100 soldiers, in fact. The Limas would be reluctant to fire on a semi because it could contain a huge quantity of food that their civilians needed. This was not because the Limas were humanitarians, they just didn't want to deal with the rioting that would come from blowing up a load of food that hungry people had been waiting for. And the Limas would want to take a cut of the food, so they didn't want to shoot up their loot.

A few weeks earlier, Grant had told Ted and Sap that he knew just where to get a semi. Grant would get one from Doug Smithson, the

Pierce Point "postman" who ran the parcel delivery system and owned a couple of semis. He was the one who donated the semi-trailer to show the cops when Gideon brought the load of food in. Smithson was a solid Patriot and could be trusted. He even had a few hundred gallons of diesel in his underground tank.

Ted devised a back-up plan in case Smithson didn't loan them a semi. He didn't tell Grant about the plan because it involved "persuading" Smithson to give up the keys or just outright stealing the semi. He hoped it wouldn't be necessary, but as Ted often said, "This ain't tiddlie winks." Ted would kill to get that semi.

Ted also had a back-up plan in case no semis were available. It wasn't ideal, but they could use Rich's short school bus. It didn't hold nearly as many troops, so they would supplement the bus with as many civilian cars and trucks as they could get.

During the planning a few weeks back, Ted, Sap, and Grant discussed the details of moving the unit by semi. A semi-trailer has about four hundred square feet of floor space, which is four square feet for one soldier. That would be enough standing room for the unit, and a little room for gear. They would rig up some ropes for the troops to hold onto during turns, accelerations, and braking. It wouldn't be comfortable, but it sure beat walking and getting shot at.

Each of the soldiers would be traveling very, very lightly. A rifle and, for most, a small civilian backpack. Only a few had kit or military pouches. Most used student backpacks that Grant scrounged up at the Grange and that some of them brought with them from Boston Harbor. Grant drew the line at kids' backpacks with cartoon characters. He wouldn't use those because they looked so stupid.

Civilian backpacks were okay with Grant even though they didn't look "badass." The civilian backpacks, coupled with the civilian hunting clothes some had, reinforced the reality that this was an irregular unit partly made up of civilians. But the civilian backpacks did what they needed to do: they held a few magazines of ammo, a water bottle, and a jacket. Not "tacticool," but they worked. Besides, the soldiers wouldn't be marching for miles. Hopefully.

The unit would have a few pickup trucks. There would be one in the lead and one in the rear, at least. They would split up the supplies among the trucks and the semi. That way, if one were lost, not all their eggs would have been in one basket. Each vehicle would have cases of ammo, plenty of diesel in various containers, some water containers, and some MREs.

They didn't have enough food for all the days they would

likely be out in the field on the march to Olympia. They only had forty-three cases of MREs, most of which came in from HQ, so that was about five MREs per soldier. That was five days of food, tops. They figured it would take at least that long, probably longer, to get to Olympia. They would try to find some food on the way there — as in steal it, though they hoped any Patriots along the way would come out and feed them. Franny would pack up a very basic field kitchen so they could cook any food they acquired. They didn't have a solid plan for food; they were "free stylin'" it. This was not like traditional military operations where Ted could radio in and have a helicopter deliver pallets of food.

The unit had plenty of diesel, but only a few gas cans. Luckily, diesel didn't melt regular plastic containers on contact like gasoline does. They could store diesel in any plastic container, even old milk jugs. So, for the semi, they had diesel and a way to carry it.

But, what about the pickups? Rich and Dan had diesel pickups and would loan them to the unit. Problem solved. This way, they would only have to bring one kind of fuel, and it could go into any plastic container. Thank God they had diesel vehicles and a bunch of diesel.

Another "coincidence," the outside thought said, with some satisfaction.

Chapter 262

Rules of Engagement

(December 26)

The rest of the day after Christmas was taken up by more and more planning. Each squad leader would need to know the details of the plan, so they were brought in and briefed. This took a few hours. They had good questions and good suggestions, and some of the final details got ironed out in the squad-leader briefings.

With the squad leaders knowing the date of the Tet operation, the cat was out of the bag about New Year's Day. That night at dinner, Grant and Ted would tell the entire unit about the operation. Franny did some amazing things with the Christmas dinner leftovers. It was a fabulous day-after-Christmas dinner. The troops were still in a good mood from Christmas, so t seemed like a good time to tell them about Tet. Grant stood up and started to talk.

"Well, ladies and gentlemen," Grant said in his booming "command" voice that he was getting better and better at using, "you've known this was coming. You've been waiting to put your skills to good use. Well, we have a mission."

It was silent. There was no whooping or bravado. Everyone was focused intently on Grant.

"Very soon," Grant explained, "we will be moving out. You've probably noticed that the tempo of training and planning has increased. That's for a good reason."

Grant pointed at Ted, "We are supremely confident that you are ready to go. Ready to fight. Ready to get even with these bastards. Ready to take our state back." That got a cheer. Grant gave the troops the basic overview of the plan. They would hit the Limas on New Year's at midnight, when they would be hung over and their guard would be down. They'd move through Frederickson, travel in the semi down Highway 101, come in behind the regular units into Olympia, occupy the state capitol, and perform civil affairs functions, like getting basic services back up and running. They would feed people and provide policing to control the gangs, all with an eye toward showing the general population in Olympia that the Patriot way works.

Grant didn't give all the details like the operation name or that

Bennington would take out Winters and the rest of Frederickson's command and control in advance. They trusted everyone in camp not to talk to the outside world, but there was no sense in giving away details that the troops didn't need to know right then.

"Sgt. Malloy, do you have anything to add?" Grant asked. He wanted to make sure that Ted was seen as the detail guy. That was fair because he was.

"Nothing further, sir," Ted replied.

There were questions about food and fuel for the trip, which other units would be there in Olympia with the 17th, how long they'd be in Olympia, and what kind of resistance they should expect. Ted answered the questions and emphasized that the Limas were collapsing in Olympia. He described the intelligence, how people were fleeing Olympia and heading to Seattle.

"Will we go to Seattle next?" one of the soldiers asked.

"That is not the current plan, but that could change," Ted answered. He didn't know himself whether they would go to Seattle, but he suspected that they would not. It seemed like the Patriots would let all the Limas gather in Seattle and then starve them out. The Patriots, while currently stronger than the Limas, would be fools to waste men and supplies trying to take Seattle. For what? To claim they controlled some lines on a map? Big deal.

Let the arrogant hipsters in Seattle rot, Grant thought. Seattle probably wouldn't make it through the winter anyway. "You can't eat snarkiness," Grant thought to himself. In the spring, the hungry and gang-terrorized inhabitants would be begging the Patriots to take them back. Good. This would be when the sorting between guilty Limas and innocent go-along-to-get-along civilians would begin.

"I'm not a quitter, but I need to ask something that others are thinking," one of the squad leaders said. "How long will this take and will it be done when our year is up?" As members of the Washington State Guard, the troops in the 17th had one-year enlistments.

"A fair question," Grant said, butting in on Ted. He did so because this was a political issue, not an operational detail. Grant recalled how critical the expiring one-year enlistments were to George Washington; it was a critical topic that needed to be handled at the commanding officer level.

"The answer is that we anticipate this taking a few weeks," Grant said. What he didn't say was that the Patriot units in Olympia would only have enough supplies for about two weeks of fighting unless Loyalist units defected and brought their supplies. If they couldn't take Olympia in about one week, the 17th would retreat back to Pierce Point or some defensible area on the way back. This wasn't like the old days when massive armies faced off with great supplies. The battle for Olympia would be fought by some regular units and lots of irregular units getting together and hitting a hollowed out den of thieves. It was closer to gang warfare than the grand campaigns of World War II.

"We anticipate that we will need to occupy Olympia for a few months to get it up and running again," Grant said. He didn't want to use the term "civil affairs" because they'd all think they were in a weenie unit of paper pushers; however, he wanted the unit to have a rough idea of what they'd be doing and for how long. They were entitled to know that. Besides, it was better to set expectations now than to overpromise and suffer the resentment later. So Grant took this opportunity to get expectations where they needed to be.

"To be honest," Grant said, which had everyone's attention since the topic was so important, "I think you guys will be bored after Olympia falls. You'll be guarding facilities. You'll be processing prisoners and handing out supplies. You'll be well-armed in case any dumbass is thinking about stealing from us. That kind of thing." The 11B squad and others who had been in combat were nodding. The experienced soldiers knew that, for every second of glory, there would be a week of boredom. The less glory the better, Grant thought; glory got people killed, maimed, and mentally scarred for life. Boredom was just … boring. It was safe.

"In fact," Grant said with a smile, "It's my goal that you are bitching to me about being bored. I would consider that a victory, because it means my people are safe." That got a lot of smiles.

"Will we be together as a unit all the time or will we be split up once we get there?" Ryan asked.

"Dunno," Grant said. "It depends on the ground conditions in Olympia, and the orders I get from HQ I would want to keep us together since we work so well together, but you never know what the mission requires."

The next question came from one of the infantrymen in the 11B squad.

"What are the rules of engagement?" he asked. He had detailed rules of engagement when he was in Afghanistan that prevented them from shooting back most of the time. They were idiotic and demoralizing, and they got guys killed. The infantryman was down with this whole Patriot thing, but he didn't want to go through the pansy-ass rules of engagement from Afghanistan again.

Grant and Ted had anticipated this question. Several squad leaders had told them earlier that the 11B squad was complaining about the possibility of stupid rules of engagement.

Ted looked at Grant and Grant nodded to signify that he would take this question. It was a quasi-legal question and Grant was the lawyer.

"Rules of engagement are very simple," Grant said. "Defend yourself. Use your judgment. Better safe than sorry." That got some smiles.

"Hey, this isn't some politically correct war being shown on CNN or Al-Jazeera," Grant said. "We're not in some host country that hates us—we're in America." That got some applause.

"All the detailed rules of the Geneva Convention don't apply, but decency does," Grant said. Well, technically, the Geneva Convention probably did apply, but Grant wasn't about to learn all the details and insist that his troops do the same. Something like "decency" was easier for these irregular troops to remember.

"Decency is your rule of engagement," Grant said, letting that sink in for a few moments.

"Remember," he continued, "you have to account for your life when you die, in my opinion. I'm not trying to get religious on you, but I'm telling you what I firmly believe. Do you want to try to explain to God why you intentionally killed an innocent person? I don't. I won't have to because I won't ever intentionally kill an innocent." He let that sink in, too.

"Who are innocent people?" Grant asked. "Unarmed people, kids, old people, most women. This isn't the movies where there are lots of booby-trapped civilians trying to blow you up. That makes for a great film, but it's not realistic here. Remember: the civilians in Olympia are hungry, most of them, and they want the gang and government terror to end. They won't be running up to you with grenades. They don't have grenades and they want you to feed them more than they want to kill you."

Grant paused and repeated, "The civilians want you to feed them more than they want to kill you."

Ted was getting a little uncomfortable. The troops shouldn't be lulled into thinking all the civilians were nice. Grant could tell he overstated the lack of civilian threats.

"This doesn't mean you should expect hugs and kisses from civilians," Grant said. "Some percentage of them will be trying to kill you. Also, beware of Lima military or police in civilian clothes. So be careful, but don't think of all civilians as suicide bombers. They aren't. Most aren't."

This got Ted nodding, which was a sign Grant was looking for. He was making this stuff up so he was starving for guidance from experienced professionals.

"If you see a civilian with a weapon, get ready to shoot," Grant said. "If you see a weapon pointed at you, definitely shoot. If they are stupid enough to point a weapon at you, they deserve to die. It's not your fault that some dumbass civilian decided to be John Wayne. Not your problem. You're just there doing a job, okay?" Grant was trying to prevent some of the guilt that often haunted those who shot civilians. He couldn't eliminate it, but he could set the tone for things now.

"Limas in uniform—military or law enforcement—are a different story," Grant said. "They are not poor civilians trapped in a government town. If they have a uniform, they're trying to kill you. Kill them first. Period. We're going to all the trouble of training and deploying in an effort to kill the bad guys. If they have a uniform, they're a bad guy. Period. Kill them. And that applies to those stupid Freedom Corps assholes in their stupid hard hats." That got a couple of cheers. Some in the unit had very bad experiences with the FCorps before coming to the unit.

"But, that being said," Grant said, "if someone in uniform is trying to surrender, then don't shoot them. Unless it's a ruse, and it might be." Grant thought about the inconsistency of what he'd just said. "I guess what I'm saying is don't automatically shoot someone who is trying to surrender. Give them a chance to surrender if that's safe to do."

"Don't try this alone," Ted interjected. "Have a second guy cover them. That way one of you is concentrating on the surrender part and another is concentrating on the killing them part if it's a ruse."

"The Limas will just shoot us without thinking, so why don't we do the same?" Corporal Sherryton asked. She was the one whose family was butchered by the gangs in Chicago.

"We're not animals," Grant quickly answered. "We're better than the Limas." Grant looked right at Sherryton and said, "I mean, Corporal, that's why you're here, right? Because we're better and we want to stop the things they do. You're here because you're better than they are. We have to be better." Grant let that sink in. "We treat people better," he continued. "We set the example for the civilian population. We want them to come over to our side. That's winning: the population wanting to come over to our side. Winning isn't piling up Lima bodies."

Grant didn't want to overemphasize restraint at the expense of fighting.

"That doesn't mean we do stupid shit just to make the Limas happy," Grant said. "We kill the enemy. We're soldiers and killing the enemy is our job. We protect ourselves and others. We do that with lethal force. If you have to choose between doing what you think you need to do and worrying about the law, pull the trigger first and we'll figure it out later. You won't be in trouble with Patriot forces unless you do something that everyone would recognize as a crime."

"Killing innocents for no reason," Grant said. "That will get you in trouble. I am ordering you not to do that. Does everyone understand?"

"Yes, sir!" everyone said, nearly in unison.

"Rape," Grant said, "will not—I repeat, not—get you in legal trouble." The crowd was stunned.

"It will get you shot," he said, drawing his pistol. "By me."

Silence.

"Everyone understand?" Grant asked.

"Yes, sir!" was the response.

"So, to review, what happens to rapists in this unit?" Grant asked.

"Boom!" someone yelled.

"Exactly," Grant said. "See, these rules of engagement aren't complicated." That got some laughs.

There were no more questions. Then Grant did something that he made up on the spot. "It's dark by now and, for once, it's not raining," Grant said. "Let's have a fire out there in the fire pit and just talk informally about things. No rank, everything off the record. Just hanging out before we ship out." That got some nods.

"Okay, you're dismissed," Grant said.

Someone started clapping. Then everyone stood up and cheered. Next, everyone was whooping and hollering. No one knew what, exactly, they were cheering for. They were just cheering. They were a family. And they were about to do something big.

Chapter 263

Padre Pete

(December 26)

Grant, Ted, and Sap were some of the first out at the fire pit. They got a fire going rather quickly. The pit, which saw quite a bit of use in the summer when it was nice out, hadn't been used in a few months. It had some crude benches around it. There were two picnic tables, too. They dried them off. Pretty soon, soldiers were showing up with lawn chairs. Some sat on the ground.

For the first few hours, they talked about everything and nothing. Hometowns, sports (well, former sports teams since there were no more games), food, and funny stories. There were many funny stories, many laughs.

Pastor Pete arrived and pulled up a lawn chair. He had been struggling with the issue of whether he would deploy to Olympia with the unit as its chaplain. He knew they would need the comfort he brought when they were out on the battlefield. They would see the absolute worst of humanity out there; they would need some answers about why all of this was happening. But the civilians at Pierce Point needed him, too. They had plenty of their own troubles.

Pastor Pete had finally decided to tell Grant that he would be deploying. He knew that the troops would be in even more danger and horrible conditions than the civilians in Pierce Point, so he would go where the need was the greatest, even if that meant people would be shooting at him. He was terrified of dying. Not about death—he actually welcomed that because he knew he was going to a better place—but about letting the men down by doing something stupid and getting killed, and then not being able to help them with the terrible things they would face.

"Hey, Padre Pete," one of the troops said. That was a nickname given to him by the Hispanic soldiers who appreciated that he had gone to such lengths to give them something like a traditional Catholic Christmas Mass in Spanish.

It was inevitable. Whenever Pastor Pete showed up, people quit swearing and were on their best behavior. The previous storytelling—some of which had involved women and liquor, and all of which involved swearing—stopped.

Things got serious. Finally, one of the soldiers asked Pastor Pete, "What about the innocent civilians in Olympia and Seattle? What did they do to deserve what we're about to do there?" Several guys nodded. They had been wondering this, too.

"They made a bunch of choices," Pastor Pete said. "They chose slavery. Yeah, that's a word we don't use much anymore. But 'slavery' isn't just people on plantations in the 1800s. It's having other people in control of your life. It's being totally dependent on others. It's trading your liberty for 'being taken care of.' It's selling yourself." People were silent.

"Most slavery is voluntary," Pastor Pete said. "Not the kind like in the old days in the South. That was anything but voluntary. It wasn't the plantation slaves' fault they were slaves. But, unlike that time, most slaves throughout history willingly sold themselves into it."

More silence. Every single person was glued to Pastor Pete's words. They had never really thought about this topic.

"Yep," Pastor Pete continued very firmly, "Those people in Olympia and Seattle—and all over America—sold themselves into slavery." This was a much heavier topic than the previous one they'd been on, which was sharing the wildest location they'd ever had sex. (Wes had won that contest.)

"Oh, they didn't make some big decision and say, 'I hereby sell myself into slavery,'" Pastor Pete said. "Not in one big decision. It took many small ones over the past few years … decades, even. You know, they chose to accept the money that the politicians took from other people. They chose to believe that they could get something for nothing, and they helped the government go out and get it from other people. Maybe it was just voting for the people who promised to take more from others and give it to them. Maybe it was more than just voting. Maybe they joined the FCorps to get some more FCard credits. They made a bunch of choices." More silence.

"Purely voluntary choices," Pastor Pete continued, "Where they knew, at some level, that what they were doing was wrong. Maybe they thought they couldn't stop what was going on. Maybe they thought that if they didn't do it, the next guy would, so why not get something out of it for themselves? Maybe they had talked themselves into thinking that taking things from others via the government was fair and the best for the majority. Maybe. But, whatever was in their hearts, they kept choosing to do the wrong thing. And they knew it. At some level."

82

It was silent except for the wood crackling in the fire.

"Think about it," Pastor Pete said, deciding to give more concrete examples they could relate to before going into the theology of it. "They voted for people promising them 'free' medical care, 'progressive' tax rates where, pretty soon, they weren't paying any taxes, but getting lots of free goods and services. They convinced themselves that the little bit they paid into Social Security entitled them to the much bigger amounts they took out of the system."

More silence and crackling of the fire.

"They chose to spend money the government didn't have," Pastor Pete said. "They chose to let the country get into ridiculous debt. They chose to expect a lavish lifestyle, like a perfect retirement where they'd have plenty. So they demanded more and more from the government, like Social Security and Medicare, to make sure their high expectations about retirement would come true."

"And guns," Pastor Pete quickly added. "They chose not to be a 'weirdo' or a 'redneck' by not owning a gun. Then—surprise, surprise—the gangs were running wild and they had no way to protect themselves. They had the chance to get a gun, but they didn't want to look like a nut job by having one. They made lots of little choices to do the wrong thing. Now they're in a world of hurt."

He continued, "You know, people in those Lima cities are getting what they wanted. Exactly what they wanted. They rejected liberty. They wanted 'free' stuff. Well, they got what they wanted: no liberty and free FCard food. They got what they wanted."

A soldier spoke up. "But do they really 'want' all the gangs and the fact that we're coming?" she asked.

"Yes and no," Pastor Pete answered. "They don't want the gangs and hunger. Who would? But here's the thing: they could see with their own eyes that the natural result of trying to get something for nothing was the eventual collapse of the system. Every single adult in a Lima town has said to themselves at one point or another, 'This is headed toward something bad.' But they all said, 'Oh well. It's the other guy who will get screwed, not me.'"

More silence as he let that sink in. "So it's not that people really want all this, it's that they had to know—had to—that it would be coming. So when it actually comes, they can't say 'I had no idea.' They had an idea; it occurred to them several times, actually. They were just too greedy and too pathetic to do the right thing. That is the same thing as doing the wrong thing. There is no one in a Lima city who didn't have a chance to get out of there and start making an honest living.

Hell, we all did." It was odd to hear Pastor Pete say, "Hell."

"Speaking of hell," Pastor Pete said, finally getting to his main point, "this whole situation they're in is a lot like hell, if you don't mind me saying. I believe hell is a place where people go and get what they want: no God. They have rejected God their whole lives. Over and over again, in little ways. Just like the Limas rejecting liberty over and over again. Well, in hell, God gives people who rejected Him what they want: a place where He isn't around. They can do their own thing. And live with each other, with no God to intervene. They get to be on their own, totally. Which means human beings will look out only for themselves. So it's a place no one can leave where everyone is only looking out for themselves. And preying on each other. Like prison."

The wood crackled loudly.

"Think about it: the Lima cities are just like a prison," Pastor Pete said. "No liberty, gangs in control, but free food — just like prison. Sometimes, prisoners even choose to go back to prison. They can't handle the freedom of the outside world, where no one tells them when to eat and what to wear, so they commit a crime just to go back to what they know. Back to what's comfortable, even if it's horrible. It's comfortable."

Pastor Pete was silent. He had made his point.

"Yep," Grant said finally. "And, here's another similarity between the Lima cities and prison: barbed wire. The Limas love the barbed wire around their cities," Grant said. "They think the barbed wire is protecting them from you guys. But it's keeping them in their prison. Dumbasses."

Pastor Pete nodded and said, "The people in those cities are just being used by the people who are supposedly taking care of them. But it's still their choice to be there, to be slaves. They sold themselves out to be 'taken care of.'"

"If I may get theological on you for a moment," Pastor Pete said, "another analogy between the Lima cities and prisons and hell is that all the bad guys are in one place away from us." He let that sink in. "Prisoners are placed away from us, and people in hell are there so they won't mess up heaven. Well, we should be glad that the Limas have all decided to cluster together. We can keep them away from the rest of us so they can't hurt them."

Grant had never thought of that. Maybe there was a good reason all the Limas were in places like Olympia and Seattle. The Limas had actually done the Patriots a favor by turning a few cities into walled off fortresses and thereby keeping the haters of liberty in one place—in one crumbling, predatory, starving place. The goal of the revolution—which the Patriots called the Restoration—was to bring liberty. Letting the sheeple out of the prison (that they put themselves in) would only increase the number of enemy personnel to deal with. If the cities don't want liberty, fine. They won't have it. The rural areas will. Pierce Point was living proof of this.

"Yeah," one of the soldiers said to Pastor Pete, "but people in prison or hell are in there because they did something bad. It's their punishment. They've already been punished by being there. That doesn't mean we can go in there and punish them more, right?"

Pastor Pete hadn't thought of that. After a moment of pondering, he said, "My point is that the people in a Lima city have made choices to be there and to, unfortunately, suffer whatever is coming their way. That includes us forcibly taking their city. They made choices; they aren't innocent."

Pastor Pete thought more and said, "Besides, we're not going into Olympia to punish people. We're going there to free them. We're also freeing ourselves from their control of us. We won't hurt people there if we don't have to. In fact, they're fortunate we're decent people. They wouldn't be decent to us. They haven't been for the past months and years."

Most soldiers were struggling with the idea of hurting innocent people in Olympia. This had been hanging over their heads and it was finally being discussed around the fire pit. They wanted to resolve this dilemma, so they asked questions.

"But," said the soldier, "even in prison, some people are innocent. Why should they suffer like the guilty?"

"Yeah," another soldier said, "what about the kids in a Lima city? What have they done to deserve this?"

There was silence; a long silence. The wood crackled several times.

The first soldier, who was clearly struggling with this idea of hurting innocent people, especially kids, asked, "Could we tell the sheeple that we'll let their kids come out safely and we'll take care of them?"

Grant instantly saw the political and propaganda flaw in this otherwise perfectly sensible and humanitarian suggestion. He said to the soldier, "If we did that, they would say the 'terrorists' are stealing kids and probably eating them. It could actually make the Limas fight harder against us."

All Grant could think of to get his troops around this moral dilemma was to say, "Remember, we're here to take down the system that takes away those kids' future. Those kids will have miserable lives if we don't change things for them. Remember that." Grant knew that was true, but he also knew that innocent kids and grown-ups would be dying in Olympia at the hands of his troops.

People started to look to Pastor Pete for some wise words or some explanation for this. His eyes welled up with tears and he softly said, "Their parents will be judged in the afterlife for what they did to those innocent kids." It was silent, except for one female soldier who was quietly crying. The crackling of the wood had stopped.

"That's the only answer I have, guys," Pastor Pete said. "It's not good enough, but it's all I got." He got up and left so the troops wouldn't see their chaplain bawling his head off.

"War is full of shitty situations," Ted said as the fire crackled.

Chapter 264

Telling Lisa

(December 26)

The fire pit discussion was over. Pastor Pete didn't mean for it to happen, but the discussion about innocent kids was so depressing that people just got up and left. Despite the depressing tone, Grant thought that it was important to air the topic out. That was something that each solider needed to wrap his or her head around. Hopefully it would just be theoretical.

It was about 7:30 p.m. Grant needed to go home. He'd been away the previous night so he needed to get home.

It could be the last night he would spend with Lisa. It was the night of heavy topics. Innocent kids dying. Ending his marriage. "God, I wish this Collapse had never happened," Grant said out loud as he headed back to his cabin. The Team was staying out at Marion Farm now that deployment was so close. Grant drove home alone in Mark's truck.

He pulled up to Gideon at the guard shack and waved.

"Where are the boys?" Gideon asked.

"Working," Grant said. "They'll be there day and night for a while. They might come back to get their stuff, but that'll be it."

Gideon nodded. He knew what was going on. He was one of only a handful at Pierce Point who did. As the guard adjacent Grant and the Team's cabins, he had to know the comings and goings of those people.

Grant parked Mark's truck and looked at his cabin. There it was. Beautiful. Well lit. Warm. Lived in. A happy family lived in there. A happy, safe family.

"I did my job," Grant said out loud to himself. "I took care of them." Grant felt a moment of satisfaction. He realized that the hours of stressing over preparations and the days of agony before his family came out to the cabin were worth it. He did his job. They would make it. Without him. He would just tell Lisa. He'd been going over this in his mind for months. He was tired of it. He would just tell her.

He walked in and there was his family. Manda and Cole were playing a board game. Drew was on the couch reading the Pierce Point newspaper and talking to Eileen. Lisa was in a chair relaxing with a glass of wine. They had about a dozen bottles out there before the Collapse, which had lasted this long because Lisa only had a couple glasses of wine a week.

Lisa smiled, winked, and said "There's my husband." Grant knew he was typically in for a great night with that wink.

But not that night. Or any night for the rest of his life. This is what I'm sacrificing, he said to himself. My lovely wife. And my kids. That's my sacrifice. Oh, and I might get killed, too.

"Hey, dear, let's go for a walk," Grant said, which caught Lisa by surprise.

"I'd rather sit here," she said. She was tired from a busy day at the medical clinic.

Grant didn't want to annoy her by insisting that they go for a walk. Wait, Grant said to himself. Annoy her? Getting up and going for a walk will be the least of her concerns in a minute.

"Finish up your wine, dear, and then we need to go for a walk," Grant said.

Lisa could tell something was up, something big. She couldn't wait to find out what it was. The relaxation of her glass of wine was ruined so she might as well find out what was going on.

She got a jacket and went outside. Grant was standing on the deck.

"Let's walk the beach," he said.

"Now?" Lisa asked.

Might as well get used to her being pissed, Grant thought. "Yes, now," he said.

Lisa didn't know what got into Grant, but she didn't like it. She walked down the steps to the beach. Grant didn't offer to hold her hand, which was unusual. Lisa felt very nervous about what he was going to tell her.

When they got to the beach, and away from the kids' hearing, Grant held both of her hands and looked her in the eye.

"I'm going to war in a few days," he said.

"What?" Lisa asked. She assumed it was a joke. A stupid joke, but a joke.

"I'm going to war," Grant said.

"What do you mean?" Lisa asked.

"I am the commanding officer of a Patriot irregular unit and we're heading out in a few days," Grant said. What a relief. He finally got it off his chest.

"Shut up," Lisa said in a joking way. He was kidding. Right?

Grant just looked at her. He wasn't crying like he thought he would be.

Slowly it started sinking in to Lisa. The "Lt. Matson" comment from that Tony guy with the amputated leg. Grant being away all the time.

"The rental team?" Lisa asked. She had suspected this was a fake story and had feared that Grant was in some insane guerilla army, but she had put it out of her mind.

"A cover story," Grant said. "There is no rental team. It's a Patriot military unit. I'm leaving with them."

Lisa just stared at Grant. This wasn't happening. This was some cruel joke he was playing. Things were going so well out there now. He couldn't leave.

"I love you so much, honey," Grant said. "I love the kids. But I have to go."

"The hell you do!" screamed Lisa. "The hell you do!"

"Yes, I do," Grant said. "They are counting on me."

"They? Who the hell are they?" Lisa screamed again. "They're not your family. They're your little political buddies. All this 'Don't Tread on Me' shit."

Grant wasn't even going to try to persuade her. His job tonight was merely to get her to understand that he didn't hate her or the kids. That was how low he set the bar. He wanted her to understand that this really wasn't his choice, and that he had to go away with the unit. But, Grant thought, without knowing all the things that he knew, like the meetings at Boston Harbor, how could Lisa possibly understand why he needed to do this?

"I love you and the kids very much," Grant said meekly. "I don't expect you to understand this. You don't know all the things I know. I don't talk about them with you because you don't like hearing about them. And they're classified."

"Classified?" Lisa screamed. "Listen to you, Mr. Big Spy Man. 'Classified'? You are so important, aren't you? You and your little 'Don't Tread on Me' Army buddies are more important than your own family. More important than us."

Grant had nothing to say.

"Instead of being some spy or whatever you're pretending to be," Lisa screamed with a shaking voice, "why don't you try to be a husband and a father?"

Grant would not take that insult. He would take a lot tonight, but not that.

"I have done a great job of being a husband and father," Grant said, trying not to scream at her. "You have this safe place, food, and everything you need. If I would have listened to you, we'd be rotting away in Olympia."

Grant instantly wished he hadn't said that. He didn't want to re-fight past battles.

"Oh, I'm wrong about everything?" Lisa screamed. "It's all my fault you decided to play Army? Yeah, that's my fault." She started sobbing uncontrollably.

"No, it's not your fault," Grant said. "It's the government. They did all of this to us. And there are other people like me who are going to fix it." He realized how crazy that must sound to a woman who is finding out her husband is leaving.

Grant just stood there. Lisa was expecting him to say, "I'm sorry. I won't go away. I'll tell them I can't do it." But the longer Grant just stood there, the more Lisa realized he was really going to leave.

Grant decided to give her more details on how well protected she and the kids were so she wouldn't think he was a bad husband and father. "Pierce Point will be well protected," he said. "The vast majority of the gate guards will stay. So will Gideon. We made sure that our operations wouldn't endanger Pierce Point."

"Are you out of your mind?" Lisa yelled and threw up her arms. "They'll find out where you're from and come and get us. How stupid are you!"

Grant was slipping into argument mode where he had to rebut each point she made. He told himself he wouldn't do this, but Lisa was out of her league when it came to military and political affairs. Grant thought of a dozen detailed reasons why she was wrong and why they would be worse off if they didn't go on offense against Olympia. He started to tell her the first reason, but he held back.

She wanted to get into a big argument about some little detail and then tell herself she was right about that detail. She needed a little thing to feel right about instead of acknowledging the reality that they were in a war and her husband was leaving to fight it.

"There are a lot of things you don't know," Grant said calmly, to avoid the debate on details that she wanted. "Trust me. You are safe."

"Trust you!" Lisa shrieked. "Yeah, trust the guy who has now left his family twice." She put her face in her hands and started crying.

"It was hard enough to trust you after you left the first time!"

she sobbed. "Now this. How stupid am I?"

That was when Grant knew his marriage was over. If Lisa, who was always the smartest person in the room, thought she'd been fooled, then she would never, ever let that happen again. She would never trust him again. Period. He knew it.

Suddenly, Grant was cold all over. He got dizzy and started losing his balance. He regained it. He felt like all the blood had drained out of him. He must be going into shock.

Lives, fortunes, and sacred honor, the outside thought said remorsefully. *This is your sacrifice.*

Things immediately became clear. Crystal clear.

Everyone was suffering in some way during the Collapse. Most people were becoming hungrier with each passing day. Most were scared of gangs or the government. Grant had done extremely well when it came to food and security. He was going to come out of the Collapse a winner. So he had thought, but he was wrong.

His sacrifice wasn't being hungry or his family being scared of gangs in their neighborhood. His sacrifice was having to leave his wife and kids.

Grant thought about all the Revolutionary War heroes and the sacrifices they had to make. Seventeen of the signers of the Declaration of Independence left their families and fought for years on the battlefield. Five were captured by the British, one dying a horrific death while incarcerated. Others lived like animals, constantly being hunted by the British. Many had children killed or captured. Eleven signers lost their entire fortunes, many with their homes being burned to ground by the British and their families captured.

Looking at the sacrifices of those around him, Grant thought about Lt. Col. Hammond. He was married, but his family was hiding somewhere. He might never see them again. Gideon's family was in Philadelphia going through who knows what. Nick, the medic, was separated from his wife and new baby. Many of the soldiers had wives and girlfriends that they would never see again.

And these were the only sacrifices Grant knew about. In a few days, many people—including him—might be dead, maimed, or captured and tortured. The sacrifices were only starting.

This was the price for fixing things. This was the price a society pays for letting itself fall apart. For getting fat, lazy, and stupid. This was the price for constantly choosing big government over liberty. Collapse—brutal, painful collapse—was inevitable. Even the innocent, like Grant, would have to suffer in order to restore things.

"Why do you hate me?" Lisa sobbed. "Why are you doing this to me? And to the kids?"

"I don't hate you," Grant said. "I love you and the only way for us to have any kind of life is to end this situation. I'm ending it. I'm stepping up to end it." That seemed pretty reasonable to Grant.

"You're leaving," she cried. "You're trying to fix the government, but you won't stay here and fix us. I don't get it. We need you."

Grant just listened. He would not try to persuade her. She was taking a war personally. Grant realized how impossible it was to reason with someone who was taking a war as a personal insult. He couldn't help. He couldn't persuade anyone when emotion was running this high.

"The only 'normal' thing I have anymore is you," Lisa said. "My job, my house, my friends … nothing is normal anymore. All I have is you. And the kids. But you are leaving us."

Grant let her cry for a while more. Might as well get it all out of her system. She calmed down after a while.

"Where are you going?" she asked.

"I can't say," he answered.

"Classified?" she retorted sarcastically.

"Who are you going with?" she asked. She had to know what was happening to her husband.

"My unit," he said without emotion.

"You said they aren't gate guards," she said. "So who are they?" Grant realized that she wanted to find out if he was with people who were good soldiers or not; she wanted to see if he was on some suicide mission. He could reassure her on this point.

"Some extremely good soldiers," he said. "Special Forces, regular Army infantry, some Marines, and some Navy and Air Force, then there's the Team, and … lil' ole' me." He left out the part about untrained civilians. That would only worry her.

"Wait," she said, as her razor sharp intellect kicked back in and she re-established some control over her emotions. "You are the commander or whatever of Special Forces? You?"

Grant laughed. That broke the tension. "Yep," he said. "Believe it or not. But only a couple guys are Special Forces. They tell me what to do."

Lisa laughed. That was a good sign.

"Why are you the commander?" she asked. Her very logical mind could not leave this illogical situation alone.

"Because I know how to get communities up and running," he said with a shrug. "They call it 'civil affairs.' You know, getting people fed, working together, medical care, a newspaper, postal service, a library … that kind of stuff. They looked at the success of Pierce Point and said they needed that in the rest of the state." This wasn't exactly true. Grant had not been sought out by Patriots as much as Ted knew that his young shooting buddies had a basement full of AR-15s in a cabin out near Olympia. The civil affairs stuff was an afterthought. And Grant had jumped at the opportunity to join the unit.

"How does this make you a commander?" she asked.

"Our mission is not to fight the bad guys head-on, but to come in after the real troops beat the bad guys and we will get things back up and running," he said. That was partially true. There would be lots of fighting once they occupied the city, but he wouldn't worry her with that.

"So you won't be in combat?" she asked, praying the answer was no.

"Nope, not really," he said. "We have guns, of course, but we have guns out here at Pierce Point and nothing big ever happens."

Lisa's immediate concern that her husband was going to die had passed. It sounded like he wouldn't be in real combat, he'd just be feeding people, or whatever. But then she wondered, how could she trust him now after months of lying? She couldn't possibly believe that he was going off to feed people without any risk to himself, but she didn't want to learn more about what he was doing and then worry about how dangerous it was. She would rather know he was lying about the low risk of what he was going to do than know exactly what he would be doing.

Now her concern returned to her husband lying to her for months.

"So all the times you told me about the 'rental team'?" she asked.

"Was a lie," he admitted. "I'm sorry. We have to keep the unit a secret. We don't want to give the Limas any reason to poke around out here."

"Limas?" she asked.

"Oh," he said, realizing that she had never heard that term before. He had been living in another world for months. Not in her world. He explained what "Lima" meant.

She started crying again, but softly this time. "You lied," she said. "You lied to me. You made me look stupid by believing you for

93

months." She was also hurt that he didn't believe she could be trusted with the truth about the unit. She would have never told anyone because that could get her husband hurt. Why didn't he trust her?

All Grant could say was "I had to." He didn't expect to persuade her, but he needed to explain to her why he did what he did. He had to.

"Go away," Lisa said. "Leave. Go be with your little Army buddies."

Grant knew that was coming. This conversation was over. He went to hug her. She pushed him away.

He had half expected her to hug him, but she wouldn't. He reminded her, "You said the last time that if I hugged you everything would have been okay," referring to when he left her in Olympia and went out to the cabin.

"That was last time," she said coldly. "That was before you'd done this a second time. I can never trust you again, Grant. Never again." She walked off.

That was that. It was over.

Grant waited a few seconds for her to turn around and run back to him. He laughed at himself for being so sappy. Of course a hug that made everything okay wasn't going to happen. Be a man, he said to himself. Get your gear, say goodbye to your kids, and go fight a war. That's what men do. That's what Grandpa did. This is your sacrifice, he said to himself again.

As they headed up the stairs to the cabin, he remembered a very practical detail.

"Hey, you can't tell anyone about the unit," he said to her.

"Oh, I owe you a favor?" she snapped back. "Sure, you've just left me and the kids for a second time. Is there anything else I can do for you?"

"Seriously, you can't tell anyone about this until after we leave," he said. He hadn't thought through this part of his confession to her, and knew he was pushing his luck. Maybe he should have waited until right before they left. He probably should have. But he couldn't be around her anymore without telling her.

"What happens if I do?" she shot back. "Are you going to 'court martial' me?"

"Kind of," he said. "Seriously, if you are planning on telling anyone about this, I need to let the unit know and they'll have to do something about it."

"Now you're threatening me!" she yelled. She said it loud

enough for the kids to hear in the cabin. He needed to calm her down.

"Okay, no one is going to court martial you," he said. "But if you tell people what's going on with us, me and about …" he almost said, "one hundred," but didn't want her to know the size of the unit, "… several people, including me, will get killed or captured," he said. "Is that what you want? To get even with me by having me killed?" He had been resisting getting some licks in on her in this argument, but couldn't hold back any more.

She started crying again. "You said there was no danger and now you say you'll get killed if I tell anyone. Which is it?" She was quick.

"There won't be any danger if you don't tell people," Grant said, surprised that he came up with that one so quickly. It wasn't a bad comeback.

He pointed at her and said, "You just said I'm a bad husband and father because I am leaving you and the kids. Now it's my turn to throw out an outrageous charge. Do you want to get me killed?"

"I'm thinking about it," she said and a laugh erupted out of her, against her will. Then she became totally emotionless. It scared her.

"Make you a deal," she said calmly, coldly. "You get the hell out of here and never come back and I won't tell the authorities about your little Army buddies."

That was chilling. All the emotion had left her; she was speaking far too calmly. She couldn't possibly love him if she could say what she just said. She wanted to be rid of him. He knew it.

After a few seconds, Grant's next thought was that he was relieved that she wouldn't tell anyone about the unit. Then he realized this was a trap. If he agreed to leave in exchange for protecting his "Army buddies," then she'd tell herself that he picked them over her. He was in a no win situation.

"No deal," he said. "I'll go turn myself in, if that's what you want." He called her bluff, which she didn't expect.

She thought for a moment, knowing that she had no intention of turning him in or telling anyone about the unit. She didn't want to get him killed or captured. She was just seeing if he cared more about his little guerilla friends than her. He had passed the test.

"Okay, I won't tell anyone about this, but you get the hell out of here," she said with a coldness that terrified Grant … and herself.

He nodded and began wondering what he'd tell the kids.

Chapter 265

"Are You Going to Put Bad Guys in Jail?"

(December 26)

Grant walked into the cabin for what he assumed to be the last time. He had been thinking about what this moment would be like for months and, now that it had actually arrived, he had no idea how it would go.

Leaving Olympia, and his family, at the beginning of the Collapse had been relatively easy. He had just shot some looters while the riots were going on. He was a marked man given his political ties. He had a safe place to go. Leaving a second time was not as easy, however. It was way harder.

Instead of leaving danger for safety like he did the first time, he was now leaving safety for danger. Grant thought about not going. He actually thought for a split second about just quitting the unit. Ted could take care of things.

No, the outside thought said firmly. *You have been placed in this position for a reason. Make your sacrifice. You won't regret it. Your family will be fine.*

Okay, then. There was no arguing with that. Once again, Grant could see clearly what needed to be done, and he had the strength to do it.

He motioned for Manda to come outside.

"What's up, padre?" she said. She was so innocent. She had no idea what he was about to do.

"I need to go work for a while," he said. That didn't surprise her. She'd seen him go for a few days at a time.

"Okay," she said, turning around to go back inside.

"No, hon, for a long time," he said. "Like, maybe for a few weeks. Maybe a few months, but maybe longer."

"Oh," she said. "What will you be doing?"

"I can't really talk about it," he said, "but it's fixing things. You know, the government. Fixing that."

She was starting to understand. "Will it be dangerous?" she asked.

"Nah," he said like it was no big deal. "I'm with some very

96

good people, like the Team." He shrugged. "They won't let anything bad happen to me. You know how they are."

She nodded. She still didn't understand what he was going to do. "Is that the 'rental team' thing?" she asked.

"Kind of," he said. "Basically, yes."

She would miss him for a while but it wasn't the end of the world. He'd be coming back. She knew he would.

Then she started thinking about it. All the guns, all the soldiers, all the danger she'd heard about in the cities. There was a reason the Team and her dad trained so hard. They would be doing something with guns in the dangerous cities. She knew what danger and guns were all about from when she had to shoot Randy Greene. She didn't want her dad to have nightmares like she was having. He had been so good to her and their family. She didn't want anything bad to happen to him. But she had to be a tough chick so he wouldn't worry about her. Like after she shot Greene and tried bravely to say, "Two to the chest, one to the head." She would put on a confident face so her dad wouldn't worry.

"Well," she said, "I'll miss you, but go do whatever it is you need to do."

Grant's heart melted. If only her mom had seen things that way. Then again, Manda was more like him than her mom. Grant got choked up. "Yep," was all he could get out.

"Your mom is kinda mad at me right now for going," he said.

"Of course," she said. "She thinks guns are dangerous and all that stuff. She'll get over it."

Grant's heart melted a second time. God, he prayed, please let Manda be right. Her statement that Lisa would get over it would give Grant the strength to go out and do all the horrible things he would be doing in the next few days. Manda's statement that Lisa would get over it might save his life, he thought.

Grant started to cry. "You're right, honey," Grant said. "She will get over it."

He recovered and said, "So, there are tons of people protecting you and Cole and mom."

Manda nodded. "Yeah," she said like Grant just stated the most obvious thing.

Grant pointed toward the guard shack. "There's Gideon at night and Jon or Mary Anne during the day. There's Chip and the Crew." They would be staying behind at Pierce Point. "There's Dan and the gate guards. There's Rich. There are a lot of people."

Manda nodded. "There's Jordan, too," she said. Ah ha, Grant thought, this is the reason it's so easy for Manda to see Grant leave. She had Jordan. Grant wasn't offended that he'd been replaced. He was relieved. She was no longer a little girl. She was a young woman. Grant needed to make room for the next man in her life.

"Right," Grant said, "there's Jordan." Grant hugged her. "Lots of people will take care of you, but you always have to take care of yourself."

She nodded.

"You did a great job of taking care of yourself when someone tried to hurt you," Grant said. "You did a great job. You didn't do anything wrong."

Manda started to cry. "I know," she said. She was not the same perky teenager she'd been before the shooting. She seemed okay, but Grant wondered if she'd ever be the same. Sacrifices, he thought. Sacrifices.

"I'm not worried at all about your brother," Grant said. "Know why?"

Manda shook her head.

"'Cause of you," he said. "I know you'll take great care of him. You already have. It's been remarkable how much you've helped him," Grant said. "Keep it up, Amanda."

Manda nodded. There was silence for a while.

"Daddy," she said in her sweet voice, "can I ask you for something?"

"Sure," Grant said. He could never say no to her "Daddy" voice.

She started to cry. "Daddy, I want to have a prom. A real prom. In a real prom dress."

Normal. She wanted normal. He couldn't fault her for that.

"You got it, dear," Grant said. He had no idea how he'd fight a war and, in the ashes of brutal urban combat, get a real high school prom for his daughter. But he would find a way.

Yes, you will.

When Grant heard those words from the outside thought, he was so relieved and at peace that he couldn't put into words. He just hugged Manda and repeated, "A prom."

Finally, he said, "I need to say goodbye to your brother." Manda nodded and gave her dad a big hug. It was a long hug; an everything-will-be-fine hug.

Grant went inside. Fortunately, Lisa wasn't around. She was in their bedroom crying with the door closed. Cole was upstairs getting ready for bed. Drew and Eileen were up there, too. He knew running into them was going to be awkward and he was dreading it. They were going to be furious at their son-in-law for leaving their daughter and grandchildren. Once again.

Grant went upstairs. Cole was stretched out on the bed. He occupied most of the mattress. He was turning into a tall and handsome 13 year-old boy.

"Hey, lil' buddy," Grant said to Cole. "I need to talk to you."

Cole smiled. His dad was home after being gone for a few days.

"Are you here to tuck me in?" Cole asked.

Grant burst into tears. He lost complete control of himself. This is what he was sacrificing. Tucking in Cole. Worse than that, Cole was sacrificing getting tucked in by his dad, but he had nothing to deserve that.

Eileen led Drew downstairs. She could tell from Grant's crying, and from hearing Lisa cry, that something big was happening and she wanted to let Grant have time alone with Cole.

"Why are you sad, Dad?" Cole asked. Cole smiled, "I made a rhyme: sad and Dad."

He was so innocent. So decent and so undeserving of everything that was happening, and was about to happen.

Grant kept crying. He couldn't stop. Months of dreading this moment were pent up and bursting out. He kept looking at Cole knowing that this would probably be the last time he would ever see him. Grant tried to get his mind to fully appreciate that. He was having a hard time doing so.

Quit thinking about yourself and your feelings, Grant told himself. You're a soldier, now act like one, he told himself. Grant slowly gained control of himself. The clarity of his mission was coming back to him. He had a once-in-a-lifetime job, a once-in-a-century job, to go do. This was his sacrifice. He needed to get it over with and start focusing on the historic job he must do. An amazing calm came over him. Again.

"Cole, I have to go away for a while and work," Grant said. Cole was listening attentively. Grant had told him before that he was going away for a few days and he had always come back. Cole didn't comprehend that Grant might not be coming back. That made this moment easier, but Grant knew it would be harder once Cole learned the truth. Even if Grant wasn't killed or captured, Lisa would never let him back. There was no way he'd be coming back to his family.

"That's okay, Dad," Cole said. "You'll be back to tuck me in." Cole smiled.

"I'll sure try," Grant said. He felt like he needed to be honest with his son. He couldn't promise he'd return and then not.

"You will tuck me in soon," Cole said. "You're a good dad."

Grant crumbled up onto Cole's bed and started crying again. Cole knew Grant was a good dad. That meant everything.

"Thank you, lil' buddy," Grant said. "Thank you for saying I'm a good dad."

"Sure, dad," Cole said. "Are you going to put bad guys in jail?"

Grant burst out in tears even harder. Cole got it. Thank God. Literally.

"Yes, I'm going to put some bad guys in jail," Grant answered. "I need to leave here to do it. I'm going to catch some bad guys back in Olympia where we used to live."

"Like the mean lady who came to our house and hurt me and Mom?" Cole asked, referring to Nancy Ringman's bizarre attack on them in Olympia.

More tears rolled down Grant's cheeks. "Yes, lil' buddy. People like that mean lady. She is bad and needs to stop hurting people."

"Thanks, Dad," Cole said. "I know the mean people will try to hurt you, but you will have guns. You will win." Cole was smiling and nodding. Grant melted again. Cole's confidence and enthusiasm was exactly what Grant needed right then.

I know, said the outside thought. *I work through the weakest, like your son.*

"I will be okay when you're gone," Cole said. "I have Missy to play with. I'm helping her with her talking. She is my friend. We don't like talking, so we just play together." Cole was nodding and smiling. He was proud of himself, as he should have been.

"And Sissy is here to help you, too," Grant said. Cole nodded.

Grant realized that he needed to wrap up the conversation. Cole was so positive. Grant wanted to end the talk on a positive note. Any bad word that Cole may utter would replay through Grant's mind thousands of times. He couldn't chance that happening. Grant needed only positive thoughts replaying. He needed that to survive. He needed hope.

"Well, Cole, I'm going to leave now for a while," Grant said. "But I want you to know that I love you very much and I'm very, very proud of you. You are a great son and I'm very happy you're my son."

Cole smiled. "Thanks, Dad," he said. "I'm glad you're my dad.

I love you, Dad." Cole hugged Grant. He felt soft; precious.

"Okay, Cole," Grant finally said. "I'm going to go put bad guys in jail. See you as soon as I can."

"Bye, Dad," Cole said and waved. I can do this, Grant said to himself. I can get up and walk out of this room. I can do it.

Indeed, Grant's legs did work and he was soon walking down the stairs from Cole's room in the loft. Now the bad part was coming: seeing Lisa again. Some of Grant's clothes that he'd need were in their bedroom with her.

Grant would delay this as long as possible by first going into the bathroom and getting his personal effects, like his toothbrush. But he had to walk past Drew and Eileen to get there. That would be unpleasant.

Drew was standing there. "Lisa told Eileen what's going on," he said. Drew wasn't mad. Not at all.

"Go do what you have to do," Drew said softly. "I understand. I know things that those two don't." Drew was referring to the fact that, as the person at Pierce Point who kept track of people's contributions to the community effort, he knew that people were helping with the effort to supply the "rental team" at Marion Farm. Drew also knew that the "rental team" was really a guerilla unit.

"It's about time someone did something about this whole shitty situation," Drew said. That was the first time Grant had ever heard Drew swear. "I'd go if I could, but I'm too old."

"And you're needed here, Drew," Grant said. "You've done a magnificent job and I need people here who can take care of my family. You'll be great at that."

Drew forced a smile. He felt guilty that he wasn't going off to war, but he knew how much good he would do by staying behind and looking after things.

"Thanks, Grant," Drew said. "Thanks for everything you've done for Lisa and us. For having this place and seeing what was coming before it hit. We owe you everything."

"Not really," Grant said. "I'm a man. I take care of my family. It's what a man does. You did it. I did it more dramatically, but you have always taken care of your family. And, when things got bad in Olympia, you pretty much told Eileen that you were leaving for the cabin with or without her. That was being a man."

Drew nodded and smiled. He was proud of how he stepped up at the end and got his wife to the cabin. It had saved their lives, and he knew it. He would forever be proud of himself for that.

"Well, you have work to go do," Drew said.

Grant just stood there. "I need to get some clothes and they're in my room with Lisa and Eileen." Grant smiled. "Here I am, a soldier, afraid to go into that room." They laughed. Grant needed that laugh.

Grant and Drew talked for a few minutes about things at Pierce Point. Drew wanted to get updated on everything he needed to know … in case Grant wasn't coming back.

Finally, Eileen came out of the bedroom. She was crying. She couldn't look Grant in the eye. She had believed everything Lisa said. Of course. She took her crying daughter's side. That's what moms do.

Grant looked at Drew and said, "I'm going in" like he was attacking an enemy machine gun nest. Drew nodded.

"I'm proud of you," Drew said. Eileen saw this and was shocked that Drew wasn't taking Lisa's side.

Grant nodded and walked toward the bedroom. I can do this, he said to himself.

He wanted to try to convince Lisa one more time. He wanted to leave on a positive note. The idea of having her hate him would weigh on his mind constantly as he was off doing some very difficult things. He needed to focus on the positive sentiment that Cole had given him.

Lisa was thinking the same thing. She had some very stressful times ahead of her and she wanted to end this on a positive note, as positive as possible. She wasn't giving in to him; she still would not let him come back, ever. But she also needed him more than ever, which was why she was so furious that he was leaving.

Grant walked into their room and Lisa was sitting on the bed with her face buried in her hands. She was crying exactly like she had been when Grant had left the first time in Olympia. That uncontrolled crying that Grant had never seen up until that point. He had the misfortune of seeing it a second time.

Grant got his clothes. The fact that he was getting his clothes only reinforced to Lisa that he was actually leaving.

He set his clothes on the bed and walked over to where she was sitting. He got on his knees in front of her. He hugged her while he was on his knees and she hugged him back. It felt so amazing. She didn't hate him. They hugged for a long time; Grant lost track of time. The hug lasted long enough for Grant to remember a lifetime of the wonderful things they had done together.

"You're the best thing that ever happened to me," Grant said to her. He didn't want to say "I love you" because he knew she'd say, "Then why are you leaving?"

"The kids are amazing," Grant said. "Thank you for them." Lisa softly nodded as they were hugging.

Finally she spoke. "Thank you for getting us out here and all the food and everything." Grant was surprised. He never expected her to thank him for that. She was admitting she had been wrong about preparing. Well, she was admitting it indirectly, which was as close to admitting it as Grant could imagine her doing.

Grant thought that Lisa might not be mad at him anymore. Wishful thinking.

"But," Lisa said, "While I'm thankful for everything you've done, I can never trust you again. You lied to me for a long time and you're leaving to do something ..." she wanted to say "stupid," but didn't want to have him out on the battlefield wondering if what he was doing was stupid. That might get him killed. "... Something I disagree that you have to go do," she said. "Other people can do it. So go and do your job, but you can't come back home."

"Okay," Grant said. This was better than her screaming at him a second time, like he'd expected. He hugged her quickly and got up. He needed to end this before she started yelling at him, which he knew he'd dwell on for the next few months.

He got his clothes and walked past her. "I love you," he said.

"Love you, too," she said. "Goodbye." That word echoed in his ears. She said it calmly. It sounded casual, like he was leaving to go to do an errand. Her calmness terrified him. It really was over.

Grant just kept walking. He couldn't say "goodbye" because that would be an admission that it was truly over. She could tell him goodbye, but he didn't have to agree. She could kick him out, but it wouldn't be his idea to leave. He didn't want to leave. He wanted his wife and family back. She could end it, but he wouldn't be the one who did.

Grant walked out of the cabin as quickly as possible. He needed to get out of there before someone said something that he'd obsess over for the weeks, months, or years.

He got into Mark's truck and headed out, waving at Gideon along the way. He stopped the truck to say goodbye. He owed that to Gideon. He rolled down the window. "See you on the other side."

"Roger that," Gideon said and saluted.

Grant returned the salute. It felt completely natural. He was no longer a family man. He was a soldier now.

Chapter 266

A Soldier Now

(December 26)

Driving away from his family on his way to the Marion Farm, Grant had the overpowering feeling that he was leaving all that was good, and that he was leaving light, warmth, and love for darkness, cold, and hate. "Why would anyone do that?" he kept asking himself.

But, just like when he left Olympia and left his family the first time, he knew that he had no choice. As hard as it was, he had to do it. Had to.

Grant was even more convinced of that now. He knew that his family would be okay and that this was his sacrifice. The outside thought had said so and it was never wrong.

Grant actually smiled. He felt warm inside. He smiled because he knew that he had the privilege, the high privilege, of doing exactly what he was supposed to do. Everything over the past few years had led up to this moment. The prepping, getting the cabin, bugging out from Olympia, setting up things in Pierce Point, the unit. This drive out to Marion Farm was a drive toward Grant's destiny.

He laughed at himself. "Driving toward his destiny"? That sounded a little corny. Then he thought about it. It was true. A complicated and amazing destiny had been laid out for him, and he was literally driving toward it.

He decided to savor the moments of the drive, to soak it all in, so he could remember it later. He started smiling. He couldn't help it. He was so calm, peaceful, and joyous that he couldn't contain himself.

As he pulled up to the Marion Farm guard station, Grant realized that he needed to take this positive energy and channel it into the unit. He needed to make this unit the very best, to improve their chances of living through what was to come. He would boost their morale and create a band of energized warriors. They would not just achieve their objective, they would kick ass and enjoy it. Those Lima bastards had an old school ass kickin' awaiting them. They were about to pay for everything they'd done. He would make them pay.

"How the hell are you, Northrup?" Grant asked the guard.

"Fine, sir," he answered. That boisterous greeting had caught him off guard.

"Good," Grant said. "We're going to kick some ass here in a few days. You ready to have the time of your life?"

"Yes, sir," Northrup said, wondering if Grant was drunk.

"Good. This is our time to get even. Do you want to get even with them?"

"Yes, sir," Northrup replied. He was a little concerned about Lt. Matson.

"I need to hear some enthusiasm, soldier!" Grant yelled.

"Time to kick ass, sir!" Northrup yelled back with a giant grin on his face.

"That's what I'm talkin' about!" Grant said. He flashed Northrup the 17th's sign and gave a "yee-haw!" rebel yell. Northrup grinned and flashed the "1-7" sign back at Grant and gave a rebel yell.

In that moment, Grant decided that he would enjoy the next few days. He'd had enough of all this gloom and doom, all this "I'm leaving my family" boo hoo crap. Quit crying, you little baby, Grant told himself. It was time to fight.

He was ready for a good old fashioned fight. Like when he beat his dad's ass the first time. The thrill from smacking a bully around and settling a score. The fear in the bully's eyes when he realizes he's getting beaten and he can no longer hurt others. The fear. Grant wanted to see the fear in the Limas' faces. He wanted to laugh and hit them over and over until they stopped hurting people.

Grant went into the farmhouse and found Ted in the den working on plans. Grant closed the door.

"Ted, I'm all in," Grant said with a huge smile. "All in, baby." Ted wondered why Grant was so hopped up. Maybe he was drunk.

"Okay," Ted said slowly. "Are you okay?"

"Yeah," Grant said. "I'm fine, man. Here's the thing: I just left my family. I feel great."

Ted looked at him like he was insane.

"No, I'm not happy that I left my family. That sucked and was the worst moment of my life," Grant said, waving his hands to gesture that it had happened in the past. "But, here's the good part: I have nothing to lose," Grant said excitedly. "I am the walking dead. My life is basically over, dude. I'm okay with that. I can't get my family back, so let's focus on the future. The future is whipping the 17th into the very best unit on earth and beating the shit out of those Lima bastards."

Ted smiled. This was exactly what he wanted to see out of

Grant. The enthusiasm would be contagious. Pretty soon, the whole unit would be chomping at the bit to go into combat. Ted had seen this before. A reluctant commanding officer usually meant disaster. An enthusiastic one usually meant success. Lots of people might die, but the mission would succeed.

Ted leaned back in his chair.

"Welcome to my world, Grant. Welcome." Ted smiled. "I got nothin' to lose either, man. Nothin'. No wife. Not sure where my kids are. All I got is you assholes."

Grant laughed. There was nothing more to say. Ted and Grant just nodded. If they weren't tough-guy soldiers, they would have hugged.

Grant stood up and said, "I gotta go. I have some contagious enthusiasm to go distribute."

Ted stood up at attention. "Hell, yes, Lieutenant!"

Chapter 267

A New Year Under New Management

(December 26 – December 30)

The next few days were a blur to Grant. He ran full speed for about twenty hours a day motivating people and getting things done. He talked to every single soldier in the unit and told them how important the mission was and how the Limas had it coming. He asked each soldier why they hated the Limas and received some stunning answers: rapes, murders, theft, destroying lives, missing relatives. Grant's message was the same: it was time to get even. You are lucky to be in a position to be able to get even with these bastards, Grant would tell the soldiers. You're not in some pathetic line with your FCard begging for cornbread mix like most people. You can fix this.

The troops loved it. They were charged. Everywhere Grant went, the troops flashed him the "gang sign." It was euphoric.

The best part of Grant's day was the morning runs. He would get up early and roust everyone out of bed while radiating enthusiasm and energy. It was, indeed, contagious. The soldiers would jump out of bed enthused and ready to go.

They ran to the Warrior Song, their unit's official song. Grant would scream out the lyrics and the whole unit would scream them back. The song was only four and a half minutes long so they ran to it on a loop several times.

After a few days of telling the troops that this was their chance to get even, Grant realized he might be overdoing it. Some of the soldiers made comments about not shedding a tear if they indiscriminately killed the residents of Olympia. That was not what Grant had in mind; not at all. He meant getting even with the guilty Limas—the FUSA and National Guard soldiers who didn't surrender, the cops still on the force and fighting, the gang bangers, the FCorps, and assorted sympathizers and enablers in the civilian population, like politicians.

Grant realized how moldable these soldiers were right at this point. They'd been cooped up in a compound for months with no contact to the outside world. When the Collapse hit, they saw everything they thought they knew about the world change overnight.

Then Grant was soon telling them it was time to "get even."

Upon this realization, Grant compensated—well, tried to compensate—by making it a point in each conversation to say they'd be getting even with the "guilty Limas." He then went on to remind them that the civilians, unless they presented a threat like pointing a weapon, were to be protected.

"That's why we're doing this," Grant would say. "We're going in to fix things, not kill innocent people." Most of the troops understood the difference. A handful, mostly the ones who had the worst things happen to them by the Limas, seemed to not understand the difference as well. Grant worried that he'd turned a few of his soldiers into killing machines of innocents and talked to Ted about his concerns. The potential innocent-killers, as Grant and Ted called them, would be watched more carefully.

Grant also worked hard on the planning of the mission. He, Ted, and Sap went through a million contingencies. What if the semi breaks down near Frederickson? What about near Olympia? They had a rough plan for most of these contingencies. For some, however, they had no plan whatsoever. They had very limited resources. Ted and Sap would constantly start to suggest a solution they had in the FUSA Army, like helicopters, and then remind themselves that they were going "third world" on this mission.

Grant also worked his ass off physically on the many heavy lifting jobs that came up as the unit was packing. If cases of ammo needed to be loaded, Grant was there doing it. He was a ball of energy and he wanted his men to see he would never ask them to do something he wasn't prepared to do himself.

Grant went into Pierce Point to get Smithson's semi. Smithson volunteered to drive his semi into combat in Olympia. He had not fully joined the unit a few months ago because he'd be away from his family during all the training, but he volunteered to do the driving job. Right then and there, the 17th got its first PMC, which stood for Private Military Contractor. It turned out there were quite a few PMCs who did brave and important things for the Patriots during the Collapse, just like in the Revolutionary War. They were Patriots doing dangerous things that needed to be done, sometimes for profit, but usually not.

At night, so no one in Pierce Point would see, members of the unit came to the Smithson place with all the diesel containers they could find and filled them up with the fuel from his underground tank. That diesel was worth a fortune now, and Smithson had willingly donated it, which was good because Grant would have shot him and taken it. He wasn't kidding. Grant knew he wouldn't have to do that, but had a conversation with himself going over what to do if this became necessary. They had come this far and nothing would stop them now from taking Olympia and ending this nightmare. Grant was going to finish this fight. He was impatient to get it started. Not only did he want to end the nightmare of the Limas' tyranny, but he wanted get on with his new, post-war life. The sooner he started the fight, the sooner his post-war life could begin. Plus, he really wanted to hit back at the bullies.

One thing terrified Grant, and it wasn't going into combat. It was Grant going to the Grange for some reason and accidently seeing Lisa. That was the last thing he needed right then. He was mentally in the game of being an "all-in" soldier and didn't need any downers like that, so he didn't go where he might run into her. Instead, he asked Rich and Dan to meet with him at the gate.

They came to the gate a few days before New Year's. It was cold, rainy, and miserable. They met in the little office at the volunteer fire station, which was one of the few dry and warm places near the gate. Now that it was nasty outside, the guards were given several small travel trailers and RVs to stay in rather than stand outside all day. They still patrolled, but they frequently came in to keep as dry as possible.

Rich and Dan knew what this meeting was about.

"Haven't seen much of you lately," Rich said with a smile. Dan laughed.

"I've been working on a big project," Grant said with a smile. Not knowing if the volunteer fire station walls were completely sound proof, Grant decided to talk in generalities.

"We'll be kicking things off at midnight on New Year's Eve, or, I guess, technically at the very beginning of New Year's Day," Grant said.

Rich and Dan nodded.

"Had you heard this before?" Grant asked, testing to see if word had leaked out.

Rich and Dan shook their heads. Good. Grant was a bit surprised this news hadn't gotten out. He was relieved.

Grant told Rich and Dan the basic plan. The unit would leave right before midnight on New Year's Day in a semi and two diesel pick-ups, fight through Frederickson, fight all the way down Highway 101 to Olympia where, hopefully, regular forces had taken the city. Then the unit would perform civil affairs work.

"What do you need from us?" Dan asked.

"From the guards?" Grant asked. "Just keep doing what you're doing. Beef up when we go. If people realize we're gone, they'll know Pierce Point has less capabilities and might pick this time to attack. We don't know of anyone planning on doing this, but it would be the time to do it if someone wanted to."

"I have reserves and a plan for calling them up," Dan said, with considerable pride. "I'll tell them they're working on New Year's Eve and I'll keep them for … how long?"

"A week if we're lucky," Grant said, "A month if we're not."

"What's the cover story for Judge Matson, the Team, and eight of the guards being gone?" Rich asked. "The 'rental team'?"

"Yep," Grant said. "It's been working so far. The story will be that we left to get the rental team up and running in the nearby — but still unnamed — community."

"Okay, sounds good," Rich said as he leaned back in his chair. He was still amazed that this rental team cover story had worked as long as it had.

Grant paused. He didn't know if Dan knew about Bennington, and he took the vow of secrecy he gave to Rich very seriously. So he said to Rich, "New Year's Eve night is when you'll need to activate your friend."

"Bennington?" Dan whispered. Rich had either told him or Dan had guessed.

"Yep, Bennington," Grant whispered back. "We're going through Frederickson. It would be much, much easier if the local officials and gang leaders were dead."

Rich looked very serious. This was for real. It was go time. "I'll activate him. A couple hours ahead of your arrival."

"Great," Grant said. "Like one to two hours ahead of us. I don't want to give them time to regroup or to be ready for us if Bennington fails to take them out."

"I have a way to communicate with him," Rich said. "Both to activate him and to get a report that the job's been done." Grant and Rich talked about how Rich would radio the news to Grant. Rich would use one of the powerful ham radios Curt Copeland had with a code phrase. Jim Q. and Scotty had ham radios that could receive the message.

When all the details were worked out, there was a long silence. All three men just stared at the little table in the room. They didn't want to say what was coming up next, but finally, Grant did.

"Well, I guess this is it for a while," Grant said as he stood up. He hated long goodbyes. Besides, these were guys. What were they going to do? Hug and cry?

"See you in a few days or weeks when Olympia is under new management," Grant said with a smile. It was a forced smile; one to show confidence in the mission, not a happy smile. It was a smile to motivate and reassure Rich and Dan.

"That's it, huh?" Dan said. "'See you around'? It all comes down to that?" Dan was trying to comprehend that Grant and the others really were leaving for war. He knew this day had been coming, but it always seemed off in the distance. Now it was here.

"Yep," Grant said, trying to act casual and confident. "That's pretty much it." He was confident, but he needed to be extra reassuring now. He knew whatever sense Rich and Dan had of the Olympia mission would color how they would communicate it to others in Pierce Point. It was important for Grant to convey confidence in the success of the mission.

"We'll be back in, I'd say, two weeks," Grant said with a shrug as if to say, "No big deal." He went on to tell them how weak the Limas were and how people were leaving Olympia for Seattle. He needed them to tell this to people after the unit left. He really needed Lisa to hear this from Rich and Dan.

"You guys will do just fine here without us," Grant said. "You'll realize just how fine and not want us back eating your food," he said, trying to make light of everything.

That comment brought up the topic of the diminishing food supplies. The FCard food would no longer be available from Frederickson after the unit attacked the town.

"We'll need to break into the semi," Rich said. "Are you okay with that?" he asked Grant.

"It's your call, gentlemen," Grant said. "I'm taking a leave of absence for a few weeks from political decisions here. I'm just glad we got through the calendar year without cracking that thing open."

Grant didn't share with them that he had been worrying about the food situation at Pierce Point. If Tet succeeded, the FUSA would no longer have control over the areas outside of Seattle, like Frederickson, so the meager government food supplies going there would cease. Not only would Pierce Point residents no longer have any FCard food from the daily runs into town, but the hungry in Frederickson would begin moving toward Pierce Point because news would spread that there was at least a little food there. It would be hard to keep the news of the semi-trailer secret when people a few miles away had no food whatsoever.

Tet would mean hunger at Pierce Point. Not just the smaller meals and lack of variety people had already been putting up with, it meant actual malnutrition. People would go to bed hungry, see their kids go hungry. Parents would hear their kids ask, "why didn't we have dinner? We didn't have any lunch or breakfast. My tummy hurts." Older people and others with weakened bodies would die from common illnesses, even from colds and the flu. There would be more Sunday funerals at the Grange. Many more.

There was also a good chance that the Utility Treaty would break down, at least in Washington State, once there was full-scale war. The Limas had been trying to keep Undecided military units on the sidelines by promising to let the utilities stay on. The Limas would no longer have anything to lose by turning them off in the rural areas, like Pierce Point, that were supplying the units attacking Lima strongholds. Surely, the Limas had a plan to take down the utilities, if attacked.

Grant's family was prepared for this, as much as they could be. Grant had that Berkey water filter at the cabin, which would treat any kind of water and make it drinkable. It was amazing technology. He had told Manda where it was and how to use it. At least his family would have drinking water.

They had firewood and a woodstove, so they'd be relatively warm. Many people in Pierce Point, however, didn't have water filters or woodstoves. Everything in American society, even after the Collapse, ran on electricity. One critical example was the refrigerators at the Grange kitchen. Maybe they would have enough generators and gas for critical things, like the Grange refrigerators. Maybe. If not, perishable food could not be stored. This would happen at the worst possible time: in the winter, when people were malnourished and needed fruit, vegetables, and meat the most. There were some healthy home canned foods but not nearly enough. Instead of these nutritious foods, the people of Pierce Point would have to fight off illness with mashed potato mix and cornbread, and even that would be in dwindling supply.

"This will suck, guys," Grant said to Rich and Dan. "But Pierce Point is amazingly well-prepared." Grant reminded them of all the ways the community had pulled together and all they had accomplished over the summer and fall: the semi-trailer, the meal cards, the gardening and hunting. "We'll make it through this, and, best of all, this will end. This year will be the last year of this crap. Next year will be different."

Grant looked them right in the eyes and said, "It will be a new year under new management."

Chapter 268

Redemption Time

(December 30)

"Breaker nine, breaker nine," Rich said on the CB radio, sounding like he was dying, "This is former Deputy Rich Gentry for Lt. Bennington. We have a serious illness out at Pierce Point, copy?"

There was static for a while until a voice came on and said, "We'll try to patch you through."

This was followed by more static for another two or three minutes until another voice came on. "Patching through."

Rich was realizing how bad things must be in Frederickson. They couldn't even get radio messages through quickly. Grant and the "rental team" might have it a little easier than they thought.

Finally, Bennington came on. He sounded calm. "Yeah, Rich," he said. "What is it?"

"I'll switch over to get off Channel 9," Rich said. Bennington knew that the next channel was 11. They had come up with this when Bennington had brought little Lucia out to get her away from Winters.

"Roger that," Bennington said. "Switching."

Rich turned the CB to channel 11 and waited a few seconds. "John, this is Rich," he said. "You copy?"

"Yep," Bennington said. "What's the emergency out there?" Bennington was playing along perfectly.

"Ruptured gall bladder," Rich said weakly, like he was in pain.

"Who?" Bennington asked, knowing the answer.

"Me," Rich said. "I have a ruptured gall bladder. I'm coming in to the hospital."

"When?" Bennington asked, with a touch of excitement in his voice. He knew that "ruptured gall bladder" was code for activating him to kill Winters, and as many of the others, as possible.

"They got me stabilized here," Rich said, "but I need to get to the hospital by about 9:00 tomorrow night. To repeat: 9:00 p.m. on December 31. Copy?"

There was a pause. Maybe Bennington was writing it down. This was a pretty big detail to get right.

"Copy," Bennington said, "9:00 p.m. on December 31. I'll let the

114

hospital know and we'll be ready for you. We'll all be ready."
Bennington sounded confident about just how ready they would be.

"Roger that," Rich said. "See you then. Gentry out."

"Bennington out," John said.

So that was it. An inside assassination job had been put into motion.

Rich changed the CB channel to 31. "Giraffe 7, this is Fred 1. You copy?"

There was a pause. Then a voice Rich didn't recognize, Jim Q.'s, came on. "Giraffe 7 is busy. I can take a message."

Rich didn't trust anyone, especially a voice he didn't know. "Have him call me on this channel."

"Roger that," Jim Q. said. He knew that the person trying to reach Grant was a friendly because he used the call sign "Giraffe 7."

A few minutes later, Grant came on. "This is Giraffe 7."

"Giraffe 7, this is Fred 1," Rich said. "Hey, man, sorry to bother you, but I wanted to let you know I called in the gall bladder situation. Everything is fine. Looks like everything is taken care of."

Grant knew what "gall bladder" meant. "Glad to hear that," Grant said. "Thanks for the update. Giraffe 7 out."

"Fred 1 out."

Rich looked around. He was alone in the radio room of Curt Copeland's house. Curt was Pierce Point's ham radio guy with the CB that had the big, powerful antenna, the one that could get out to Frederickson without a problem. Rich had asked Curt to stand outside and not listen. Rich didn't give a reason and Curt didn't ask.

"All done," Rich said to Curt once he was outside. "Thanks for your radios."

"No problem," Curt said. "Anything I can do to help." Curt was more than happy to be considered important after years of people thinking he was odd for liking radios.

Rich excused himself and went back to the Grange.

In Frederickson, Bennington sat in his car. He felt the adrenaline surge through him. His face got hot and he felt a burst of energy. In the privacy of his patrol, where no one could hear him, he started pounding the dashboard of his car and screaming. For months, he had been holding back his rage at Winters, the County, the gangs, the Collapse, his ex-wife, and all those children like Lucia, the little Mexican girl who Winters raped. Lucia was the last straw for Bennington He was screaming at the top of his lungs to get all of the anger out of him. He felt strong and powerful hitting the dashboard and screaming. He was out of control; the hatred and revenge was pouring out against his will. At first, he was afraid of how much fury he had, but he quickly realized that the rage was good. It was giving him strength and purpose. He needed the rage to do what he was going to do. Lucia and the others needed his rage to fuel the revenge he was about to dish out.

After a minute or two of pounding the dashboard, his fists hurt and his voice was hoarse. He began calming himself down. He needed to be one hundred percent normal for the next thirty-six hours in order to pull this off.

Bennington knew he'd probably die. There was a part of him that actually looked forward to it. It would be better than what he was doing now, which was helping bullies and gangs commit their crimes. He had brought shame to himself by helping them. Now he would bring honor to himself. For generations, they'd talk about this and what a hero he was. He had to admit that he wanted that, to make up for what he'd done up until now. To redeem himself.

Bennington went over the plan he'd been refining in his mind for weeks. It was a solid plan. Ambitious, but solid. He knew he would have to do this all alone. Although he knew plenty of fellow officers who were disgusted with Winters and the gangs, he wasn't sure he could trust them. This was too big to gamble with. Not only would trusting the wrong person get him killed, but whatever the Patriots were going to do in the next thirty-six hours would be jeopardized, too. This plan—in which he did the job without any help—would either succeed or fail. It was that simple.

Bennington wished the timing was different. He was glad it was going to be over soon, but New Year's Eve was a hard time to get things done. People would be taking the day off and partying. Well, the county officials and gang leaders would be partying since they were the ones with the booze and girls.

Then he thought about it. The partying would actually be an opportunity. Bennington readjusted his plan accordingly. Hey, he thought, this might actually work out better than I thought. Wow, he thought, doing this on New Year's Eve will actually be a good thing. He thought back to George Washington crossing the Delaware River on Christmas Day when the enemy was hung over and sleeping. It worked.

Bennington started to smile as the new plan unfolded in his head. Pretty soon, he was laughing out loud. This would be perfect.

Time to get it going. Redemption time.

Chapter 269

Strap It On

(December 31)

Grant was taking a nap. He had been doing that on an increasing basis. Instead of sleeping all night, he'd work hard for eight or ten hours planning, organizing, and motivating people and then take a two-hour nap. This was happening naturally; he didn't plan it. But, he figured, it was good he was getting in this rhythm because that's how it would be on the battlefield. Well, it would probably be twenty-four hours up and then a two-hour nap, if he was lucky. Either way, napping would be the only sleep he'd get. It was remarkable how well he was adapting to this napping schedule. It was almost like the human body was made to nap.

Without a regular work or meal schedule, Grant quickly lost touch of the time on a clock. In his world, it was either dark or light. He was either working or not. He was either hungry or not. Up until now, he had almost never looked at his watch—he had almost not brought a watch from Olympia to his cabin—but now he looked at it all the time. It was the only way to tell what part of the day it was.

Grant wasn't even tired. He felt alive and alert. He was operating at peak efficiency. He knew that every second counted right now. Every little detail of planning could mean life or death. Everything was serious.

Grant was riding this feeling and remaining extremely upbeat and enthusiastic. He had every member of the 17th motivated at peak levels, too. Grant would go around asking them, "How the hell are you, soldier?" "Out-fucking-standing, sir!" was the answer he'd get. Everyone was amped.

The last-minute preparations were like a final practice exam before the big test. They worked on unit-wide movements where all the members of the 17th would advance on the farmhouse, each squad covering another squad and then advancing themselves. They practiced communications, which were crucial. It was like a big ballet. They were going at full speed now and doing things flawlessly after months of working up to this point.

They had a plan for everything. They planned out what to do

117

with casualties. How to treat them and, unfortunately, how to preserve the bodies until they could be taken out with dignity. They had a plan for various communication failures. Simple, yet ingenious plans to switch frequencies. Ways to identify friendly fighters. They even had a plan for dealing with enemy prisoners when they didn't have enough men to guard them. They would use zip ties, thin plastic straps used to hold wires and cables in place, but big enough to encompass two wrists, as makeshift handcuffs. They would mark the forehead of each Lima prisoner with a big "L" in permanent marker. This would tell other Patriot units that the prisoner was an enemy soldier and prevent him from trying to blend back into the civilian population if he escaped. Tagging the enemy with an "L" would also allow the general population to exact any revenge they felt. Marking prisoners for possible civilian reprisals wasn't exactly following the Geneva Convention, but the Patriots had received reports of how the Limas were treating Patriot prisoners. An "L" on the forehead was much more humane than what the Limas did to Patriots.

They went over the route they would be taking to Olympia and the rally points, spots where they'd meet other members of the unit if they became scattered. Having stray soldiers wandering around the battlefield was a waste of strength and got people killed, so they reviewed rally points over and over again. They had a few highway maps and one detailed street map of Olympia, but that was it. Far less mapping than a "real" military unit would have. But they made do.

They had a plan for regrouping if the unit was disbursed at just about every one of the forty mile-markers from Pierce Point to the state capitol. For example, if the unit was bogged down or split apart right outside Frederickson, they would rally at the high school right outside the city limits. They would gather around the gym. The squad leaders were tasked with fitting all these details in their brains. Constantly going over them helped them remember the finer points. Repetition was the only way to retain all this information. Pretty soon, tired troops could recite the answers without even thinking. It was perfect.

The closer they got to launching, the food changed. They'd been eating well lately because they were getting rid of the hard-to-cook foods. Now, as they were close to shipping out, the meals got simpler. Food and supplies were getting packed up and the KP crews who cleaned up after a cooked meal were needed for unit-wide movements and to attend briefings. This meant less cooked food and more cold food, which was okay. They could handle it. Besides, they might as well get used to eating whatever they could find. The battlefield was not known for fine dining.

Ted and Sap felt good that the unit was ready. They knew the details of what a unit needed to know. They had trained lots of irregular troops before.

New Year's Eve, the day before the mission, was a rest day. The troops got to relax. They were encouraged to sleep during the day since they'd be up that night, as well as the next, and the next, and for who knows how long. Grant expected them to be too nervous to rest. He was wrong, though. All the work they'd put in over the past few days, mental and physical, wore everyone out. And they were now used to napping, so they slept well that day.

They were roused at 5:00 p.m. on New Year's Eve. They had a good dinner; better than the previous few days. The big treat was coffee. All the coffee they wanted. That had never happened before. Franny wouldn't have any coffee makers or a place to make coffee in the next few days, so he figured he might as well use it all up.

Grant and Ted wanted them all jacked up on caffeine to psych them up, and to keep them up for the next thirty-six to forty-eight hours.

They only had three little coffee makers and about a hundred coffee drinkers. "You ever tried to make coffee for a hundred guys?" Franny asked when Ted inquired about how to make all the coffee. Franny started in the afternoon with the little coffee makers and put each pot into a few big ice coolers with a spigot at the bottom to let melting ice water out. It worked fine. By dinner time, everyone was jacked up on coffee. Of course, those ice coolers would forever smell like coffee, but that was less important than the troops being tired.

Pastor Pete was there, as he would be moving out with the unit. He gave a very short prayer before dinner.

"Remember," he told the unit, "you have to account for your life. Just remember that. You will spend eternity stuck with what you did down here. If you intentionally kill innocents, you'll live with that forever. If you make an honest mistake, it will be an honest mistake. If you risk yourself for your unit mates, you'll be remembered forever for that."

Pastor Pete paused. "Think of this way," he said. "Everything you're about to do will be recorded like a movie. You, and everyone else, will be able to view it for a million years. Remember: you're on camera. Act accordingly."

That was it. Short, free of Bible quotes and verses, and completely non-denominational. Yet profound.

Grant was the next to speak. He, too, would keep it short and hopefully profound.

"Remember when you got here?" Grant asked. "Remember what you knew: just about nothing. Now look at you. Myers," Grant said pointing to one of the soldiers.

"What is the rally point for mile marker twelve?" Grant asked.

"KOA camp ground," Myers said without thinking.

"See," Grant said. "You guys are ready. Very ready. You know why you're doing this; we've talked about that a thousand times. Now it's time to go do it. I trust each and every one of you with my life."

Grant was not qualified to give the next speech, so he had the person who was give it. He had worked this out in advance.

"Sgt. Malloy has some thoughts for you," Grant said, as Ted stood up. Ted nodded to Grant to thank him for giving him the floor.

"You'll be scared," Ted said. "And you should be. You're doing something extremely important and your unit mates are counting on you. You want to do this right. You'll go through a lot of emotions out there. But that's normal. I've been there. Several times." He looked over at Sap who nodded.

"When you have emotions you haven't had before, realize that's because you haven't done this before," Ted said. "Your emotions are normal in this situation, it's just not normal for you to actually be in this situation. That's all. Don't think you're weird when weird things start to happen. Just accept it and keep your mind on doing your job."

Ted looked around the room to make eye contact with every single person. "You will be scared. But you will be surprised how instinctually your training takes over. You will just do the right thing and not even know it. It's weird, but a lifesaver. It's what we've been doing for months out here. You'll see why we did what we did out here when you're out there."

"Some of you," Ted said, "will have to kill people. Do it. You'll know when you need to. It's usually when someone is trying to kill you. There is something about someone trying to kill you that will clarify your thinking. It makes decision making very easy. In fact, you won't even know you're making decisions. You'll just be doing what you trained to do without even thinking. Trust me. You will just do it. That's normal."

"What happens," Ted asked, "if you stop to have a debate with yourself and spend a few seconds trying to decide if each person trying to kill you deserves to die? Well, two things happen. One is bad and the other is worse. The first thing is that you're dead. That's bad. But

120

what's worse is that your unit mates will probably also get killed. You see, it's not just you out there. It's all of us. We work together as one. So if you decide to choke, you're choking the rest of us. So forget about yourself and do the right thing for all of us. You'll see what I mean when this is over.

And one final thought." Ted then became very serious.

"Like Lt. Matson, I trust each and every one of you with my life. There is no higher honor I can bestow on you. Odds are one of you will probably save my life in the next few days. Thank you in advance." Ted pointed at Sap, which was Sap's signal to get things going. "Okay, ladies and gentlemen, it's time to gear up. Strap it on and report to your squad leader back here. Let's go fix things."

A cheer went up. Grant couldn't resist the opportunity to fire them up even more. He yelled, "How the hell are you?"

"Out-fucking-standing!" they yelled back in unison. Even Pastor Pete.

Grant was already in his kit with his rifle. He was ready to go. So was the Team. They huddled together with the rest of the HQ/Team squad. The Team had done this before—well, not this exact same thing, but they'd geared up to go into a fight numerous times. This was no big deal they kept telling themselves, but they were scared. And hiding it well.

So was Grant. He wasn't scared to die because he knew he'd be going to heaven. But he was scared about being captured and tortured. Thinking about what the Limas would do to him was terrifying; he planned on shooting himself with his little Ruger LCP .380 auto pistol he kept in his pocket before they could get to him. He wasn't sure if he would have the courage to shoot himself, but at least he'd have a pistol to point at an enemy soldier and then the enemy could shoot him.

He was also scared about being maimed, especially being paralyzed. He was really scared about the mental aftershocks of combat. He knew he'd be changed after this. He thought about what happened to Sniper Mike, who still had the feeling he was being watched by enemy snipers, even though he knew it wasn't true. Grant knew he would have nightmares and sleeplessness, at a bare minimum. There was no way to go into combat and have things work out well. There would be some damage; the only question was how much.

Off in the distance, Grant heard Smithson start up the diesel semi and get it idling. This was really going to happen. The sound of the diesel engine suddenly made this very, very real. A wave of excitement and fear swelled up in Grant.

Grant, Ted, and Sap oversaw the gathering of the squads and made sure they had all their gear. The squads assembled in the pre-arranged order and headed out to the semi.

The other vehicles were parked in the order they would be in during the convoy. The first vehicle was the scout car. They had made a last-minute change from the original plan, which had been to have Mark's truck with the Team in the lead, but then an opportunity presented itself. They got a car. And they had a former Army scout in the unit. So the first vehicle would be a nondescript car with three men, one of whom was the scout, the other two were experienced infantrymen. They had a radio and would probe ahead and radio in any threats. Their car ran on gasoline, unfortunately, and they only had a few gas cans for it. Oh well. The car wouldn't use that much gas and it wasn't too far to Olympia. They could always ditch the car if they ran out of gas and have the scout ride in Mark's truck.

The second vehicle was Mark's black Chevy truck with the extended cab. It was a diesel and held the Team. Bobby would drive and Scotty would be up front on the radio. Pow and Grant would be in the rear seats. Ryan and Wes drew the short straws and would be in the back of the truck with a tarp over them. The tarp could be thrown off and those two could get into the fight quickly, if they had to. That way, the truck wouldn't have a bunch of well-armed men visible in the back, which would draw far too much attention. The tarp was also nice if it rained, which it probably would, given the time of year.

The third vehicle was the semi, which Smithson drove. Jim Q. and Ted were in the cab with him. With communications from Jim Q., Ted could lead the unit if the Team's truck was hit and Grant was out of the fight. Not that Grant would actually be leading the fight, but he was the lieutenant.

Most of the soldiers were in the back of the semi. Those who might have to get in and out frequently, like those who would be fighting a lot, were packed by the trailer door. The further up front a person was, the less elite he or she was. The Chairborne squad was at the very front of the truck.

The fourth vehicle was the chase truck. It got that name because it was originally planned to be the last vehicle. The chase truck was Rich's green Ford diesel pickup. It, too, had an extended cab and was driven by one of the former Pierce Point guards who was now in the unit. He was actually Rich's neighbor and had promised him that he'd take good care of his truck. There were a bunch of supplies and two men under a tarp in the back of the chase truck. There were two people in the rear cab who would likely get in and out often: Nick, the medic, and Donnie Tailorman, the sniper.

Donnie was a Pierce Point civilian. He wasn't a sniper in the sense of sneaking into enemy territory for days and taking a shot. He was just a really good shot with a really good rifle. He was more aptly called a "marksman."

Donnie, who was in his mid-fifties and in spectacular shape, was one of the Pierce Point guards poached by the 17th. He was a plumber by trade and really helped with getting the farm up and running, but his passion in life, and the reason he was in the 17th, was that he was an amazing hunter. He loved to go to Idaho and Montana and hunt elk at long ranges. He had a 300 Win. Mag. with a powerful scope. He could hit man-sized targets out to eight hundred yards. He wasn't a military-grade sniper, but damned close and an extremely good guy to have around.

At the last minute, they added two utility vehicles in the rear, which hadn't been part of the original plan until Sap asked at one meeting how they would move their wounded and dead. No one had an answer. There was no room in any other vehicle. They also needed to have some miscellaneous hauling capability.

The call went out in camp for vehicles. One of the poached Pierce Point guards came forward and volunteered his pickup. A second guard volunteered his car.

There were two problems with the utility vehicles, neither of which was insurmountable. The first problem was that neither one ran on diesel. "Gotta play the hand you're dealt," Ted would say, stealing the line Grant always used. It was better to have two utility vehicles than none, even if they ran on gasoline. The worst case scenario was to abandon them if they ran out of gas.

The second problem was that using these vehicles, which were kept in Pierce Point, meant that the owners would have to explain where they went. Luckily, both guards were single, so they didn't have to explain to wives or girlfriends where they'd been for the past few months, why they needed their vehicles (when no one had gas), and where they would be going for the next few days, weeks, or months. Thank God for single guys.

The utility truck and utility car were manned by the Pierce Point guard who owned each one and a second man who provided security. It was important for these two rear-echelon vehicles, both of which could easily get cut off from the main convoy, to be driven by local Pierce Point guys who knew how to get around the territory from there to Olympia. Getting lost could get you, and others, killed.

The utility truck and utility car each had a hand-held CB, but that was it. The 17th was short on secure intra-unit radios from Boston Harbor and the squad leaders needed those. The CB-only comms in the utility truck and car meant that Jim Q. would need to remember to send out messages separately to them on the CB. This was not ideal, but nothing about this situation was ideal. It was a war; a ragtag and low-tech war. They were just damned happy to have troops, weapons, and food. Radios were a luxury.

Finally, the unit was saddled up and ready to roll out. Everyone got in their place. No one talked much. They headed out without any fanfare. They'd been rehearsing and planning for this moment for so long that it was anti-climactic when it actually happened. Everyone was preoccupied with doing their jobs; there was no time for public drama, like a goodbye speech. Every man and woman had inner drama going on about going into combat; there was no need to add to it. Grant thought that being low-key and seeming calm would communicate confidence to the unit, so he just got into his vehicle as if he were running an errand.

The radios crackled and the scout car started to move, followed by Mark's truck. The semi lurched forward followed by Rich's truck and the two utility vehicles. They were finally moving toward Olympia. Upon feeling the truck moving, and realizing that this time was for real, Grant sat up straight in his seat. He looked out the window and smiled. They were finally going to fix things.

When they left the guard gate at Marion Farm, it seemed weird. Most of the troops hadn't seen anything outside of Marion Farm since they got there several months ago. Most came in at night by boat to the landing and had never left. The troops who had window seats and hadn't lived in Pierce Point before were looking around at the new sights. They were gawking like tourists.

The convoy slowly rumbled down the road toward the Pierce Point gate. "Let Dan know we're coming," Grant said to Scotty.

Scotty grabbed his radio, set the frequency, and said "Badger 9, this is Pine 6, copy?"

After a while, Dan came on. "Pine 6, this is Badger 9."

"Bringing some New Year's Eve fireworks," Scotty said, which was the pre-arranged code for the unit coming through the gate.

"Roger that," Dan said. "Badger 9 out."

Dan activated his plan for the unit moving through the gate. He had a few minutes before the slow-rumbling semi and the other vehicles would be coming. He sounded the administrative alarm, which was a whistle he had. The administrative alarm was different than the attack alarm.

The gate guards started to gather around Dan, who was in the fire station. Guards were getting out of their RVs and trailers.

Once most of the guards were there, Dan said, "Okay, folks, something's about to happen that you didn't see. You got that? You didn't see what's about to happen."

The gate guards had become fairly used to "you didn't see this" moments, like when Bennington came to the gate with a little Mexican girl, dropped her off, and drove away. That didn't happen.

"There will be a car, pickup, semi, a second pickup and two last vehicles that will be going through the gate in a few minutes," Dan said. "You didn't see it." The gate guards nodded.

"Now go out and tell those still on post about this," Dan said to the gate guard squad leaders. "Dismissed." The squad leaders ran out of the fire station to go tell the others. None of the guards went back into their warm RVs and trailers. They all wanted to see what it was that they didn't officially see.

Dan went out to each station, especially the snipers up on the hill, to make sure they all knew friendlies were coming. The squad leaders had gotten the word out. Dan found Heidi, the comm chick, and made sure that Sniper Mike across the road knew what was going on. Heidi gave Dan a thumbs up.

Just then, the headlights of a car hit the guards. That was so rare. No one drove anymore, especially at night. It was like a UFO was shining a light on them.

Dan was standing there in the lights waving them through. One of the guards was opening the gate to let them out. Then more headlights appeared, together with the pinging hum of diesel engines.

The driver of the lead car saluted Dan and the gate guards. The passengers of the lead car had their hands out the window with a thumbs up. The Team's truck did the same, as did the semi and the chase vehicle.

As the last vehicle cleared the gate and it was closing, Dan saluted them.

"That's the 'rental team,' right?" a gate guard whispered to Dan.

"Something like that," Dan said with a smile.

Chapter 270

Blowout New Year's Eve Party

(December 31)

New Year's Eve in Frederickson was a relaxed affair. People were ready to have a party. The year had been so hard. People really needed a mental break. Much like in the former Soviet Union, New Year's Eve was a huge party. People living like that needed to believe the new year would be better than the last one. It probably wouldn't, but it was a good excuse to get drunk in the middle of a bleak and hopeless life.

After breakfast on New Year's Eve, Bennington got all the booze he could from the "evidence locker," as they called it, which was where they locked up all the contraband they stole and used for themselves or sold. Bennington had a lot of booze.

He took an armload of bottles up the stairs to Commissioner Winter's office. There was Julie Mathers, the poor receptionist who Winters repeatedly raped and then showed off the pictures to everyone. She was a shell of a person. She looked dead. She was too pathetic to look at. Bennington felt guilty for not wanting to look at her. He hoped that this would be the last day of humiliation she would suffer. "Hey, Julie," Bennington said. "Just setting up for the party tonight."

It took Julie a while to realize what Bennington was saying. She was always in a daze of varying intensities.

"I don't have that down," Julie finally said.

"Oh," Bennington said, "I talked to Commissioner Winters about it right before Christmas. Weird. He must have forgotten. Lots going on this time of the year."

Julie was getting scared. If Winters thought she had made a mistake…

"Put it down on his schedule for 8:00 p.m. and I'll tell him he forgot," Bennington said. "I'll take the fall for not reminding him."

Julie was relieved. "Who's coming?" she asked.

"Department heads, community leaders, the usual," Bennington said. "Community leaders" was the phrase for gang leaders.

"I have some refreshments," Bennington said, pointing his head down at the bottles in his arms. "And there will be some girls who want to come." The "girls" they always had at the "community leader" parties were hookers and soon-to-be rape victims, of course. Julie knew that.

"I'll put the refreshments in the conference room and lock it," Bennington said. "Wouldn't want this valuable stuff to walk off."

Julie just stared. It was horrible to look at her. She was so wrecked.

Bennington walked up to Julie and looked her in the eye. "Tonight would be a good night for you to stay in your room," Bennington said, referring to her quarters in the courthouse. "Julie, do you understand?"

She looked puzzled.

"Julie," Bennington said to her very sincerely, "promise me you'll stay in your room tonight and not come out." He was taking a huge risk about letting someone on to what was going to happen, even if it was only a vague mention of it, but he couldn't resist. He couldn't have anything happen to that poor, innocent woman who had been through so much.

"Okay," she said. She had no idea why, but she could tell that Bennington was trying to protect her.

"You should be 'sick' tonight, Julie," he said, staring her straight in the eye. "Trust me, you need to be sick tonight. Okay?"

Julie nodded. Bennington was talking to her in that "wink, wink" tone meaning they were breaking the rules. That was a common tone in the courthouse. As in, "this came from the evidence room," wink, wink.

"Okay, I'll be sick tonight," she said.

"This is our little secret," Bennington said. "Have I ever done anything mean to you, Julie?"

She shook her head. Bennington was just about the only man in that whole courthouse who hadn't done something awful to her. She had always thought of him as the one man not trying to hurt her. He was one of the good guys.

"Our little secret," Julie finally said.

Bennington nodded. "See you tomorrow morning," he said to her. Hopefully he would see her tomorrow morning, but the odds of him still being alive by then were pretty slim. The prospect of seeing her in the morning was a silver lining in this cloud of doom. He chose that to be his goal; fight hard, stay alive, and see her face tomorrow.

Bennington spent the rest of the day going around the courthouse inviting the department heads—the Sheriff, Emergency Management coordinator, County Manager, the FCorps liaison—to Commissioner Winters' big blow out New Year's Eve party.

"The chicas will be outrageous," Bennington promised all of them. "We've got some new ones," Bennington told them. "Some girls who managed to get themselves in jail and are now looking for a way out," he said with a big, fake smile.

Bennington went to the gate at the entrance to the MexiZone, which was the Mexican area of town run by the gangs. The MexiZone looked like a small town in Mexico: broken down cars, dogs running wild, and little kids everywhere. The buildings were dilapidated at best, and barely habitable at worst. Several families were packed into an apartment or small house. It was a horrible place, by design. Winters herded the Mexicans into one corner of the town so he could control them. The day-to-day control of the MexiZone – the protection money, the drug trade, the prostitutes – was administered by the gangs, who reported to Winters and gave him a cut of all the rackets. Just like a small town in Mexico, the vast majority of the people in the MexiZone were decent, hardworking people who were tyrannized by a few thugs.

Bennington was let in at the gate to the MexiZone, of course, because Winters was protecting the gangs and Bennington worked for him. The gangs in the MexiZone were "good" ones, the ones Winters could work with. There were still other gangs, but they had largely been run out of town by the "good" gangs and Winters' police.

"I need to talk to Moco," Bennington said, referring to the chief of staff for Señor Hernandez, the leader of the main gang in town. Hernandez had taken over from the Senorita, who was much kinder than him.

The guard had Bennington wait until a black Cadillac Escalade SUV came up. Those gang bangers drove in style while the rest of the population walked.

Moco rolled down his window. His eyes were bloodshot. He looked hung over, or high, or both.

"Party tonight," Bennington said to Moco. "Big one. Lots of refreshments and lots of girls. New ones." Bennington smiled a big smile.

Moco grinned back. He knew what goodies were in store tonight. "Carne fresca," he said, which meant "fresh meat."

"Yep," Bennington said, forcing a big smile. "About 8:00

128

tonight at the Commissioner's office. That's when the 'carne fresca' will be there. They'll go fast, so get there on time. Señor Hernandez and any of his guests are, of course, invited."

Moco smiled and nodded. He waved and rolled his window back up.

The rest of the day, Bennington found excuses to go see department heads and senior gang officials to make sure they heard him talk up the big party. There was a buzz in the circles that ran Frederickson about this big blowout New Year's Eve party.

Bennington had one more errand to run before the party. He went to the armory and checked out some items. When he was questioned about it, he said to the clerk, "Can't go into it, man. Secret shit." The clerk nodded. Bennington was a lieutenant. He got what he wanted. Besides, the clerk thought, Bennington had been in on a lot of stuff the police department had done. Like all the stuff in the "evidence room." Bennington was solid. He could be trusted.

It had just turned dark, which was about 4:30 p.m. Bennington thought he should eat some dinner. His stomach had been queasy all day as he gave out invitations to the party and therefore saw the faces of all the people he planned to kill that night. He analyzed every way he could be killed while trying to carry out his very ambitious plan. He kept wondering how much it must hurt to be shot. He had been surging on adrenaline all day and his stomach finally had enough. He took one bite of dinner and started to puke. After he quit throwing up, he drank some water. He realized that he would be hungry later that night. "No last supper," he muttered under his breath.

Over the next few hours, he paced around the courthouse. He thought about his life, focusing on all the good things he'd done until recently, how he had wanted to help people and joined the Sheriff's Department. He had done good things there: he caught criminals, comforted crime victims, and steered kids in the right direction. He saved lives from car accidents, heart attacks, and once ran into a burning mobile home to save a two-year old boy. He was a good man.

Then the Crisis started. Everything turned shitty. He saw good people turn into criminals just to survive. He ended up shooting two of them, a mother and her adult son stealing some food. He watched as he and his fellow police officers became armed enforcers for corrupt politicians and gangs. He had to watch as gang thugs beat men and raped women; he couldn't help them. He had to let it happen. That was the worst part of it: helping the gangs terrorize the innocent people of the MexiZone. To top it all off, his wife left him and took his daughter.

He went into his patrol car in the parking lot just to get away from all the people in the courthouse. He put his face in hands and started to cry about all the bad things he'd done and let happen. He had a long conversation with God and asked to be forgiven for all the things he'd done. It was a long conversation. By about 7:30 p.m., he felt relieved. He knew exactly what he needed to do. He even smiled. For real, this time.

He went up to Commissioner Winters' office and was glad to see a handwritten note on Julie's desk that said "Out sick." Thank God.

Bennington unlocked the conference room and took a bottle of Jack Daniels. He took a swig. He would allow himself one swig. He went into the bathroom with the bottle.

He poured out the whiskey. He got a water bottle out of his small backpack he brought with him. He filled the empty whiskey bottle with ice tea. It was light brown and looked just like whiskey. He would "drink" out of that bottle all night so everyone would assume he was as drunk as they were.

He looked at the other items in his backpack. They were perfect. Perfect for this job. He couldn't wait.

He looked in the mirror. He smiled again. A real smile. He hadn't seen the "old John" in the mirror in quite some time. There he was: the old, good John. The one who helped people instead of allowing people to get hurt. "Let's go," he said to himself.

Bennington went back into the conference room. On the way, he put his backpack in one of the cubicles by the conference room.

The first guest arrived at 7:55 p.m. He was the Emergency Services coordinator. He was a total douche bag; a complete hack. A felon—seriously, a convicted felon before the Crisis, who was picked by Winters to run the "racket," as they privately called county government. Bennington made small talk with him, the whole time thinking, "I can't wait to kill you." Bennington was halfway scared that he was thinking things like "I can't wait to kill you" and half wondering why it took him so long to come up with the courage to finally do it.

Shortly after 8:00 p.m., more guests began to arrive, mostly the rest of the department heads. A couple brought "girlfriends" who were well-known hookers. Too bad, Bennington thought, as he saw them come in. They'll have to die, too. They hadn't done anything too bad. They would be in the wrong place at the wrong time. Bennington had a great plan, but he couldn't make it so perfect that only truly guilty people would die. He'd struggled with this for weeks but just couldn't come up with any other way. Besides, he told himself, the hookers were guilty in some way. Instead of making an honest living like everyone else, they were partying it up with the government and gangs, and thereby living in luxury from all the ill-gotten gains. That made it a little easier to do what he was going to do, but not much. Those girls were someone's daughters.

Everyone was getting roaring drunk. Some came pretty buzzed and others came high. The hookers sure were. They had to be pretty blasted to crawl into bed with these fat, old bureaucrats.

All the men were sitting back in the conference room chairs. They were kings. They had all the booze and hookers they could want. They had it made. They were the winners. All those poor dirtbag citizens outside the courthouse who were cold and hungry. What chumps. Losers. They just didn't have the drive to succeed like the people in that conference room.

"Where's the new girls?" the Sheriff asked. That's what he'd come to the party for.

"Weird, Sheriff," Bennington said. "They were supposed to be here by now. I'll check," he said, getting on his radio and stepping outside where there was less noise. He knew the Sheriff would be listening to his radio back in the conference room.

"Jonesy," Bennington said to Jones, who was the night-shift jailer, "where are those new girls you had?"

"What?" Jonesy said. "We don't have any new girls." He wondered what the hell Bennington was talking about; he would have remembered some new girls. Jonesy often got the first crack at them when they came in. He would have remembered that.

"Sure you do," Bennington said. "You know, the young ones who came in last night?"

"Dunno, man," Jonesy said.

Bennington snickered to himself. This was perfect. It was almost like Jonesy was part of the plan. He wasn't, but he was cooperating nonetheless.

"That's bullshit," Bennington said. "I'll be down in a couple of minutes to straighten this out."

Bennington went back into the conference room. The Sheriff looked at him and said, "I heard it all. Go find those girls."

"Will do," Bennington said.

Moco and Señor Hernandez arrived as Bennington was leaving the conference room. They brought their own girls. The department heads liked the Mexican girls and Señor Hernandez liked to share them. It was just business. More gang members came in a minute later. Bennington counted six of them.

He was making the rounds getting everyone fired up. He was explaining the mix up in the jail and how he'd be going down there in a few minutes to get the girls up there to the conference room.

"Hey, man," the FCorps liaison said to Bennington, "I love that stuff," pointing to his bottle of Jack Daniels that was actually iced tea.

"Oh, hey, sorry man," Bennington said. "I'm really sick. You don't want to catch what I have. I got some other good stuff for you," he said as he walked over to pour the guy a drink.

"Okay," the FCorps guy said as he gulped down the drink Bennington made him. Bennington was glad he had planned things down to the very detail of the story about being sick.

It was 8:45 p.m. and all the government and gang luminaries were in the conference room. Shortly, Winters strolled in. He was always up for some "carne fresca."

Bennington looked at everyone in the conference room, which now included the last piece to his plan: Winters. There he was. He had no idea he was about to die.

Bennington could not believe how calm he was. His heart was racing, but he was still calm. His body had found a way to have peace, while adrenaline was racing through his veins.

Bennington went over to the Sheriff, who was making out with a Mexican hooker in the corner of the conference room near the door to the hallway. It looked so pathetic to see the middle aged and fat Sheriff making out with a scantily clad, beautiful woman. Pathetic. The Sherriff probably really believed she was attracted to him. He looked stupid and grotesque, like everything else in the courthouse.

Bennington interrupted him, "I'm going down to the jail now to get the girls."

The Sheriff waved his hand as if to say, "Okay. I'm busy now."

Bennington radioed the jail, "I'm coming down, Jonesy. The Sheriff is pissed."

Bennington didn't go down the stairs toward the jail. Instead, he went to the cubicle right outside the conference room and got his backpack. It was still there. Of course it was, he thought. Given what was in it, the place would be on lock down if someone had found it.

Bennington got the first item out of the backpack and put it in the outside pouch. He didn't zip it up. He could grab it easily. He looked in the main compartment of the backpack. All the other items were there too. Perfect.

Bennington walked to the doorway of the conference room. He looked at those people one last time. He looked right in their faces. He would remember these faces the rest of his life.

Chapter 271

New Year's Fireworks

(December 31)

Bennington stepped back behind the door to the conference room so he was behind the wall. He got the flash-bang concussion grenade out of the outside pouch of the backpack. These grenades, used by SWAT teams, were also called "stun grenades." They were not deadly. Instead, they produced a deafening sound and light so bright it temporarily blinded anyone within several yards. They were used to disorient people before a team went in.

Bennington calmly pulled the pin and threw it in the conference room. He was trying to have it land on top of the conference room table so the blast would radiate outward. He didn't want it to go under the table because the tabletop would absorb some of the blast.

Everything seemed to be in slow motion. Bennington heard the people talking and laughing. His hearing was heightened. He could hear things like he was right there, but he was outside the door. He heard the grenade bounce on the floor. He went to his backpack and pulled out a regular grenade. He was grasping the pin right as the flash-bang went off.

"Boom!" There was a blinding white flash out of the conference room door, the loudest noise he'd ever heard, and a blast wave came out the door.

It was silent in the conference room for a split second, except for the deafening ring of their ears. No one could believe what had just happened. That's when Bennington lobbed the second grenade in, a fragmentation grenade this time that would shred anyone within several yards of its blast radius. He knew the people in the conference room would be temporarily blinded and deaf from the stun grenade. They wouldn't see or hear the next thing to land in the room.

"Boom!" Another explosion. It was a different kind. A different sound and different blast. Luckily, Bennington was behind the wall when it went off. He pulled the pin on the second fragmentation grenade and threw it in.

"Boom!" Another one. By now, people were screaming. Blood curdling screams. But only a couple were. They sounded like the hookers.

Bennington swung into the conference room doorway, drew his pistol, and started shooting all the men. He'd spare the hookers with the pistol. They hadn't done anything wrong.

The closest one to the door was the Sheriff. Or what was left of him. He was literally blown apart. His chest and head looked like hamburger. Bennington had never seen so much blood.

The Sheriff was on the floor deader than a doornail. The hooker was alive. The Sheriff, in his last official act of bravery, had shielded her from the blast with his fat and flabby body while he was making out with her. He no idea he was doing it, but he had managed to save her life. Unintentionally.

Bennington was moving at lightning speed. He went on to the next men he could find. The Emergency Management director was on the floor, still alive but badly wounded. Bennington delivered a .40 round to his head. Instant hamburger. Red mist everywhere.

The FCorps liaison was trying to stand up and had a pistol. Bennington put a double tap in his chest. Another shower of red mist.

Bennington made his way from the door area to the back of the conference room where the gang bangers had been standing. They were farther away from the conference room door, where the two fragmentation grenades reach wasn't as great.

One of the gang bangers drew a pistol with his bloody arm. Bennington was already drawn, no contest.

Señor Hernandez tried to stand up, but that didn't last very long. A .40 to the head ended that attempt. That bastard deserved it.

The last gang banger was on the floor trying to use one of the injured hookers as a shield. He was a real gentleman. Bennington, who was standing, had an easy, downward angle on him and effortlessly put a round in his head without endangering the hooker. The air was filled with more red mist.

The last one in the room was Winters. He was injured on the floor. It looked like his arms and legs were torn up from grenade fragments. He was still conscious, but stunned. Upon seeing him, Bennington got a surge of joy. Joy. An odd emotion now with all this killing. But it was joy.

Bennington calmly walked up to Winters and could tell that Winters was still temporarily blinded by the flash-bang grenade.

"It's me, boss," Bennington yelled down to Winters on the floor. "It's me."

Winters was relieved. "I'm glad you're here, John. Help me."

"Sure, boss," Bennington said. "I'm here to help." Bennington raised his right foot and then he stomped Winters' throat with his boot. There was the sound of small bones breaking. "That's for Julie."

Bennington realized that he needed to get out of there. He looked behind him in case one of them was alive and conscious enough to draw on him. Nope. He looked at each one on the way out of the room. All the men were dead. That was what mattered.

Bennington wasn't done. His work that night had only begun. He grabbed the backpack and ran down the stairs. He got on the radio, which was full of screaming people talking about explosions in the courthouse up on the Commissioner's floor.

"This is Bennington, I need all personnel on the third floor now!" he yelled into the radio. Pretty soon, fellow officers were running up the stairs and into the lobby area. Bennington pointed to the conference room. All the officers ran into the conference room.

Guilty as hell. Each one of his fellow officers running into the conference room was guilty as hell. Sanders, Jimenez, Boddleman, Tipton. In a split second, Bennington could remember all the horrible things those four had done. The bribery. Putting innocent people in jail, and worse. Stealing from people. Every one of them was guilty. All the decent cops, which had been the majority, had already left the force, like Bennington should have done.

When the four cops ran into the conference room, Bennington ran to the doorway and looked in. Then he looked around behind him. When no one was looking, he tossed another fragmentation grenade in.

"Boom!" Bennington came running from the conference room doorway toward the lobby, which had filled up with more cops, and yelled, "Booby trapped! Watch out for booby traps!" That would slow them down so he could perform the second phase of his plan.

Bennington motioned for the other officers to follow him. He ran down into the communications room and yelled at the comm guy, "The gangs attacked the Commissioner and the department heads! I saw it all! Call out Code Orange! Code Orange!"

That was the code phrase the county had for an attack on the gangs, even the "good" ones who were doing business with the county. Winters had planned for the gangs trying to take over if there had been a business disagreement between the government and the gangs. "Code Orange" meant all police, FCorps, and Blue Ribbon Boys needed to go straight to the MexiZone and start killing all the male gang bangers possible. It would be an all-out war. Perfect.

The comm guy started screaming, "Code Orange!" into the

radio. Units out on patrol started radioing in that they copied and were heading to the MexiZone to start the operation. They had a meet-up point a block from the entrance to the MexiZone.

"Let's go!" Bennington yelled. About a dozen men started to follow him out into the parking lot to get into their cars.

"Shouldn't we secure the courthouse?" one of the astute sergeants asked.

"No time! No time! Move! Move!" Bennington yelled. These people were used to taking orders and Bennington was a lieutenant. He had planned on this and knew that the people who were still cops or FCorps were conformists who would take orders. They would do whatever he said. That was how things worked in the courthouse.

A group of about twenty men were streaming out into the parking lot. They were jumping into police cars and heading out. Bennington drove the lead car. He was in charge and everyone was following the leader.

They sped to the staging area without their lights or sirens on. When they got there, about a dozen other cops and Blue Ribbon Boys had assembled. The regular police were putting on body armor. The Blue Ribbon Boys looked terrified. They were supposed to have an easy job standing at a gate. Now they had to go into the MexiZone?

The cops, who now had their body armor on, seemed more confident. Of course they were. They had body armor. Everyone huddled around Bennington.

"Okay," he yelled to everyone. "The gang bangers are probably drunk now so this should be easy. Go in and just start killing every last one of them. You'll know them when you see them. You probably see them all over town. Leave the women, children, and old people alone. Now go get the bangers before they take over the whole town! Go! Go! Go!"

The men broke out of the huddle and ran toward the Mexican gate. There was no real plan or any communications of any kind. They were just running toward the "enemy." Perfect.

Bennington, who had put on his body armor, got his AR out of the trunk and ran behind them. He heard the first shots from the MexiZone guards and then the cops unloaded on the guards. The shooting quickly stopped.

Lights started coming on in the Mexican houses near the entrance to the MexiZone. Dog started barking. The cops began fanning out into groups of two or three. Perfect.

Bennington was running around giving orders. His men had no

clue what they were doing. They were just going house-to-house looking for young males. It was total chaos, just like Bennington had planned.

The number of gunshots was increasing. Now it started to sound like a bunch of firefights. Bennington ran up to a group of two Blue Ribbon Boys who were cowering behind a car. He knew both of them. They were bullies and thieves. They were the perfect government employees under the Winters administration.

"Go! Go!" Bennington yelled and pointed toward a house. The two got up and ran toward it. Bennington used the car roof as a rest and covered them. He looked around and didn't see anyone. Bennington put the red dot of his Aimpoint sight on back of the head of the closest Blue Ribbon Boy and pulled the trigger. He quickly did the same for the second one.

"Snipers!" Bennington yelled into the radio. "Snipers!" he screamed again. The fear of Mexican snipers would slow them down. Perfect.

Bennington ran up to another group, this time, it was three cops in body armor hiding behind a car. "I think fire is coming from over there," he yelled pointing toward a house. He ran back to a car for cover and then he shot all three of them in the back of the head.

Bennington realized that there might be too many of them. The plan was for the gang bangers and government people to kill each other. As many as possible. If Bennington kept killing too many on the government side, the gangs just might win. That wasn't part of the plan. But then again, with most of the gang bangers high or drunk on this New Year's Eve, the government had the element of surprise. Oh well, Bennington couldn't plan out all the details. This was war. It could not be precisely managed, just guided, which Bennington had done.

He had set the plan in motion. Now it was time for it to play out. The government and gangs would be fighting each other for the next several hours, maybe days. And they'd be doing it in the MexiZone. That would leave the highway wide open for people to go right past everything.

Then Bennington realized he had another important thing to do in order to complete the plan. He found his car and headed back to the courthouse.

Chapter 272

Everything Can Change on a New Year's Day

(December 31)

It was New Year's Eve in Times Square in New York.

"Three, two, one!" everyone chanted as the glowing ball dropped, signifying it was officially the New Year on the East Coast.

Everyone was cheering. Jeanie was watching it on TV in the big meeting room back in Camp Murray, Washington. It was 9:00 p.m. Pacific time, but midnight, and officially the New Year, in New York.

Jeanie, the media expert, couldn't help but notice that the ball drop was different this year. She could tell from the camera angles that the crowd was much, much smaller than in the past. A big crowd like in the past would be too juicy of a terrorist target so they must have limited the crowd size. A lot.

The crowd seemed surprisingly racially mixed. And they all had "We Support the Recovery!" signs. It was pretty obvious, at least to a PR expert like her, that the few hundred people on the TV screen were actors with props.

But Jeanie didn't care. She was mesmerized by the familiar ball dropping in Times Square, even if everything about this year was different. For decades, she'd watched this on TV every New Year's. Well, not every New Year's. The past few years, when she was in college and then a graduate, she spent her New Year's Eves partying instead of watching TV. But when she was a kid and a teenager, her family would all get together to watch the Times Square ball drop on TV.

Sitting there watching the ball drop, and feeling the many glasses of champagne kicking in, Jeanie was transported back in time. She remembered when she was a girl, watching the huge 2000 New Year's Eve ball drop. A new millennium. Everything seemed so new and fresh back then. The future was wide open. Everything was going great. She had a brand new millennium to go out and make her mark in. She remembered her mom and dad telling her on that particular New Year's Eve that she was lucky to be alive then. That her generation had it made and would have wonderful lives. It was their millennium. America was the only world super power in 2000.

Everything was perfect.

Jeanie needed the comfort provided by the drop of the Times Square ball. It made everything seem ... normal which meant that the upcoming year would be great, as they always should be.

Things could suck all year, but seeing that ball drop meant some things never change. Hey, Jeanie thought, America has had a rough couple of years—this year in particular—but America will bounce back. It always does, right? Jeanie was upbeat and optimistic for the first time in months. Things would get better.

Suddenly, the TV went off. Jason was standing in front of it with the power cord in his hand. He looked very serious. And worried.

"Sorry, everyone," Jason said. "We have a general alert. Everyone needs to go to their duty stations. There have been several attacks tonight all over western Washington."

Everyone was stunned. Now? New Year's Eve? This was a holiday. The Patriots were savages. They couldn't even give the legitimate authorities one night off? They were animals.

Jeanie and everyone else took a second or two to fully comprehend what was going on. Attacks? All over western Washington? Was this the beginning of the war? The real war? The big one?

Then Jeanie started to tear up. The new year. The new year would suck. It was actually going to be worse than the previous one. This wasn't going to get better. Last year wasn't a fluke bad year. Things would suck forever. There would never be a good year again. They were only going to become worse and worse.

Jeanie started running to her "duty station," which was at the visitors' barracks. That was the few rooms they had for visitors to stay. Since Jeanie handled the NVIPs, the "not very important persons" who got tours of Camp Murray, the visitors' barracks was her duty station. It was a humiliation to have a lame "duty station" like that, but that was just one of the humiliations she suffered at Camp Murray because she was not fully trusted.

There she sat for about twenty minutes, which was an excruciatingly long time, in the visitors' barracks. She could hear people running around. Jeanie was obviously useless there where nothing was happening. That gave her twenty minutes to think about New Year's Eves past ... and, unfortunately, future. Christmas had been so bleak trapped there in the prison of Camp Murray, but this was worse. Far worse. Hope was being attacked on New Year's Eve. Which was exactly what the Patriots wanted, she realized.

Finally, Jeanie couldn't take it anymore. She went back to the cafeteria to talk to people. She needed to find out what was going on.

"There has been a series of apparently coordinated attacks tonight," one of her State Patrol friends told her as he ran into the next room. "All around Olympia. And in Seattle. Even in the JBLM ring. All over the state."

"Are they attacking us here?" Jeanie asked.

"Nope," her friend said. "Not yet." He ran off.

That was reassuring. "Not yet." Boy, that would help her sleep tonight.

Jeanie was starving for information. She went back into the big meeting room with the TV. It was on again, replaying the ball drop. She checked all the channels. Same thing: New Year's programs. The news stations were replaying the President's New Year's speech about how last year was a challenge, but everything would be better this year. Duh, Jeanie, the political media expert, thought. Of course TV won't be covering the attacks.

Jeanie realized that she couldn't find out what was going on. She'd have to just wait and see if they were attacked. It was the most helpless feeling she'd ever had. Just sit and wait to see if a fight is coming to you.

She went back to her "duty station" and sat there. Pretty soon, she was crying. Softly at first, but when she realized no one was around to hear her, loudly. She was remembering all the things she'd seen and heard about how weak the "legitimate authorities" were. The speculation about whether they could withstand an attack. Now she had to sit and wonder whether they could. And then what would happen to people like her, if they couldn't.

Jeanie lost track of time that night. She thought about each of the lies she told all day long. The biggest lie she told visitors was that the population overwhelmingly supported the legitimate authorities. That would be tested tonight. She would tell the visitors that the military units were loyal. That would be tested. She told them that Camp Murray had a plan for everything. That would be tested.

She knew how it would turn out. She started crying even louder.

Chapter 273

The Clear Out Crew

(December 31)

"All clear to mile post two," a voice said on the radio. The voice was "Nineteen Delta," who was Josiah Wallingford, a former Army scout. The code 19D was the MOS (Military Occupational Specialty) for a scout. So, in Army lingo, a scout was a 19D.

Josiah insisted on being called "Nineteen Delta." It wasn't an ego thing about being a scout. He really, really didn't want his real name used. He seemed to have some deep reason why, but he wouldn't say why when he was asked. That was cool. Many people in the Patriot movement were using fake names or going exclusively by code names. It was accepted.

Ted and Grant were extremely grateful to have a scout in the unit. Nineteen Delta was the eyes of the unit. He would go ahead of them and spot any problems.

Nineteen Delta was in the little lead car, the "scout car," with two other soldiers, Jake "Meerkat" Herman and Corporal DeShante Anderson. Meerkat grew up a poor white kid in Nashville. Anderson, who was black, grew up in Chicago. He had invented the "1-7" "gang sign" for the unit.

These two guys knew how to fight in urban settings. They'd had to do it all their lives; they just refined their skills and got better gear in the Army.

Nineteen Delta, Meerkat, and Anderson were called the "Clear Out Crew" because the three of them would work together to clear out any obstacles, like enemy guards.

The Clear Out Crew dressed in civilian clothes so they could blend in, if necessary. Their civilian car even had a "We Support the Recovery!" bumper sticker. They had a set of fake identities supplied by HQ and they could operate independently in Lima-controlled areas for several days, if necessary. The Clear Out Crew was one of the prizes of the 17th. Most irregular units didn't have guys like that.

It was silent in Mark's truck. Bobby was driving and Scotty was in the front cab working the radios. Grant and Pow were in the rear cab, which also had loads of gear. Ryan and Wes were under a tarp in

142

the back of the truck with additional supplies.

Everyone was silent because they wanted to listen to the radio and pay attention. They were constantly scanning their surroundings. It was like hunting. Serious hunters focus on their surroundings. Bad ones relax and talk. The price for being a bad hunter was not getting a deer. The price for relaxing and talking out here was dying.

So far, so good, Ted thought. They'd only gone two miles, but the roads were totally clear. It was eight more miles to the Blue Ribbon Boys' gate at the entrance to Frederickson, which would be the first battle, unless Bennington had taken care of things.

Nineteen Delta gave "all clear" reports at each mile marker all the way up to mile post nine.

"Going on foot," Nineteen Delta said as they were approaching mile post ten and the Frederickson gate manned by the Blue Ribbon Boys. Nineteen Delta grew up on a Montana ranch and had hunted since he was seven years old. He knew how to move silently quite well.

All the 17th's convoy vehicles pulled off the road to wait. They were sitting ducks there, so the troops in pickups and utility vehicles got out and patrolled around. Grant would have joined them but, as the commanding officer, he wasn't supposed to unnecessarily expose himself to fire. Bobby was driving, so he wasn't supposed to leave the truck except in an emergency. Scotty was doing comms for Grant, so he needed to stay put. And Ryan and Wes were under the tarp, so they weren't going anywhere. This left Pow to be the one to get out and check things over.

A few minutes went by, which seemed like a few hours. Grant rolled down the window in Mark's truck so he could hear anything, and sure enough, he heard something.

The soft sound of gunfire in the distance. Faint "pop, pop, pops." It sounded like a few fire fights in Frederickson. Good. Probably.

"Two guards at the gate," Nineteen Delta whispered into the radio. "Clear Out Crew, link up with me." His voice was very calm, which reassured everyone else in the unit who was listening on the radio.

Grant was gung ho, but he could not do what the Clear Out Crew did. Because they had to be so silent, their primary weapon was a knife. When Grant watched them training, he realized that the one thing he couldn't do was sneak up on a guy and slit his throat. He just couldn't do it. But the Clear Out Crew could. And they could do it extremely well.

After a few minutes, Nineteen Bravo came on the radio. "Objective secure. No further guards. Just two. Go ahead and roll in."

Bobby put the truck in gear. They kept the engine idling so they could quickly take off, if necessary. Besides, it was a diesel. It needed to idle.

Grant was glad to be moving. It was better than being a sitting duck. But, then again, maybe they were heading closer to an ambush, he thought. Sitting somewhere relatively safe or moving forward? Grant would pick moving because that put them closer to Olympia, and getting there was their job. Everything they'd done for months was about getting to Olympia.

The Frederickson gate was well lit. As Mark's truck came up on the guards, Grant could see the lead car and the Clear Out Crew. They had face masks on and they looked terrifying. Nineteen Delta came over to Mark's truck. Bobby rolled the window down.

"Got two prisoners," Nineteen Delta said. "A couple teenage punks were taking a piss when we took out their two colleagues. They came back to their posts, saw us, and instantly surrendered. Hammer and tag?"

"Yep," Grant said. "Hammer and tag." This was the phrase they had come up with for how they would take care of prisoners they didn't want to take with them because they didn't have the transport space, the resources to guard them, or food to feed them. They wouldn't have any of those things for prisoners, except maybe high-value ones, on the ride into Olympia. Once they got to Olympia, they would have temporary facilities to house prisoners, but not now.

"Hammer and tag" meant the unit would take a hammer or other heavy object, like a pistol, and smash the hands of the prisoner. They wouldn't count on zip ties to handcuff them because unattended prisoners could wriggle out of them after a few hours. Smashing the prisoner's hands meant they couldn't fight for a few weeks or maybe months while they healed. Smashing their hands was more humane than shooting them. The unit would then "tag" the prisoner by marking his face in permanent marker with an "L" for Lima. That way, others could know that the prisoner was a Lima. And, with broken or severely bruised hands, the prisoner wasn't a threat.

Grant had no moral problem with hammer and tagging enemy prisoners. If Lima combatants got out of this fight with just smashed hands, they were getting off easy. Under any set of morals, Lima combatants deserved to die. Most armies would have shot them without even thinking about it. So, as harsh as smashing their hands was, it was still far more humane than shooting them. And it solved the Patriot's problem of transporting, guarding, and feeding the prisoners.

Nineteen Delta whispered "hammer and tag" to the Clear Out Crew. Anderson put the hands of the two terrified guards on the metal gate while Nineteen Delta held Scotty's silenced .22 pistol, the "Hush Puppy," to the guards' heads.

The guards had a piece of duct tape on their mouths so they couldn't scream. Meerkat took out his pistol. The guards started to scream into the duct tape. They were screaming for their lives, but no one else could hear them. It sounded pathetic. They were so helpless.

Meerkat used the butt of his pistol, a heavy 1911, to smash the hands of the first guard. He screamed out in pain, muffled by the tape. Meerkat smashed the hands of the second guard. He then took out a Sharpie pen and wrote a huge "L" on the guards' faces. The Clear Out Crew walked away, opened up the gate, and got in the lead car. The guards rolled around on the ground screaming into their duct tape gags, like squealing pigs.

That was it? Grant thought. The Frederickson gate was taken? It couldn't be that easy.

Things were going to become harder now that they were in Frederickson, Grant realized. They could roll down a country road on the way into town, but now they were in town, where every block had a dozen possible ambush points, full of people. More people meant more Lima sympathizers calling in to the authorities that a strange convoy was there. It also meant more people shooting at them. And it meant more innocent civilians to navigate.

Moving through town took forever. They spent more time idling than moving. Ted had made a calculated decision to do it this way and Grant had agreed. They could just ram through Frederickson and keep going, but if they left Frederickson in Lima hands, they would have their escape route back to Pierce Point cut off. And Pierce Point would be exposed to a strong Lima force that could roll down the road and take on the Pierce Point guards; guards who were weakened without the Team with eight guards, now in the 17th. By blowing through an unsecured Frederickson and racing to Olympia, the 17th would have effectively divided themselves and Pierce Point. Besides, the 17th was merely an irregular unit sent in behind the regular forces taking Olympia. They weren't in a rush to get there.

Bennington was the other reason Ted and Grant decided to go slowly through Frederickson and make sure it was secured. If Bennington had taken out the town's leadership and successfully created chaos right when the 17th was rolling through, then it would be much easier to take Frederickson. Maybe even possible for an irregular unit of just one hundred troops. Maybe.

As the 17th crept through Frederickson, the sound of gunfire was getting louder and louder. There was still no contact with the enemy. They got about a mile in when the inevitable happened.

An FCorps volunteer in Frederickson, Levi Millsaps, saw the convoy. He knew that a semi with lead and chase cars and trucks wasn't normal. It was New Year's Eve. No one had a reason to be driving at 10:00 p.m. on New Year's Eve. The only semis that ever came through town went to the grocery store or courthouse. This convoy wasn't going in that direction, besides there was gunfire throughout the city. Something was going on. He had earlier heard on his FCorps radio that there was a "Code Orange." He didn't know what that meant, but calling out a code, along with the gunfire in the distance, must mean something was going on.

"County EM dispatch," he radioed in to County Emergency Management. "This is Levi Millsaps. Copy?"

"Millsaps, County EM dispatch," a dispatcher said. "Go ahead." It wasn't the voice of the regular dispatcher, but someone new.

"Yeah, I'm here by the Lions Park and I'm seeing something strange," Millsaps said.

"What do you see?" crackled the voice.

"A semi-truck with a lead car and pickup and a couple pickups and car behind it. And the pickup behind the semi has several armed men in the back of the truck."

"Excellent," said the dispatcher. "The food semi finally got here. The cars and pickup are the escorts. Thanks for the report, Millsaps."

Millsaps felt proud. He had helped. He had observed something and reported it. Millsaps was a hard core Loyalist, a true believer in the legitimate authorities. He had retired from the Post Office and volunteered back in 2011 for the Department of Homeland Security's "see something, say something" campaign. Millsaps thought it was important to watch people. There were terrorists everywhere. He wanted to protect his fellow citizens from them, and keeping a watchful eye on them was the way to do it.

"What's all the gunfire about?" Millsaps asked.

"Can't say on the radio," the dispatcher said. "It'll be over soon, though."

"OK," Millsaps said. "I'm on standby if you need me."

"Thanks," the dispatcher said. "Bennington out."

Chapter 274

"There's a New Sheriff in Town"

(December 31)

About a half hour before the Pierce Point convoy descended upon Frederickson, Bennington had returned from the fighting at the MexiZone and went straight to the courthouse.

He headed to Julie Mather's room and pounded on the door.

"Julie, it's John Bennington," he said. "I need you to come out."

Julie was terrified. She had heard all those explosions in the courthouse. She had no idea what was going on, but knew it had to be big … and bad. She had been hurt by so many men, including plenty in the courthouse. She would never open her door to one of them pounding on the door.

Except John. He was the one man there who had never hurt her. He never tried to get her into bed. In fact, he even tried to protect her from Winters and the others. He was always respectful.

"Julie, you are in danger," Bennington said. "The explosions were in the conference room. Who was it that told you to be 'sick' tonight?" Bennington hoped no one heard him say that, but this part of the courthouse was now empty, except for Julie.

That's right! Julie thought. Bennington had saved her. He must be behind the explosions. He must be … now she understood what was going on. Bennington had killed all the people in the conference room. She had no idea why he would risk his own life to kill those people, but somehow it made sense. Bennington had been the only person to be nice to her, so it made sense that he would be the only person who would finally do something.

"Winters is dead," Bennington said through the door, remembering the sound of his neck bones snapping under his boot. "Lots of the others, too. No one is left to hurt you. I saved you, Julie, and now I need to help you some more. You are not safe in this building. Trust me."

She unlocked, and slowly opened, the door. There he was. He looked so handsome. More than that, he was there to help her. Unlike all the others. He was there to protect her. She couldn't believe how lucky she was.

"Grab any medications or other things you need," Bennington said. "Right now! I need to get you out of here. Grab everything you need."

Julie got her glasses. She wore contacts for work. She wouldn't need those anymore. "Okay," she said. "Where are we going?"

"The radio room," Bennington said. "You'll see what's going on in a second. Let's move."

Bennington couldn't believe the risk he was taking by getting Julie and yelling through her door that he had told her to be sick. If someone heard him, he was dead. Dead.

These were the details and things he had gone over in his head countless times over the past few weeks, and he was prepared for whatever was coming his way. If he lived through the grenades and shooting, he knew that he would try to do something good: saving Julie. And that meant being with Julie. He was madly in love with her, he finally admitted to himself. He had loved her from afar for months, but could never admit that to himself because he expected Winters to kill her. He couldn't get too attached to her. Luckily, Winters wasn't a threat to her anymore. Now she could have a normal life – and he desperately wanted that to be with him.

This was more than just a normal man-loves-woman thing. Julie was the perfect example of what had been done to the people. She had been violated and humiliated by people with power. She needed to be rescued. Like all the other people.

Bennington was in a unique position to rescue her. To make up for all the bad things that happened. Well, not totally make up for them, but to at least try to stop further harm, and help guide her toward a better life.

Bennington grabbed her by the hand and started running through the courthouse. People were running around and yelling about attacks, where to send reinforcements, and screaming, asking why there were no reinforcements. It was total chaos. Perfect.

Bennington had to admit to himself that he'd done a fine job handling his task. The leadership was dead. All of them. The cops and FCorps had been so controlled by the political elite that they couldn't tie their shoes without approval. And all the approvers were now dead.

Bennington took Julie to the radio room in the courthouse, which was part of the plan. "Get me Mendez," he said to the comm guy, whose name he always forgot. Paul Mendez was the one active duty cop Bennington trusted. They had talked gingerly and in code about how bad things were. Mendez reminded Bennington of himself as a young man. A sheepdog who wanted to help people. Bennington had no idea why Mendez was still on the force. That was another similarity between them. Bennington was taking another big risk by trusting Mendez, but what the hell.

"Mendez is on his way," the comm guy said. He pointed at Julie. "What's she doing here?"

"Shut your fucking mouth and do your job," Bennington barked. The comm guy froze with fear. He slowly recovered and returned to his dispatch work.

The radio was erupting with screams for reinforcements. The gangs were putting up fierce resistance. The scattered cops, FCorps, and Blue Ribbon Boys that had rushed into the MexiZone without a plan, leadership, or communications were dead retreating. Now the gangs had regrouped and were coming out of the MexiZone for a counter attack.

Mendez came rushing in. "Yeah, boss?" he said breathlessly.

Bennington motioned for him to come out into the hall, and he did.

"Paul, I need you to take Julie, the receptionist, to your place," Bennington whispered to Mendez. "Make sure she's safe with your family. Got it?"

Mendez nodded. He had no idea why he was doing this, but he figured that the vague conversations he had with Bennington about how out of control things were in the courthouse were now coming to fruition.

"After you get her to your place," Bennington continued to whisper, "I need you to round up all the ex-cops. All the good guys. All the guys who quit the force. I need you to get as many good guys as possible, even if they're not former cops, and get them here. The Sheriff is dead and I'm the next in command. I'm the Sheriff and I'm calling out for a posse. I need good men, Paul, not corrupt bastards."

Mendez nodded. He knew exactly what Bennington was doing. "We need good guys to take out corrupt ones," he said.

Bennington nodded. "Yep, Paul, it's come to this. Finally. You and I had talked around this for a long time. But now it's time to do it. I'm the new Sheriff and I'm going to get this under control. You're my second in command. Now, go get Julie to your place and get me a posse."

Mendez saluted and ran off with Julie. That went well, Bennington thought.

Bennington went back into the radio room. He looked at the

comm guy and drew his pistol.

"You're done here," Bennington said to the terrified comm guy. The comm guy put his hands up. He was unarmed.

"Hands behind your back," Bennington said and the comm guy complied. Bennington holstered his pistol and handcuffed him.

"I'm not going to kill you unless you give me a reason to," Bennington said. "You're under arrest for …" Bennington had to think of what the charge would be, "aiding and abetting … racketeering." That was close enough.

Bennington took him to an office down the hall. Bennington had the master key. "You'll be staying here until we sort things out," Bennington said to the guy, who was now shaking and crying. "Some of your former colleagues on the force will be joining you here. It's our temporary jail. People who prove their loyalty to the Constitution will not be killed. Understand?" Bennington wanted the rumor to start going around that he wouldn't kill everyone; only the guilty ones. People from the old regime would be spared as long as they fully supported the new management.

The comm guy nodded.

"As this room fills up," Bennington said to the comm guy, "tell your buddies something."

Bennington pulled out his pistol and put it up to the comm guy's head. Then he put it back in his holster.

Bennington smiled. "There's a new Sheriff in town."

Chapter 275

"Good Evening, Officer"

(December 31)

After putting the comm guy in the makeshift jail, Bennington returned to the comm room and started running the radios. He was starving—he'd thrown up earlier and it was now close to midnight—but he didn't have time to eat, or the desire. He had other things to do.

The radio room was an extremely strategic asset. With it, Bennington could control the fight between the gangs and corrupt cops. That is, he could misdirect the cops and have them killing the gangs and vice versa. He didn't want to destroy the radios. He had thought about it in the initial phases of his planning, and it would have been easy, but he realized that he'd need the radio system to direct the good cops, his posse.

Bennington knew enough about the radios to get the job done. He got the report from the FCorps guy about the semi and vehicles, which he assumed to be the Pierce Point guys. They were right on time. Now that he had the cavalry here, Bennington's options expanded significantly.

About forty-five minutes after he left, Mendez called Bennington on the secondary police frequency.

"Dropped off the package, talked to people and now I'm on my way back," Mendez said.

"Roger that," Bennington said.

The sound of gunfire had subsided by now. There was an ominous feeling that a storm was brewing, and would soon unleash its havoc. The cops were terrified that they had rushed in and haphazardly attacked the gangs—and now the gangs were pissed.

This calm before the storm was a critical time in the battle. One little mistake now, Bennington thought, and they could lose it all.

After a few minutes, Mendez came running in. "What's next, boss?" he asked.

Bennington handed him a piece of paper. "Take this and link up with a semi that's over by Lions Park. It is between Lions Park and here, somewhere. There is a lead car and pickup and a chase pickup. They're armed." Bennington smiled. "They're our reinforcements."

Bennington looked around the room crammed with radios and computers. They didn't have what he was looking for. He ran into the next room where he found it. He tore it down and brought it into the radio room.

"Here," Bennington said, handing Mendez an American flag that had been hanging on the wall in the adjoining meeting room. "Approach the convoy with this flag. Waive it around. This is how they'll know you're a friendly."

Mendez nodded. This was awesome. Awesome. Reinforcements.

"How's the posse coming along?" Bennington asked.

"I've got several guys ready to go," Mendez said. "Everyone understands what's going on. We've been waiting for it. I told the posse to report here. They're already coming in."

Bennington smiled. Support, like Mendez, was key. Bennington realized that he was getting lucky. He should have had other guys in on this plan, but he hadn't been able to fully trust them so he didn't get anyone involved. Bennington would rely on the luck of having guys like Mendez helping, even if he didn't plan for it.

"How does the posse know what to do?" Bennington asked.

Mendez smiled, "I got Paulson organizing things." Paulson had been kicked off the Frederickson city police force when he was outed as an Oath Keeper. Paulson was a great guy.

"Paulson's there in the lobby getting guys organized," Mendez said. "He's telling everyone that this posse is being called by you, and that it's for the legitimate government, but he knows what's really going on. He's giving the new guys winks when he says this is for the 'legitimate government.'"

"Outstanding," Bennington said. "Couldn't do this without you guys."

Bennington got on a CB and set it to channel 11, the prearranged channel to communicate with the Pierce Point troops. He would be taking more risks by talking to them on an unsecure CB, but that's all he had. This whole thing wasn't exactly planned out in great detail. They were free styling it.

"Breaker, breaker one-one," Bennington said. "This is the gall bladder surgeon."

In the cab of the semi, Jim Q. had a CB. It was on channel 11 as Rich had told him to be. Jim Q. and Ted knew about the "gall bladder" story, so they figured it was that friendly cop in Frederickson who was clearing things out before they rolled through.

Ted grabbed the handset. "Gall bladder surgeon, go ahead."

"There will be a police officer with an American flag approaching you," Bennington said, praying that no one was listening to channel 11 who would recognize his voice. "He's a friendly. He has a piece of paper with him that you need. Copy?"

"Copy," Ted said. "I will let my guys know that an LEO with an American flag is a friendly and get back to you when I see the paper."

"Roger that," Bennington said. "Gall bladder surgeon out."

Ted pointed at Jim Q. who got on the inter-unit radios and made sure each vehicle knew about the LEO with an American flag. They all confirmed that they got the message. Soon, a police car with its lights on, but no siren, came slowly toward the 17th. Mendez had decided that he was more at risk from well-trained reinforcements mistaking him for a bad guy than he was from the gangs seeing his lights. Besides, the gangs were pretty much concentrated at the entrance to the MexiZone, so the odds were that the only risk to him in the area by Lions Park was friendly fire from the reinforcements.

"Cop car," Nineteen Delta said into his radio as he was looking through his rifle scope. "Coming our way."

Meerkat and Anderson saw the lights and rested their rifles on the hood of the scout car. They could tear the cop car to pieces if they had to.

The unit was tense. Those of them who could hear the radio traffic knew that a cop car was coming. It was probably the friendly. Probably.

"I see the flag," Nineteen Delta said into the radio. "He's friendly. Do not fire on the cop car. Repeat: Do not fire on the cop car."

Everyone with an inter-unit radio confirmed that they got the message.

The police car stopped abruptly. Mendez had finally seen the semi. He opened his door and waved the flag out of the open door. Then he slowly got out. He knew several rifles were aimed at him and that he should make no sudden moves.. Now that he was out of his car, he started slowly, turning three-hundred-sixty degrees while displaying the flag. After two full turns around with the flag, he carefully walked up to the lead pickup. He had never seen the scout car. Good.

Bobby casually rolled the window down and said, almost comically, "Good evening, officer."

Chapter 276

"Let's Go to Work"

(December 31)

"I have a piece of paper for the semi," Mendez said to Bobby. "It's from the gall bladder surgeon."

Mendez started to hand it to Bobby, but he still wasn't one hundred percent sure Bobby and the pickup truck were with the semi people. Things had been moving too fast to have pre-planned codes. Mendez would have to make it up as he went.

He pulled the paper back and said to Bobby, "You need to tell me what channel the gall bladder surgeon talks to you on."

Bobby nodded and looked at Scotty.

"Eleven," Scotty yelled across the cab and out the window to Mendez.

"That's what I thought, but you can't be too careful with things like this," Mendez said and handed the paper to Bobby. Bobby handed it to Grant, in the rear of the cab.

"I'll be sitting in my cruiser for a while," Mendez said as he walked back to his police car. He got in and turned the lights off. Now that he had made contact with the reinforcements, he could turn the lights off and not be giving away his position to the gangs any longer.

Grant looked at the paper. It was addressed to "Rich's guys." Grant scanned it and smiled. He got out of the truck and walked over to the semi cab, where Ted was.

"This is fucking brilliant," Grant said to Ted. "Rich's cop friend, who is named Bennington, killed a bunch of the cop and gang leadership, started a war between the two, and now is in the radio room at the courthouse. He gave us 144.75 as the frequency to talk to him on and a code phrase to authenticate ourselves."

Grant pointed over toward the courthouse, which was at least a mile away. "And, get this," he said. "Bennington has called out a posse of the Patriot cops who got fired. Now they, the good cops, will start popping the gangs and bad cops."

"Chaos," Ted said with a smile. "Exactly what we need right now."

"Bennington needs some help from us," Grant said, scanning

the paper again. "He needs us to make a show of force where the gangs are rallying and planning an attack on the courthouse." Grant pointed to the handwritten map Bennington had drawn and told Ted the plan Bennington had written down.

"This is great," Ted said. "Let's do it."

Grant ran back to Mark's truck. The inter-unit radios were crackling. Ted got on the radio and briefed Sap, who was in the back of the semi. Ted knew everyone in the semi-trailer could hear the radio, so he was effectively talking to everyone. His voice was always calm, but he paid extra attention to sounding calm so everyone in the semi-trailer would know things were under control. Hearing the briefing, even one delivered by a calm leader like Ted, increased the emotions in the semi-trailer. The nervousness level went up in the trailer, as did the excitement level. This was real. It was go time. They were heading into a big fight.

Ted quickly briefed the chase truck and the scout car so now everyone knew the plan. He made sure every car had drawn out a map of where they needed to be. There would be no GPS for this maneuver. Thank God, Ted thought, that some people still knew how to use a map. After years of relying on GPS, many people had lost this knowledge.

Jim Q. got on the 144.75 mHz frequency on the ham radio band and said, "Gall Bladder Surgeon, this is Cavalry 1," which was the code phrase Bennington had given the 17th.

"Do you copy?"

Bennington came on the radio. "Cavalry 1, this is Gall Bladder Surgeon, copy."

"We have the paper and are proceeding as instructed," Jim Q. said.

"Roger that," Bennington said. "See you in a few."

Mendez would drive the lead car and direct them where they needed to go. Even with a guide, someone in each vehicle was acting as the navigator with the hand drawn maps they had quickly scribbled. They made sure that the direction they were going in was consistent with the map. The convoy was now rolling.

The 17th could hear an increase in the rate of fire, and it was getting louder as they got closer to their objective. It was now getting frighteningly loud and constant. There were wild bursts of fire; high-volume, "spray and pray" fire that seemed random instead of well-aimed. Then there would be single shots that seemed more deliberate and careful. It was impossible to know if the gangs were doing the spray and pray or if the cops were terrified and doing it. It seemed like after a wild burst, a few single shots would put an end to the bursts.

There was a real firefight going on — and they were heading straight into it. Just as they had been all day, the soldiers of the 17th were a combination of excited and afraid – but even more so now that they heard the fight they were about get into. Everyone was silent, straining to hear any little noise that could tell them more about what they were facing. No one wanted to talk and distract the others.

"One more block and then we dismount," Nineteen Delta said into the radio. The convoy slowed and then came to a gentle stop.

When the scout vehicle stopped, everyone paused. For a second or two, all the vehicles just sat there. Ted's voice came on the intra-unit radios in each vehicle.

"This is it," he said.

Grant motioned for Scotty to hand him the radio. "Let's go to work," he said to the whole unit.

With that, they plunged into the darkness and went into combat for the first time.

Chapter 277

"We Got It From Here"

(January 1)

Grant couldn't feel his legs. He was so jacked up on adrenaline, he was just gliding around. He didn't have solid control over his muscles. He was just going through motions, like an automated robot. He felt stronger than he'd ever felt. His vision seemed crystal clear, his hearing was sharp. It was like when he shot the looters. His body was pumping adrenaline—human rocket fuel. He was firing on all cylinders.

Grant first ran up to Mendez's car and the scout car. They were in some scary part of town. All the businesses were abandoned. The street lights were on and they cast a weird yellow shadow on everything. There was garbage blowing around. The place looked terrifying, like a foreboding scene from a movie where only bad things happened.

"You know what you need to do?" Grant asked Nineteen Delta.

"Yes, sir. We're heading out to get a look," he said, motioning for Meerkat and Anderson to take up observation positions.

Grant gave him the thumbs up and turned around to run to the semi. Ted was already out of the cab and the semi-trailer door was up. Sap was getting the troops out of the trailer. From a block away, they were dismounting from the semi and running out on foot for two reasons. First, it was important for them to get out now, before the shooting started. Second, they didn't want any enemy to see that they were traveling in a semi. The enemy could radio that in and then their cover would be blown on the road to Olympia.

The troops were running out and grouping by squad behind trash dumpsters or any other cover they could find. It was interesting, Grant thought. They had practiced rolling out of the trailer back in training. But they never knew exactly what setting they'd be rolling out into. So when the guys exited the trailer for real this time, they were scrambling to find cover to get behind. Oh well. You can't rehearse for everything.

The Team had gone ahead to help the scouts. Grant and Ted were with the main group of troops from the semi. The chase truck was guarding the rear.

Grant was terrified. Not of the gunfire; he'd been through that before and hadn't been shot. He was afraid of himself—of making a mistake. Grant realized he had no idea what to do because he had never been in command during combat. Actually, it was worse: he'd never been in combat. But he was in command. He blurted out, "Okay, Ted, what do we do?"

Ted turned and said, "We get in a fight." He smiled. He loved this. Good.

Ted told Jim. Q to radio to Bennington that they were in place.

"Give the order to move out whenever you're ready," Grant said to Ted, embarrassed that he didn't know what to do, but glad that he wasn't trying to do it.

Ted got on the inter-unit radio. "Move out. Follow the scouts and Team. Guard the flanks and rear. Let's go!"

That's how it started. Everyone just started running, taking cover along the way if possible, and scrambling up the street. The street lights were illuminating them. Grant wished those things were off, but he didn't want to fire shots to take them out. They still had the element of surprise.

They all ran down street, sweeping the areas in front of them with their rifles. They were moving like a real military unit, just like in training. For the first time, Grant could see how all that training—constantly practicing how to move as a unit—was paying off. As they moved down the street, the 17th Irregulars projected deadly military power and professionalism.

Something else struck Grant: the loudness of their boots. They sounded like a stampede of bulls. But in boots.

"Boom! Boom! Boom!" Grant was terrified. He felt another surge of adrenaline, which he didn't think was possible, given all the adrenaline he had pumping through his body already. The gun shots were louder than he expected. He always wore hearing protection while practicing, but he didn't have hearing protection now. And it wasn't practice. It was all very, very real.

The troops instinctively dropped down and took cover where they could. Ted and Sap were motioning and yelling for them to get up and keep advancing. Most did. A few froze. Ted and Sap were keeping track of who froze. Grant just kept running forward. He wanted to go up the street and be with the Team, even though the gunfire was up there. He was being drawn like a magnet toward his guys. And the gunfire. Because that was where his guys were.

The gunfire stopped as quickly as it began. A car alarm was going off. It was hard to hear anything else but that alarm. Everyone's ears were ringing. Finally, Grant heard some voices yelling in Spanish in the distance. They sounded scared.

There were also voices in English much closer. "Oh, shit!" one of them said. "Who are these guys?"

Grant had made it up to the Team by now. Mendez was right behind him. All of them and the scouts were taking cover behind some fancy gang cars and SUVs that were shot full of holes. That's where the car alarm was coming from. Fifty yards away, toward the apparent entrance to the Mexican neighborhood with its guard gate, was a small group of cops. Fifty yards beyond that at the neighborhood guard gate, was a large group of gang-looking young men.

Grant looked back at the 17th. In the street light, he could see most of the unit. They filled up the street and sidewalks and overflowed everywhere. It looked like there were a thousand of them. Grant couldn't believe how overpowering and badass they looked. Everyone was standing up straight or aiming their weapon properly. Every single person looked serious and attentive. They looked professional.

Grant tried to imagine what a cop or gang banger's reaction to the sight of the 17th would be. The troops in that street looked like a real military unit. Well, since most had beards and irregular uniforms, maybe they looked more like a unit full of experienced military contractors. But that made them seem even scarier. They looked like mercenaries. Maybe even a rival gang of former military men, not a tightly directed military unit.

The troops looked like they could go off — and in a big way — at any moment they chose. They looked military enough to be very effective, but uncontrolled enough to flip into revenge mode and destroy anything. It was the worst combination for anyone in their way. Good.

"This is Deputy Mendez!" Mendez yelled in English toward the voice that had hollered out. "All of you put your hands up! Cops and gangbangers. All of you. You're all under arrest."

The cops were stunned. They had assumed the well-armed soldiers were from the Army or something and were there to reinforce them.

Not one of the cops put his hands up. They were still trying to figure out what was going on.

"Don't fuck with us!" Anderson yelled out. "Hands up,

bitches!" he said in a voice that sounded like he'd wanted to say that to cops for some time.

Hearing that, the cops started putting their weapons down and raising their hands. The Team covered them while the Clear Out Crew cuffed them with zip ties. It was a very dangerous part of the fight.

Soon, lights started coming on in the Mexican neighborhood. People were yelling and vehicles were starting up. It quickly sounded like everyone in that neighborhood who could possibly leave was racing out of there. Dogs were barking and kids were crying.

It took a while to safely cuff all the cops. "Who are you guys?" one of them asked Nineteen Delta.

"Shut up," Nineteen Delta snapped back. "Don't distract me or I will fucking kill you. Understand?" He wanted to use his voice to assert that he and his people were in full command of this situation, and that they had the power of life and death over their prisoners. If he could use his voice as a weapon, instead of his rifle, pistol, or knife, Nineteen Delta was a happy man.

"They're getting away," one cop yelled as the sound of people fleeing the Mexican neighborhood grew louder.

"Shut up!" Mendez yelled. "Shut the fuck up!" Mendez, too, was trying to use his voice instead of weapons to accomplish what needed to be done.

"Are there any more of you?" Wes asked one of the cops with sergeant's stripes, assuming he was in command.

Mendez pointed at the sergeant and said, "Yep. He'll know."

The dazed sergeant counted up the cuffed prisoners and said, "I guess so."

"If there are any more of you and they decide to fight us, there could be a crossfire and you bastards will get cut to pieces," Ryan said. "So, we'll ask again: is this all of you?"

The sergeant counted again. "There may be three missing."

"Thank you, Sergeant," Grant said. He motioned for the scouts to go find them. They took off. The scouts knew they didn't need to risk themselves just to get three more prisoners; they were only trying to intercept the three who might be trying to get reinforcements.

The Team took over as the observers and then covered the scouts as they advanced forward.

"So," Grant motioned Ryan as the two were up front as observers, "what was all that shooting about?"

Ryan shrugged. "Dunno. This happened all the time in Afghanistan. People would start shooting. It was hard to tell right away what set it off. This is war, Grant. Crazy shit happens," he said with another shrug.

After a few minutes, which seemed like hours, the scouts came back.

Nineteen Delta came over to Grant, Ted, and Mendez. "Okay, here's what it looks like. We got all the cops in this area. Three, or whatever, got away. Most of the gang bangers took off. It sounds like lots of women and children got left behind. Real gentlemen, huh? The women and children are terrified. There are probably enemies in that neighborhood," he said, pointing to the MexiZone, "But, I gotta think, most of the armed men took off."

Ted looked at Nineteen Delta, and shrugged. "Guess we'll see." He paused. "Now it gets interesting." The last thing Ted wanted was some distraction, like urban fighting in Frederickson, which would slow them down on getting to Olympia. But if that's what was required, he'd do it.

Jim Q. came up to them and handed Ted the radio. "Gall Bladder Surgeon wants to talk to you."

Ted took the radio. "Gall Bladder Surgeon, this is … you can call me Ted. I'm with the cavalry."

"You in a place where what I say won't get to the wrong ears?" Bennington asked. The prisoners heard the voice of Bennington, who they assumed was on their side, and were even more confused than ever.

Ted looked around and saw the prisoners watching him. "Standby," Ted said and he motioned for several guys to stand around him so they would shield the sound of the radio from the prisoners.

When the sound was successfully muffled, Ted turned the volume down. "Okay, go ahead."

"I've got a posse here at the courthouse," Bennington said. "They're coming down to you. Same deal: draped in an American flag. We'll take over. The gangs took off from what we can tell. They're heading toward Olympia. We have their radio frequencies and are hearing them say that the whole Army showed up. They're scared to death. They are running away. Not what I expected."

"Need anything more from us?" Ted asked.

"Are you free from enemy ears?" Bennington asked.

"Affirmative," Ted said.

"Okay, I'm going to say that we have another unit like yours coming into town any minute. I want the prisoners to hear that so they spread that rumor. Get back to a place where they can hear you and I'll

162

shout out a head fake."

Ted liked his idea. This Bennington guy was pretty bright and crafty. He was exactly what they needed to pull something like this off.

"Will do," Ted said to Bennington. Ted turned the volume back up, motioned for the human sound shield to break up, and then walked over toward the prisoners.

Ted acted like he was oblivious to them standing there. "Say again?" he said into the radio.

"Your reinforcements are coming down from Bremerton," Bennington said. "Two more platoons. Some Marines from the Bremerton naval base who are now under Patriot command. Bradleys. The whole shebang." Bradleys referred to Bradley fighting vehicles, which were armored personnel carriers. No one in Frederickson had any defense against them.

"Roger that," Ted said, half remembering the Marines used LAVs instead of Bradleys, but who would pick up on that? "When they getting' here?" Ted asked, playing along with the charade.

"They radioed in with an ETA of twenty minutes," Bennington said.

"Great," Ted responded. "We can get back to our Humvees."

Which, of course, didn't exist. Ted wanted the enemy to be on the lookout for Humvees, not for a harmless looking semi-truck and a couple of pickups.

Ted and Bennington were trying not to laugh out loud. The rumor of two platoons of Patriot Marines just about to arrive in Bradleys and that a bunch of Patriot fighters were moving in Humvees would spread among the Limas in Frederickson, and out to Olympia, in no time. The bad cops would surrender. The gangs, if any were left, would probably take off.

Ted decided to have some fun with the prisoners, who were hanging on every word he and Bennington were saying. "You want us to shoot the prisoners?" Ted asked.

"Negative," Bennington said, playing along. "We have the posse coming to you in a minute or two. We have a jail for them. We'll give them a chance to change sides or we'll kill them." That wasn't true but the rumor would spread instantly among them. Perfect.

"You sure you don't want us to kill them?" Ted said, while acting like no one was around to hear it. "It's no problem. It'll save you guys time and resources."

"Nah," Bennington said casually. "We'll give them a chance to give us some intel and change sides first."

"Okay," Ted said like he disagreed. "We're out of here unless you need something else."

"Nope," Bennington said, deciding at the last minute to throw in some more disinformation. "Your unit can head to Seattle as planned." That added even more confusion.

"Roger that," Ted said. "Grim Reaper out." He added that call sign just to screw with the prisoners and add another crazy detail to the rumor that would undoubtedly be spreading. Ted was trying not to laugh. It was almost childish, but all of the disinformation had a powerful tactical effect. Rumors in the enemy's head could have more effect than bullets.

Ted walked back to the main group of the troops and started telling them to prepare to head back to the staging point once they got the order. He reminded them to be alert for a counter attack.

Everything was quiet. There were occasional shots, but not many. The wind started to blow. It was weird: a hundred well-armed troops staring silently at about a dozen handcuffed cops, surrounded by silence. No one had anything to say, and it would seem unprofessional to chat. The troops' job was to quietly hold their positions and cover the prisoners until they were ordered to do something different.

Pretty soon, the posse showed up and, to everyone's surprise, Bennington was with them. He should have stayed in the radio room, but he really wanted to see this Pierce Point unit firsthand.

When Bennington arrived, he asked the Team, "Who's in command?" They pointed to Grant.

He went over to Grant. "Thanks for stoppin' by."

"No problem," Grant said. "Thanks for preparing things for us. Couldn't have done it without you."

Bennington nodded. He couldn't contain his pride. He broke into a smile, saluted, and said, "We got it from here."

Chapter 278

The Lake Isabella Boys

(January 1)

It was time to get out of Frederickson and off to Olympia. Grant motioned for the Team to head back to Mark's truck.

As soon as they got to the truck and started getting in, Pow smiled and said to the them, "This never gets old." It was a huge tension breaker and a sign that things had calmed down, at least momentarily. No one was talking like that when they headed out from Pierce Point. Everyone was silent and serious. Now, with their first engagement having gone so well, they could relax a little.

As the Team got into the truck, they regained their swagger. They weren't cocky, because they never were, but they were enjoying this again. They had taken a few hours off from their normal gung-ho smiling selves. The old Team was now back.

Grant could feel it and emphasized it. He wanted to fire them up, as well as himself. As Ryan and Wes were getting under the tarp, he said to the whole Team, "Is there any place you'd rather be?"

"Hell no!" they said in near unison.

Pow was smiling to himself. When he and Grant got into the rear cab, Grant asked, "So you were a little quieter than usual a while ago. I see the old Pow is back."

Pow nodded and seemed relieved. "I haven't killed anyone in a couple of months," he said, in a matter of fact tone, referring to the raid on the Richardson meth house. "I didn't enjoy doing it." Pow looked a little embarrassed. "I've had some dreams lately, as the trip to Olympia got closer."

"Dreams about what?" Grant asked.

"Having to do it again," Pow said. He looked out the window. Smiling Pow was gone again and deep thinking Pow had replaced him.

Suddenly, Pow turned back to Grant and smiled again. "But I got over it. You know how, bro?"

Grant shook his head.

"I've been talking to Pastor Pete a lot. He helped me figure it out. I'm supposed to be doin' this. You, me, us," Pow said, pointing to all the troops around him. "All of us. We're supposed to be doing this.

165

We've been put here to do this. There's no other explanation. Too many coincidences, bro, too many coincidences."

Pow paused and looked Grant right in the eye. "It's an honor, man. An honor to be trusted with this job. Enjoy it. That's what I've figured out. Enjoy the job, just don't enjoy the killing."

Pow did a press check of his AR, which was contagious. Grant did one, too, and Scotty looked back from the front cab and, seeing Grant and Pow do one, did the same. Bobby, who was in the driver's seat, got his AR from his left side where it was riding between his seat and the driver's side door. He grabbed it with this left hand and did a press check, which wasn't easy, given that he was right handed. He saw the brass cartridge case in the chamber and gave Scotty a thumbs up. Things were settling back into their regular flow. The Team was press checking and heading off to something big.

Scotty's radio crackled. The unit was getting ready to move out. All the vehicles were ready and the drivers and their navigators had their directions and maps. Gas levels were okay. They'd stop in a few hours and refuel.

And eat. Everyone was starving. They had a big dinner several hours ago, but the constant stress and tension burned up a lot of calories. At first, most of the troops were too nervous to eat. But, now that they'd survived their first "battle," they relaxed. And got hungry.

Oh well, Grant thought. They'd be hungry for a while. One of the things Ted and Sap consciously did in training, without the troops realizing it, was to change their expectations about hunger. In peacetime, everyone in the unit ate normal meals before they came out to Marion Farm. Back then, the refrigerator, fast food, or convenience store was never more than a minute away. They never had to go eight hours without eating and worry about getting hungry, but they did at Marion Farm, on occasion. When they pulled a twelve-hour guard shift and maybe had been working before that and hadn't gotten a chance to eat. It was rare for them to go without eating all day, but it was relatively common for them to go without a meal, given the training cycle and their jobs around camp, like guard duty and unloading the boat.

Grant was now realizing how beneficial it was that he and the others in the unit didn't bat an eye at going long periods without a meal. Now they could handle not eating for a while without thinking it was the end of the world. They had experienced some discomfort and made it through just fine. So, as the troops were hungry now after midnight, they knew they'd live just fine. They'd get some chow whenever it was possible.

They rolled out of Frederickson onto the main road to Olympia. They had alternate routes planned out but, unless there was a reason to do otherwise, the main road still made the most sense. It would all depend on how much resistance they met.

It can't be this easy, Grant kept thinking. There's no way this will be a cakewalk. Frederickson had gone surprisingly well, but they had gotten lucky. Bennington had pulled that off almost single handedly. That couldn't be expected in Olympia.

If they suffered massive casualties, it would be in the next few hours, Grant thought. They'd have several troops picked off in Olympia during the occupation, Grant figured, but a massive hit would come on the road when they were all in one place. Hopefully the semi- trailer wouldn't get hit.

The main road turned into Frederickson eventually became the main street through town. They traveled slowly. Nineteen Delta was a very cautious guy. Thank God.

It took an hour and a half to get out of Frederickson. The troops were quietly talking to pass the time. They weren't goofing around — there was still a serious mood — but they were keeping the mood light as they crept through the dark and seemingly empty town. There were probably people in town, but it was impossible to tell. There were no lights on, no activity. Everyone was probably hiding under their beds.

A few minutes outside of Frederickson, Nineteen Delta came on the radio. "Roadblock. Halt. Take cover. We'll check it out."

Things got tense again. After a few minutes, Nineteen Delta came back on the radio. "They claim to be friendlies and want to join up."

Grant and Pow looked at each other. Pow mouthed, "What the fuck?" They had a plan for this. Sort of.

"Tell him to have their CO," meaning commanding officer, "at the roadblock and I'll talk to him," Grant said to Scotty. This involved political stuff, which was his thing. Grant wanted to ask Ted what he thought, but Scotty telling Nineteen Delta on the intra-unit radios that Grant was getting out to talk to the guards would tell Ted what was going on. If Ted thought it was a terrible idea, he could say so on the radio.

"No need to handcuff them all," Grant said to Scotty. "Just have the Clean Up Crew cover them extra well. This could be an ambush." Scotty relayed that through the intra-unit radio to Nineteen Delta, but didn't use the word "ambush." There was no need to alarm the rest of the unit.

Meerkat and Anderson had the handful of guards covered while Nineteen Delta was searching a wide radius around the roadblock for an ambush. There didn't appear to be one. It was dark, so Nineteen Delta couldn't be sure that there weren't mines or IEDs there, but he wasn't too concerned. The guards, four of them, looked pretty ragtag. He doubted they were sophisticated bomb makers. They were "duck hunter" guards, typical guys with hunting rifles and shotguns wearing hunting clothes. Their roadblock was very crude: two cars across the road. But it was effective; it caused the 17th to stop.

When the area around the roadblock was secure, Nineteen Delta radioed it in. Ted got on the radio. "Have the flank checkers get out."

They had a plan for being stopped. They would have the flank checkers — two members of the Team in the lead truck and the six or so men in the chase truck — get out and check the right and left flanks of the convoy and the rear.

This meant Pow and Scotty in the lead truck. Bobby, the driver, stayed in the truck, as did Grant, since losing the CO in a routine flank check made no sense. Ryan and Wes would stay under the tarp since it was so hard to get in and out.

Grant was embarrassed that he hadn't immediately thought of doing the flank check the moment the convoy stopped at a blockage. Oh well, he thought. Ted thought of it. That was why he was around.

Besides, Grant had been analyzing what to do with these unknown roadblock guards. Solving this political problem was Grant's job; the flank check was Ted's. Things worked better when people had well defined roles.

"I want to talk to these guys," he said to Bobby as Grant got out of the rear cab. Bobby nodded, and kept his attention focused on punching the gas pedal and getting the hell out of there if an ambush started.

As Pow and Scotty got out, Pow pointed to a clump of trees about a hundred yards ahead and said to Bobby, "Rally point." If possible, that would be where Bobby would go, in an emergency to wait for Pow, Scotty, and Grant before Bobby took off. It was critical that everyone knew where to get back into the convoy so no one got left behind. Then again, anyone left behind by their own vehicle could grab a ride with another vehicle.

This would not be ideal, though, because there would be confusion whether that person made it back to the convoy. The driver of each vehicle (other than the semi) was responsible for making sure all of his men were accounted for. The squad leaders in the back of the semi would account for each of their troops and report to Sap, who was ultimately responsible for making sure all eighty-four troops in the semi were accounted for. This was the kind of thing they had gone over for hours in meetings and had practiced for days, which was why Grant didn't want to have these roadblock guys join up. There were way too many moving pieces to that. Four random guys would get confused and throw the plans off. There wasn't much room for them in the back of the semi, anyway. They had a little room back there, but it was for other things. Besides, they really didn't need four duck hunters.

Grant realized how much his thinking had changed since the Collapse began. A year ago, if Grant had been approached because four armed men wanted to join the Patriots in an armed battle, he would have said, "Sure, the more the merrier." Grant would have thought of them wanting to join as a validation of how right the Patriots were and how wrong the Loyalists were, of how triumphant the Patriot cause was. Sort of like some children's book where the good citizens out in the country enthusiastically join George Washington's army, with drums, flutes and waving flags.

Now Grant realized that these guys would be a liability, a distraction, a monkey wrench. He had gone from an idealist to a manager of military details, but that didn't mean these guys were useless. Far from it. Grant approached them with his right thumb on the safety of his AR. He could click it off and fire in a split second. He treated these guys as hostile until he had reason to think otherwise.

As Grant approached them, he could see that there were four of them and their weapons were leaning up against their truck. Meerkat and Anderson were covering them while Nineteen Delta was talking to them with a flashlight in his left hand and his Glock in his right hand, lowered, but ready to go.

"Good evening, gentlemen," Grant said. "I'm ... well, it doesn't matter who I am. I understand you guys want to join up. I have a few questions, but I'll make this quick because I don't like having my guys sitting here for long. No offense."

They nodded. These guys were happy and excited. They didn't seem like they were setting up an ambush. They appeared interested in helping.

"You guys know which side we're on, right?" Grant asked.

"Yep," replied the oldest one, who was in his mid-forties.

"Patriots. Just like us."

"We are, indeed, Patriots," Grant said. "But we don't know whether you are or not. It's not like we get official membership cards."

They nodded again. They thought this might happen where they'd have to prove that they were the good guys.

"Here's the deal, gentlemen," Grant said. "You're more valuable to the cause doing what you're doing. Making sure no bad guys come into or out of Frederickson. Manning this roadblock."

"Like blocking the passage of the gangs that have been speeding out of there all night?" the youngest one said with great enthusiasm. "We got here too late to stop them ... and there's only four of us," he said with some embarrassment.

"Don't apologize," Grant said. "We need you to stop gangs. Or Limas."

"What are Limas?" the oldest one asked. Grant remembered that these guys had probably been hunkered down for the past several months trying to feed their families and protect themselves from gangs and corrupt cops. They didn't sit around making military plans or using slang like the 17th did, so Grant explained what a Lima was.

They smiled. They liked this kind of talk. They had been whispering among themselves for months about how much they hated the Loyalists, but they couldn't do much about it. Now there were all these Patriot military guys who were out in the open and about to kick somebody's ass. The good guys were out and fighting. Finally. These four had been dreaming for months that this would happen, and now it was.

"We also need you guys to make sure no Limas come up from Frederickson to chase us," Grant said. He smiled and said, "As unlikely as that is."

The four nodded again. They were mesmerized by Grant and the others. Real live Patriot military was here. Well, little did they know, Patriot irregulars, but, from the perspective of a good ole' boy out there in the country just trying to survive, the 17th Irregulars seemed like Green Berets. They kind of were. Kind of, but not really. They were trained by Green Berets, which was better than nothing.

"What can we do to help?" the oldest one, and apparent leader, asked.

"Tell us everything you know about any obstacles or enemy up the road," Grant said pointing toward Olympia. He would not tell these four the 17th's objective, but they had probably figured it out.

"None, at least that we know of," the oldest one said. "But we don't get out on the road much. Gas is impossible to get out here."

"Okay, here's another thing you can do," Grant said. "There's a new Sheriff in Frederickson. He has a posse. You can link up with them and do whatever they need. They're the new cops, not the old ones you've been dealing with. The old ones are in jail," Grant said with a grin. "You'll know the posse is the real posse if you ask whether they're with the 'gall bladder surgeon.'"

"The what?" the oldest asked.

"Gall bladder surgeon," Grant said. "Just roll with it."

"Which reminds me," Grant added, "you guys need a call sign. It's how we know people are good guys. Pick one."

"Lake Isabella," the young one said. "That's right over there. It's where we live."

"Okay," Grant said. "You're now the Lake Isabella Boys. I'll call that into HQ and tell them that there is a Patriot roadblock here going by the call sign 'Lake Isabella Boys.'"

Grant looked at the Lake Isabella Boys' gear. They had obviously just thrown their guns into the truck and headed over here with the two blocking cars. That's all they had.

"Let me guess," Grant said, "you don't have a radio."

"Nope," said the oldest one.

"Can you get a CB?" Grant asked.

"Yep," one of them said. "I got an old one. It's at home."

"Get it fired up and at your post here," Grant said. He was consciously trying to use military terms like "post" so these guys would feel like they were part of a military unit. That would make them take this … war, that's the word, more seriously. Feeling like they were part of a military operation would also make them more likely to take orders, which was key.

"Use channel 11," Grant continued, "and talk to the new cops on it. That'll get you squared away. Remember to mention the gall bladder surgeon on channel 11 so the new cops know you're on the team. Don't use the gall bladder thing after that. Just once. We don't want anyone listening to know our codes, okay?"

They all nodded. This was the most exciting thing, by far, that had happened since this whole Collapse thing started. They even had a code name!

Grant basically trusted these Lake Isabella Boys, but he needed to make absolute sure. He thought of a way to test their loyalty.

"Any of you got little kids?" Grant asked. Two of them raised their hands.

"Good," Grant said. "We might need them. We have a special operation to perform that requires a couple of little kids as decoys. Can we borrow your kids for a couple of weeks?"

What an outlandish request. "Borrow" kids for a few weeks? To be decoys in a special operations military mission? Insane.

"Is thirteen too young?" one of the guys asked. "My boy would love to help."

"Would you go get him?" Grant asked. The guy started walking toward the truck to drive back home to get his son.

"Okay, okay," Grant said and stopped the man. "You passed the test." The Lake Isabella Boys looked stunned. So did Meerkat and Anderson who were covering them.

"We don't need your kids," Grant said. "I just wanted to see if you'd give them up. That shows you are Patriots."

The men smiled. They had just been fooled. But in a good way.

"You guys are officially fighting for the good guys now," Grant said to the Lake Isabella Boys. "Welcome to the Patriots. And have a happy New Year."

Grant shook their hands and then realized he was wasting precious time. He saluted them, which was part of his effort to impress upon them that this was a real live military operation and they were now part of it. They saluted back. Their salutes weren't official military ones since they had no military training, but were the kind of salutes they'd seen in movies, which was fine. They'd be a great roadblock and, once they got their CB, an observation point. Both of these would be a big help. It would at least slow down any Limas who would be coming from Frederickson to attack the 17th from the rear.

As he walked back to Mark's truck, Grant realized that Ted needed to know what was going on, so he went up to the semi cab and motioned for Ted to get out. Grant told him what had happened and that Jim Q. should call into HQ and tell them that some friendlies at Lake Isabella were manning a roadblock and what their code name was.

"How did you know they were Patriots?" Ted asked.

Grant told the story about asking them for a kid.

"King Solomon," Ted said, "Nice one." He was referring to the story in the Bible of King Solomon who used a similar trick . The king was asked to judge which of two women was the real mother of a child. He said the baby would be cut in half and each woman given a piece. The real mother cried out that the other woman should have the baby just so he could live. This revealed that she was the real mother, because the real mother would not want her child cut in half.

Ted had figured out where Grant got the idea. It showed what kind of books Ted read.

Chapter 279

Casualties

(January 1)

As they went slowly—very, very slowly—down Highway 101 toward Olympia for the next couple of hours, Grant couldn't stop thinking about the Lake Isabella Boys. There must be thousands of guys like them who were just waiting for a real military push to bring them out of the woodwork, guys who had been keeping their heads down and taking care of their families for months. They had a gun and were willing to risk it all to make things better. They were enthused and would do anything, including giving their kids to strangers who promised to use them as decoys in a special operations mission, to get this horrible nightmare of the Collapse over with. The political significance of the Lake Isabella Boys was loud and clear: the people were damned sick and tired of the "legitimate authorities." Grant had assumed a high level of civilian support for the march on Olympia, but maybe it would be even higher than he thought, making it easier than he predicted.

His peaceful thought was rudely interrupted by the loud boom of a rifle shot up ahead. Even through the windows of Mark's truck, the shots outside startled him. The noise was followed by a loud thud and the sound of crunching metal and glass.

Grant and the convoy were idling along at about five miles per hour as the scout car was up ahead checking out an overpass. The overpass, which Grant knew well from driving to and from his cabin so many times, was about a half mile ahead. Bobby put on the brakes and Scotty got on the radio to Nineteen Delta.

There was no response. Oh God, Grant thought, they were experiencing their first combat casualties. Grant had a horrible feeling about what was around the corner at the overpass. Grant's biggest fear was a Lima tank column, as unlikely as that was. Or it could be one of those Homeland Security MRAP armored cars.

Everyone was silent as they slowly rounded the corner on the highway. They were afraid of what was on the other side. Grant mentally rehearsed what he'd do if he saw Lima armor or other superior forces. He quickly assumed he would initially hit them as hard as possible and then fall back to assess the situation. This was where Ted's expertise would come in.

The lights from the highway were shining on a terrible sight.

It was a wrecked car; the scout car.

"Stop," Grant said to Bobby. "Let's see what's ahead." He wanted to speed up ahead to see if the scout car needed help, but he didn't want to dash into an ambush. He had to fight his urge to rush toward the overpass.

Bobby stopped the truck and Scotty radioed to unit that they were stopping. "Why isn't the Clear Out Crew doing this?" Ted radioed back.

"They're not responding," Scotty said. He didn't want to alarm anyone by saying, "I think they crashed." But everyone hearing the intra-unit radio needed to know what was going on.

When they stopped, Pow, Scotty, and Grant got out. As they got out, Ryan yelled from under the tarp, "What's up?"

"Something happened to the scout car at the overpass," Grant said. "Be ready."

"Roger that," Ryan said from under the tarp.

Pow, Scotty, and Grant got out and moved quickly, trying to find cover. There wasn't much on the side of a highway. Luckily, they stopped the truck in between highway lights so they weren't silhouetted. It was dark and damned hard to see them from a distance.

"Boom!" Another rifle shot. They heard a bullet impact about 100 yards ahead and way to their left, in the median of the highway. It was at least 600 yards to the overpass.

"Boom!" Another shot that was way short and to their left. Whoever was shooting at them was doing a shitty job; this made them relax a little bit.

"Boom!"

"I got a muzzle flash on the overpass," Pow said.

"Sniper on the overpass," Scotty radioed in. "About 600 to 1,000 yards ahead. Shots are way short and to our left."

"Flank checkers out," Ted said. "Everyone be ready to go. And get me Donnie." This was a perfect project for a sniper: to counter another sniper.

Jim Q. radioed on the CB to the chase truck that Donnie needed to get out and go meet up with the Team.

Hearing that, Donnie jumped out of the chase truck with his hunting rifle. He ran as fast as he could, which wasn't as fast at fifty-four, as he had been at eighteen. He was the oldest guy in the unit. And he was the first one to get to shoot someone.

As he was running, Donnie realized that he would arrive with his pulse racing too much. The microscopic movement from the normal beating of a heart—especially the added movement from an increased pulse from running—could actually throw a shot off target. When the target was several hundred yards away, a tiny fraction of a degree of angle translated into several feet of deviation.

Donnie tried his hardest to keep his heart rate down, but he was running into combat and running fast. He knew there was no way to slow down his heart, and that he just had get there fast without getting shot.

"Looks like a sniper on the overpass," Pow said to Donnie when he got up to where the Team was down on the ground. "About 600 to 800 yards," Pow said. "Not a very good shooter."

Donnie was excited. He would finally get to do some work. He wanted to prove that an old guy like him, with no military experience, could be useful.

"Right there," Pow said, pointing toward the overpass. "Can you hit him?"

Donnie nodded, although he wasn't sure if he could. He got down on the ground with a good angle toward the overpass. He got out his laser range finder. It was 872 yards, outside his optimal range. "Man-sized target" he thought. That's pretty big. There was a lot of room for error, though. The sniper on the overpass would be hunched down and not a full man-sized target. Odds were, he would miss a couple of times, but then get closer with each successive shot after he made adjustments. This was unlike the big-game hunting he'd done where he basically got one shot in before the animal ran away. This animal on the overpass was sitting in one place.

Donnie was glad that Pow had found them some decent cover. He took off his backpack, which he used for a rest, just like when he was hunting. He took out his good binoculars and gave them to Pow.

"Spot me," Donnie said. Pow took the binos and found a good place to lie down.

"Boom!" Another shot hit. It was still short and to the left, but closer this time.

"This guy sucks," Pow said. "He has no idea where his shots are hitting. He must not have a spotter."

Grant came running up to them, "Let's go, gentlemen. I've got wounded men in that car up there."

"Don't rush us," Pow said, a little annoyed. "We're working

here."

Grant realized that he shouldn't have tried to rush Donnie and Pow. He knew that Pow knew they needed to hurry up so they could go get the scouts out of the car.

Donnie made a few adjustments on his scope for the 872-yard shot.

"Target," Donnie said, which meant he had the target in sight. He had a shadowy blob in his scope. The crosshairs of his scope were jumping around because his heart was beating so hard.

"Send it," Pow said, which meant there were no obstructions or friendlies in the way and it was okay to shoot.

Donnie waited a few seconds until he had the shot. Well, he kind of had the shot. The crosshairs were still jumping around and he couldn't tell for sure if the target was the enemy sniper. But he knew that the shadowy blob with a rifle wasn't a Girl Scout, so he didn't feel bad about taking a shot. Besides, going on the offense by taking a shot at the sniper would help out the situation because it would cause the enemy sniper to hide, which would reduce the number of shots he could take at the 17th.

"Boom!" His shot wasn't faint like the others. It was ear-ringing. A 300 Win. Mag. is not a quiet gun. It kicked up a spray of pooled rainwater and dirt from the side of the road where they were lying. That was the first shot from the 17th Irregulars. This was for real.

"Inconclusive," Pow said, looking through his binos. "Can't tell if that's a hit or not. Too dark."

It was quiet, except for their ringing ears.

"Send another," Grant said. He was feeling desperate to get the scout car rescued. Those guys could be bleeding to death.

"No target," Pow said, peering through his binos.

"Send it to the same place," Grant said. "Keep his head down while we go get the scouts."

"That's stupid," Pow said. "We can't go running up there until we take this guy out."

Pow's tone didn't bother Grant; everyone on the Team was an equal and the best idea won, which meant that a person proposing a bad idea would be told so in not-too-gentle terms. That was fine for when the Team was just the Team, but now Grant was a lieutenant in combat, and a non-Team member, like Donnie, was hearing this. Grant started to tell Pow not to talk to a lieutenant that way when Pow interrupted.

"He's running away!" Pow said, still looking through the binos.

"He's running across the overpass!"

Donnie tried to follow the dark figure across the overpass, which was hard to do at night. He fired another round, but knew as he pulled the trigger that he hadn't led the target enough.

"Gone!" Pow said. "I lost him."

There were a few seconds of silence followed by a loud crashing noise. It sounded like something was falling; rumbling and crashing. Like something heavy was crashing down onto the road.

"What was that?" Grant yelled, realizing that he needed to keep his voice down because, for all he knew, they were surrounded by the enemy and about to be ambushed. If this was an ambush, it sure was effective to have one sniper holding everything up. Even if the sniper didn't hit anyone, it was a great way to slow things down and create opportunities for regular troops to hit you. The military guys had always talked about how much they hated enemy snipers. Now Grant was seeing why.

"Dunno," Pow said. "Wait."

It was silent for another few seconds as Pow looked through the binos.

"What the hell?" Pow said. Everyone was hanging on his every word.

"Logs?" Pow said. "It looks like there is a bunch of logs, or telephone poles, or something across the highway."

Of course, Grant thought, the sniper bought some time while others put up an obstacle. They were now officially trapped on the highway. Sitting ducks. Grant might have led his men into a giant trap.

"Vehicle leaving," Pow said after a while. "Car lights." He could see the tail lights after they went past the log jam and headed up the highway toward Olympia.

Grant and Donnie could see the lights now.

Donnie took a shot at the car lights. Just trying to get lucky.

"Miss," Pow said. "They're taking off."

"Now we can go get the scout car," Grant said. He ran over to Scotty to radio in what had gone on.

Pow got up and headed for Mark's truck. Donnie looked around, wondering what to do.

Pow yelled, "Jump onto the bumper of our truck and ride it. We'll get you closer and you can cover us while we get to the scout car." Grant radioed Scotty asking him to yell back to Ryan and Wes under the tarp in the truck bed to expect someone to jump onto the rear bumper.

Donnie nodded, got up, slung his rifle, and grabbed his backpack. He ran over to Mark's truck and jumped on rear bumper and held onto the tailgate.

Grant and Pow got into the rear cab.

"Go to the overpass!" Grant yelled to Bobby, who instantly put the truck into gear and quickly took off.

"Whoa!" Grant yelled to Bobby. "Donnie's on the bumper. It's hard to hold on."

Bobby slowed down to about ten miles an hour. They were plowing ahead toward the overpass. The slower speed allowed them to keep their eyes on signs of an ambush.

Grant looked back and there was Donnie, with a rifle and backpack, holding on for dear life.

"Stop!" Grant said about three hundred yards from the overpass. He could see a crumpled car that looked like the scout car.

"Pow, Donnie," Grant yelled, "cover me and Scotty." Scotty gave Bobby the CB radio but kept the intra-unit one. This allowed Bobby to have radio contact with the unit because Jim Q. could relay messages from the intra-unit radio to the CB, and therefore, to Bobby. The driver had to be in the loop in case he needed to go pick people up.

Pow and Donnie got out and started setting up a quick sniper position to cover Grant and Scotty. Right behind them came Grant and Scotty, who started finding cover before running up to the crashed scout car.

Bobby yelled back to Ryan and Wes, "Get ready to jump up and cover Grant and Scotty. Enemy was last seen on the overpass."

"Got it," Wes yelled back.

By now, Grant wasn't feeling so brave. He was scared. Scared that he had wasted too much time getting to the scout car and its dead or dying occupants. Because no one was currently shooting at them, Grant assumed that the enemy had left and that there was no danger getting to the scout car ... unless this was a big ambush.

Grant ran up to the crash, which took a while given that it was about three hundred yards away and he was running between cover the whole time. Scotty was right behind him.

It was horrible. The little car was not built to withstand a crash, and it didn't.

Grant realized that the term "twisted" metal was not a car accident cliché. It was real. Everything was twisted and smashed, strewn all over. The "We Support the Recovery!" bumper sticker was still intact.

This was the most scared Grant had been, so far. Some of his men were dead or about to die in that crushed car. He had known that this would probably happen at some point in the march to Olympia. But now that it had, he was scared. He didn't know what he was scared of. He was just scared.

Grant heard Scotty radioing in. "Crash site. Scout car. Looks bad."

It was. It was dark, but the highway lights illuminated parts of the crash site. Grant could see someone. It was Anderson. He was wrapped around the steering wheel; literally wrapped around it. The top of his head was gone.. All that was left was his face, which was soaked in blood with bits of broken glass stuck to it.

Grant and Scotty searched for Nineteen Delta, who was on the other side of the crash, the side that wasn't in the highway light. They found him outside of the car. He must have been flung from the car, which made sense. The scouts didn't wear seatbelts when they had to be able to get out of the car on a moment's notice. Traffic safety wasn't their highest concern.

Nineteen Delta was dead, too. His blood was everywhere. Grant shined the flashlight all over the area; it looked like he had bled out. Grant immediately started feeling guilty that they hadn't rushed in to help, despite the sniper and possible ambush. Maybe he should have not worried about the sniper, who turned out to be a shitty shot, and just rushed to the scene of the crash. Maybe Nineteen Delta wouldn't have bled out.

Grant quickly snapped out of feeling guilty. He had to make sure this wasn't an ambush. He and Scotty kept looking around with their flashlights. At first, Grant was worried that any enemy about to ambush them would zero in on the flashlights. Then he realized that the odds of an ambush were getting smaller and smaller. He also realized that Pow and Donnie would know the flashlights were him and Scotty. Hopefully. Friendly fire was almost as big a concern as enemy fire.

They heard some groaning. Thank God. It was Meerkat, who was under a car door. He, too, must have been thrown from the car.

"Medic!" Scotty yelled into the radio, which Ted had already thought of and had told Nick to take the chase truck up to the crash site. Right as he called in for the medic, Scotty saw the headlights of a truck coming. He assumed, and hoped, it was the chase truck.

"Medic on the way in the chase truck," Jim Q. said into the intra-unit radio just before Scotty decided to take up a kneeling position and potentially engage the truck speeding toward him. "Flashing headlights now," Jim Q. said right before the truck flashed its headlights, which allowed Scotty to return to treating Meerkat.

"Can you hear me, man?" Grant yelled to Meerkat. Grant noticed that his fear showed in his voice. He sounded terrified and knew that he needed to be more calm so his men didn't get scared, especially Meerkat, who needed to think everything was okay.

"Over here," Meerkat managed to get out. Right then, the headlights of a truck appeared and lit up everything. Nick jumped out.

"Nick's here, bro," Grant said to Meerkat as he and Scotty were getting the car door off him. "You'll be fine. Things don't look too bad."

This was kind of true. Meerkat had all his limbs and there wasn't a ton of blood. It could have been much worse.

Nick got to work with Grant's assistance.

"Some broken bones, but basically okay," Nick said after a quick assessment.

Grant felt a surge of relief. He immediately started to think of the plan for getting the wounded out.

"Get the utility truck here," Grant said to Scotty, who started to call it in.

"Car," Meerkat said. "Take the utility car. I'll be okay in it. Save the truck for hauling."

Amazing. Meerkat was seriously wounded and he was thinking more clearly than Grant. What a soldier.

"Yeah, that makes sense," Grant said and pointed to Scotty, who nodded. Grant looked at Nick, who looked up and nodded.

"Car will work," Nick said.

Scotty got on the radio. "Get the utility car here. Utility truck can sit tight. We're taking a man back."

Back where? Pierce Point?

"Tell the Frederickson hospital we've got a car crash coming in," Nick said to Scotty.

Frederickson hospital. Of course, Grant thought. He had forgotten it existed. Luckily, Nick always knew the location and general direction to the nearest hospital. He was good at what he did.

Scotty radioed it in. A few minutes later, word came that Frederickson hospital was back in operation. They had lots of wounded of their own from "Code Orange," but they had room for one more. Thank God Frederickson was in Patriot hands.

"You're going to the hospital; a real hospital," Nick said to

Meerkat. "You'll be fine."

"Thanks, man," Meerkat said, with a pained wince.

"Don't talk," Nick said. He knew Meerkat had broken ribs.

Meerkat was quickly stabilized and in the back of the utility car heading off. Now the work began.

Chapter 280

Combat Cheeseburger

(January 1)

Bodies. Grant had to deal with bodies of Anderson and Nineteen Delta. These weren't the bodies of strangers. They were his guys. Guys he knew and liked. Brothers, actually.

Grant looked over at Anderson. There was the fun-loving guy who invented the 17th's "gang sign." He was dead. Mangled. In pieces. A guy who was so alive, so animated, always smiling and joking was now crumpled up and missing the top of his head. Grant thought about his missing forehead. That's where Anderson's smiles and jokes came from: his brain. Now his brain was splattered all over the dash and windshield of that stupid little car. Anderson's joking and smiling was gone. It went away when his head did.

And there was Nineteen Delta. A heart of gold. A tough, tough kid. Well, Grant thought, a man in his late twenties, but still a "kid" to an old guy like Grant. Nineteen Delta was kind and always looked after the weaker members of the unit. Now he was split apart, parts of him hanging out of his body. All that kindness was now gone. He was now just parts of a person, covered in blood.

"Get the utility truck over here to take away their bodies," Grant said to Scotty. "Take them to Frederickson. Bennington will make sure they get the burial they deserve."

"We need the utility truck over here," Scotty said into the radio. He didn't want to say "To pick up two bodies." The guys, especially back in the semi-trailer, would be speculating and getting scared. They needed to have their edge now. There was no use worrying about whose bodies they were. There would be more.

The utility truck came up. The Pierce Point guard driving it got out and, seeing the bodies in his headlights, threw up. He was embarrassed, but returned to work and did what needed to be done.

"Don't worry about barfing," Grant said. "I've done it."

But not this time, Grant thought. Something had changed in him. He had become less sensitive to these things. He was still moved by the tragedies, just not as much as when he was back in Pierce Point. He realized that when he left his family to ship out with the unit, he mentally transitioned to being a soldier. He was no longer "father, husband, attorney" Grant Matson. He was simply "soldier" Grant Matson now, and his mental change was being reflected in his ability to react as such to tragedies.

The convoy was about one hundred yards from the overpass. They were parked on the side of the highway on one of those nice, wide shoulders designed to fit a semi so it's still off the road. They had enough room on the shoulder, especially with the pickups, to get out and move around. The shoulder was like a long, thin parking lot.

They were parked near a highway light which provided a decent amount of light for their long convoy on the shoulder. Grant didn't like that they—a big, fat target—were illuminated but, so far, it seemed like there was no enemy around, so he appreciated the light.

The Pierce Point guard driving the chase truck got a chainsaw out. He went over to the logjam and started up the saw.

During all the craziness, Grant had forgotten all about the obstacle that lay ahead of them. Oh crap. They were a stalled, sitting duck, he remembered. It was time to get out of this.

He went over to the guard, who knew how to use a chainsaw.

"We'll cut this," he said pointing to logs. "Here, here, and here," he said. Grant was glad that this ole' boy from rural western Washington knew a thing or two about cutting wood. Grant was extremely grateful that someone had thought to bring the chainsaw. And the bolt cutters. They'd probably need those later, too.

"How long?" Grant asked.

"A half hour, if we get people to move the pieces," he said.

Grant ran over to Scotty and told him to have the semi unload the troops. It would take many, many muscles to get the cut up logs off the highway.

They made short work of the logjam. Thank God they had that chainsaw. Grant was praying that the chain didn't break. Then again, they could have someone jump in the utility truck and go get a chainsaw or two from the Lake Isabella Boys a few miles back.

"Pretty sophisticated," Ted said as he shined his flashlight on the ropes used to hold the logs up on the embankment and then release them. "Somebody knows what they're doing."

Grant looked at Ted and started to say that this was not good news.

Ted nodded before Grant could speak. "Yep," Ted said, as if he were reading Grant's mind. "There will be more of these obstacles up the road. And they'd be crazy not to have an ambush or two attached

184

to each obstacle. We got lucky on this first one."

Ted looked again at the ropes for the log release. "They were ready for us to come. Well, not us, per se, but people like us. It might take a couple of days to get Olympia." Ted looked down the highway in that direction and just stared. He was calculating how much time, and how many lives, it would take to get down the damned highway.

Get to Olympia, Grant thought. We have to get to Olympia. He looked at his watch. It was 6:17 a.m. It was still dark.

Grant looked around. The men were exhausted. They'd slept, most of them at least, until yesterday afternoon, but they were mentally and emotionally drained.

They'd been keyed up with anxiety and action all night, and it had been a long one. In the street lights by the overpass, Grant could see his breath. He assumed the temperature was in the high thirties. Most soldiers had fleece jackets and pants under their fatigues and civilian clothes. They weren't freezing, but the cold still burned up lots of calories.

Grant's stomach rumbled. He was really hungry. He found Ted and whispered, "Should we feed these guys?" Grant didn't trust his judgment on this issue; he needed Ted's input. They only had about five MREs per person and they needed to get moving. Then again, they were hungry and tired and needed a mental break. These guys, including Grant, were not Special Forces. They were irregular volunteers. They couldn't be ordered to march for two days straight without food like a regular Army unit could.

"Just thinkin' the same thing," Ted said. "When the highway is clear, we'll have breakfast."

When the road was fully clear, he ordered the troops to reassemble by their vehicles. They knew that this meant they were going back on the road. They were tired and hungry, but no one whined about going back out, which was what Ted wanted to see. He had lowered their expectations. They thought they were going back to work.

"Breakfast time, ladies and gentlemen," he announced. The troops relaxed and felt relieved. There were a couple fist pumps at this news, but most soldiers didn't want to show how glad they were to eat because they didn't want to look like sissies. But they were all damned glad to get some chow.

Franny was breaking out the MREs. They were in cases in the back of the utility truck. The sound of Franny busting into the thick cardboard boxes was a sweet sound. Most people hadn't realized how hungry they were until they thought they would actually be eating. It had been over twelve hours since they last had any food and for the past half hour or so, they'd been doing hard work clearing the logs off the highway. They were hungry.

Without being told, the troops lined up by squad on the shoulder of the highway behind the chase truck, at the very rear of the convoy, where the MREs were.

The military had a reason to organize people the way it did; it wasn't just to boss people around. It was a very practical way to have a large group of people do the same thing at the same time.

The HQ/Team squad was pulling guard duty while the others ate. Someone had to be out there looking for threats. And the HQ/Team squad, as the leaders, had an obligation to make sure everyone ate before they did. It was part of the deal in a military unit. Leadership got certain perks, but also had duties to others. Eating last was one of those duties.

The unit had not eaten MREs during training as they were too valuable when there was regular food to cook. Some of the military members of the unit, like the Air Force and Navy people, had never really eaten MREs when they were in the FUSA military. Maybe they did a couple of times, but it was almost novelty food back then. Almost all of the civilians in the unit had never eaten an MRE.

There were a lot of urban legends and myths about MREs. Most people thought they tasted bad, but they didn't (for the most part). They were actually very nutritious, designed to give troops strength and nourishment in situations exactly like the one facing the 17th Irregulars there on the side of Highway 101. The troops were too hungry to worry about what their MREs tasted like.

Franny was giving a quick refresher class on what is in an MRE, how to open them, how to use the heating unit, and how to pack the wrappers back into the bag. He had done this for the troops during training, but that was a few months ago.

Guys were getting out their pocket knives because it took a knife to open up an MRE. They could be opened without one, but it was hard. "Can I borrow that knife you guys have?" one of the soldiers asked Wes, who was guarding the flank closest to the utility truck where the MREs were being handed out. The soldier was referring to the big Zero Tolerance folding knives that belonged to each member of the Team.

"I ain't dulling my blade for some MRE, dude," Wes said in his southern drawl. His Zero Tolerance would hold an edge forever, but there was a tradition. Fighting knives are not used for day-to-day things. A person's fighting knife was a tool for a specific job; not used for little jobs when another tool would do. Wes got out his cheapo pocket knife and tossed it to the soldier. "Use this, bro."

One of the soldiers was using his flashlight to see what entrée his buddy got. The highway light wasn't sufficient to see the black writing on the brown MRE bag.

"Egg omelet!" he said. "You do not want to eat that. Worst food on the planet. Inedible. We called those things 'chicken shit' back at my old unit 'cause we were pretty sure they just had chickens shit in a bag and then call it an 'omelet.'"

Just like in any American military unit out in the field, MRE entrees and, especially side dishes, were being traded like the stock exchange. The winners were the ones who got fudge brownies and pound cake in their meals. The losers were those who got the egg omelets as their entrees. There was not much of a market for MRE egg omelets.

"I'll trade you some crackers for that that chicken shit," one of the infantrymen said to the hapless soldier who was stuck with the egg omelet. The infantryman had previously eaten plenty of MREs. He knew that the reputation of MRE egg omelets was overblown. They didn't taste great, but were certainly edible. There was more protein in one of those omelets than in the crackers; much more filling.

"Done," said the soldier with the omelet. He was a former civilian who had never eaten an MRE, so he believed the reputation of the egg omelet, but the good news for him was that the egg omelet also came with hash browns and Pop Tarts. Not bad.

"Clam chowder?" another soldier said as he shined a flashlight on his. "Are you kidding me? How disgusting is that? Cold clam chowder out of a bag?"

"I'll take it," said another soldier, who had MRE chowder before and knew that it was pretty good. "Loves me my chowder."

Ted and Grant were watching all this as they were guarding. Ted looked over at Grant and had a big grin on his face. So did Grant. Over just a few months, this ragtag collection of military people and civilians had come together as a solid unit. Now they sounded like experienced military personnel, trading MREs and complaining about egg omelets.

It only took a few minutes for most people to finish their meals. They were wolfing them down. A couple were taking longer because they were using the heating packets to heat up entrees and hot drinks.

Franny went around and collected all the spare accessory packets, which had salt and pepper and matches, and all the unused heating packets. Those were valuable.

A squad leader saw that all his men were done eating. Without being told, he rounded them up and got them onto guard duty so the HQ/Team squad could eat.

Grant went over to the utility truck. Franny handed him an MRE. It felt so good in his hand. A big square block of food. It was weird. It was just an MRE, but Grant was so hungry. He hadn't realized how hungry he was until he was holding a meal.

But he had work to do. They could eat their MREs in the trucks. Grant found Ted and said, "Let's get out of here." Ted nodded and told the squad leaders to start packing everyone up.

It would take a few minutes to get everyone into the semi-trailer. Enough time for Grant to start eating. He took the precious cargo over to the rear seat of the extended cab of Mark's truck and unpacked the little packages of food inside and put them on the seat. He was standing outside the truck with the MRE on the seat. The truck's indoor lights were on so he could see what meal he got.

"Beef patty." Decent. And it was even better covered in the BBQ sauce that it came with. Mexican macaroni and cheese. Pretty good, actually. Nacho cheese pretzels and a packet of cheese spread like Velveeta, which he squirted on the two wheat snack breads, which were really good. Way better than you'd think with a name like "wheat snack bread."

"Hey, look, a combat cheeseburger," Grant said to Bobby about his two pieces of wheat snack bread with cheese spread and a beef patty. Bobby laughed.

"Beef stew and one of those awesome HOOAH bars," Bobby said about his MRE. The HOOAH bars were like a military version of an energy bar. They were really good, though it was rumored that anyone who ate one would be unable to take a crap for a week after.

About halfway through Grant's meal, Ted was walking up to each vehicle yelling, "Mount up!" It was time to get back on the road.

The guys on the Team gobbled the food from their opened pouches and threw the unopened ones into their cargo pockets. They knew to gather all the wrappers. Franny came around collecting them in one of the empty MRE case boxes. This was not done out of some desire to recycle for the environment, but to make sure no one could tell how many men had eaten there. OPSEC required that litter be picked up.

188

Grant did a final count of the men in the truck. He ran out to the bed of the truck and said, "Any ugly homos under that tarp?"

"Just us two," Wes said from underneath. "Ryan said I have to put out for my MRE. He said Marines do that all the time."

"Fuck you, hillbilly," Ryan said with a laugh.

"That's exactly what you're trying to do to me under this tarp," Wes shot back.

Things were back to normal.

Grant heard the diesel engine of the semi rev up. It was time to go back to work.

Chapter 281

The New Scouts

(January 1)

Before heading out again, Grant went over to Ted for some last minute instructions. He ran up to the cab of the semi where Ted was and climbed up to the passenger side. Ted had his window down and the heat from the cab was flowing out. It felt great against the cold from outside. It felt like it was about to rain. Grant could tell from the way the wind was starting to pick up.

"You got point," Ted said to Grant.

Oh great, Grant thought. Now the Team was the scout unit. Except they had no scout training. Oh well. He couldn't sweat it. They didn't have any formal military or law enforcement training, but look at all they'd done so far.

"Roger that," Grant said. "We need to boogie to Olympia."

"Be careful," Ted said. He could tell Grant was anxious to get to Olympia. A little too much. Patience was a virtue—especially when people were trying to kill you with snipers, booby traps, and ambushes. It was even more important for scouts to be patient, and Grant wasn't.

"Sure," Grant said, trying to act like he wasn't scared out of his mind about being in the lead vehicle. He thought it was crazy to have the commanding officer in the lead vehicle and scouting … but, he had to admit that the real operational commander of this unit was in the cab of the semi.

"No, seriously, Grant, slow it down," Ted said. "Be very cautious. Get us there alive. Don't give those Lima bastards anything to brag about, like shooting up the 17th Irregulars."

Grant nodded. This was a rare rebuke from Ted. It was a soft rebuke, but a rebuke nonetheless. Ted was serious.

"Got it," Grant finally said. "We'll try to be as cautious as possible."

Ted smiled. "Besides, we're getting radio traffic, in Jim Q.'s totally incomprehensible language, and things are going well." Jim Q. looked over at Grant and nodded.

Grant felt a shot of warm adrenaline and joy soar through his body. He'd been waiting to hear that. He wanted to know every detail.

"The main fighting," Ted said, "is along I-5 from JBLM down into Olympia. That's the frontal assault from the regular forces. That's the brunt of the fighting. The Patriot regulars have pushed the Limas back into Olympia. We have guys like us coming up I-5 from the south, a couple of Lewis County units. They're not meeting much resistance. Mostly these overpass things like we got. Snipers and road obstacles. No helos or artillery. So far."

Grant was thrilled. This might actually work, he thought for the first time. He knew things would work out in the end, but he had no idea things were going to go this well this quickly. So far.

"Why?" Grant asked. "Why are we having it so easy?" He wanted to understand everything about this that he could.

Ted shrugged. "Best we can figure is that morale is at rock bottom for the Limas. All they have, for the most part, are kids in National Guard uniforms. Their officers or the gangs, or both, have looted their supplies and equipment. There are some cops, a splinter group of State Patrol, who are putting up a good fight against us, especially in the urban areas of Olympia. But, overall, these poor Lima kids have no idea why they're fighting. They don't believe their bosses any more. They're just there. Pointing their rifles in the direction they're told."

This was exactly what Grant thought might happen, but just not so quickly. This was fantastic.

Ted looked around to make sure no one else was listening. "We're going to win this. We're going to take Olympia. I have two questions, though."

Grant was hanging on his every word. "Yeah?"

"First," Ted said, "will we hold Olympia after a counter attack?" He paused and said, "And, second, will the 17th get to Olympia in one piece?" Ted looked at Grant and said, "Get us there, Lieutenant, in one piece. Scout us in. Be patient. They don't need us there right now. They need us there in a while, alive and ready to kick ass inside Olympia, not dead on the highway outside of town. You don't want to come this far and then not get to Olympia, do you?"

"Got it," Grant said. He did. Knowing that the battle was going well reduced the pressure to quickly get to Olympia. And, Grant now had to admit to himself, he was being a little too competitive. He used to think the amazing, wonderful, fantastic 17th Irregulars, who seemed to pull rabbits out of their hats and wildly exceed the expectations placed on an irregular unit, should be the first ones into Olympia and wave a Don't Tread on Me flag. He had wanted some glory, but now he felt ashamed of that desire. Glory was an abstract, theoretical idea. Anderson, Meerkat, and Nineteen Delta were real. Limiting the casualties to just those three would be the glory. Not waving a flag.

"Got it," Grant repeated. He didn't want to say, "I'll quit being an overexcited and inexperienced military commander with visions of flag-waving in my head."

Ted smiled and saluted, which was not customary in the battlefield, or in the cab of a vehicle, but Ted realized that Grant needed a salute.

Grant returned the salute. Man, that felt good, he thought. He jumped down from the running board on the cab. He ran, full sprint, to Mark's truck. He was re-energized. It could have been the good news about the regular units advancing, or it could have been the food. Perhaps, though, it was the realization that he was now the scout leader who was going to get them there alive.

"We're the scouts," Grant yelled to the Team as he got up to Mark's truck. He yelled so Ryan and Wes could hear from the back and all the occupants in the front and rear cabs could also hear.

"Hell, yeah!" Pow said. He had been itching to do some fancy work, and now he was going to have the chance. He loved fighting. He especially loved fighting alongside these guys. His guys. Guys who were way better than the jack-ass punks they'd gone up against so far. This was the time of Pow's life. Right now. The next few hours heading into Olympia. This was when legends would be born. And William Kung "Pow," a tough-ass Korean, would be a Patriot legend.

Bobby and Scotty soaked it in. Scouts, huh? Okay. They were up to it. So were Ryan and Wes. They felt a little exposed in the back of the truck with only a tarp to shield them from bullets and shrapnel, instead of the cab of the truck like the others had.

"Hey," Pow said, coming to life. He was on fire. "That sniper and spotter thing me and Donnie did worked pretty good. We can spot for you guys as we head up toward an overpass."

"Great idea," Grant said. "He can fit back here," he said, referring to Donnie in the rear cab. Grant pointed at Pow. "You two can get out a few hundred yards behind us and watch for problems as we move ahead."

"They'll need a radio," Scotty said.

"Yep," Grant agreed and then ran over the semi. He went up to the cab and told Ted the plan to use Donnie and Pow and that they needed a radio, an intra-unit radio, not some CB that required Scotty to carry two and communicate between both.

Ted nodded. They had two extra intra-unit radios. HQ sent the extras for this type of situation. "One is none; two is one" was the phrase Ted always used to describe why extra equipment was always needed. It was amazing how many things broke or got lost in operations.

Ted gave Grant an extra radio. It was exactly like Scotty's. They had all been trained on them back at Marion Farm. The Team and others had received more intensive training. But, then again, the Team had been using radios of various kinds for months to talk to each other in tactical situations. Pow would have no problem using the radio and using it well.

Grant ran to the chase truck and got Donnie.

"Grab your gear and all the 300 Win. Mag. ammo you have," Grant said to a surprised Donnie. "You're coming with us. We're the new scouts."

Donnie nodded. He'd had an enormous adrenaline rush working with Pow and taking those shots earlier. He loved it and wanted more.

"You got a pistol?" Grant asked, looking at Donnie sitting in the rear cab of the chase truck.

"Yep," Donnie said. He purchased a Glock 21 right before the Collapse, when he realized his hunting guns were not precisely suited for what he suspected was coming. A Glock 21, chambered in .45, was extremely well-suited for what came.

"You got rain gear?" Grant asked as he looked at the trees, which were starting to blow from the increasing wind.

Donnie shook his head. Grant looked at the driver, who had a Gore-Tex jacket. "Give him your jacket," Grant ordered, knowing that the driver wouldn't need it since he would stay dry in the cab. The driver jumped out of the cab and handed Donnie his jacket.

"Let's go," Grant said to Donnie, who was out of the cab and assembling his gear together.

Grant and Donnie ran over to Mark's truck. There was some light from the highway light, which was helpful because running in the dark was a bad idea. A twisted ankle right then would be a very, very big deal. How could Grant tell his grandkids that he was the commander of a brave irregular unit and almost got to Olympia for the big battle ... but he twisted his ankle and had to spend the war sitting in the back of a pickup.

Pow scooted over to the middle of the rear cab. It would be tight for three full-sized guys with gear. Once they were sitting in the cab, Grant and Pow checked their ARs to make sure they were on safe. Of course they were. Grant and Pow smoothly put their ARs between their legs; it was like putting on a seatbelt or something they'd done a million times before.

Donnie was a little nervous about having a loaded gun in the truck. He was an experienced hunter and hunters just didn't carry guns around like that. They put them in the back or, better yet, in a gun case. But years of safe hunting practices had been thrown out the window. He needed to travel in a cramped cab with his rifle in hand. This wasn't a hunting trip in Montana.

Donnie pointed the muzzle up instead of putting it on the floor. "Protecting the crown," he said, referring to the part of the gun at the very end of the barrel. The crown was the last point of contact between the bullet and the barrel as the bullet flies out. A microscopic nick in the crown could cause the bullet to wiggle just a millionth of an inch and set the bullet on an incorrect path. Donnie's rifle had a recessed crown that minimized this risk. But still, Donnie could not bring himself to put his muzzle down on a floor. Grant's and Pow's ARs had flash hiders on the end of the barrels protecting the crown so they thought nothing of putting the muzzle down on the floor.

Donnie looked at Grant and Pow seated next to him. He knew that Grant was a lawyer before the Collapse and that Pow was some insurance salesman. Now they looked like experienced military contractors. He was struck by how quickly things changed after the Collapse; how reality had completely shifted.

This was true of Donnie, too, to an extent. He was riding around in a truck with a loaded rifle between his legs. He would never have done that in the past. He would likely be pointing his rifle in unsafe directions, potentially at human beings, which was a strict no-no in his decades of hunting. Donnie was breaking years and years of ingrained safety rules. He, too, had gone from a normal person to a fighter.

Everyone was silent as they went slowly from the shoulder onto the highway and under the overpass. Scotty was using Donnie's good binos.

Bobby knew that Scotty needed it dark in the cab so he wouldn't lose his natural night vision. And Bobby knew that they needed to be as stealthy as possible as they drove down the highway. So, without saying a word, Bobby turned off the headlights. It was terrifying. Even without normal traffic, driving down a highway without headlights was frightening.

No one was talking. They had important work to do, observing for threats. Especially Scotty. This was no time for chitchat.

Luckily, the highway lights provided some illumination on the road. But there were dark spots in between the lights; dark spots where a log could be hiding.

"We're only going about ten miles per hour," Bobby finally said, to break the tension. "And we have air bags—up front at least. Too bad for you guys in the back," he said jokingly.

They crept along. Grant looked behind them. The rest of the convoy was not behind them. They were waiting to get the word that the next overpass was clear.

Decades of zooming down highways at sixty, seventy, or eighty miles an hour made it hard to go so slow. Grant's impatience was coming back. "Let's go!" he wanted to yell. But he knew that this was as fast as they could go.

Everyone was looking out their windows, which were rolled down even though it was cold outside.

"Why are the windows rolled down?" Donnie asked. "To see better?"

"That's one reason," Pow said. "And because you could shoot out of an open window and not spray yourself and your buddies with glass."

"'That's what the heater's for,'" Bobby said. "Remember when Ted used to say that?" That was a few years ago, back when Ted was still an active duty soldier spending his weekends at the range with the guys who became the Team. Ted taught them so much, like driving around with their windows down when they might need to shoot out of the car. Ted taught them PSDs, which stood for Personal Security Details. Riding with someone who was being protected, getting out and moving the person, and engaging the enemy and then getting back into the car and taking off. They did all this. It was this unusual training – unusual for civilians – that allowed the Team to be so effective when they picked up Grant's family right after the Collapse and got them out to the cabin.

"Remember how Ted used to …" Pow started.

"Sorry, man," Grant interrupted. "We gotta concentrate here. When we take Olympia, we'll have several beers and talk about this stuff. Okay?"

"Yep," Pow said. Grant was right.

Everyone was silent and peered out the window. No threats. Just pitch black. The highway lights were gone because they were on a stretch of highway without them. It was absolutely black, even a few feet in front of them. Bobby slowed down to a crawl. The truck was hardly moving at all.

Grant, who knew the highway well from all the trips over the years he'd made back and forth to his cabin, knew that an overpass was coming up around the next bend.

"Full alert, gentlemen," he said to everyone in the truck. "There's an overpass right ahead."

Sure enough, as they slowly rounded the bend, there was the overpass. That overpass that he sped past many times before without giving it a second thought now felt ominous.

"How far to the overpass from here?" Pow asked.

"Dunno, never had to think about it," Grant said. "Let's get out and see."

Grant, Pow, and Donnie got out and looked at the overpass. There did not appear to be anything on it, or around it. But that wasn't good enough.

"How far?" Pow whispered to Donnie, who was getting his laser range finder.

"Seven hundred fifty-six yards," Donnie said.

"We'll get closer for you two to watch us," Grant said to Pow and Donnie. They got back in the truck and slowly crept toward the overpass. Scotty radioed in what was happening.

Donnie was getting new laser readings as they inched forward.

"How about, say, four hundred yards?" Grant asked Pow. "That should be far enough away that anyone on the overpass will have a hard time hitting us, but close enough that Donnie can hit them."

Pow nodded. "Four hundred yards means an amateur like that last guy can't hit us," he said. "But a trained guy can take us at that range. Easy."

Grant shrugged. They would have to take this chance. The Limas probably didn't have trained snipers out tonight, at least not in this area. If they did, they would have put their good ones on the first overpass and really tied up any advancing Patriot units. Besides, Donnie wasn't a pro, and four hundred yards was about his effective range given his nerves and experience level. So they needed to be within Donnie's range.

"Four twenty six," Donnie read off of this laser range finder.

"That's good," Grant said. "Let's go."

Bobby stopped the truck. Scotty handed Pow a radio set to the intra-unit frequency.

"Test," Scotty said into the radio, which came through loud and clear on Pow's radio, with a little feedback.

"Test," Pow replied and his voice came through on Scotty's radio, also with feedback.

"Time to go to work," Pow said to Donnie with a smile. Donnie grinned back.

They got out and set up with a good angle on the overpass.

"Let's go be scouts, Mr. Doggett," Grant said to Scotty.

Scotty nodded, got out of the truck and did a press check. He had a round in the chamber and the safety was on. Of course. He checked his Aimpoint red-dot sight. It was on. Of course. They had a battery life of several years.

Grant did the same. Same deal: round in the chamber, safety on, and his EOTech red-dot was on.

"I'm ready to go get you guys if there's trouble," Bobby said. "And I know where Pow and Donnie are, so I'll get them, too."

Well, kind of. No one really knew how to be a scout. They were making it up as they went. What else could they do? This was an irregular unit in an irregular war. "Play the cards you've been dealt," Ted would always say.

Scotty took the point. Grant was spread out from him, so a mortar or grenade would only kill one of them. Nice thought, Grant remarked to himself. Very cheery.

They walked slowly, but not too slowly. Their hearing was sharp. They could hear every tree rustle. Without all the usual noises of modern life, the wind sounded amazingly loud as it swayed through the huge evergreen trees surrounding them.

Grant and Scotty alternated by looking through their weapons' optics and then without them. They wanted to be able to have their rifle up and ready to shoot, but they also wanted to have the wider field of vision that came from not straining through an optic. They were grateful for their red-dot sights. They were also glad that they had flashlights on their rifles. This was no time to be fumbling for a flashlight and trying to use one hand to shine and the other to point a rifle.

Grant and Scotty moved effortlessly toward the overpass with weapons up, then down, searching and assessing. They had the "combat glide" down, which was the term Ted used for describing how to walk while advancing on a target with their rifle up. They looked very professional doing that. It took no effort to move like pros. They'd done it for hours in training at Pierce Point and before the Collapse, and they'd moved in on real targets, raiding the meth house and on several other call-outs in Pierce Point that never resulted in shots fired.

Pretty soon, Scotty and Grant were right up on the overpass. All they heard was the humming of the sodium highway lights and the wind. The lights were surprisingly loud.

From training so long together, Scotty and Grant knew what each other would do without saying a word. They went under the overpass, each one on different sides of the highway—Scotty on the right and Grant on the left—scanning it for obvious booby traps. They wouldn't turn on their flashlights and do a real search until they knew that no one was around waiting for something easy to shoot at, like a beam coming out of their flashlights.

They moved on the highway and went under the overpass where they immediately turned their rifles upward to see if anyone was above them or on their flank. Nope. No one.

Then they kept their rifles on their flanks and looked to see if anyone was along the onramp to their sides. Nope.

They kept moving this way, silently in the dark. Without their lights on, and with their dark colored fleece jackets, it was nearly impossible to see them. The highway lights illuminated them somewhat, but not too much. They kept looking for their next piece of cover as they advanced, just like they'd done a thousand times. They had this down.

They went all the way down to where the onramp merged onto the highway, which was several hundred yards. Grant realized that they'd overrun their sniper coverage. The sniper team was four hundred yards back from the overpass, which was now a thousand yards from where Scotty and Grant were. They would need to come up with a better plan for this next time.

Then again, Grant thought, maybe not. The main attack would come from the side of an overpass facing the convoy, not the back side, which was what the enemy on the overpass would want to stop: the coming convoy, not two scouts that had gone past the overpass. So the sniper team would stay where they were in future scoutings to protect against an attack on the convoy.

Once they got to the end of the onramp, Grant pointed up toward the on-ramps and made a motion for them to go up it and meet back up on the overpass. Scotty knew exactly what Grant would want to do, so his motions made sense to him, even if they wouldn't have made sense to anyone else.

"Making this shit up was we go," Grant whispered to himself. They were. Like that thing about going up the on-ramp and back to the overpass. They just made it up. "Free styling" as Lt. Col. Hammond said back at the Boston Harbor briefing. Free styling, indeed.

Scotty and Grant were moving up the onramp and getting closer to the overpass.

Oh God. Grant had a horrible thought. He and Scotty would be on the overpass and Pow and Donnie wouldn't know it was them. The sniper team might think they were bad guys. Grant wanted to yell to Scotty to radio in that they were the ones about to be on the overpass, but he couldn't yell, and Scotty was far away.

Of all the ways to die, getting shot by your own sniper was the worst one. Oh well. He had to secure this overpass, and fast. The convoy was idling back there and needed to get to Olympia to get in the fight.

Grant got to the overpass. He looked over and Scotty was there, too, on the other side. Scotty looked, and to Grant's relief, he was on the radio and waving his arm for the sniper team to see. Scotty knew to radio in that they were the ones on the overpass. Grant was relieved to have smart and well-trained team members. They went down the off ramp and headed back toward the truck, moving much more quickly now that they knew that there were no obvious ambushes or booby traps.

Now they could use their lights. When they were down the off ramp where it met the highway, Grant turned on his weapon's light and motioned for Scotty to go down the highway with his light and look for any booby traps, which he did.

They took their time on this phase. They had just done a semi-quick sweep of the area without their lights. Now they could look for odd packages on the side of the road or wires, although those were hard to see even with the 200 lumens from their Surefire weapon lights.

It took a few minutes to go the length of the highway and then past the overpass with the lights on. Grant was getting tired. He had walked a lot with a tactical load, and was concentrating very hard. He was shouldering his rifle and sweeping the areas in front of him. His rifle was relatively light, but after about twenty minutes of moving with it, he was tired.

Finally, when they got to the far end of the back side of the overpass where the onramp met the highway, they were satisfied the area was clear. Grant gave a thumbs up to Scotty and he did the same. They jogged back to the truck with their weapons' lights on and swept the area one last time.

That jog was getting tougher as Grant went. He was in good shape, but this was hard work. Plus, he had that fleece jacket on. He was boiling. He felt sweat on his baseball cap. It was his favorite one, the tan Survival Podcast "ant" hat. He didn't want to get sweat stains in his favorite hat.

Wait, he thought. "You're in combat and don't want to get a hat dirty?" he asked himself. That hat was going to get sweat stained. It would give it character.

They jogged up to the area where Pow and Donnie were. They couldn't see them because the sniper team was hidden and Grant and Scotty's night vision was gone with all the lights they'd been using.

As they ran by Pow and Donnie's area, Grant heard Pow's voice.

"Cover us."

Grant and Scotty stopped and got down on the ground in a prone shooting position. They covered the overpass, which they knew was clear, while Pow and Donnie ran back to the truck.

It felt natural for Grant and Scotty to get on the ground and cover their teammates. They'd done it so many times in training that they didn't even think about it.

Grant enjoyed the time on the ground to rest. His heart rate was so high from all the running that his EO Tech red-dot was jumping all over the overpass target. He would be worthless as a sharpshooter at this point. That was okay. There wasn't anyone on that overpass to shoot at.

Scotty's radio crackled. "At the truck," said Pow.

Grant and Scotty got up and jogged back, slower than before. They were tired. Even twenty-three year-old Scotty was slowing down. Grant, who was twenty years older, didn't feel so bad about being tired.

Mark's truck never looked so good. They had made it back safely and now they could rest. They took off their tactical vests so they could remove their fleece jackets and cool off. It felt great to get that jacket off.

"Get in guys," Bobby said. "I want to be all the way past the overpass when the convoy comes through. I want to be well ahead of them." He was smart.

Grant and Scotty threw their vests into the truck and got in. Mark's black Silverado slowly started up and drove straight toward the overpass that had seemed like a death trap earlier. It was a regular overpass now; a dark, empty overpass. They went under it and everyone breathed a sigh of relief. Now on to the next one.

Chapter 282

Road Trip

(January 1)

The sun was starting to come up. It was 7:20 a.m. according to Grant's watch. There he sat, with all his friends cruising through a sunrise. It was just like a road trip: his buddies, a long ride, a sunrise; except for the part about people trying to kill him.

With the sun rising and the fact that the last few overpasses had been clear, everyone was lightening up on the strict no-talking atmosphere from the beginning of that long night.

"Dudes, I'm starvin'," Grant said. That MRE wasn't keeping him satisfied. They were pretty filling, but he'd burned off several hundred calories running around overpasses since he last ate.

"Want my HOOAH bar?" Bobby asked. "I've been just sitting here in the truck. I haven't been running all over like you. And I'm not an old man."

"Hell, yes, I want your HOOAH bar," Grant said. "And your momma says I'm in great shape."

Everyone laughed. They needed that release. It had been the first laugh in hours, which was rare for the Team. They realized that they were making lifetime memories right then. This would probably be the biggest and most memorable day of their lives. They were soaking it in. After a couple minutes of joking around, mainly about Bobby's momma, it was lighter outside and they were going fairly fast.

"Hey, next overpass. Let's get Ryan and Wes out of the back to come along," Pow said. "They're probably getting sore back there and we could use the extra rifles."

Great idea. Plus, after doing one overpass, Ryan and Wes would know how to get through them in the future and could teach others, if necessary.

"Whoa," Bobby said as he put on the brakes. It was barely light, but Bobby could see a vehicle ahead, parked on the side of the road.

"SUV on the side of the road at…" Scotty said into the radio. He checked the area and his map and added, "At about mile marker 21. We will check it out. Stop the convoy."

"Roger," Jim Q. said over the radio. Pow had his radio off to prevent feedback.

"Time for Ryan and Wes's first scouting mission," Grant said. They stopped the truck four hundred thirty-five yards from the SUV, according to Donnie's laser range finder.

"Escalade," Scotty said after looking through Donnie's good binoculars. "Fancy one."

Gang. That was a gang vehicle. They were the only ones who drove Escalades, and just about the only ones who could get gas.

Donnie and Pow set up near the truck. Grant and Scotty got out. Grant went to the back of the truck. "Get out, guys. We have a vehicle on the side of the road to check out."

The tarp flew up and Ryan and Wes sprang out of the pickup bed. They were ready to finally see some action.

Grant quickly explained how it would work with the sniper team cover and the four of them moving up on the vehicle.

"Ten bucks says it's an abandoned gang rig because they ran out of gas," Ryan guessed. He was probably right.

The four of them took off toward the Escalade. They were spread out and had four different angles of fire on the vehicle, but not into each other. Dang, Grant thought to himself as he watched Scotty, Ryan, and Wes advance on the target. They had a very smooth combat glide.

Scotty was the first to get close. "Looks abandoned," he whispered into the radio mic he had clipped to the left shoulder of his tac vest. There wasn't much highway light on the SUV and there wasn't much sunlight from the dawn yet. Scotty was basing his assessment of abandonment on the fact that no lights were on and there was no movement. That didn't mean there weren't people in it. Or hiding near it.

How to see if there were people in the SUV? Wes beat him to it. Wes motioned for everyone to hold their positions, which were about twenty-five yards from the SUV. Wes bent down and got a rock, which he threw at the SUV.

He missed. He tried it again and made contact.

"Ping!" The rock hit the rear door of the Escalade.

Nothing. Wes threw another rock. It hit and nothing happened. Finally, Wes got closer, got a bigger rock, and threw it at the rear window. It cracked.

Nothing. The Team advanced on the SUV. It was locked. Ryan took the muzzle of his AR and broke the driver's side window. It took a couple of good thrusts to do that. The safety glass wasn't shattering, just staying together like it was made out of fabric. But after a couple of good pops, Ryan had the window broken.

"Trick I learned in the Marines," he said with a big smile and pointing to the flash hider. Those brakes were coming in handy, Grant thought, as he remembered how he had used one to disable an oncoming threat at the meth house.

Ryan had gloves on, as did most of them, so he could unlock the door and open it without worrying about broken glass.

Nothing. The thing was empty.

"They're into the vehicle," Pow's voice said over Scotty's radio. Everyone looked at Scotty. He had forgotten to turn down the volume. He quickly fixed that.

"Probably ran out of gas," Ryan said. They searched the SUV quickly. No bombs or booby traps, but that wasn't a surprise. These were just gang bangers, not sophisticated terrorists.

Grant found some notes written in Spanish. He took them and would get them to Ted later so that one of the Spanish speakers in the unit could see if they were of importance. Probably not, but it didn't hurt.

"Let's let everyone coming past thing in the future know that it's not a threat," Grant said. He took his AR and started using the flash hider to break out a window. The rest of the Team did, too. It felt great to be smashing up a gang car. Everyone else in a fifty-mile radius would be terrified of that Escalade. The Team felt somewhat powerful breaking something that others would be afraid to mess with.

"We'll be doing more to the gangs than just smashing their windows when we get to Olympia," Wes said. "Their teeth. They'll be lucky if that's all we smash."

"Testicles," Ryan said. It felt great to talk shit and break stuff. It was a tremendous release.

Grant realized that their work was done. He opened up all the doors on the SUV and popped the hood, which would make it clear to anyone that this vehicle was not going anywhere.

Ryan took out his K-Bar knife, the one he got in the Marine Corp, and was under the hood about to cut lines to render the vehicle inoperable.

"Stop!" Grant yelled. "Our guys might need a gang-looking car for when we're cruising around Olympia. I mean, its windows are smashed up, but we still might be able to use it."

Ryan nodded. Good idea.

After getting some pent-up aggression out on that SUV, they all went back to Mark's truck.

"Have fun?" Pow asked.

"Yep," said Wes. "We'll let you break stuff next time."

They all got back in the truck. "Safe to proceed," Scotty said into the radio. "Vehicle abandoned and neutralized."

The Team took off, a little faster than they had before. Everyone felt like they were going quicker and quicker, and conditions were becoming safer and safer.

They were heading toward the next overpass when raindrops started to hit the windshield.

"Great," Bobby said. "It's fucking raining."

"This actually *is* great," Grant said.

"Why?"

"Politics."

"Politics?"

"Yep," Grant answered. "We're motivated. They're not. They won't stay out in the rain. We will."

"Are you serious?" Pow asked. "You don't think they'll fight just because it's raining?"

"No, I don't think they'll fight nearly as hard now," Grant said. "I think these National Guard kids, who have no idea why they're fighting us, will huddle under overpasses in the rain and see our convoy as a place to get warm and dry after they surrender."

They all thought about that.

"Gun fights aren't just about guns," Grant said. "They're about the will to fight, and politics affects that." It made sense.

They saw another overpass and slowly came to a stop. They were four hundred seventy-one yards to the overpass. It was almost light now. That overpass was much less scary in the light where they could see there were no apparent tank columns waiting for them.

In a matter of minutes, they had that overpass cleared. They found one of those log obstruction booby traps, still all bound up with the ropes. Whoever was supposed to release it, took off. Scotty radioed all this in.

"Proceed at full speed," Scotty said.

"Wait!" Ryan yelled out.

Everyone froze and quickly turned toward Ryan.

"I got a body here," Ryan yelled. Everyone took up defensive positions and formed a hasty perimeter. They were ready for an attack. They weren't sure why they'd be attacked for finding a body, but they reflexively got ready for an ambush.

Scotty radioed in for the convoy to stop.

Ryan, who had done this several times, walked up to the body, looked for obvious booby traps, and put the flash hider of his rifle on one of the dead man's eyes. If the apparent dead man was faking it, that would get a reaction out of him. It was physiologically impossible for a flash hider on an eye to not produce a jerking reaction.

Nothing. The dead man had a gunshot to the back of the head. Nearby, was a yellow hard hat.

"FCorps!" Ryan yelled. "Some FCorps douche bag."

"He musta been the one who was supposed to pull the rope on the logs when we came," Grant said.

"But the gang bangers must have needed a ride," Pow said. "His ride."

"Yep," said Scotty, who called in that there was an enemy body, but that the convoy could roll on.

Ryan got the FCorps helmet. "We might be able to use this," he said.

They all ran back to the truck. The rain was growing steadier. Their fleece jackets were getting wet and heavy.

Seeing Ryan put his rifle in that man's eyes was haunting Grant. This war shit was nasty. There was something sacred about a person's eyes; it was barbaric to stick something in a person's eye, even if he were an enemy soldier. Grant couldn't remove the mental image of Ryan jabbing a rifle into that man's eye. War was different than normal life. Different things happened in war, and jabbing a man in the eye was one of them.

They got back in the truck and kept going. Grant got a bottle of water and popped a caffeine pill. Even with all this excitement, he was getting tired and could feel his senses were getting dull. He offered caffeine pills to everyone else, and they gladly took him up on the offer. He made a mental note to get some to Wes and Ryan in the back of the truck the next time they stopped.

They went along for the next three hours, crawling along and checking out overpasses. They found another with the log booby traps, but no one to pull the rope. They didn't find a body this time. The Lima assigned to pull the rope must have just taken off or been taken by the gang. Who knew? Who cared? The Lima wasn't around to attack them and the convoy could keep rolling. That was all that mattered.

"Next overpass is Delphi Road," Grant said. He remembered that was the exit to Jeff Prosser's house and wondered how Jeff was doing on his farm. Was he okay? Was he hiding any WAB people?

Grant hoped he was.

Grant hadn't thought about his WAB colleagues in a while. They were POI, like Grant. They didn't have a cabin to go to. Grant would have offered up his place, but things moved too quickly when he shot the looters and had to bug out. Besides, Grant remembered them as the guys who never took him up on his suggestions that they prepare for what was coming. If he'd invited them to his cabin, they would have shown up without any supplies. Grant had the room, and the obligation, to have a place at the cabin for his family and the Team. Co-workers, even close friends, were a second priority. It was just how it was.

Grant assumed Tom, Ben, and Brian had probably been rounded up in Olympia. God only knew what had happened to them and their families. Grant tried to put it out of his mind. Then he thought back to smashing the Escalade's windows. That felt good. The reason it felt so good was wondering what the government and the gangs had done to good people like the Fosters, Trentons, and Jenkins. Killing those Lima bastards who had done this to good people like them would feel even better.

No. Don't enjoy that. You need to set an example.

Whoa. That came from nowhere. But Grant thought about it. He could see that path again, like he had before. He was supposed to stop the killing once the bad guys had been chased out. He was supposed to make this more like the American Revolution, with reconciliation and rebuilding, than the French Revolution, with decades of terror and revenge killings.

Yes.

Chapter 283

Pumpkin Pie ... with Whipped Cream

(January 1)

The rain sucked. Those wearing fleece were soaked. A few guys on the Team had Gore-Tex jackets, which were very common in a rainy place, like the Seattle area. Gore-Tex kept them dry.

But no one really noticed the rain. They were focused on clearing each overpass, and in between overpasses, they were in the truck with the heater cranked and the windows down, joking around and having the time of their lives. It was actually fun. Less fun for Ryan and Wes in the back without the heater, but still fun.

"HQ reports that the exit after mile marker 32 is held by friendlies," Jim Q. said over the intra-unit radio. Delphi Road, Grant thought. That made sense. Grant knew, from his visits out to Jeff Prosser's farm before the Collapse, that Delphi Road was full of self-reliant country people. They were a lot like the Pierce Point people. And, being this close to Olympia, people on Delphi Road were probably being abused by gangs and government officials coming out on looting runs.

"We're about a mile from there," Grant told Bobby. "We'll take this overpass slowly. There will probably be pickets and guards on it. Friendlies. Supposedly. But we'll see. So this one isn't a quickie look-n-cruise like the others." Everyone nodded.

They saw the sign for the Delphi Road exit. "Go ahead and park here," Grant said to Bobby. "We'll walk it in to the guards up there."

"You sure they're friendlies?" Pow asked.

"Pretty sure," Grant said. "HQ says so and, from what I know about people out here, they probably are, but we shouldn't assume. They could shoot at us by mistake. Proceed accordingly."

By now, the truck had stopped. Pow and Donnie set up to cover the overpass.

"We don't need to cover this overpass," Grant said. "We'll need cover for the people at the exit."

Scotty's radio crackled. "Standby for runner with code phrases," Jim Q. said on the radio. "Utility truck will be coming up on your rear to deliver the message."

"Roger that," Scotty said. He turned to Grant in the back seat. "Radios aren't secure enough, especially this close to Olympia, for us to relay code phrases." Everyone nodded.

"We'll need Ryan and Wes," Grant said. Pow was closest to the door so, without a word, he got out and got them out of the bed of the truck.

In the few minutes it took for the utility truck to arrive, the Team and Donnie established a perimeter, scanned the overpass, and planned cover points to leapfrog between.

"Vehicle approaching," Ryan said as the utility truck was coming down the highway toward them. "Utility truck," he said.

The truck pulled up and a soldier got out and ran up to Grant. "Code phrase for friendlies is 'pumpkin pie,'" the soldier said. "Response code is 'whipped cream.'"

"Roger that," Grant said, "'Pumpkin pie' and response 'whipped cream.' Got it." The soldier got back in the utility truck and it sped back to the rear of the convoy.

Grant was walking to each member of the Team on the perimeter to tell them the code phrases, and then he heard something alarming, the sound of gunfire and explosions in the distance. The noise was faint, but unmistakable. It was like the gunfire in Olympia off in the distance at the beginning of the Collapse, but way more shots were being fired. Strings of automatic fire. Loud, explosive booms.. There was a full-on battle going on a few miles away. Grant thought about it. This was a real war. A real frickin' war. He knew in his head that this was a war and that he was heading into it, but now he felt in his heart that it was real. It sounded like a real war, like some news report from the Middle East. It was much more serious than the small gunfight between a gang and some police, like he'd experienced in Frederickson. This was a real war, with real military equipment, including whatever it was that was causing the loud explosions. For a moment, Grant thought his little irregular unit was no match for the regular units with the real military equipment. He wondered if the 17th was up to the task ahead in Olympia, where the explosions were coming from.

Yes, you are.

"Time to get to work," Grant said, with that surge of relief that came when the outside thought reassured him.

The Team and Donnie were hearing the battle for themselves. They were focused on the directions the sounds were coming from and straining to see what was going on. A few of them looked at each other and nodded slowly, as if to say, "So this is what a real war sounds like." The only one who wasn't reacting at all was Ryan, the Afghanistan veteran. He realized that everyone else was hearing these sounds for first time and, just like him the first time, they'd be concerned about what lies ahead.

"Pretty light, actually," Ryan said. "This ain't shit," he said with a shrug. The shrug was an act. Inside, he was scared that a real war was happening in his own country. He knew how much killing, maiming, and terrifying those explosions did. But that was why he was heading into the explosions: to make them stop.

Everyone did a press check. Round chambered, safety on, and optics on. Every gun. Of course. They checked their magazines. All were full. They hadn't fired a shot yet. They checked their magazines on their tac vests. All full. Press check of pistols.

Everyone knew that, while the people on the Delphi overpass were supposedly friendlies, they were still people, and that meant the possibility of human error like friendly fire.

"Radios turned down?" Grant asked Scotty and Pow. They checked. Yep. Radio volume was turned down so only they could hear it.

Grant gave a caffeine pill to Ryan and Wes and then popped another one himself. He needed it. He could feel his alertness decreasing. It was plummeting, actually. He needed to be on the top of his game for this overpass.

"Can I take point, LT?" Ryan asked Grant, referring his lieutenant rank by the military slang for it, "LT." He whispered, "I've done this before." Grant appreciated the whisper so the other guys weren't reminded that Grant had never done this before.

"Yep," Grant whispered back. "Thanks." Ryan gave a thumbs up and headed to the front of the pack.

They fanned out and advanced down Highway 101 toward the beginning of the exit off ramp. After a while—a long while because they were walking instead of driving—they were getting close to the exit.

They grabbed all the cover they could, but there wasn't much on the side of the off ramp. When they got to the beginning of the exit, they leapfrogged up the off ramp. They provided cover for those ahead of them and then moved forward themselves. They moved like professionals; even Donnie.

They got about two thirds of the way up the off ramp when

Ryan heard some bushes rustling. He put up his fist, the hand signal for the group to freeze. They did, some noticing the signal instantly and others taking a few seconds. Then they scanned around with their weapons. They could feel that they were being watched.

They were friendlies. Supposedly.

After a while, they continued advancing up the off ramp, staying in the brush on each side of the pavement. As they got to the top of the off ramp, there was more rustling. They saw someone run from where the off ramp and the bridge over the highway met and then to the right, down the road. They were headed right toward where Grant assumed the guards would be. Whoever was running was small and fast, maybe a kid. Grant thought about how horrible it would be kill a kid by mistake.

He gave the hand signal for "keep your eyes open," though he didn't need to. All of them were extremely focused. It was the most danger they'd been in so far in this whole Collapse. It made taking down the meth house seem easy. The meth-house people weren't armed to the teeth and the Team wasn't in the open there. They were here; the brush on the side of the pavement only partially concealed them and was not bullet-proof. And it was daylight. They felt exposed and vulnerable. In one short burst of fire from the rustling bushes, they'd be cut to pieces.

This was less of taking an overpass than it was meeting up with friendly forces, Grant kept telling himself. Because, if they were advancing on the enemy, they'd be dead. Those rustling bushes would have been quickly followed by bursts of fire. Grant looked at the Team advancing up that off ramp; they were in a terrible position. It was daylight and the advancing Team was relatively bunched up. Grant didn't have two hours to properly inch up this off ramp. He hoped HQ was right about this being a friendly exit.

Grant came up to the road and motioned for Pow to come up to him. Pow had the good binoculars. He motioned for Pow to look down the road.

"Guards and a gate," he whispered. "Guys running around. They know we're here."

Grant didn't know what to do. The safe thing would be to wait until the guards either walked down the road to meet them ... or started to attack them.

Grant began analyzing the situation. He crouched behind some brush thinking for about ten seconds, which was longer than he liked to take. He just couldn't decide what to do. Then he realized that this "analysis paralysis" is what got people killed. He needed to act. Freestyle it.

"I'm going to walk up to them," Grant whispered to the half of the Team on his side of the pavement. "HQ says they're friendlies. If they're not, I'll tell them that I'm with some Lima — I mean 'legitimate authorities' — unit and that I got separated from my unit."

Grant looked at all of them very seriously. "If it looks like they're Limas, run the hell away. Get back to the truck. Fast. I'll distract them and hopefully get shot. I don't want to go to one of their prisons. I'm a wimp."

"Dude," Pow whispered, sensing that Grant's recent caffeine pill was entering his blood stream and amping him up too much. "That 'pumpkin pie' and 'whipped cream' shit means these guys are friendlies. Don't stress about it."

"Probably," Grant whispered, "But we need a plan for if things go bad."

They all nodded; he was right. Grant handed Donnie his AR. There was no need to scare the guards by walking up with one of those. He would have just his pistol. Besides, if this was an ambush, Grant was done for and Donnie could use the AR to get back to the truck.

Ryan gave hand signals to Scotty on the other side of the pavement describing that Grant would walk up to the guards and to run back to the truck if Grant took fire. Ryan used a mixture of official infantry hand signals and ones he made up, but they were basic enough for Scotty to understand the overall plan. Scotty told the plan to the half of the Team on his side of the pavement.

Grant slowly got out of the semi-concealment of the brush. He put his hands out to his side and walked to the center of the road. He could feel that guns were pointed at him. He couldn't really see any. The guards and gate were about a hundred yards from where the off ramp met the exit. Grant was scared; he knew guns were pointed at him, by people who very well might be the enemy or, even if they were friendlies, might be inexperienced duck hunters who would panic and shoot him. But his overriding thought was to be brave for the Team. He had to let them see that he wasn't scared, because then they wouldn't be scared. His obligation was to the Team. He kept thinking about the Team behind him and what they thought of how he was handling this.

Soon, he could see guards were, indeed, pointing rifles at him. He focused on keeping his hands to his side and just walking slowly. And confidently. He had nothing to hide. If they were friendlies, he was one of them. If they were Limas, he was just a Loyalist separated from his unit. Either way, he was one of them. Walk that way. Walk like you're one of them.

He got about fifty yards from the gate. The guards looked pretty squared away. A little on the duck hunter side, but they didn't look like the punk-ass Blue Ribbon Boys. They looked dedicated, not like they were guarding some gang's loot.

"Stop!" someone yelled. Grant did.

"Pumpkin pie!" Grant yelled. "You got any pumpkin pie? I'm hungry."

After a little while someone yelled back, "You like whipped cream on that?"

Grant smiled. "I sure the hell do."

There was a silence.

"Please proceed," someone yelled. Grant kept walking toward them, with his hands still out to his sides. He knew to be very cautious and not make sudden moves with what looked like two dozen rifles pointed in his direction. Grant got up to the gate and could see the guards. The leader-looking man came up to him.

"Ned Ford," the leader said. He was wearing civilian clothes.

"Lt. Matson," Grant said. He still avoided using this first and last name. He was POI, after all.

"Welcome, lieutenant," Ford said. "How can we assist you?"

Before Grant spilled the beans and exposed his men to an ambush, he had to make extra sure these guys were Patriots. So he made something up.

"Find me some of those teabagger bastards," Grant said. "You seen any?"

Ford smiled. "Yep." He pointed to himself and all the guards. "Us."

"You need any more assurance that I'm who I say I am?" he asked Ford. "I can get a secure radio here and you can talk to my commander at headquarters if you'd like."

"Not necessary," Ford said. "We've been expecting you."

Ford motioned for his guards to lower their weapons, which they did. Grant walked up to Ford, who pointed to Grant's 17th Irregulars patch. "What unit?" he asked Grant.

"Seventeenth Irregulars, Washington State Guard," Grant said with pride.

Ned saluted him and Grant returned the salute. "Welcome to Delphi Road," Ned said.

"Glad to be here," Grant replied. But it was time to get down to business; his men were sitting ducks on the off ramp and especially parked in the convoy.

"I have five men down there," Grant said. It was raining, so he didn't want them to stand out in it more than he had to.

"We know," Ford said. "Been watchin' you guys the whole time."

"I know," Grant said. "May I bring them up here?"

"Sure," Ford said. "Just you guys?"

"Nope," Grant said. "We have a convoy. A lead pickup, a semi, a chase pickup, and two utility vehicles that should be rejoining us."

Grant suddenly had the nagging feeling that he shouldn't be telling Ford all of these operational details like which unit he was with and their strength. He couldn't put his finger on where the feeling was coming from, but he was definitely feeling that he shouldn't have disclosed these important pieces of information. Regardless, the cat was now out of the bag. He hoped he hadn't just made a huge mistake.

Ford was impressed with the size of the convoy. They hadn't seen that many fighters ever. They thought their two dozen or so guards were a pretty big force.

"Joining the battle?" Ford asked as he pointed off toward Olympia.

Grant hesitated to answer. Secrecy about the unit and its mission had been ingrained in him for months. Then he thought about it. What else explains this convoy and the code phrases that show they're Patriots? Any one at the Delphi Road guard station knew exactly what the 17th was up to even before Grant had said a word.

"Yes, sir," Grant said. Grant made it a point to call Ford "sir" because, while Ford might not have any official military rank, he was the commanding officer of the guards. He deserved Grant's respect.

"You guys hungry?" Ford asked.

"Absolutely," Grant said. They were slightly ahead of schedule, so they could take the time to eat. And schmoozing with friendlies would boost the morale of the unit—and of the friendlies. The unit would see that the people were on their side, which was critical to a unit's morale.

"Let me get my radio guy here so I can tell my convoy to get here," Grant said. "You got enough food for about a hundred men?" There went another operation detail.

"We will in about a half hour," Ford said as he motioned for people to get the food ready.

Grant nodded and pointed back toward where the Team was. "I'm going to go get my guys." He was still being cautious not to make any sudden moves.

Ford nodded.

Grant turned around and jogged back to the Team. He told them what was going on. Scotty got on the radio and told the convoy to take the Delphi exit and pull in for some food with friendlies.

Pow ran down to Bobby, who was still in Mark's truck, and had him come up the off ramp and give the Team and Donnie a ride all the way up to the guard station. Might as well save a few calories and take the ride.

After a few minutes of the Team and Donnie standing in the rain, Bobby came by with the truck. They all got in and rode up to the Delphi guards. They were talking about how awesome a meal would be and guessing what might be on the menu.

When the Team pulled up to the Delphi gate, it was obvious that the guards were in awe of them. The Team had cool equipment, especially those tac vests and radios. And, reassuringly, the guards noticed that a "duck hunter" like them, Donnie, was with the Team. This reinforced that even with all these wiz-bang tactical gadgets, there was still a place in this fight for good ole' boys like them.

The guards had a million questions for the Team. How many other units were going into Olympia? How was the battle going? Did the Limas have helicopters and artillery? There was a rumor that the Limas had tanks; what had the Team heard about that? Was the rumor true that the Limas were shooting civilians in Olympia? This was the most eventful time of the guards' lives, but they had no information from the outside world. Now there was a fellow Patriot unit standing in front of them and they had radios. The guards were desperate for information.

One of the Delphi guards in particular, a young guy, had a zillion questions for Grant. He asked how many were in the unit, what the semi looked like, and what kind of frequencies they were using.

Grant got a bad feeling about him, especially that last question about frequencies. There was no reason a normal person would ask that. After a while, Grant started to blow him off by giving vague answers to his questions and changing the subject.

"Scotty," Grant said. "I need to go over some operational details with you."

When they were out of earshot of everyone, Grant whispered, "See that young guy?"

"The one asking all the questions?" Scotty asked.

Grant nodded.

"He's way too nosy," Scotty said. "Our frequencies? Are you kidding me? Want me to watch him?"

"Like a hawk," Grant said.

Chapter 284

"Reconciliation Starts Today"

(January 1)

Scotty's radio crackled. The convoy was a few minutes out. Bobby volunteered to go back and guide them in. Not that they needed it, but getting lost was such a big deal in this environment. Such a misstep could get a hundred guys killed.

Some civilian trucks started arriving from down Delphi Road. That must be the food, Grant thought. There was an RV that appeared to be the field kitchen, but they needed to bring in more food for their hundred or so lunch guests.

Pretty soon, the convoy was there. Smithson parked the semi on the ramp so he wouldn't have to turn it around. It looked like a normal semi parked on an off ramp with a driver taking a nap in it like back before the Collapse. Nothing out of the ordinary. The troops got out of the semi and headed to the promised food. They had been standing in the semi for hours and were anxious to stretch their legs, were hungry, and wanted to meet fellow Patriots who were joining them in this war.

The food was great. The fact that they were so hungry had something to do with that. The first wave of food was venison and elk steak. They were served cold because they'd been cooked that morning for the guards' lunches. The RV field kitchen was firing up and putting out as much food as they could. The trucks brought in a big load of already baked biscuits and cornbread, which was for the guards' lunches and dinners. The big hit of the meal was the dozens of Mason jars of home-canned fruit; tons and tons of canned pears and cherries, both of which grew well in western Washington State. The guards normally went through that much canned fruit in a few days, but they wanted to feed their guests from the 17th.

There were a few picnic tables for the guards; the female soldiers were offered the first seats. The women were fully qualified soldiers and respected members of the unit, but the men were still gentlemen. The rest of the 17th and the Delphi guards stood and quickly devoured plates of food. There weren't enough plates, so each person ate their food quickly and then took their plates back to the field kitchen, where they were quickly washed and handed to the next person. There were plenty of handshakes and high-fives among the 17th and the Delphi guards. Both groups were glad the other one was there to share in this fight. It was a joyous occasion. Eating a nice meal with fellow fighters. It was a feast. A New Year's Day feast.

After everyone had eaten, Grant raised a cup of water and motioned for Ford to stand.

"Here's a toast to a New Year," Grant said. "A happy New Year." Everyone cheered.

In the middle of all the celebration and hospitality, Scotty came running over to Grant.

"He's texting," Scotty whispered, half out of breath. "The young guy is texting." He ran off toward the bushes around the gate and Grant followed him, right in the middle of the toast. He knew it appeared rude, but he had no other choice.

When Grant caught up to Scotty, Scotty had his rifle pointed at the young guy. A cell phone was on the ground. The young guy was crying and begging for his life.

"Please! Please!" the young guy was screaming. He looked like he was in high school, maybe seventeen or eighteen years old. "I didn't mean to hurt anyone!" He was completely coming apart.

"Shut up!" Scotty yelled in his command voice.

Grant came up and drew his rifle, too. "Got him," Grant said to Scotty. "What's going on?"

By now, a crowd had followed Scotty and Grant. An audience was forming.

"That fucker was texting," Scotty said, still with his rifle pointed at the young guy's forehead. "After asking all those questions. Like our frequencies? Our fucking frequencies he wanted to know."

"They have my girlfriend!" the young guy screamed.

"What's going on?" Ford asked. "And, why are you pointing a rifle at one of my men?"

"Because," Grant said calmly, "it appears that he's a spy." There was a gasp.

"What?" Ford screamed. "Listen," he yelled at Grant. "We are feeding you but now you're trying to kill my men? Explain yourself!"

Grant and Scotty explained all the weird questions followed by the texting.

While they were explaining this Ford, Ted yelled, "Perimeter!" and the 17th started to form a circle around the Delphi guards. Who knew if other guards were spies, too?

Some of the Delphi guards shouldered their rifles or drew their pistols. The 17th did the same. A Mexican standoff. Except there were way more soldiers than guards.

"We need to make sure there aren't any more spies," Grant said. "Sorry, Mr. Ford, but we need to secure this place."

"What the hell is wrong with you?" Ford asked. Things were very tense. The Delphi guards were looking to Ford for instructions. "We've got four or five times more guys than you do," Ted said to Ford. "Let's just calm down and see if there are any more people who have picked today as a day to text their girlfriends or others."

Ford knew that the 17th outnumbered them. He didn't want a bunch of people, especially his own, to get killed.

"Okay," Ford said reluctantly. "We'll put our weapons down." His men started to do so.

Ted motioned for the 17th to do the same.

"We're going to see if any of your people have their cell phones on them and have texted recently," Ted said.

Ford nodded. He could not defend any of his men if they were texting information about the soldiers.

Ted motioned for the soldiers to start patting down the guards.

While all this was happening, the young guy was bawling like a baby. He kept talking about his girlfriend.

"Shut up!" Grant yelled at him. By now, Scotty had the young guy's cell phone and was reading the texts.

Scotty started yelling out the texts on his phone. "'Convoy. Semi-truck. About 100 troops, 17th Irregulars of State Guard. Heading to Oly down Highway 101. At Delphi exit now.'"

"Do you have an explanation?" Grant asked the young guy. He was going into judge mode. He could feel it.

"My girlfriend is in Olympia," the young guy said. "Her dad is an FCorps high-ranking guy. He said that if I helped them that I could be with her."

"Are you fucking kidding me?" Grant screamed. Selling out a hundred men just to make out with some girl? Treason was bad enough, but treason for a chick was even worse.

Scotty, who was normally very calm, thrust the muzzle of his AR right at the young guy's face. He ducked out of the way. Scotty clicked the safety off his AR. It made the very distinctive "click" sound of an AR safety. He pointed it right between the kid's eyes.

"Stop!" Grant yelled at Scotty. "Stand down, Scotty. Stand

down," Grant said in his command voice. Scotty obeyed the order and clicked the safety back on, lowering his rifle. A wet spot appeared on the young guy's crotch. He had just pissed his pants.

It was silent for a moment. No one could believe what was happening. Thirty seconds ago, they had all been toasting the New Year, now this.

"Do you want to do this or should I?" Grant asked Ford. "He's one of your men, so it's your responsibility, but I can take that responsibility off your hands." Everyone knew what Grant was talking about. Especially the kid. He started crying even more.

"C'mon," Ford said. "He's just a kid."

"I don't give a fuck," Ted said, walking up to Ford and getting in his face. "He tried to get us killed and he just might have succeeded. That fucking text has already gone out."

Ford was dumbfounded. He didn't know what to do. He had no plan for this; he had never even thought that one of his own would do this.

Grant knew what to do: shoot this little fucker in the head, finish lunch, and get back on the road.

Mercy. Be the example. This will set the tone for all that follows.

Grant thought about that. The outside thought had been right every time so far. He needed to follow what it said. Another thought quickly jumped into Grant's head, though he couldn't shake the feeling that it wasn't actually his thought. It was a brilliant thought and one that came from somewhere else.

"Give me that cell phone," Grant said. Someone handed it to him. Grant read aloud as he typed, "'False alarm. No semi coming to Oly. It was a rumor. I verified it's false. All quiet at Delphi.'" He quickly hit the send button.

"There," Grant said. "That solves that military problem. Now, onto the human problem."

The kid was shaking so hard he fell down, trembling and whimpering on the ground. He was pathetic.

"You can't kill him!" one of the Delphi guards yelled. "He's my cousin."

"The hell I can't kill him," Grant screamed at the guard. "I can kill him." Grant drew his pistol. "I sure as shit can!"

It was silent again. Grant, with his pistol in hand, walked up to the kid and thundered, "Stand up!" The kid couldn't. Or didn't want to, knowing what was coming. A couple of soldiers grabbed him and forced him to stand.

"What's your name, you little shit?" Grant screamed. "Name! Now!"

"Zack Knight," the kid said slowly. He was ashamed of himself and didn't want people to hear his name, even though all the Delphi guards knew who he was.

Grant walked right up to Zack, waved his pistol in the kid's face, screaming, "Traitor! You deserve to die, you little fuck!" Grant was feeling a rage he didn't know he had in him. He was starting to think he would shoot this kid right then and there. He started thinking about angle of the bullet and whether there was a safe backstop behind the kid's head. He knew that would be disobeying the outside thought, but he couldn't control himself.

Then a calm came over him. He casually put his pistol up to the kid's head. Grant took a breath like he was getting mentally prepared to do something big.

More silence. And whimpering. People started to cover their ears, preparing for the loud noise that was coming.

"But not today," Grant said as he calmly holstered his pistol. "Because you are no longer a direct threat to my men. You can't do any more spying and I cancelled the effect of your little dispatch."

Grant stepped back from Zack. "Killing you wouldn't solve any problem. The problem is over. Killing you would just have your family hate us. That accomplishes nothing. And you're not exactly a badass we're taking out from the Lima side. You're a pathetic, selfish, horny little piece of shit."

Grant stepped back even further and started to talk to the crowd. He needed to make a political point. "We only kill people who are a threat to us," Grant said. "Directly. A direct threat. People who are capable of hurting us. Not pathetic little boys who piss their pants." That felt good to say, Grant had to admit. He really wanted to kill this guy. He would settle for humiliating him if the outside thought said to spare him.

Grant looked at Ford. "We have a little something we call 'hammer and tag.' I won't shoot this kid today, but he will pay." Grant motioned and Sap came up to Zack and zip tied his hands in front of him. The troops hauled the cuffed kid to a nearby picnic table. They forcibly sat him down. Neither Zack nor the Delphi guards had any idea what was about to happen.

Grant pulled out his pistol. Ford was confused. Didn't Grant just say he wouldn't shoot him?

Sap and the others held Zack's hands down on the table. Grant took his Glock, with its polymer lower, and flipped it around so he was holding it by the end of the metal barrel. His Surefire flashlight was mounted on the bottom of the barrel, so it filled up his hand. He held his pistol like a hammer, except that the grip was pointing toward Grant and the flat top of the metal barrel, with the rear sight was pointing toward the kid. Grant's upside down pistol was now a crude metal club.

Grant raised his hand high and smashed Zack's hands. He screamed out in pain. Grant saw that he had mangled his left hand. Sap wrestled the kid, who was much easier to control now that one of his hands was smashed, so that his right hand was on the table. Grant raised the pistol and smashed Zack's remaining hand. A second scream of pain shot out.

Grant looked at his pistol for any damage. The notched rear sight was the part of the barrel that slammed into his hands. The rear sight had blood all over it. He handed his pistol to Bobby, who was standing nearby. Bobby cleaned it off on his jacket and handed it back to Grant.

One of Grant's soldiers was standing there with a permanent marker. Sap and the others held Zack down while Grant wrote a big "L" on his face. It was a little crooked because the kid was squirming so much. And his face was scrunched up in pain so it was hard to write on it, but the purpose of the "L" wasn't to put a nice looking letter on a person's face.

"There," Grant said to Ford. "That's 'hammer and tag.' It's better than killing them. And now, he's no longer a threat. And everyone will know not to trust him. Forever."

After the hammer and tagging, Zack fell to the ground again, still sobbing like a baby.

"Stand up, you little shit," Grant yelled at him. Grant had to admit how good it felt to smash that kid's hands and humiliate him. After all, that little dirtbag was trying to get them all killed just to be with a stupid girl. Grant knew it was wrong to enjoy it, but he still managed to have a surge of warm adrenaline and joy pulsing through him. It was like a drug. He loved it. But, ultimately, Grant had an obligation to set a good example, and this was his chance so he decided to take it.

Grant motioned to Sap to get Zack standing up. Zack was balled up in a fetal position on the ground crying. Sap kicked him lightly. Sap wanted to give him a second, much harder kick but realized that would exceed the hammer and tag punishment.

"Get up, you stupid fuck," Sap said. Zack was in too much pain to stand. Realizing the political opportunity this presented, Grant motioned for Sap and Bobby to help Zack up. After a couple of tries, Zack was finally standing. He stared Grant in the eye. Grant laughed at Zack's pathetic attempt at intimidation and stared Zack right back in the eyes.

He said loudly to Zack, but really speaking to the crowd around him, "When people ask what happened to you, tell them 'reconciliation.'" Grant turned to the whole crowd and repeated, "Reconciliation."

"We have to live with each other when this is all over," he said and pointed to Zack, "and judging by the piss-poor performance of his Lima colleagues, that won't be too long from now. We can't kill all of the shits like this. Well, we can, but that would mean revenge killings from their side. And more from ours. And more from theirs. And so on."

Grant paused and looked at the crowd. "Reconciliation starts today." He let that sink in with them. Then he repeated, "Reconciliation starts today."

"Instead of killing this traitor, like I had every right to do," Grant said to the crowd, "we took him out of the fight. But we let him live. He'll be a productive member of society in a few weeks when his hands heal. The 'L' on his face will wear off in a few weeks. That's reconciliation."

Grant walked up a few inches from Zack's face and softly, but eerily, said, "You understand me, young man?"

Zack nodded slowly. He had stopped crying by now.

Everyone was silent.

"No other texting," Ted said after coming back from searching all the guards. "All the others are clean."

Grant turned to Ford. "I trust that you will keep all your guards' cell phones, so if we have another little shit like this that a hundred of my men don't get killed."

Ford nodded. He didn't like being ordered around by Grant but, he had to admit, Grant made sense. Actually, as Ford thought about it, his anger was not at Grant, but rather, it was embarrassment that one of his men had been a spy.

"Okay," Grant said. "Let's get back to work."

The soldiers shuffled around and got their gear together.

"Okay, 17th," Grant said. "Let's get in our rigs and roll. Thanks for lunch Mr. Ford."

Chapter 285

Meanwhile, In Olympia

(January 1)

In the Cedars, Ron Spencer was just waking up late on New Year's Day morning. He'd been out all New Year's Eve night tagging slogans in town. Ron's contact with the Patriots, Matt Collins, had been arrested a few weeks ago and hadn't been heard of since. A new contact, Joel Edwards, took over for Matt and gave Ron instructions. Joel's instruction for New Year's Eve was to spray paint "Welcome, Patriots!" all over Olympia.

Welcome. That must explain the gun fire and explosions Ron heard all night. They sounded far away, but slowly got closer. And then there were bursts of fire nearby from random directions, like people were going on shooting sprees inside the various neighborhoods. It was all very confusing, unless you knew that Patriots were taking the city that night.

And they were going to take Olympia. Ron was sure of it. Every day he got to see how weak the Limas were, how they were hanging onto power in the city by a thread. The only reason people in this town were putting up with the gangs and government thugs was that most of the people were part of the system themselves. They were government employees—well, former government employees after the many budget cuts, or they still worked for the government in the FCorps or other capacities. Perhaps they made their living off of bribes or as white-collar gang members trafficking in "contraband" (and everything was contraband). Health care. Home repairs. Everything required a permit and no one gave out permits, so it was all underground. Just about everyone in Olympia was part of it, so they all wanted the Limas to stay in power. Not because they liked the Limas, but because they were caught up in the system.

It was sad, Ron thought. Most of these people caught up in the system weren't bad. They didn't wake up one morning and decide to be part of a corrupt government and oppress their neighbors. They started out a few years ago just doing their government job, accepting the money and benefits that came with that. Voting for people who would keep taxing other people to pay for their jobs. Then, when things got bad, these same decent people thought they could wait it out. Things would get better. They always did: this was America. In the meantime, they needed to join the FCorps or even put out a "We Support the Recovery!" yard sign. No big deal. It wasn't like they were robbing people. They just had a yard sign up.

If morality wasn't an issue, it made sense to be a government supporter in Olympia. You got more credits on your FCard. You kept your job (if you had one). You didn't get visited by the FCorps. Your friends liked you because you weren't a "teabagger." You were just like everyone else.

It happened slowly. One little compromise, one little "practical" decision after another. Harmless little decisions, like accepting an FCard with more credits than your neighbor who didn't have a "We Support the Recovery!" yard sign. Little decisions like that. Just doing what everyone else was doing. If everyone else was doing it, it couldn't be wrong, could it?

Closely related to the slow process of accepting more and more government controls was the fact that most people in Olympia could not take care of themselves. They were dependent, totally dependent on the government. Without food in the stores and the credits on the FCard, they would starve. Deciding not to go along with the government meant starving, and your kids going hungry. That was too high a price to pay for some idealistic emotional decision like not putting up a yard sign. It was *just* a yard sign, compared to your family starving. It was an easy decision to make.

Another reason why the population of Olympia put up with the Limas was that they were disarmed. While Ron and a few others in his neighborhood secretly had guns, almost no one else in the city was that fortunate. The general population had long ago been told that guns were evil and dangerous. Having a gun meant you were a redneck teabagger, so the population was largely unarmed and, not surprisingly, had no way to push the gangs and government back.

Ron thought about how most of the people around him had slowly morphed into what they had become, how they were dependent and disarmed. He had been seeing it going on the whole time. At first, he said something and tried to persuade people, but they looked at him like he was crazy, and a little dangerous. At first they were polite. Then they weren't. Then they refused to talk to him. He was lucky he wasn't hauled off. The only reason that he wasn't was that the government had too few prisons. And Ron could bribe his way out of it with the silver he had stashed away.

225

He realized how close he could have been to being one of them. He could have bought into the "way it is," that big government was necessary, and even a compassionate way to make sure the poor were fed. He could have been dependent if it weren't for that silver. He could have listened to his neighbors and not owned a gun.

So Ron couldn't really hate all his neighbors. He could have been just like them; he was just a few decisions away from being one of them. That didn't excuse what they had done; they had hurt people and ruined lives. They had to be stopped. Ron wanted them to pay for what they'd done; it was just that revenge wasn't his strongest urge. What he really wanted was for all of this to stop. For all his neighbors to admit they had made a mistake and start a new way of life. One that didn't depend on taking things from other people.

Ron wasn't just going to sit around and dream about how to make it stop. He was doing something about it, concrete and dangerous things. At least he could die knowing he tried.

Ron thought back on everything he had done. He had tagged numerous Patriot slogans all over town. On Christmas Eve, he tagged the Lima "Carlos cabal" members in his neighborhood with big "L" on their doors. That freaked them out. They were terrified and angry. They had actually believed that they were popular in the neighborhood. Their sense of popularity and security had been shaken to the core. They suspected Ron and even came to his house on Christmas morning. But Ron's wife, and even his adorable little kids, lied for him and said he was with them that night. They looked throughout the house but never found any spray paint. They looked on Ron's hands and didn't find any traces of paint. Duh. He used disposable latex gloves.

Ron had to quit patting himself on the back about his Christmas Eve tagging and focus on what he would be doing in the next few hours and days. He was on standby for a big mission. He had to let the Patriot forces coming through know who the Limas and Patriots were in the neighborhood. Ron knew. He had a list of addresses and a handwritten map, but it was unknown if Patriot forces would come through Ron's specific area, so he may never be activated for that mission.

But Ron would still be the Patriot's liaison for this neighborhood. He would handle any problems that came up before the city was finally taken. If Limas in the neighborhood went on a rampage against him or his Patriot and ULP neighbors, Ron would lead the effort to fight back, which could be house-to-house fighting. That would mean shooting his neighbors at close range. Ron had a shotgun and a few pistols. He made sure his wife, Sherri, was ready to use them, if needed.

Ron was on his own for this phase. Free styling, as the Patriots called it. Ron had been getting instructions from Joel Edwards, but that required face-to-face discussions. Joel would be hunkered down in his own neighborhood during the attack on the city. Cell phones would be down, of course, and they weren't secure enough to talk on, anyway. Besides, there wasn't much that needed to be communicated. Just make your neighborhood as helpful to the Patriots as possible and take out any Limas coming after you. Other than that, just wait for the Patriots to establish order throughout the city. Then, when the Patriots get to your neighborhood, tell them who the Limas are. No detailed plan was necessary.

"It's finally happening," Ron said to himself. Finally, all the corruption would be over. All the stealing. All the violence they did, or allowed to be done. All the gangs. All the FCorps thugs, their FCards to politically connected people. All the neighbors spying on neighbors just to get extra FCard credits. Finally, it would be over.

Ron's wife was up and came into the kitchen that morning. "Happy New Year's," he said, giving her a big kiss.

Chapter 286

Mr. Shipley

(January 1)

"Kill him," Mr. Shipley told Freddy, handing him a lead pipe. "They did it to us. Remember what they did to us."

Freddy was shaking under the street light in a really crappy part of Olympia. Garbage was blowing around and the whole place smelled like piss and people who hadn't taken a bath in months. It was loud out on the street. There was gunfire and explosions about a mile away. People were running around screaming. Some were screaming in pain and others were screaming with joy at hunting people down to kill them.

"Remember what they did, Freddy," Mr. Shipley said again. Mr. Shipley was in his sixties, and with a long beard, he looked like one of the ZZ Top guys. He was like a father figure to Freddy, who was a mildly developmentally disabled homeless man in his thirties.

Freddy nodded. Mr. Shipley was right. He was always right. But Freddy had never killed anyone. He had never actually hurt anyone.

"Go ahead," Mr. Shipley said. "Go ahead, Freddy. Remember what they've done."

Horrible and sickening visions passed through Freddy's head. They were vivid memories. He remembered what the yellow helmets had done. Freddy felt a surge of adrenaline. Of hateful adrenaline. He gripped the pipe. He looked the terrified FCorps man in the eyes. The FCorps man was trying to scream, but the duct tape on his mouth prevented that. The man communicated his horror with his eyes. Those eyes.

That man wasn't a human being, Freddy told himself. That man was one of them. One of them, who hurt people. Just for fun. Then, Freddy started to remember what the FCorps men had done to Freddy and his friends. Freddy was fighting this feeling. He was trying not to hate, but he couldn't resist it anymore.

Freddy sensed that someone had hit the FCorps man in the head with a pipe. The man's head exploded with blood spurting everywhere. Freddy looked. The pipe was in his hand. He was the one who hit the man.

He kept hitting the man in the head. The man's eyes were crossed. He was trying to scream, but no sound was coming out. Freddy looked as the pipe just kept hitting the man's head.

Pretty soon, the man's eyes closed and he slumped to the concrete.

"Nice, Freddy, very nice," Mr. Shipley said. "He had it coming. You know he did, right?"

Freddy nodded. He didn't feel bad about killing this man. He thought he would, but he wanted to fit in and please Mr. Shipley who had done so much for him and all the guys. Mr. Shipley would never ask him to do something wrong.

"OK, Freddy, go back to the line and we'll try to get into that building," Mr. Shipley said, pointing to a storage unit warehouse. "There might be some of them in there."

Freddy nodded and put the now bloody lead pipe in his back pocket. He might need it again.

"Oh," Mr. Shipley said. "Don't forget the helmet. Take that and give it to one of the guys. We can use it to trick them into thinking we're one of them."

Freddy nodded, picked up the helmet, and started heading back to his guys.

Holding the helmet felt weird. Freddy hated those helmets, but now he was holding one. He couldn't believe how strange it felt to actually hold one. The helmet terrified him, but he was in control. He had the helmet, and the guy wearing it was now dead.

"I did good, Mr. Shipley," Freddy said.

"Yes you did, Freddy," Mr. Shipley said with a big smile. "Yes, you did. Very good."

Freddy smiled, too. That was rare. Shipley had never seen Freddy smile before. Freddy had been through a lot, more than most people would ever know. Times ten.

Allen Shipley looked at the dead man. He walked over and kicked his head with his boot. "Bastard. That's for Larry."

What has happened to me? Shipley asked himself. He grew up in a nice family. His dad was a preacher and his mom was a nurse. He had the most loving family imaginable. He had rebelled against their apple pie and goodness but, in hindsight, they were fine people.

It was hard being a preacher's kid. Everyone expects you to be a goodie-goodie, but Allen Shipley was no goodie-goodie. He was a tough guy. With a twist: he protected the weak.

Allen was bigger than most kids and instinctively knew how to fight. He ruled the playground in school. He ruled it by beating up bullies. He had protected the weak since he was a little kid, when he started protecting his younger sister and brother. He would just walk up to a situation, see if someone weaker was getting abused, and start fighting the bully or bullies doing it. He couldn't control it. His instincts took over and he went into ass-kicking mode, even if it left him with split knuckles and bruises.

Allen was an excellent student, but he hated school. He was very intelligent, but he thought just about everything they were teaching him in school was stupid. He was bored. All day in class he would think about the flag pole after school, which was where the fights were. He was either fighting someone that day or figuring out who to support or which bullies to get the next day.

The geeks and losers loved Allen. There was Allen, with a black leather jacket, looking like a junior criminal, checking in with them to make sure no one was picking on them. That never happened to geeks and losers. Guys in black leather jackets weren't nice to the weaklings.

Allen got kicked out of school all the time. He would get so frustrated with how stupid the teachers were. He was solving their bullying problem, but he was the one who got in trouble, which was when he started to hate corruption. Those bureaucrat teachers just wanted to get rid of trouble makers, even when the "troublemaker" was doing the right thing that the teachers were too weak or lazy to deal with themselves. They should have given him a medal for all the wrongs he was righting at that school.

Allen remembered the day he got kicked out of high school for the last time. It was a permanent suspension. His mom was in the principal's office crying. Allen looked at the principal, a hateful little man who loved to boss people around, especially little kids who couldn't fight back, and said, "Well, sir, no good deed goes unpunished." Allen got up and walked out. He wouldn't see his family again for thirty years.

Allen stayed for the next several months at the homes of the geeks and losers he'd helped. Everyone wanted to support him. He was constantly amazed how much respect and thanks he received. He loved the losers. He felt at home with them. He realized that he, too, was a loser, just not in the traditional sense. He was a loser because he couldn't manage to stay in school and fit in with everyone else – well, he couldn't fit in with all the stupid people and bullies. Fitting in was overrated, anyway.

Allen needed to leave his town of Cupertino, California. His parents were there and they constantly carped on him to cut his hair, dress different, and go back to school. He loved and respected them, but he couldn't live in the same house with them. He needed to do his own thing, so he spent his late teens and early twenties in Los Angeles. It was the 1970s, when there were actually jobs for a young hard-working person. He did all kinds of jobs, from fast food to construction. He'd rent an apartment with a bunch of friends and have a good time.

When he turned twenty one, he got a job as a bouncer at a bar. Then he got offers at better and better bars. Pretty soon it was clubs, very fancy ones with A-list stars. This was LA, after all.

Allen earned tons of money, but he wasn't happy. There were no losers around. Allen missed them. He missed fighting bullies. He couldn't shake the strong feeling that he was supposed to fight bullies. So he got on a Greyhound bus one day and rode north. He'd just get off in some town and start over. That was the extent of his plan.

The bus stopped in Olympia, Washington. Allen looked around. It seemed like a nice town. The dome of the state capitol was visible from the Greyhound station. That was different. Maybe this would be a good place to be.

"Stop it!" Allen heard a man scream. Two big guys were grabbing a retarded man and taking his little cassette player with headphones. Allen ran over and beat the living hell out of them, quickly and thoroughly. In the process, the retarded man's cassette player fell to the ground and broke. He was crying. That cassette player was everything to him. With it, he was cool like everyone else.

Allen came over to the man. "Don't worry. I'll get you a new one." The man couldn't believe it. Allen took out a $50 bill and said, "Let's go get you another one."

They walked a few blocks to an electronics store downtown. He told the man to pick out whichever cassette player he wanted.

"My name is Monte," the man said.

"I'm Mr. Shipley," Allen said. He didn't want to use his first name. He didn't know why. He just didn't. Maybe because Allen was his dad's name, too.

"Thank you, Mr. Shipley," Monte said. "Why are you doing this?" Monte was used to people trying to take advantage of him. His mom was always telling him to be careful of strangers, but for some reason Monte felt safe around Mr. Shipley.

"Because people did something wrong and I can fix it," Allen said. "That's why. It's a good enough reason, don't you think, Monte?"

"Yes, I do, Mr. Shipley," Monte said. "Yes I do." Monte smiled. That was why he was doing this, Allen thought to himself. That smile. Monte's self-respect and dignity. That's why he was doing this.

They got a really good cassette player with headphones, a Sony Walkman. It was an upgrade from the one Monte had back at the bus station. Monte was so happy he couldn't believe it.

When it was time to leave, Monte wondered if this Mr. Shipley man would want to take naked pictures of him like one of the other men who had helped him before. Monte had said no to that other man. Monte knew that naked things were wrong. That man eventually left him alone.

"Stay safe, Monte," Allen said as he shook Monte's hand. "And remember that God has never made an insignificant person."

Monte swelled up with pride. No one had ever said anything like that to him.

"Are you a preacher?" Monte asked.

Allen laughed. "No, not even close."

"You should be," Monte said. "You help people and, just now, you made me believe in God. Thank you, Mr. Shipley."

Allen cried for the first time in his life. That was it. He would be a preacher. But, a preacher with long hair and a leather jacket. Not like his dad. He'd help people on his terms, not by some rule book.

"There are some God people I know," Monte said. "Let's go see them." Monte knew he shouldn't do that. He told his mom that he'd be home by 3:30 and it was already 4:10, but he needed to show Mr. Shipley the God people.

They walked a few blocks in downtown Olympia from the retail area north to an industrial area. The neighborhood got progressively worse as they went north. Not dangerous, just sketchy.

"Union Gospel Mission," said the sign. The place was a dump. There were various homeless men and some women standing around in the parking lot. Losers. Allen's kind of people.

Allen felt at home the second he saw the place. Monte introduced him to people and pretty soon, Big Reggie, the "deacon," greeted Allen.

"I want to be a preacher here," Allen blurted out.

Big Reggie didn't pay any attention. People came in high or drunk all the time. They said all kinds of crazy things.

"No, seriously," Allen said. "I want to be a preacher here." Allen spent the next twenty plus years of his life there at the Union

Gospel Mission. He ministered. He protected people. He called his parents one day to tell them that he was a preacher. On his terms. They cried and took the first plane to come and see him. They were not judgmental at all; they were so proud of their son. He was proud to be their son.

As time went on, things got rougher and rougher in the industrial area, which was near the port of Olympia. More gang graffiti, more dangerous and deranged street people, not the decent ones that Allen could work with. Most street people were harmless and gentle. They got picked on by the mean ones. There were more and more mean ones.

Soon, constant crime became a fixture of activity down by the port. On occasion, Allen would have to go out and knock some heads. Pretty soon, the word got out that Mr. Shipley was not the guy to screw with. People left him and his mission people alone.

When the economy tanked, things got even worse. There were tons more people coming to the mission. Allen had never seen so many. They were different: lots and lots of "normal" people, not drunks and crazies. All these decent people who lost their jobs were now at the mission, trying to find a place to stay and some food to eat.

The economy continued to spiral downward. More and more people became increasingly desperate. There were no jobs. None. Not for these people. And the cops were getting meaner and meaner. They had no tolerance for the "bums" and would do anything, including beat them, to keep them in "their areas." That was "Bum Town," which was the area around the mission and the port.

Not all cops were bad, but a couple definitely were. And the good cops didn't stop it. Allen would see that and get furious. Here were people who could stop bullying, but did nothing, just like the teachers who kicked him out of school.

One night, two of the bad cops—the two worst—were beating one of Allen's homeless guys. Allen charged at them and beat the crap out of them. They were shocked. All those stun guns and batons were useless against an experienced street fighter like Allen.

"Stay the hell out of my area," Allen said. "This is Mr. Shipley's territory. Cops are dead here."

The cops stayed away from Bum Town after that. It became a police "no go" area. Right about this time, the Olympia Police Department was having massive layoffs due to the dropping tax receipts. The city would double taxes, but get less revenue.

The Olympia Police Department was now down to one third of

their pre-Collapse strength. One third - but crime had exploded. They had eight times the murders, and were on pace for a twenty-fold increase. Theft went uninvestigated. They didn't even try to do anything about stolen cars anymore. If a car was stolen, a victim filled out a report on a website and got an email back saying the police were working "diligently" on the case. That's was it. An email. That was the extent of the investigation.

So the police, who didn't enjoy getting their ass kicked by some biker-looking preacher, didn't come back. They had other things to do. They let Mr. Shipley run Bum Town.

The warehouse across the street from the mission had been abandoned for a few years now. The state fish and game department used it to print materials — yes, the state fish and game department had its own print shop and produced printed materials that no one read because everything was on the internet. After one of the many rounds of budget cuts, even the "vital" fish and wildlife printing facility had to close. The warehouse was boarded up.

The mission was bulging at the seams, so Allen took a crow bar, a bunch of guys, and "converted" the warehouse into the "mission annex." The state was in such disarray at that point that they didn't even care that one of their abandoned buildings was being used by the mission.

Allen was a genius at getting donations, so pretty soon the "annex" was up and running, housing two hundred homeless people.

Punk kids were coming into Bum Town and trying to beat up Mr. Shipley's people for fun. Bad idea. Allen organized patrols and, on three occasions, beat the hell out of the kids. One of them ended up dying. Oops. Shouldn't have beaten up one of Mr. Shipley's people. No cops ever came around to investigate. They were scared of Bum Town.

The news right around this time was full of stories about the "teabaggers." Allen would watch the news and think about how the Patriots were doing what he was doing: fighting government bullies. One of his big donors had a Don't Tread on Me sticker on a locker in his metal shop. Allen asked him about it and a conversation ensued. Pretty soon, Allen was in the Patriot underground.

The Patriots used Bum Town to hide out. Mr. Shipley told his homeless people which strangers were cool; everyone treated the Patriot soldiers and plainclothes operatives with maximum respect because Mr. Shipley said so.

The Patriots also used the abandoned warehouses — Allen had taken over several by then — to store things, like weapons. The Patriots even had full time guards in Bum Town to protect the goods.

The Patriots gathered intelligence there, too. They would ask the homeless to keep their eyes peeled for things when they ventured into other parts of town.

Everyone in the normal parts of town ignored "bums." They pretended like they weren't there. Several Lima officials would have highly sensitive discussions and describe classified operational details right in front of a "bum." They assumed the homeless person was too drunk or stupid to understand what they were saying. How wrong they were. Pretty soon, the FCorps started to get nasty with Bum Town. It was an open secret that the Patriots were in there, it was just that the cops and FCorps had too many other problems to deal with. But FCorps would make periodic forays into Mr. Shipley's territory. They were usually bullies who, like the punk kids previously, just wanted to beat people up. The bully FCorps would justify the forays into Bum Town as "fighting terrorism."

Pretty soon, the FCorps with their stupid yellow helmets, would do what they called "bum fucks" where they would beat and rape homeless people — men or women. Mostly men. The FCorps wanted to humiliate and dominate them. It was widely known that if you wanted to rape and torture, join the FCorps. You were above the law.

The first "bum fuck" took Allen by surprise. He hated those FCorps dicks, but this? This shocked even him. He wouldn't let it happen a second time. Pretty soon, having a yellow helmet in Bum Town was a death sentence. The FCorps started staying away.

Around Christmas, Allen's big Patriot donor came to see him. Allen only knew him as "Mr. Smith." Allen had found out his real name but, out of respect for the risks he was taking, only referred to him as "Mr. Smith."

"Some heavy shit is gonna go down around New Year's," Mr. Smith said to Allen. "Some heavy shit."

"Okay," Allen said. "Let me know what I need to do."

"Secure Bum Town so we can use it as a staging area," Mr. Smith said. He smiled and said, "Gee, the port is right here. What a great way to land some guys. Right in the heart of the state capitol."

"You know," Allen said, "two of my guys were down by the water and heard the port people talking about how no one would be working there on New Year's Eve. They're having some big party." Allen couldn't remember if he had passed that on to the Patriots or not. There had been so much going on.

Mr. Smith smiled. "Yep. Your guys passed that on to HQ and, based partially on the port people being gone on New Year's Eve, they came up with a naval landing. A small one, but a landing, nonetheless. Instead of a 'naval' landing, it'd be more accurate to say a 'pirate' landing, but good guy pirates. The Limas are so weak right now that just a small water landing like this will have a huge impact."

Allen smiled. Brilliant. Landing forces six blocks from downtown and a mile and a half from the capitol. And Allen was perfectly positioned to help. It was like his twenty plus years of work there had been leading up to this, even though he didn't know it back then.

"I need you to take out as many FCorps as possible," Mr. Smith said. "About an hour before the main operation."

"I know just how to do it," Allen said. He described his plan to get word to the FCorps through some Patriots inside the FCorps that a big, epic bum fuck was going to happen on New Year's Eve. Lure in as many FCorps as possible. Surround them. Let his people exact their revenge. Especially on captured yellow helmets. Let them feel what it was like to be on the receiving end for a change.

"Perfect," Mr. Smith said. They worked out the details.

Now it was New Year's Eve and Allen was leading his people in the hand-to-hand fighting with the FCorps in Bum Town.

"Freddy," Allen said, "nice work. Now go back and join up with the others. The yellow helmets are on the run and we need to get as many as possible tonight."

"There's some boats coming!" someone yelled. Allen ran the two blocks to the port. He hoped to see many boats. They were finally going to take Olympia and end all this! No more bum fucks. No more corrupt cops. No more of this.

Allen saw the lights of big and small boats. There were about a dozen of them. He watched as they came in. When the first boat got close, he could see it was flying the Don't Tread on Me flag. The largest boat had an armored car on it.

The side of the armored car read, "Tantori Security Co."

Chapter 287

"We're Winning!"

(January 1)

Back at the Prosser Farm, the EPU agents were excited. They were professionals and rarely showed emotion, but they were giddy with excitement on New Year's morning. When they weren't out at a guard station on the farm, they were huddled near the radio in the living room.

"Amazing," said Mike Turner, one of the EPU agents. "They're crumbling. I've never seen anything like this." Mike went on to tell the WAB adults — the kids were off in separate rooms playing because they didn't need to worry about all this military stuff — about how the Patriots were advancing on Olympia.

"We've entered the city from multiple directions," Mike said. "Get this: we landed amphibious forces right at the port of Olympia! Amphibious forces! Like this is some real war, or something."

Mike drew a crude map of Olympia and showed everyone roughly where the good guys were. "We're holding the bridge at the Pierce/Thurston County line on I-5." That bridge was necessary for the Limas to come down from JBLM to reinforce Olympia. "It's like the Limas aren't even trying to come into Olympia. I dunno. It's like they're letting Olympia fend for itself." Mike was beaming. He had bet his life on the Patriots winning. And it seemed like they were.

Karen, Brian's wife who was not exactly gung ho about all this military stuff, had been concerned that her husband was being sucked into some big military adventure without thinking. So she asked Mike, "What's the source of this information? Patriot reports?"

Mike's eyes lit up. "No! That's the cool thing," he said, losing his normal professional restraint. "All these reports I'm giving you come from the State Patrol's own radios. We have the frequencies. We listen in on them. No, all this good news is coming straight from the Limas. You can hear how scared they are. I even recognize a few voices from my days back at the Patrol. I know them. They are terrified. We're winning." He put his hands up to the sky. "We're winning!"

Brian wanted to change the subject a bit. He didn't want his wife to look like she had been wrong, even though he knew she was.

"What's happening inside Olympia?" Brian asked. He was wondering how his former neighbors still back in the city were doing.

"We don't know too much about details inside the city," Mike said. "The Lima reports about the civilians are very general. But, from our limited number of Patriot observers inside the city, we know there is a lot of shooting. Not sure if it's gangs or military or police, or Patriot gray men and resistance. Lots of shooting, though. Detailed reports are hard to come by. Most of our guys are still on the outskirts and comin' in."

Brad Finehoff, the head of the EPU unit, came into the room, "A Patriot irregular unit came down Highway 101 an hour ago, linked up with the Delphi guards, and is now heading into Olympia."

"When do we go in?" Ben asked.

"When it's safe, Governor," Brad said. "Not sure when that will be, but in a few days, probably."

Everyone was silent. They just looked around and soaked it all in. There they were in the living room of a farmhouse getting updates on a war in their own town. And getting ready to go into it and become the Governor. Who would have thought this was possible a few years, or even months, earlier?

Chapter 288

HVT on Film

(January 1)

"I am Attorney General Jerry Harvey... and I have joined the Patriots," said the small, slim, prominent looking man. He was the Loyalist Washington State Attorney General – well, now he was the former Attorney General. He was broadcasting live on every television in western Washington State and several internet news sites. The Patriots had finally hacked the stations and sites, broadcasting directly into the homes of millions of Washington residents late in the morning, when a huge audience was tuning in to find out what was causing all the gunfire and explosions they'd been hearing.

The Limas' psychological devastation from having their own Attorney General switch sides was absolutely enormous. It was a gigantic propaganda coup, one of the most important events in the whole war. The Attorney General's broadcast would show the Undecideds in Lima territory that the "legitimate authorities" were not invincible. If their own Attorney General was switching sides, what did that say to rank-and-file Loyalists?

"I ordered the killing and detention of hundreds of innocent people, all in violation of the Constitution," the Attorney General said. "I did not stop the state and federal government from violating just about every law and principal of decency. I didn't stop them. I did terrible things and am sincerely sorry. I make this confession freely. I have been treated well. I have been cooperating with Patriot prosecutors to identify my former colleagues who committed crimes so they can be held accountable. Soon. Very soon." He said that with confidence.

"The Patriots have been very fair to me," he continued. "I have been offered a full pardon. My family was rescued by Patriot forces and relocated to a safe location in one of the free areas of New Washington." He paused and looked directly into the camera.

"The so-called 'legitimate authorities' are losing. You know it; you feel it. Listen to the voice in your heart. This can't go on. Your kids deserve a better life. You see the lack of food, all the crime everywhere, and the corruption. You know the Loyalists are wrong. Switch sides. I did, and I'll forever be grateful I did. Join me. Join the Patriots." He paused to allow the camera to fade out. He looked relieved and at peace when he finished speaking.

"Okay, that's a wrap, Jerry," said Patriot intelligence officer Dutch Hillenburg, signaling that the video shoot was over. "Thanks, man. That was perfect." He hugged Jerry, who began to cry. Jerry was crying tears of relief that the ordeal was over and everything had turned out so well.

"I need to be honest," he said to Dutch. "Coming over to your side wasn't my idea in the beginning. You had to kidnap me." He started to cry again. "I don't deserve any credit for making the right decision, but now that this has been forced on me, I can say that I'm glad I'm on your side. We were wrong, Dutch. I did bad things. You got me to realize that. Thank you." Dutch nodded. He actually believed Jerry was now sorry for what he'd done.

"Sir," a soldier said to Dutch as she walked into the conference room. "We have the special guests for you and General Harvey." The formal title of an Attorney General is "General," even though the Attorney General is a civilian, so Jerry was technically "General Harvey."

"You'll love this, Jerry," Dutch said. He had grown so close to the former Attorney General that he could call him "Jerry." Dutch motioned to the soldier to send in the special guests.

Helicopter pilot, Lt. Enrique "Paco" Mendez, came in with a woman, Jessica Aylesworth, and three other men; Terry Rose, a burly airborne Ranger; Tom Kirkland, a Special Forces soldier who coordinated the helicopter strikes for the Limas at Camp Murray; and Roy Chopping, a former New York City detective. They "bro hugged" and fist-bumped Dutch. Jerry looked on, not knowing any of them.

"Where are my manners?" Dutch asked. "General Harvey, this is 'Paco,' the helicopter pilot who picked you up in August. You probably didn't recognize him without his helmet and visor."

"Pleased to meet you." Jerry said. "Under somewhat better circumstances this time," he said, referring to the fact that when Jerry and Paco first met, it seemed like Paco was trying to kidnap him.

"General," Paco said, tipping his head. He didn't salute because they were indoors and Jerry was a civilian.

"And you remember Terry," Dutch said to Jerry. "He punched you in the face and handcuffed you."

"How could I forget?" Jerry said with a slight smile. Jerry had almost no sense of humor and seeing Terry again was terrifying. A slight smile was all he could manage.

"Sorry, General," Terry said. "Nothing personal. Just business. I had to get you out of that building and into the bird," he said, referring to the helicopter.

"You've never met Tom Kirkland," Dutch said, motioning for Tom to shake the Attorney General's hand. "He's a Special Forces solider who was actually at Camp Murray coordinating the ground forces who rode on the Loyalists' helicopter strikes. He is the one who got Terry's people onto the helicopter Paco flew to the hospital to retrieve you."

"You know Jessica," Dutch said to Jerry. "She is, of course, your personal assistant."

"Jess," Jerry said, "I'm so glad to see you're okay." He hugged her and she started to cry.

"Sorry I had to do this, General Harvey," she said. "But it all worked out. Are Linda and the kids okay?" she asked, referring to his family.

"They're fine," he said, "and you actually did me a favor. Now I'm not in Olympia, which will soon be under the control of people who wouldn't like the old me." He smiled. Getting kidnapped by the Patriots wasn't his idea, but now he was working for the side that appeared to be winning.

"Finally," Dutch said as he pointed to a civilian, "this is Roy Chopping, who used to work for you at the Attorney General's Office. He was code-named 'Trigger' and is the guy who arranged for your – shall we say – 'evacuation' from Olympia and your new life here."

"General, it's a pleasure," Roy said, in his thick New York accent and shook Jerry's hand. "Glad things turned out well." Roy truly was glad Jerry decided to work with the Patriots because he had been ready to kill him. And Roy didn't like killing people.

"Hey, Jerry," Dutch said, "they're just here to tell the story about your evacuation from Olympia." He motioned toward the video camera. "We're going to make a video about what happened, you know, for historical purposes. We're documenting lots of stuff like this for the historians, for after we win."

Jerry stared at them, trying to process what was going on. Historical purposes?

"Jerry, kids in high school history class will watch this for a couple decades to come," Dutch said. "You'll be famous – in a good way."

That stirred another slight smile from Jerry. He was a politician, after all.

"Okay," Jerry said. "Let's do this." He paused, "Actually, I've never heard the whole story of what happened, so I'm as curious as anyone else."

Dutch smiled and directed each of the men to sit around the conference room table. When they were seated, the cameraman looked through the view finder and gave a thumbs up. They were ready to film.

"So," Dutch said, "introduce yourselves and describe how you all came together back in August."

After introductions, Paco started to tell the story. "I got the mission from Tom Kirkland, who was a Patriot Special Forces solider volunteering to run missions from a Lima base. He pulled me aside and told me that we needed to pick up an HVT," a high value target. "He said the HVT was in St. Peter's Hospital in Olympia, courtesy of a Patriot operative working within the Attorney General's Office." Everyone looked at Roy.

Paco continued, "We had to pick up a team of SOF guys," meaning Special Operations Forces, "to do the extraction from the hospital. We had to pick up Terry and his team at a landing site on the way to the hospital, but the pilot was a Lima so we had to make him think Terry's people were Lima contractors. Tom made sure Terry's people were at the landing zone."

Paco paused, "I had to take the helicopter over; I was the co-pilot, so I did." He kept it vague because he had to shoot the pilot. "Then we picked up Terry and his team at a landing site and I took them to the hospital."

"That's where my guys took over," Terry said. "We had the perfect cover: bringing a wounded helicopter pilot to the hospital. They let us walk right in. We knew right where to go because of Trigger."

Roy grinned, "Okay," he said, "this is the best part of the story." He paused. "Well, Jessica gets a lot of the credit. Wanna tell the story?"

She shook her head and motioned for Roy to tell the story.

"You're too modest," he said to her. "Jessica worked for Jerry in the AG's Office and so did I. She approached me when things were getting bad with her concerns about what was happening in the office. We became friends. We are similarly minded and we decided to work together. I had contacts in the Patriot community. She faked an appendicitis attack and I told General Harvey that she was in the hospital. I took him there to see her, except he ended up seeing Terry instead." They all laughed, even Jerry.

Chapter 289

Survival of the Scaredest

(January 1)

It had been light now for several hours. Jeanie Thompson could hear an increasing amount of gunfire and explosions. The sounds seemed to surge in intensity around 2:00 a.m. and then they tapered off. Now, there were just occasional "pop, pop, pops" and an occasional "boom." They seemed far away, but then again, she was in a big, armored building at Camp Murray so the sounds could be close and were just being muffled by the building's thick walls.

Camp Murray—the Emergency Operations Center for the legitimate Washington state government—was evacuating. Key personnel, most notably the new Governor and his people, had already left, before all this started. The rumor was that they'd gone to Seattle.

Convoys of progressively less important people were leaving in armored caravans up I-5 to Seattle. The longer a person had to stay showed how unimportant they were. Jeanie knew she'd be in the last convoy or get left behind entirely. She knew she was dead when the teabaggers came through the gates of Camp Murray, but she didn't even try to get a spot on a convoy leaving. She couldn't be trusted because of her past friendship with some WAB people. That put her on the bottom rung of everything at Camp Murray. Maybe her past friendships would persuade the Patriots not to kill her. That was her plan: get captured and drop some names. She knew it wasn't much of a plan.

Word came back that the second and third convoys got hit a mile outside of Camp Murray, right on the grounds of JBLM! The Patriots knew they were coming and had regular military units ambush them! Oh my God, Jeanie thought. No one was safe.

Wait, Jeanie thought. Maybe her plan of being captured and dropping names was better than the others' plan of leaving in a convoy. For the first time since she saw the ball drop in Times Square on TV a few hours ago, Jeanie smiled. She might be the survivor here.

That thought ended her gloom. It opened up her mind. All the old gloomy thoughts she'd been thinking had become a loop of repetition. Now she was thinking fresh. She had ties to the Patriots and that meant she might actually live through this. What had been a liability for months was suddenly an asset.

"Hey, Jeanie," Roger said as he ran up to her "duty station" at the visitors' barracks. "Can we talk?" It was Roger, the Emergency Management Department computer guy.

"Sure," Jeanie said. She was political enough to know exactly what he was going to say.

"Um, you know some teabaggers," Roger said. "I mean Patriots, right?"

"I used to," Jeanie said. She would have been suspicious in the past that they were trying to find out if she was a spy. But with the complete breakdown of everything, she knew that this was no loyalty test. This was a plea for help.

"Well, if they come in here," Roger said, but hesitated. "Will you tell them that I never believed any of this stuff. Will you?" He was terrified. Both about the Patriots coming in and about trusting Jeanie with that statement that could get him killed by the internal security people.

"Sure," Jeanie said. She had no idea if Roger really was a Patriot or just a guy trying to save his skin. Either way, he would be useful to Jeanie because he would go back and tell people that she could get you in good with the Patriots. That would bring more people to her and, who knows, maybe she could organize them here for a mass surrender. The more defectors she could deliver to the Patriots, the better the odds of her being treated better. She hated to think selfishly like that, but this was a matter of life and death. Hers.

Roger looked around to see if anyone heard what he said. He mouthed "thank you" and took off. In a few minutes more people were coming to Jeanie and asking her the same thing. The word was officially out: Jeanie can get you in good with the Patriots.

It never occurred to Jeanie to organize defectors at Camp Murray and then have them physically attack the Loyalists. That wasn't her personality. She knew how to help the Patriots. Just sit there. Don't try to help the Loyalists. Just sit there and wait for the Patriots to come. All the people coming to ask her to put in a good word with the Patriots were doing the same thing. They were just sitting in a chair not even trying to do their jobs.

"Loyalists"? Jeanie thought. Did I just call my co-workers that? Yes, she realized. Things had changed in her mind. She was now fighting the Loyalists. In her own way, not with a gun.

Just sitting there and not doing her job was very easy because there was very little work to do at Camp Murray. Most of the important people were gone. There were no computers to run, for example. Those operations had been taken over by computer centers in Seattle. Jeanie went into the computer room just to get an update on what was going on.

It was silent in there. Silent. All the computers were turned off. The silence was so strange in that room, which normally had humming noises from all the servers.

People were just sitting in their chairs staring at turned-off screens, silently contemplating their fate. Rehearsing what they'd say to the Patriots when they came through the door. The silence and the stares off into space were too much for Jeanie. It meant that this was really over. She thought hard about that: Camp Murray was over. All the people, her co-workers, and all the things they did here were over.

Jeanie was glad it was over, but it was hard to accept that it really was. Like an elderly relative in terrible pain who finally dies. You're glad the pain is gone, but it's hard to believe it's finally over. It seems so final. Because it is.

Chapter 290

Thirty Pieces of Silver

(January 1)

The sense of it really being over was also palpable at the Clover Park TDF. Nancy Ringman couldn't believe what was happening.

"Pick up!" she screamed into her cell phone. Because she was an important official, she had the one cell phone provider that was still operating. Kind of. It was supposed to be secure and up all the time, but, like with lots of other things the government promised, it didn't exactly operate as advertised.

Nancy was trying to call Linda, her boss. Linda had been ignoring her for days. Linda had told Nancy to get rid of all of those prisoners at the Clover Park TDF. Two thousand of them or whatever. Nancy had done exactly as she was told and all she wanted was to get the hell out of there. Clover Park was in the JBLM ring, but not even that was safe anymore. Some important convoys from Camp Murray had been ambushed right near Clover Park—inside the JBLM ring! Nancy wanted to get to Seattle where everyone else seemed to be going, but it took connections to get on one of those buses. Nancy had always had great connections. Always. But now it took even better connections to get anything done. She needed Linda to make arrangements for her to get to Seattle. If Linda didn't pick up … maybe Nancy would have to stay at Clover Park.

That thought started to take over in Nancy's mind. She might have to stay put.

It was late morning on New Year's Day. Nancy had been hearing the gunfire and explosions all night, but had just assumed that she'd be evacuated. She was, after all, the director of a TDF. She was important.

"Not anymore," she said out loud.

Okay, so that was it, she decided. She was being abandoned. She realized that spending hours trying to call a cell phone when there was gunfire and explosions was denial. She was in a dangerous situation, a very dangerous one, and her usual way of getting out of them, connections and networking, wasn't going to work.

She opened a bottle of wine. It was some of the really good

stuff she still had there. She just sat there, paralyzed. It was all so obvious now. She had been used. Linda had just told her to kill over two thousand helpless people and now Linda wouldn't help her get out of this war zone.

Used. She had been used. Nancy started to realize how stupid she had been. She had enjoyed all the power. She'd loved it, actually. Worshiped it was a more accurate word. She'd also loved all the goodies, like the kickbacks from the prison food contractors, including the wine.

She looked at the bottle of wine she was drinking. It was so valuable it was a shame to even be drinking it. It was probably worth an ounce of silver.

"Thirty pieces of silver," she said out loud, referring to some guy in the Bible that she had learned about as a kid. Judas, that was the guy, she remembered. Thirty pieces of silver. Thirty bottles of wine. Same thing.

Everything was so clear now. She'd done all of this. It was her fault.

She got up and walked slowly down the hall of the empty facility to the window facing the football field. There was fresh dirt on the football field. And under it were two thousand people. She had put them there.

She kept thinking about that Judas guy and silver. She tried to remember how that story ended. Then she realized that Judas killed himself. She started to think about that. It made sense. She had been used. No one was going to save her. The teabaggers would be at Clover Park soon and she could only imagine what they'd do to her.

This was a big decision, so she needed another bottle of wine. She gulped it down. She was good and drunk by now.

She looked out the window again at the fresh dirt on the football field. Maybe it was the wine, or maybe it was decades of denial suddenly disappearing, but Nancy was realizing that she'd done some terrible, terrible things. She couldn't stand herself. She'd be like that Judas guy and take herself out. And be remembered.

She staggered around and looked for a way to do the deed. She remembered that the food contractor had given her a gun for a gift. It was a fancy, shiny one, still in its box. She remembered where it was and went and to get it. She picked up the box, opened it, and looked at the gun. There were bullets in the box. She closed the box and breathed a heavy breath. She took the pistol box with her and slowly walked out to the football field.